The Queen's Necklace

by
Alexandre Dumas and Auguste Maquet

The Queen's Necklace
by Alexandre Dumas and Auguste Maquet

Copyright © 2024

All Rights reserved.

No part of this publication may be reproduced, stored in a retrieval system, or transmitted in any form or by any means, electronic, mechanical, photocopying or Otherwise, without the written permission of the publisher.
The author/editor asserts the moral right to be identified as the author/editor of this work.

ISBN: 978-93-64285-61-2

Published by
DOUBLE 9 BOOKS
2/13-B, Ansari Road
Daryaganj, New Delhi – 110002
info@double9books.com
www.double9books.com
Tel. 011-40042856

This book is under public domain

ABOUT THE AUTHOR

Alexandre Dumas (1802-1870) and Auguste Maquet (1813-1888) were two prominent French authors who collaborated on several notable works of historical fiction, including "The Queen's Necklace." Dumas is best known for his historical novels, which often blend adventure, romance, and historical detail. His most famous works include: **"The Three Musketeers" (1844):** A classic adventure novel that follows the exploits of d'Artagnan and his three musketeer friends. **"The Count of Monte Cristo" (1844-1846):** A tale of betrayal, revenge, and redemption set against the backdrop of post-Napoleonic France. **"The Man in the Iron Mask" (1859):** A sequel to "The Three Musketeers," dealing with political intrigue and mystery. Maquet is known for his collaboration with Alexandre Dumas, contributing to several major works. His role was often in developing plots and historical research. **"The Queen's Necklace" (1849):** A historical novel co-written with Dumas, exploring the scandal of Marie Antoinette's necklace. **"The Count of Monte Cristo" (1844-1846):** Contributed to the historical and narrative elements of the novel. **"The Three Musketeers" (1844):** Assisted in the creation of the plot and historical accuracy. Dumas's novels have been adapted into numerous films, television series, and stage productions, and his influence extends beyond literature into popular culture. While Maquet's name is less well-known compared to Dumas, his collaboration with the famous author significantly impacted the success and historical accuracy of their joint works. His contributions to the genre of historical fiction and adventure literature are well-regarded in literary circles.

CHAPTER XIV
M. FINGRET 116

CHAPTER XV
THE CARDINAL DE ROHAN 120

CHAPTER XVI
MESMER AND ST. MARTIN 130

CHAPTER XVII
THE BUCKET 133

CHAPTER XVIII
MADEMOISELLE OLIVA 138

CHAPTER XIX
MONSIEUR BEAUSIRE 143

CHAPTER XX
GOLD 146

CHAPTER XXI
LA PETITE MAISON 151

CHAPTER XXII
SOME WORDS ABOUT THE OPERA 160

CHAPTER XXIII
THE BALL AT THE OPERA 162

CHAPTER XXIV
THE EXAMINATION 175

CHAPTER XXV
THE ACADEMY OF M. BEAUSIRE 178

CHAPTER XXVI
THE AMBASSADOR 185

CHAPTER XXVII
MESSRS. BŒHMER AND BOSSANGE 189

CHAPTER XXVIII
THE AMBASSADOR'S HOTEL 192

CHAPTER XXIX
THE BARGAIN 197

CHAPTER XXX
THE JOURNALIST'S HOUSE 201

CONTENTS

PROLOGUE
THE PREDICTIONS 11

CHAPTER I
TWO UNKNOWN LADIES 41

CHAPTER II
AN INTERIOR 46

CHAPTER III
JEANNE DE LA MOTTE VALOIS 50

CHAPTER IV
BELUS 58

CHAPTER V
THE ROAD TO VERSAILLES 63

CHAPTER VI
LAURENT 69

CHAPTER VII
THE QUEEN'S BED-CHAMBER 79

CHAPTER VIII
THE QUEEN'S PETITE LEVEE 89

CHAPTER IX
THE SWISS LAKE 96

CHAPTER X
THE TEMPTER 100

CHAPTER XI
M. DE SUFFREN 105

CHAPTER XII
M. DE CHARNY 110

CHAPTER XIII
THE ONE HUNDRED LOUIS OF THE QUEEN 114

CHAPTER XXXI
HOW TWO FRIENDS BECAME ENEMIES.. 207

CHAPTER XXXII
THE HOUSE IN THE RUE ST. GILLES 212

CHAPTER XXXIII
THE HEAD OF THE TAVERNEY FAMILY 219

CHAPTER XXXIV
THE STANZAS OF M. DE PROVENCE 222

CHAPTER XXXV
THE PRINCESS DE LAMBALLE.. 227

CHAPTER XXXVI
THE QUEEN.. 232

CHAPTER XXXVII
AN ALIBI 240

CHAPTER XXXVIII
M. DE CROSNE.. 245

CHAPTER XXXIX
THE TEMPTRESS 249

CHAPTER XL
TWO AMBITIONS THAT WISH TO PASS
FOR TWO LOVES.. 253

CHAPTER XLI
FACES UNDER THEIR MASKS 255

CHAPTER XLII
IN WHICH M. DUCORNEAU UNDERSTANDS
NOTHING OF WHAT IS PASSING.. 262

CHAPTER XLIII
ILLUSIONS AND REALITIES 267

CHAPTER XLIV
OLIVA BEGINS TO ASK WHAT THEY WANT OF HER 269

CHAPTER XLV
THE DESERTED HOUSE.. 272

CHAPTER XLVI
JEANNE THE PROTECTRESS.. 273

CHAPTER XLVII
JEANNE PROTECTED 277

CHAPTER XLVIII
THE QUEEN'S PORTFOLIO 281

CHAPTER XLIX
IN WHICH WE FIND DR. LOUIS 284

CHAPTER L
ÆGRI SOMNIA 287

CHAPTER LI
ANDRÉE 291

CHAPTER LII
DELIRIUM 295

CHAPTER LIII
CONVALESCENCE 298

CHAPTER LIV
TWO BLEEDING HEARTS 302

CHAPTER LV
THE MINISTER OF FINANCE 306

CHAPTER LVI
THE CARDINAL DE ROHAN 309

CHAPTER LVII
DEBTOR AND CREDITOR 314

CHAPTER LVIII
FAMILY ACCOUNTS 317

CHAPTER LIX
MARIE ANTOINETTE AS QUEEN, AND MADAME
DE LA MOTTE AS WOMAN 320

CHAPTER LX
THE RECEIPT OF MM. BŒHMER AND BOSSANGE,
AND THE GRATITUDE OF THE QUEEN 323

CHAPTER LXI
THE PRISONER 326

CHAPTER LXII
THE LOOK OUT 330

CHAPTER LXIII
THE TWO NEIGHBORS 332

CHAPTER LXIV
    THE RENDEZVOUS 335
CHAPTER LXV
    THE QUEEN'S HAND 337
CHAPTER LXVI
    WOMAN AND QUEEN 339
CHAPTER LXVII
    WOMAN AND DEMON 344
CHAPTER LXVIII
    THE NIGHT 349
CHAPTER LXIX
    THE CONGÉ 352
CHAPTER LXX
    THE JEALOUSY OF THE CARDINAL 355
CHAPTER LXXI
    THE FLIGHT 361
CHAPTER LXXII
    THE LETTER AND THE RECEIPT 365
CHAPTER LXXIII
    "ROI NE PUIS, PRINCE NE DAIGNE,
    ROHAN JE SUIS"[B] 368
CHAPTER LXXIV
    LOVE AND DIPLOMACY 373
CHAPTER LXXV
    CHARNY, CARDINAL, AND QUEEN 376
CHAPTER LXXVI
    EXPLANATIONS 380
CHAPTER LXXVII
    THE ARREST 385
CHAPTER LXXVIII
    THE PROCÈS-VERBAL 390
CHAPTER LXXIX
    THE LAST ACCUSATION 393
CHAPTER LXXX
    THE PROPOSAL OF MARRIAGE 396

CHAPTER LXXXI
ST. DENIS 399

CHAPTER LXXXII
A DEAD HEART 400

CHAPTER LXXXIII
IN WHICH IT IS EXPLAINED WHY THE BARON
DE TAVERNEY GREW FAT 403

CHAPTER LXXXIV
THE FATHER AND THE FIANCÉE 405

CHAPTER LXXXV
AFTER THE DRAGON, THE VIPER 408

CHAPTER LXXXVI
HOW IT CAME TO PASS THAT M. BEAUSIRE WAS
TRACKED BY THE AGENTS OF M. DE CROSNE 412

CHAPTER LXXXVII
THE TURTLES ARE CAGED 414

CHAPTER LXXXVIII
THE LAST HOPE LOST 423

CHAPTER LXXXIX
THE BAPTISM OF THE LITTLE BEAUSIRE 425

CHAPTER XC
THE TRIAL 426

CHAPTER XCI
THE EXECUTION 429

CHAPTER XCII
THE MARRIAGE 433

PROLOGUE
THE PREDICTIONS

AN OLD NOBLEMAN AND AN OLD MAÎTRE-D'HÔTEL

It was the beginning of April, 1784, between twelve and one o'clock. Our old acquaintance, the Marshal de Richelieu, having with his own hands colored his eyebrows with a perfumed dye, pushed away the mirror which was held to him by his valet, the successor of his faithful Raffè and shaking his head in the manner peculiar to himself, "Ah!" said he, "now I look myself;" and rising from his seat with juvenile vivacity, he commenced shaking off the powder which had fallen from his wig over his blue velvet coat, then, after taking a turn or two up and down his room, called for his maître-d'hôtel.

In five minutes this personage made his appearance, elaborately dressed.

The marshal turned towards him, and with a gravity befitting the occasion, said, "Sir, I suppose you have prepared me a good dinner?"

"Certainly, your grace."

"You have the list of my guests?"

"I remember them perfectly, your grace; I have prepared a dinner for nine."

"There are two sorts of dinners, sir," said the marshal.

"True, your grace, but— —"

The marshal interrupted him with a slightly impatient movement, although still dignified.

"Do you know, sir, that whenever I have heard the word 'but,' and I have heard it many times in the course of eighty-eight years, it has been each time, I am sorry to say, the harbinger of some folly."

"Your grace— —"

"In the first place, at what time do we dine?"

"Your grace, the citizens dine at two, the bar at three, the nobility at four— —"

"And I, sir?"

"Your grace will dine to-day at five."

"Oh, at five!"

"Yes, your grace, like the king— —"

"And why like the king?"

"Because, on the list of your guests, is the name of a king."

"Not so, sir, you mistake; all my guests to-day are simply noblemen."

"Your grace is surely jesting; the Count Haga,[A] who is among the guests— —"

"Well, sir!"

"The Count Haga is a king."

"I know no king so called."

"Your grace must pardon me then," said the maître-d'hôtel, bowing, "but, I believed, supposed— —"

"Your business, sir, is neither to believe nor suppose; your business is to read, without comment, the orders I give you. When I wish a thing to be known, I tell it; when I do not tell it, I wish it unknown."

The maître-d'hôtel bowed again, more respectfully, perhaps, than he would have done to a reigning monarch.

"Therefore, sir," continued the old marshal, "you will, as I have none but noblemen to dinner, let us dine at my usual hour, four o'clock."

At this order, the countenance of the maître-d'hôtel became clouded as if he had heard his sentence of death; he grew deadly pale; then, recovering himself, with the courage of despair he said, "In any event, your grace cannot dine before five o'clock."

"Why so, sir?" cried the marshal.

"Because it is utterly impossible."

"Sir," said the marshal, with a haughty air, "it is now, I believe, twenty years since you entered my service?"

"Twenty-one years, a month, and two weeks."

"Well, sir, to these twenty-one years, a month, and two weeks, you will not add a day, nor an hour. You understand me, sir," he continued, biting his thin lips and depressing his eyebrows; "this evening you seek a new master. I do not choose that the word impossible shall be pronounced in my house; I am too old now to begin to learn its meaning."

The maître-d'hôtel bowed a third time.

"This evening," said he, "I shall have taken leave of your grace, but, at least, up to the last moment, my duty shall have been performed as it should be;" and he made two steps towards the door.

"What do you call as it should be?" cried the marshal. "Learn, sir, that to do it as it suits me is to do it as it should be. Now, I wish to dine at four, and it does not suit me, when I wish to dine at four, to be obliged to wait till five."

"Your grace," replied the maître-d'hôtel, gravely, "I have served as butler to his highness the Prince de Soubise, and as steward to his eminence the Cardinal de Rohan. With the first, his majesty, the late King of France, dined once a year; with the second, the Emperor of Austria dined once a month. I know, therefore, how a sovereign should be treated. When he visited the Prince de Soubise, Louis XV. called himself in vain the Baron de Gonesse; at the house of M. de Rohan, the Emperor Joseph was announced as the Count de Packenstein; but he was none the less emperor. To-day, your grace also receives a guest, who vainly calls himself Count Haga— Count Haga is still King of Sweden. I shall leave your service this evening, but Count Haga will have been treated like a king."

"But that," said the marshal, "is the very thing that I am tiring myself to death in forbidding; Count Haga wishes to preserve his incognito as strictly as possible. Well do I see through your absurd vanity; it is not the crown that you honor, but yourself that you wish to glorify; I repeat again, that I do not wish it imagined that I have a king here."

"What, then, does your grace take me for? It is not that I wish it known that there is a king here."

"Then in heaven's name do not be obstinate, but let us have dinner at four."

"But at four o'clock, your grace, what I am expecting will not have arrived."

"What are you expecting? a fish, like M. Vatel?"

"Does your grace wish that I should tell you?"

"On my faith, I am curious."

"Then, your grace, I wait for a bottle of wine."

"A bottle of wine! Explain yourself, sir, the thing begins to interest me."

"Listen then, your grace; his majesty the King of Sweden—I beg pardon, the Count Haga I should have said—drinks nothing but tokay."

"Well, am I so poor as to have no tokay in my cellar? If so, I must dismiss my butler."

"Not so, your grace; on the contrary, you have about sixty bottles."

"Well, do you think Count Haga will drink sixty bottles with his dinner?"

"No, your grace; but when Count Haga first visited France, when he was only prince royal, he dined with the late king, who had received twelve bottles of tokay from the Emperor of Austria. You are aware that the tokay of the finest vintages is reserved exclusively for the cellar of the emperor, and that kings themselves can only drink it when he pleases to send it to them."

"I know it."

"Then, your grace, of these twelve bottles of which the prince royal drank, only two remain. One is in the cellar of his majesty Louis XVI.——"

"And the other?"

"Ah, your grace!" said the maître-d'hôtel, with a triumphant smile, for he felt that, after the long battle he had been fighting, the moment of victory was at hand, "the other one was stolen."

"By whom, then?"

"By one of my friends, the late king's butler, who was under great obligations to me."

"Oh! and so he gave it to you."

"Certainly, your grace," said the maître-d'hôtel with pride.

"And what did you do with it?"

"I placed it carefully in my master's cellar."

"Your master! And who was your master at that time?"

"His eminence the Cardinal de Rohan."

"Ah, mon Dieu! at Strasbourg?"

"At Saverne."

"And you have sent to seek this bottle for me!" cried the old marshal.

"For you, your grace," replied the maître-d'hôtel, in a tone which plainly said, "ungrateful as you are."

The Duke de Richelieu seized the hand of the old servant and cried, "I beg pardon; you are the king of maîtres d'hôtel."

"And you would have dismissed me," he replied, with an indescribable shrug of his shoulders.

"Oh, I will pay you one hundred pistoles for this bottle of wine."

"And the expenses of its coming here will be another hundred; but you will grant that it is worth it."

"I will grant anything you please, and, to begin, from to-day I double your salary."

"I seek no reward, your grace; I have but done my duty."

"And when will your courier arrive?"

"Your grace may judge if I have lost time: on what day did I have my orders for the dinner?"

"Why, three days ago, I believe."

"It takes a courier, at his utmost speed, twenty-four hours to go, and the same to return."

"There still remain twenty-four hours," said the marshal; "how have they been employed?"

"Alas, your grace, they were lost. The idea only came to me the day after I received the list of your guests. Now calculate the time necessary for the negotiation, and you will perceive that in asking you to wait till five I am only doing what I am absolutely obliged to do."

"The bottle is not yet arrived, then?"

"No, your grace."

"Ah, sir, if your colleague at Saverne be as devoted to the Prince de Rohan as you are to me, and should refuse the bottle, as you would do in his place— —"

"I? your grace— —"

"Yes; you would not, I suppose, have given away such a bottle, had it belonged to me?"

"I beg your pardon, humbly, your grace; but had a friend, having a king to provide for, asked me for your best bottle of wine, he should have had it immediately."

"Oh!" said the marshal, with a grimace.

"It is only by helping others that we can expect help in our own need, your grace."

"Well, then, I suppose we may calculate that it will be given, but there is still another risk—if the bottle should be broken?"

"Oh! your grace, who would break a bottle of wine of that value?"

"Well, I trust not; what time, then, do you expect your courier?"

"At four o'clock precisely."

"Then why not dine at four?" replied the marshal.

"Your grace, the wine must rest for an hour; and had it not been for an invention of my own, it would have required three days to recover itself."

Beaten at all points, the marshal gave way.

"Besides," continued the old servant, "be sure, your grace, that your guests will not arrive before half-past four."

"And why not?"

"Consider, your grace: to begin with M. de Launay; he comes from the Bastile, and with the ice at present covering the streets of Paris——"

"No; but he will leave after the prisoners' dinner, at twelve o'clock."

"Pardon me, your grace, but the dinner hour at the Bastile has been changed since your grace was there; it is now one."

"Sir, you are learned on all points; pray go on."

"Madame Dubarry comes from the Luciennes, one continued descent, and in this frost."

"That would not prevent her being punctual, since she is no longer a duke's favorite; she plays the queen only among barons; but let me tell you, sir, that I desire to have dinner early on account of M. de la Pérouse, who sets off to-night, and would not wish to be late."

"But, your grace, M. de la Pérouse is with the king, discussing geography and cosmography; he will not get away too early."

"It is possible."

"It is certain, your grace, and it will be the same with M. de Favras, who is with the Count de Provence, talking, no doubt, of the new play by the Canon de Beaumarchais."

"You mean the 'Marriage of Figaro'?"

"Yes, your grace."

"Why, you are quite literary also, it seems."

"In my leisure moments I read, your grace."

"We have, however, M. de Condorcet, who, being a geometrician, should at least be punctual."

"Yes; but he will be deep in some calculation, from which, when he rouses himself, it will probably be at least half an hour too late. As for the Count Cagliostro, as he is a stranger, and not well acquainted with the customs of Versailles, he will, in all probability, make us wait for him."

"Well," said the marshal, "you have disposed of all my guests, except M. de Taverney, in a manner worthy of Homer, or of my poor Raffè."

The maître-d'hôtel bowed. "I have not," said he, "named M. de Taverney, because, being an old friend, he will probably be punctual."

"Good; and where do we dine?"

"In the great dining-room, your grace."

"But we shall freeze there."

"It has been warmed for three days, your grace; and I believe you will find it perfectly comfortable."

"Very well; but there is a clock striking! Why, it is half-past four!" cried the marshal.

"Yes, your grace; and there is the courier entering the courtyard with my bottle of tokay."

"May I continue for another twenty years to be served in this manner!" said the marshal, turning again to his looking-glass, while the maître-d'hôtel ran down-stairs.

"Twenty years!" said a laughing voice, interrupting the marshal in his survey of himself; "twenty years, my dear duke! I wish them you; but then I shall be sixty—I shall be very old."

"You, countess!" cried the marshal, "you are my first arrival, and, mon Dieu! you look as young and charming as ever."

"Duke, I am frozen."

"Come into the boudoir, then."

"Oh! tête-à-tête, marshal?"

"Not so," replied a somewhat broken voice.

"Ah! Taverney!" said the marshal; and then whispering to the countess, "Plague take him for disturbing us!"

Madame Dubarry laughed, and they all entered the adjoining room.

[A] The name of Count Haga was well known as one assumed by the King of Sweden when traveling in France.

II.—M. DE LA PEROUSE

At the same moment, the noise of carriages in the street warned the marshal that his guests were arriving; and soon after, thanks to the punctuality of his maître-d'hôtel, nine persons were seated round the oval table in the dining-room. Nine lackeys, silent as shadows, quick without bustle, and attentive without importunity, glided over the carpet, and passed among the guests, without ever touching their chairs, which were surrounded with furs, which were wrapped round the legs of the sitters. These furs, with the heat from the stoves, and the odors from the wine and the dinner, diffused a degree of comfort, which manifested itself in the gaiety of the guests, who had just finished their soup.

No sound was heard from without, and none within, save that made by the guests themselves; for the plates were changed, and the dishes moved round, with the most perfect quiet. Nor from the maître d'hôtel could a whisper be heard; he seemed to give his orders with his eyes.

The guests, therefore, began to feel as though they were alone. It seemed to them that servants so silent must also be deaf.

M. de Richelieu was the first who broke the silence, by saying to the guest on his right hand, "But, count, you drink nothing."

This was addressed to a man about thirty-eight years of age, short, fair-haired, and with high shoulders; his eye a clear blue, now bright, but oftener with a pensive expression, and with nobility stamped unmistakably on his open and manly forehead.

"I only drink water, marshal," he replied.

"Excepting with Louis XV.," returned the marshal; "I had the honor of dining at his table with you, and you deigned that day to drink wine."

"Ah! you recall a pleasing remembrance, marshal; that was in 1771. It was tokay, from the imperial cellar."

"It was like that with which my maître-d'hôtel will now have the honor to fill your glass," replied Richelieu, bowing.

Count Haga raised his glass, and looked through it. The wine sparkled in the light like liquid rubies. "It is true," said he; "marshal, I thank you."

These words were uttered in a manner so noble, that the guests, as if by a common impulse, rose, and cried,—

"Long live the king!"

"Yes," said Count Haga, "long live his majesty the King of France. What say you, M. de la Pérouse?"

"My lord," replied the captain, with that tone, at once flattering and respectful, common to those accustomed to address crowned heads, "I have just left the king, and his majesty has shown me so much kindness, that no one will more willingly cry 'Long live the king' than I. Only, as in another hour I must leave you to join the two ships which his majesty has put at my disposal, once out of this house, I shall take the liberty of saying, 'Long life to another king, whom I should be proud to serve, had I not already so good a master.'"

"This health that you propose," said Madame Dubarry, who sat on the marshal's left hand, "we are all ready to drink, but the oldest of us should take the lead."

"Is it you, that that concerns, or me, Taverney?" said the marshal, laughing.

"I do not believe," said another on the opposite side, "that M. de Richelieu is the senior of our party."

"Then it is you, Taverney," said the duke.

"No, I am eight years younger than you! I was born in 1704," returned he.

"How rude," said the marshal, "to expose my eighty-eight years."

"Impossible, duke! that you are eighty-eight," said M. de Condorcet.

"It is, however, but too true; it is a calculation easy to make, and therefore unworthy of an algebraist like you, marquis. I am of the last century—the great century, as we call it. My date is 1696."

"Impossible!" cried De Launay.

"Oh, if your father were here, he would not say impossible, he, who, when governor of the Bastile, had me for a lodger in 1714."

"The senior in age, here, however," said M. de Favras, "is the wine Count Haga is now drinking."

"You are right, M. de Favras; this wine is a hundred and twenty years old; to the wine, then, belongs the honor——"

"One moment, gentlemen," said Cagliostro, raising his eyes, beaming with intelligence and vivacity; "I claim the precedence."

"You claim precedence over the tokay!" exclaimed all the guests in chorus.

"Assuredly," returned Cagliostro, calmly; "since it was I who bottled it."

"You?"

"Yes, I; on the day of the victory won by Montecucully over the Turks in 1664."

A burst of laughter followed these words, which Cagliostro had pronounced with perfect gravity.

"By this calculation, you would be something like one hundred and thirty years old," said Madame Dubarry; "for you must have been at least ten years old when you bottled the wine."

"I was more than ten when I performed that operation, madame, as on the following day I had the honor of being deputed by his majesty the Emperor of Austria to congratulate Montecucully, who by the victory of St. Gothard had avenged the day at Especk, in Sclavonia, in which the infidels treated the imperialists so roughly, who were my friends and companions in arms in 1536."

"Oh," said Count Haga, as coldly as Cagliostro himself, "you must have been at least ten years old, when you were at that memorable battle."

"A terrible defeat, count," returned Cagliostro.

"Less terrible than Cressy, however," said Condorcet, smiling.

"True, sir, for at the battle of Cressy, it was not only an army, but all France, that was beaten; but then this defeat was scarcely a fair victory to the English; for King Edward had cannon, a circumstance of which Philip de Valois was ignorant, or rather, which he would not believe, although I warned him that I had with my own eyes seen four pieces of artillery which Edward had bought from the Venetians."

"Ah," said Madame Dubarry; "you knew Philip de Valois?"

"Madame, I had the honor to be one of the five lords who escorted him off the field of battle; I came to France with the poor old King of Bohemia, who was blind, and who threw away his life when he heard that the battle was lost."

"Ah, sir," said M. de la Pérouse, "how much I regret, that instead of the battle of Cressy, it was not that of Actium at which you assisted."

"Why so, sir?"

"Oh, because you might have given me some nautical details, which, in spite of Plutarch's fine narration, have ever been obscure to me."

"Which, sir? I should be happy to be of service to you."

"Oh, you were there, then, also?"

"No, sir; I was then in Egypt. I had been employed by Queen Cleopatra to restore the library at Alexandria—an office for which I was better qualified than any one else, from having personally known the best authors of antiquity."

"And you have seen Queen Cleopatra?" said Madame Dubarry.

"As I now see you, madame."

"Was she as pretty as they say?"

"Madame, you know beauty is only comparative; a charming queen in Egypt, in Paris she would only have been a pretty grisette."

"Say no harm of grisettes, count."

"God forbid!"

"Then Cleopatra was——"

"Little, slender, lively, and intelligent; with large almond-shaped eyes, a Grecian nose, teeth like pearls, and a hand like your own, countess—a fit hand to hold a scepter. See, here is a diamond which she gave me, and which she had had from her brother Ptolemy; she wore it on her thumb."

"On her thumb?" cried Madame Dubarry.

"Yes; it was an Egyptian fashion; and I, you see, can hardly put it on my little finger;" and taking off the ring, he handed it to Madame Dubarry.

It was a magnificent diamond, of such fine water, and so beautifully cut, as to be worth thirty thousand or forty thousand francs.

The diamond was passed round the table, and returned to Cagliostro, who, putting it quietly on his finger again, said, "Ah, I see well you are all incredulous; this fatal incredulity I have had to contend against all my life. Philip de Valois would not listen to me, when I told him to leave open a retreat to Edward; Cleopatra would not believe me when I warned her that Antony would be beaten: the Trojans would not credit me, when I said to them, with reference to the wooden horse, 'Cassandra is inspired; listen to Cassandra.'"

"Oh! it is charming," said Madame Dubarry, shaking with laughter; "I have never met a man at once so serious and so diverting."

"I assure you," replied Cagliostro, "that Jonathan was much more so. He was really a charming companion; until he was killed by Saul, he nearly drove me crazy with laughing."

"Do you know," said the Duke de Richelieu, "if you go on in this way you will drive poor Taverney crazy; he is so afraid of death, that he is staring at you with all his eyes, hoping you to be an immortal."

"Immortal I cannot say, but one thing I can affirm——"

"What?" cried Taverney, who was the most eager listener.

"That I have seen all the people and events of which I have been speaking to you."

"You have known Montecucully?"

"As well as I know you, M. de Favras; and, indeed, much better, for this is but the second or third time I have had the honor of seeing you, while I lived nearly a year under the same tent with him of whom you speak."

"You knew Philip de Valois?"

"As I have already had the honor of telling you, M. de Condorcet; but when he returned to Paris, I left France and returned to Bohemia."

"And Cleopatra."

"Yes, countess; Cleopatra, I can tell you, had eyes as black as yours, and shoulders almost as beautiful."

"But what do you know of my shoulders?"

"They are like what Cassandra's once were; and there is still a further resemblance,—she had like you, or rather, you have like her, a little black spot on your left side, just above the sixth rib."

"Oh, count, now you really are a sorcerer."

"No, no," cried the marshal, laughing; "it was I who told him."

"And pray how do you know?"

The marshal bit his lips, and replied, "Oh, it is a family secret."

"Well, really, marshal," said the countess, "one should put on a double coat of rouge before visiting you;" and turning again to Cagliostro, "then, sir, you have the art of renewing your youth? For although you say you are three or four thousand years old, you scarcely look forty."

"Yes, madame, I do possess that secret."

"Oh, then, sir, impart it to me."

"To you, madame? It is useless; your youth is already renewed; your age is only what it appears to be, and you do not look thirty."

"Ah! you flatter."

"No, madame, I speak only the truth, but it is easily explained: you have already tried my receipt."

"How so?"

"You have taken my elixir."

"I?"

"You, countess. Oh! you cannot have forgotten it. Do you not remember a certain house in the Rue St. Claude, and coming there on some business respecting M. de Sartines? You remember rendering a service to one of my friends, called Joseph Balsamo, and that this Joseph Balsamo gave you a bottle of elixir, recommending you to take three drops every morning? Do you not remember having done this regularly until the last year, when the bottle became exhausted? If you do not remember all this, countess, it is more than forgetfulness—it is ingratitude."

"Oh! M. Cagliostro, you are telling me things— —"

"Which were only known to yourself, I am aware; but what would be the use of being a sorcerer if one did not know one's neighbor's secrets?"

"Then Joseph Balsamo has, like you, the secret of this famous elixir?"

"No, madame, but he was one of my best friends, and I gave him three or four bottles."

"And has he any left?"

"Oh! I know nothing of that; for the last two or three years, poor Balsamo has disappeared. The last time I saw him was in America, on the banks of the Ohio: he was setting off on an expedition to the Rocky Mountains, and since then I have heard that he is dead."

"Come, come, count," cried the marshal; "let us have the secret, by all means."

"Are you speaking seriously, sir?" said Count Haga.

"Very seriously, sire,—I beg pardon, I mean count;" and Cagliostro bowed in such a way as to indicate that his error was a voluntary one.

"Then," said the marshal, "Madame Dubarry is not old enough to be made young again?"

"No, on my conscience."

"Well, then, I will give you another subject: here is my friend, M. Taverney—what do you say to him? Does he not look like a contemporary of Pontius Pilate? But perhaps, he, on the contrary, is too old."

Cagliostro looked at the baron. "No," said he.

"Ah! my dear count," exclaimed Richelieu; "if you will renew his youth, I will proclaim you a true pupil of Medea."

"You wish it?" asked Cagliostro of the host, and looking round at the same time on all assembled.

Every one called out, "Yes."

"And you also, M. Taverney?"

"I more than any one," said the baron.

"Well, it is easy," returned Cagliostro; and he drew from his pocket a small bottle, and poured into a glass some of the liquid it contained. Then, mixing these drops with half a glass of iced champagne, he passed it to the baron.

All eyes followed his movements eagerly.

The baron took the glass, but as he was about to drink he hesitated.

Every one began to laugh, but Cagliostro called out, "Drink, baron, or you will lose a liquor of which each drop is worth a hundred louis d'ors."

"The devil," cried Richelieu; "that is even better than tokay."

"I must then drink?" said the baron, almost trembling.

"Or pass the glass to another, sir, that some one at least may profit by it."

"Pass it here," said Richelieu, holding out his hand.

The baron raised the glass, and decided, doubtless, by the delicious smell and the beautiful rose color which those few drops had given to the champagne, he swallowed the magic liquor. In an instant a kind of shiver ran through him; he seemed to feel all his old and sluggish blood rushing quickly through his veins, from his heart to his feet, his wrinkled skin seemed to expand, his eyes, half covered by their lids, appeared to open without his will, and the pupils to grow and brighten, the trembling of his hands to cease, his voice to strengthen, and his limbs to recover their former youthful elasticity. In fact, it seemed as if the liquid in its descent had regenerated his whole body.

A cry of surprise, wonder, and admiration rang through the room.

Taverney, who had been slowly eating with his gums, began to feel famished; he seized a plate and helped himself largely to a ragout, and then demolished a partridge, bones and all, calling out that his teeth were coming back to him. He ate, laughed, and cried for joy, for half an hour, while the others remained gazing at him in stupefied wonder; then little by little he failed again, like a lamp whose oil is burning out, and all the former signs of old age returned upon him.

"Oh!" groaned he, "once more adieu to my youth," and he gave utterance to a deep sigh, while two tears rolled over his cheeks.

Instinctively, at this mournful spectacle of the old man first made young again, and then seeming to become yet older than before, from the contrast, the sigh was echoed all round the table.

"It is easy to explain, gentlemen," said Cagliostro; "I gave the baron but thirty-five drops of the elixir. He became young, therefore, for only thirty-five minutes."

"Oh more, more, count!" cried the old man eagerly.

"No, sir, for perhaps the second trial would kill you."

Of all the guests, Madame Dubarry, who had already tested the virtue of the elixir, seemed most deeply interested while old Taverney's youth seemed thus to renew itself; she had watched him with delight and triumph, and half fancied herself growing young again at the sight, while she could hardly refrain from endeavoring to snatch from Cagliostro the wonderful bottle; but now, seeing him resume his old age even quicker than he had lost it, "Alas!" she said sadly, "all is vanity and deception; the effects of this wonderful secret last for thirty-five minutes."

"That is to say," said Count Haga, "that in order to resume your youth for two years, you would have to drink a perfect river."

Every one laughed.

"Oh!" said De Condorcet, "the calculation is simple; a mere nothing of 3,153,000 drops for one year's youth."

"An inundation," said La Pérouse.

"However, sir," continued Madame Dubarry; "according to you, I have not needed so much, as a small bottle about four times the size of that you hold has been sufficient to arrest the march of time for ten years."

"Just so, madame. And you alone approach this mysterious truth. The man who has already grown old needs this large quantity to produce an immediate and powerful effect; but a woman of thirty, as you were, or a man of forty, as I was, when I began to drink this elixir, still full of life and youth, needs but ten drops at each period of decay; and with these ten drops may eternally continue his life and youth at the same point."

"What do you call the periods of decay?" asked Count Haga.

"The natural periods, count. In a state of nature, man's strength increases until thirty-five years of age. It then remains stationary until forty; and from that time forward, it begins to diminish, but almost imperceptibly, until fifty; then the process becomes quicker and quicker to the day of his death. In our state of civilization, when the body is weakened by excess, cares, and maladies, the failure begins at thirty-five. The time, then, to take nature, is when she is stationary, so as to forestall the beginning of decay. He who, possessor as I am of the secret of this elixir, knows how to seize the happy moment, will live as I live; always young, or, at least, always young enough for what he has to do in the world."

"Oh, M. Cagliostro," cried the countess; "why, if you could choose your own age, did you not stop at twenty instead of at forty?"

"Because, madame," said Cagliostro, smiling, "it suits me better to be a man of forty, still healthy and vigorous, than a raw youth of twenty."

"Oh!" said the countess.

"Doubtless, madame," continued Cagliostro, "at twenty one pleases women of thirty; at forty, we govern women of twenty, and men of sixty."

"I yield, sir," said the countess, "for you are a living proof of the truth of your own words."

"Then I," said Taverney, piteously, "am condemned; it is too late for me."

"M. de Richelieu has been more skilful than you," said La Pérouse naïvely, "and I have always heard that he had some secret."

"It is a report that the women have spread," laughed Count Haga.

"Is that a reason for disbelieving it, duke?" asked Madame Dubarry.

The old duke colored, a rare thing for him; but replied, "Do you wish, gentlemen, to have my receipt?"

"Oh, by all means."

"Well, then, it is simply to take care of yourself."

"Oh, oh!" cried all.

"But, M. Cagliostro," continued Madame Dubarry, "I must ask more about the elixir."

"Well, madame?"

"You said you first used it at forty years of age— —"

"Yes, madame."

"And that since that time, that is, since the siege of Troy— —"

"A little before, madame."

"That you have always remained forty years old?"

"You see me now."

"But then, sir," said De Condorcet, "you argue, not only the perpetuation of youth, but the preservation of life; for if since the siege of Troy you have been always forty, you have never died."

"True, marquis, I have never died."

"But are you, then, invulnerable, like Achilles, or still more so, for Achilles was killed by the arrow of Paris?"

"No. I am not invulnerable, and there is my great regret," said Cagliostro.

"Then, sir, you may be killed."

"Alas! yes."

"How, then, have you escaped all accidents for three thousand five hundred years?"

"It is chance, marquis, but will you follow my reasoning?"

"Yes, yes," cried all, with eagerness.

Cagliostro continued: "What is the first requisite to life?" he asked, spreading out his white and beautiful hands covered with rings, among which Cleopatra's shone conspicuously. "Is it not health!"

"Certainly."

"And the way to preserve health is?"

"Proper management," said Count Haga.

"Right, count. And why should not my elixir be the best possible method of treatment? And this treatment I have adopted, and with it have preserved my youth, and with youth, health, and life."

"But all things exhaust themselves; the finest constitution, as well as the worst."

"The body of Paris, like that of Vulcan," said the countess. "Perhaps, you knew Paris, by the bye?"

"Perfectly, madame; he was a fine young man, but really did not deserve all that has been said of him. In the first place, he had red hair."

"Red hair, horrible!"

"Unluckily, madame, Helen was not of your opinion: but to return to our subject. You say, M. de Taverney, that all things exhaust themselves; but you also know, that everything recovers again, regenerates, or is replaced, whichever you please to call it. The famous knife of St. Hubert, which so often changed both blade and handle, is an example, for through every change it still remained the knife of St. Hubert. The wines which the monks of Heidelberg preserve so carefully in their cellars, remain still the same wine, although each year they pour into it a fresh supply; therefore, this wine always remains clear, bright, and delicious: while the wine which Opimus and I hid in the earthen jars was, when I tried it a hundred years after, only a thick dirty substance, which might have been eaten, but certainly could not have been drunk. Well, I follow the example of the monks of Heidelberg, and preserve my body by introducing into it every year new elements, which regenerate the old. Every morning a new and fresh atom replaces in my blood, my flesh, and my bones, some particle which has perished. I stay that ruin which most men allow insensibly to invade their whole being, and I force into action all those powers which God has given to every human being, but which most people allow to lie dormant. This is the great study of my life, and as, in all things, he who does one thing constantly does that thing better than others, I am becoming more skilful than others in avoiding danger. Thus, you would not get me to enter a tottering house; I have seen too many houses not to tell at a glance the safe from the unsafe. You would not see me go out hunting with a man who managed his gun badly. From Cephalus, who killed his wife, down to the regent, who shot the prince in the eye, I have seen too many unskilful people. You could not make me accept in battle the post which many a man would take without thinking, because I should calculate in a moment the chances of danger at each point. You will tell me that one cannot foresee a stray bullet; but the man who has escaped a thousand gun-shots will hardly fall a victim to one now. Ah, you look incredulous, but am I not a living proof? I do not tell you that I am immortal, only that I know better than others how to avoid danger; for instance, I would not remain here now alone with M. de Launay, who is thinking that, if he had me in the Bastile, he would put my immortality to the test of starvation; neither would I remain with M. de Condorcet, for he is thinking that he might just empty into my glass the contents of that ring which he wears on his left hand, and which is full of poison—not with any evil intent, but just as a scientific experiment, to see if I should die."

The two people named looked at each other, and colored.

"Confess, M. de Launay, we are not in a court of justice; besides, thoughts are not punished. Did you not think what I said? And you, M. de Condorcet, would you not have liked to let me taste the poison in your ring, in the name of your beloved mistress, science?"

"Indeed," said M. de Launay, laughing, "I confess you are right; it was folly, but that folly did pass through my mind just before you accused me."

"And I," said M. de Condorcet, "will not be less candid. I did think that if you tasted the contents of my ring, I would not give much for your life."

A cry of admiration burst from the rest of the party; these avowals confirming not the immortality, but the penetration, of Count Cagliostro.

"You see," said Cagliostro, quietly, "that I divined these dangers; well, it is the same with other things. The experience of a long life reveals to me at a glance much of the past and of the future of those whom I meet. My capabilities in this way extend even to animals and inanimate objects. If I get into a carriage, I can tell from the look of the horses if they are likely to run away; and from that of the coachman, if he will overturn me. If I go on board ship, I can see if the captain is ignorant or obstinate, and consequently likely to endanger me. I should then leave the coachman or captain, escape from those horses or that ship. I do not deny chance, I only lessen it, and instead of incurring a hundred chances, like the rest of the world, I prevent ninety-nine of them, and endeavor to guard against the hundredth. This is the good of having lived three thousand years."

"Then," said La Pérouse, laughing, amidst the wonder and enthusiasm created by this speech of Cagliostro's, "you should come with me when I embark to make the tour of the world; you would render me a signal service."

Cagliostro did not reply.

"M. de Richelieu," continued La Pérouse, "as the Count Cagliostro, which is very intelligible, does not wish to quit such good company, you must permit me to do so without him. Excuse me, Count Haga, and you, madame, but it is seven o'clock, and I have promised his majesty to start at a quarter past. But since Count Cagliostro will not be tempted to come with me, and see my ships, perhaps he can tell me what will happen to me between Versailles and Brest. From Brest to the Pole I ask nothing; that is my own business."

Cagliostro looked at La Pérouse with such a melancholy air, so full both of pity and kindness, that the others were struck by it. The sailor himself, however, did not remark it. He took leave of the company, put on his fur riding coat, into one of the pockets of which Madame Dubarry pushed a bottle of delicious cordial, welcome to a traveler, but which he would not have provided for himself, to recall to him, she said, his absent friends during the long nights of a journey in such bitter cold.

La Pérouse, still full of gaiety, bowed respectfully to Count Haga, and held out his hand to the old marshal.

"Adieu, dear La Pérouse," said the latter.

"No, duke, au revoir," replied La Pérouse, "one would think I was going away forever; now I have but to circumnavigate the globe—five or six years' absence; it is scarcely worth while to say 'adieu' for that."

"Five or six years," said the marshal; "you might almost as well say five or six centuries; days are years at my age, therefore I say, adieu."

"Bah! ask the sorcerer," returned La Pérouse, still laughing; "he will promise you twenty years' more life. Will you not, Count Cagliostro? Oh, count, why did I not hear sooner of those precious drops of yours? Whatever the price, I should have shipped a tun. Madame, another kiss of that beautiful hand, I shall certainly not see such another till I return; au revoir," and he left the room.

Cagliostro still preserved the same mournful silence. They heard the steps of the captain as he left the house, his gay voice in the courtyard, and his farewells to the people assembled to see him depart. Then the horses shook their heads, covered with bells, the door of the carriage shut with some noise, and the wheels were heard rolling along the street.

La Pérouse had started on that voyage from which he was destined never to return.

When they could no longer hear a sound, all looks were again turned to Cagliostro; there seemed a kind of inspired light in his eyes.

Count Haga first broke the silence, which had lasted for some minutes. "Why did you not reply to his question?" he inquired of Cagliostro.

Cagliostro started, as if the question had roused him from a reverie. "Because," said he, "I must either have told a falsehood or a sad truth."

"How so?"

"I must have said to him,—'M. de la Pérouse, the duke is right in saying to you adieu, and not au revoir.'"

"Oh," said Richelieu, turning pale, "what do you mean?"

"Reassure yourself, marshal, this sad prediction does not concern you."

"What," cried Madame Dubarry, "this poor La Pérouse, who has just kissed my hand——"

"Not only, madame, will never kiss it again, but will never again see those he has just left," said Cagliostro, looking attentively at the glass of water he was holding up.

A cry of astonishment burst from all. The interest of the conversation deepened every moment, and you might have thought, from the solemn and anxious air with which all regarded Cagliostro, that it was some ancient and infallible oracle they were consulting.

"Pray then, count," said Madame Dubarry, "tell us what will befall poor La Pérouse."

Cagliostro shook his head.

"Oh, yes, let us hear!" cried all the rest.

"Well, then, M. de la Pérouse intends, as you know, to make the tour of the globe, and continue the researches of poor Captain Cook, who was killed in the Sandwich Islands."

"Yes, yes, we know."

"Everything should foretell a happy termination to this voyage; M. de la Pérouse is a good seaman, and his route has been most skilfully traced by the king."

"Yes," interrupted Count Haga, "the King of France is a clever geographer; is he not, M. de Condorcet?"

"More skilful than is needful for a king," replied the marquis; "kings ought to know things only slightly, then they will let themselves be guided by those who know them thoroughly."

"Is this a lesson, marquis?" said Count Haga, smiling.

"Oh, no. Only a simple reflection, a general truth."

"Well, he is gone," said Madame Dubarry, anxious to bring the conversation back to La Pérouse.

"Yes, he is gone," replied Cagliostro, "but don't believe, in spite of his haste, that he will soon embark. I foresee much time lost at Brest."

"That would be a pity," said De Condorcet; "this is the time to set out: it is even now rather late—February or March would have been better."

"Oh, do not grudge him these few months, M. de Condorcet, for, during them, he will at least live and hope."

"He has got good officers, I suppose?" said Richelieu.

"Yes, he who commands the second ship is a distinguished officer. I see him—- young, adventurous, brave, unhappily."

"Why unhappily?"

"A year after I look for him, and see him no more," said Cagliostro, anxiously consulting his glass. "No one here is related to M. de Langle?"

"No."

"No one knows him?"

"No."

"Well, death will commence with him."

A murmur of affright escaped from all the guests.

"But he, La Pérouse?" cried several voices.

"He sails, he lands, he reembarks; I see one, two years, of successful navigation; we hear news of him, and then——"

"Then?"

"Years pass——"

"But at last?"

"The sea is vast, the heavens are clouded, here and there appear unknown lands, and figures hideous as the monsters of the Grecian Archipelago. They watch the ship, which is being carried in a fog amongst the breakers, by a tempest less fearful than themselves. Oh! La Pérouse, La Pérouse, if you could hear me, I would cry to you. You set out, like Columbus, to discover a world; beware of unknown isles!"

He ceased, and an icy shiver ran through the assembly.

"But why did you not warn him?" asked Count Haga, who, in spite of himself, had succumbed to the influence of this extraordinary man.

"Yes," cried Madame Dubarry, "why not send after him and bring him back? The life of a man like La Pérouse is surely worth a courier, my dear marshal."

The marshal rose to ring the bell.

Cagliostro extended his arm to stop him. "Alas!" said he, "All advice would be useless. I can foretell destiny, but I cannot change it. M. de la Pérouse would laugh if he heard my words, as the son of Priam laughed when Cassandra prophesied; and see, you begin to laugh yourself, Count Haga, and laughing is contagious: your companions are catching it. Do not restrain yourselves, gentlemen—I am accustomed to an incredulous audience."

"Oh, we believe," said Madame Dubarry and the Duke de Richelieu; "and I believe," murmured Taverney; "and I also," said Count Haga politely.

"Yes," replied Cagliostro, "you believe, because it concerns La Pérouse; but, if I spoke of yourself, you would not believe."

"I confess that what would have made me believe, would have been, if you had said to him, 'Beware of unknown isles;' then he would, at least, have had the chance of avoiding them."

"I assure you no, count; and, if he had believed me, it would only have been more horrible, for the unfortunate man would have seen himself approaching those isles destined to be fatal to him, without the power to flee from them. Therefore he would have died, not one, but a hundred deaths, for he would have gone through it all by anticipation. Hope, of which I should have deprived him, is what best sustains a man under all trials."

"Yes," said De Condorcet; "the veil which hides from us our future is the only real good which God has vouchsafed to man."

"Nevertheless," said Count Haga, "did a man like you say to me, shun a certain man or a certain thing, I would beware, and I would thank you for the counsel."

Cagliostro shook his head, with a faint smile.

"I mean it, M. de Cagliostro," continued Count Haga; "warn me, and I will thank you."

"You wish me to tell you what I would not tell La Pérouse?"

"Yes, I wish it."

Cagliostro opened his mouth as if to begin, and then stopped, and said, "No, count, no!"

"I beg you."

Cagliostro still remained silent.

"Take care," said the count, "you are making me incredulous."

"Incredulity is better than misery."

"M. de Cagliostro," said the count, gravely, "you forget one thing, which is, that though there are men who had better remain ignorant of their destiny, there are others who should know it, as it concerns not themselves alone, but millions of others."

"Then," said Cagliostro, "command me; if your majesty commands, I will obey."

"I command you to reveal to me my destiny, M. de Cagliostro," said the king, with an air at once courteous and dignified.

At this moment, as Count Haga had dropped his incognito in speaking to Cagliostro, M. de Richelieu advanced towards him, and said, "Thanks, sire, for the honor you have done my house; will your majesty assume the place of honor?"

"Let us remain as we are, marshal; I wish to hear what M. de Cagliostro is about to say."

"One does not speak the truth to kings, sire."

"Bah! I am not in my kingdom; take your place again, duke. Proceed, M. de Cagliostro, I beg."

Cagliostro looked again through his glass, and one might have imagined the particles agitated by this look, as they danced in, the light. "Sire," said he, "tell me what you wish to know?"

"Tell me by what death I shall die."

"By a gun-shot, sire."

The eyes of Gustavus grew bright. "Ah, in a battle!" said he; "the death of a soldier! Thanks, M. de Cagliostro, a thousand times thanks; oh, I foresee battles, and Gustavus Adolphus and Charles XII. have shown me how a King of Sweden should die."

Cagliostro drooped his head, without replying.

"Oh!" cried Count Haga, "will not my wound then be given in battle?"

"No, sire."

"In a sedition?—yes, that is possible."

"No, not in a sedition, sire."

"But, where then?"

"At a ball, sire."

The king remained silent, and Cagliostro buried his head in his hands.

Every one looked pale and frightened; then M. de Condorcet took the glass of water and examined it, as if there he could solve the problem of all that had been going on; but finding nothing to satisfy him, "Well, I also," said he, "will beg our illustrious prophet to consult for me his magic mirror:

unfortunately, I am not a powerful lord; I cannot command, and my obscure life concerns no millions of people."

"Sir," said Count Haga, "you command in the name of science, and your life belongs not only to a nation, but to all mankind."

"Thanks," said De Condorcet; "but, perhaps, your opinion on this subject is not shared by M. de Cagliostro."

Cagliostro raised his head. "Yes, marquis," said he, in a manner which began to be excited, "you are indeed a powerful lord in the kingdom of intelligence; look me, then, in the face, and tell me, seriously, if you also wish that I should prophesy to you."

"Seriously, count, upon my honor."

"Well, marquis," said Cagliostro, in a hoarse voice, "you will die of that poison which you carry in your ring; you will die— —"

"Oh, but if I throw it away?"

"Throw it away!"

"You allow that that would be easy."

"Throw it away!"

"Oh, yes, marquis," cried Madame Dubarry; "throw away that horrid poison! Throw it away, if it be only to falsify this prophet of evil, who threatens us all with so many misfortunes. For if you throw it away you cannot die by it, as M. de Cagliostro predicts; so there at least he will have been wrong."

"Madame la Comtesse is right," said Count Haga.

"Bravo, countess!" said Richelieu. "Come, marquis, throw away that poison, for now I know you carry it, I shall tremble every time we drink together; the ring might open of itself, and— —"

"It is useless," said Cagliostro quietly; "M. de Condorcet will not throw it away."

"No," returned De Condorcet, "I shall not throw it away; not that I wish to aid my destiny, but because this is a unique poison, prepared by Cabanis, and which chance has completely hardened, and that chance might never occur again; therefore I will not throw it away. Triumph if you will, M. de Cagliostro."

"Destiny," replied he, "ever finds some way to work out its own ends."

"Then I shall die by poison," said the marquis; "well, so be it. It is an admirable death, I think; a little poison on the tip of the tongue, and I am gone. It is scarcely dying: it is merely ceasing to live."

"It is not necessary for you to suffer, sir," said Cagliostro.

"Then, sir," said M. de Favras, "we have a shipwreck, a gun-shot, and a poisoning which makes my mouth water. Will you not do me the favor also to predict some little pleasure of the same kind for me?"

"Oh, marquis!" replied Cagliostro, beginning to grow warm under this irony, "do not envy these gentlemen, you will have still better."

"Better!" said M. de Favras, laughing; "that is pledging yourself to a great deal. It is difficult to beat the sea, fire, and poison!"

"There remains the cord, marquis," said Cagliostro, bowing.

"The cord! what do you mean?"

"I mean that you will be hanged," replied Cagliostro, seeming no more the master of his prophetic rage.

"Hanged! the devil!" cried Richelieu.

"Monsieur forgets that I am a nobleman," said M. de Favras, coldly; "or if he means to speak of a suicide, I warn him that I shall respect myself sufficiently, even in my last moments, not to use a cord while I have a sword."

"I do not speak of a suicide, sir."

"Then you speak of a punishment?"

"Yes."

"You are a foreigner, sir, and therefore I pardon you."

"What?"

"Your ignorance, sir. In France we decapitate noblemen."

"You may arrange this, if you can, with the executioner," replied Cagliostro.

M. de Favras said no more. There was a general silence and shrinking for a few minutes.

"Do you know that I tremble at last," said M. de Launay; "my predecessors have come off so badly, that I fear for myself if I now take my turn."

"Then you are more reasonable than they; you are right. Do not seek to know the future; good or bad, let it rest—it is in the hands of God."

"Oh! M. de Launay," said Madame Dubarry, "I hope you will not be less courageous than the others have been."

"I hope so, too, madame," said the governor. Then, turning to Cagliostro, "Sir," he said, "favor me, in my turn, with my horoscope, if you please."

"It is easy," replied Cagliostro; "a blow on the head with a hatchet, and all will be over."

A look of dismay was once more general. Richelieu and Taverney begged Cagliostro to say no more, but female curiosity carried the day.

"To hear you talk, count," said Madame Dubarry, "one would think the whole universe must die a violent death. Here we were, eight of us, and five are already condemned by you."

"Oh, you understand that it is all prearranged to frighten us, and we shall only laugh at it," said M. de Favras, trying to do so.

"Certainly we will laugh," said Count Haga, "be it true or false."

"Oh, I will laugh too, then," said Madame Dubarry. "I will not dishonor the assembly by my cowardice; but, alas! I am only a woman, I cannot rank among you and be worthy of a tragical end; a woman dies in her bed. My death, a sorrowful old woman abandoned by every one, will be the worst of all. Will it not, M. de Cagliostro?"

She stopped, and seemed to wait for the prophet to reassure her. Cagliostro did not speak; so, her curiosity obtaining the mastery over her fears, she went on. "Well, M. de Cagliostro, will you not answer me?"

"What do you wish me to say, madame?"

She hesitated—then, rallying her courage, "Yes," she cried, "I will run the risk. Tell me the fate of Jeanne de Vaubernier, Countess Dubarry."

"On the scaffold, madame," replied the prophet of evil.

"A jest, sir, is it not?" said she, looking at him with a supplicating air.

Cagliostro seemed not to see it. "Why do you think I jest?" said he.

"Oh, because to die on the scaffold one must have committed some crime—stolen, or committed murder, or done something dreadful; and it is not likely I shall do that. It was a jest, was it not?"

"Oh, mon Dieu, yes," said Cagliostro; "all I have said is but a jest."

The countess laughed, but scarcely in a natural manner. "Come, M. de Favras," said she, "let us order our funerals."

"Oh, that will be needless for you, madame," said Cagliostro.

"Why so, sir?"

"Because you will go to the scaffold in a car."

"Oh, how horrible! This dreadful man, marshal! for heaven's sake choose more cheerful guests next time, or I will never visit you again."

"Excuse me, madame," said Cagliostro, "but you, like all the rest, would have me speak."

"At least I hope you will grant me time to choose my confessor."

"It will be superfluous, countess."

"Why?"

"The last person who will mount the scaffold in France with a confessor will be the King of France." And Cagliostro pronounced these words in so thrilling a voice that every one was struck with horror.

All were silent.

Cagliostro raised to his lips the glass of water in which he had read these fearful prophecies, but scarcely had he touched it, when he set it down with a movement of disgust. He turned his eyes to M. de Taverney.

"Oh," cried he, in terror, "do not tell me anything; I do not wish to know!"

"Well, then, I will ask instead of him," said Richelieu.

"You, marshal, be happy; you are the only one of us all who will die in his bed."

"Coffee, gentlemen, coffee," cried the marshal, enchanted with the prediction. Every one rose.

But before passing into the drawing-room, Count Haga, approaching Cagliostro, said, —

"Tell me what to beware of."

"Of a muff, sir," replied Cagliostro.

"And I?" said Condorcet.

"Of an omelet."

"Good; I renounce eggs," and he left the room.

"And I?" said M. de Favras; "what must I fear?"

"A letter."

"And I?" said De Launay.

"The taking of the Bastile."

"Oh, you quite reassure me." And he went away laughing.

"Now for me, sir," said the countess, trembling.

"You, beautiful countess, shun the Place Louis XV."

"Alas," said the countess, "one day already I lost myself there; that day I suffered much."

She left the room, and Cagliostro was about to follow her when Richelieu stopped him.

"One moment," said he; "there remains only Taverney and I, my dear sorcerer."

"M. de Taverney begged me to say nothing, and you, marshal, have asked me nothing."

"Oh, I do not wish to hear," again cried Taverney.

"But come, to prove your power, tell us something that only Taverney and I know," said Richelieu.

"What?" asked Cagliostro, smiling.

"Tell us what makes Taverney come to Versailles, instead of living quietly in his beautiful house at Maison-Rouge, which the king bought for him three years ago."

"Nothing more simple, marshal," said Cagliostro. "Ten years ago, M. de Taverney wished to give his daughter, Mademoiselle Andrée, to the King Louis XV., but he did not succeed."

"Oh!" growled Taverney.

"Now, monsieur wishes to give his son Philippe de Taverney, to the Queen Marie Antoinette; ask him if I speak the truth."

"On my word," said Taverney, trembling, "this man is a sorcerer; devil take me if he is not!"

"Do not speak so cavalierly of the devil, my old comrade," said the marshal.

"It is frightful," murmured Taverney, and he turned to implore Cagliostro to be discreet, but he was gone.

"Come, Taverney, to the drawing-room," said the marshal; "or they will drink their coffee without us."

But when they arrived there, the room was empty; no one had courage to face again the author of these terrible predictions.

The wax lights burned in the candelabra, the fire burned on the hearth, but all for nothing.

"Ma foi, old friend, it seems we must take our coffee tête-à-tête. Why, where the devil has he gone?" Richelieu looked all around him, but Taverney had vanished like the rest. "Never mind," said the marshal, chuckling as Voltaire might have done, and rubbing his withered though still white hands; "I shall be the only one to die in my bed. Well, Count Cagliostro, at least I believe. In my bed! that was it; I shall die in my bed, and I trust not for a long time. Hola! my valet-de-chambre and my drops."

The valet entered with the bottle, and the marshal went with him into the bedroom.

CHAPTER I
TWO UNKNOWN LADIES

The winter of 1784, that monster which devoured half France, we could not see, although he growled at the doors, while at the house of M. de Richelieu, shut in as we were in that warm and comfortable dining-room.

A little frost on the windows seems but the luxury of nature added to that of man. Winter has its diamonds, its powder, and its silvery embroidery for the rich man wrapped in his furs, and packed in his carriage, or snug among the wadding and velvet of a well-warmed room. Hoar-frost is a beauty, ice a change of decoration by the greatest of artists, which the rich admire through their windows. He who is warm can admire the withered trees, and find a somber charm in the sight of the snow-covered plain. He who, after a day without suffering, when millions of his fellow-creatures are enduring dreadful privations, throws himself on his bed of down, between his fine and well-aired sheets, may find out that all is for the best in this best of all possible worlds.

But he who is hungry sees none of these beauties of nature; he who is cold hates the sky without a sun, and consequently without a smile for such unfortunates. Now, at the time at which we write, that is, about the middle of the month of April, three hundred thousand miserable beings, dying from cold and hunger, groaned in Paris alone—in that Paris where, in spite of the boast that scarcely another city contained so many rich people, nothing had been prepared to prevent the poor from perishing of cold and wretchedness.

For the last four months, the same leaden sky had driven the poor from the villages into the town, as it sent the wolves from the woods into the villages.

No more bread. No more wood.

No more bread for those who felt this cold—no more wood to cook it. All the provisions which had been collected, Paris had devoured in a month. The Provost, short-sighted and incapable, did not know how to procure for Paris, which was under his care, the wood which might have been collected in the neighborhood. When it froze, he said the frost prevented the horses from bringing it; if it thawed, he pleaded want of horses and conveyances. Louis XVI., ever good and humane, always ready to attend to the physical wants of his people, although he overlooked their social ones, began by contributing a sum of 200,000 francs for horses and carts, and insisting on their immediate use. Still the demand continued greater than the supply. At first no one was allowed to carry away from the public timber-yard more than a cart-load of wood; then they were limited to half this quantity. Soon the long strings of people might be seen waiting outside the doors, as they were afterwards seen at the bakers' shops. The king gave away the whole of his private income in charity. He procured 3,000,000 francs by a grant and applied it to the relief of the sufferers, declaring that every other need must give way before that of cold and famine. The queen, on her part, gave 500 louis from her purse. The convents, the hospitals, and the public buildings were thrown open as places of asylum for the poor, who came in crowds for the sake of the fires that were kept there. They kept hoping for a thaw, but heaven seemed inflexible. Every evening the same copper-colored sky disappointed their hopes; and the stars shone bright and clear as funeral torches through the long, cold nights, which hardened again and again the snow which fell during the day. All day long, thousands of workmen, with spades and shovels, cleared away the snow from before the houses; so that on each side of the streets, already too narrow for the traffic, rose a high, thick wall, blocking up the way. Soon these masses of snow and ice became so large that the shops were obscured by them, and they were obliged to allow it to remain where it fell. Paris could do no more. She gave in, and allowed the winter to do its worst. December, January, February, and March passed thus, although now and then a few days' thaw changed the streets, whose sewers were blocked up, into running streams. Horses were drowned, and carriages destroyed, in the streets, some of which could only be traversed in boats. Paris, faithful to its character, sang through this destruction by the thaw as it had done through that by famine. Processions were made to the markets to see the fisherwomen serving their customers with immense leathern boots on, inside which their trousers were pushed, and with their petticoats tucked round their waists, all laughing, gesticulating, and splashing each other as they stood in the water. These thaws, however, were but transitory; the frost returned, harder and more obstinate than ever, and recourse was had to sledges, pushed along by skaters, or drawn by roughshod horses along the causeways, which were like polished mirrors. The Seine, frozen many feet deep, was become the rendezvous for all idlers, who assembled there to skate or slide, until, warmed by exercise, they ran to the nearest fire, lest the perspiration should freeze upon them. All trembled for the time when, the water communications being stopped, and the roads impassable, provisions could no longer be sent in, and began to fear that

Paris would perish from want. The king, in this extremity, called a council. They decided to implore all bishops, abbés, and monks to leave Paris and retire to their dioceses or convents; and all those magistrates and officials who, preferring the opera to their duties, had crowded to Paris, to return to their homes; for all these people used large quantities of wood in their hotels, and consumed no small amount of food. There were still the country gentlemen, who were also to be entreated to leave. But M. Lenoir, lieutenant of police, observed to the king that, as none of these people were criminals, and could not therefore be compelled to leave Paris in a day, they would probably be so long thinking about it, that the thaw would come before their departure, which would then be more hurtful than useful. All this care and pity of the king and queen, however, excited the ingenious gratitude of the people, who raised monuments to them, as ephemeral as the feelings which prompted them. Obelisks and pillars of snow and ice, engraved with their names, were to be seen all over Paris. At the end of March the thaw began, but by fits and starts, constant returns of frost prolonging the miseries of the people. Indeed, in the beginning of April it appeared to set in harder than ever, and the half-thawed streets, frozen again, became so slippery and dangerous, that nothing was seen but broken limbs and accidents of all kinds. The snow prevented the carriages from being heard, and the police had enough to do, from the reckless driving of the aristocracy, to preserve from the wheels those who were spared by cold and hunger.

It was about a week after the dinner given by M. de Richelieu that four elegant sledges entered Paris, gliding over the frozen snow which covered the Cours la Reine and the extremity of the boulevards. From thence they found it more difficult to proceed, for the sun and the traffic had begun to change the snow and ice into a wet mass of dirt.

In the foremost sledge were two men in brown riding coats with double capes. They were drawn by a black horse, and turned from time to time, as if to watch the sledge that followed them, and which contained two ladies so enveloped in furs that it was impossible to see their faces. It might even have been difficult to distinguish their sex, had it not been for the height of their coiffure, crowning which was a small hat with a plume of feathers. From the colossal edifice of this coiffure, all mingled with ribbons and jewels, escaped occasionally a cloud of white powder, as when a gust of wind shakes the snow from the trees.

These two ladies, seated side by side, were conversing so earnestly as scarcely to see the numerous spectators who watched their progress along the boulevards. One of them taller and more majestic than the other, and holding up before her face a finely-embroidered cambric handkerchief, carried her head erect and stately, in spite of the wind which swept across their sledge.

It had just struck five by the clock of the church St. Croix d'Antin and night was beginning to descend upon Paris, and with the night the bitter cold. They had just reached the Porte St. Denis, when the lady of whom we have spoken made a sign to the men in front, who thereupon quickened the pace of their horse, and soon disappeared among the evening mists, which were fast thickening around the colossal structure of the Bastile.

This signal she then repeated to the other two sledges, which also vanished along the Rue St. Denis. Meanwhile, the one in which she sat, having arrived at the Boulevard de Menilmontant, stopped.

In this place few people were to be seen; night had dispersed them. Besides, in this out-of-the-way quarter, not many citizens would trust themselves without torches and an escort, since winter had sharpened the wants of three or four thousand beggars who were easily changed into robbers.

The lady touched with her finger the shoulder of the coachman who was driving her, and said, "Weber, how long will it take you to bring the cabriolet you know where?"

"Madame wishes me to bring the cabriolet?" asked the coachman, with a strong German accent.

"Yes, I shall return by the streets; and as they are still more muddy than the boulevard, we should not get on in the sledge; besides, I begin to feel the cold. Do not you, petite?" said she, turning to the other lady.

"Yes, madame."

"Then, Weber, we will have the cabriolet."

"Very well, madame."

"What is the time, petite?"

The young lady looked at her watch, which, however, she could hardly see, as it was growing dark, and said, "A quarter to six, madame."

"Then at a quarter to seven, Weber."

Saying these words, the lady leaped lightly from the sledge, followed by her friend, and walked away quickly; while the coachman murmured, with a kind of respectful despair, sufficiently loud for his mistress to hear, "Oh, mein Gott! what imprudence."

The two ladies laughed, drew their cloaks closer round them, and went tramping along through the snow, with their little feet.

"You have good eyes, Andrée," said the lady who seemed the elder of the two, although she could not have been more than thirty or thirty-two; "try to read the name at the corner of that street."

"Rue du Pont-aux-Choux, madame."

"Rue du Pont-aux-Choux! ah, mon Dieu, we must have come wrong. They told me the second street on the right;—but what a smell of hot bread!"

"That is not astonishing," said her companion, "for here is a baker's shop."

"Well, let us ask there for the Rue St. Claude," she said, moving to the door.

"Oh! do not you go in, madame; allow me," said Andrée.

"The Rue St. Claude, my pretty ladies?" said a cheerful voice. "Are you asking for the Rue St. Claude?"

The two ladies turned towards the voice, and saw, leaning against the door of the shop, a man who, in spite of the cold, had his chest and his legs quite bare.

"Oh! a naked man!" cried the young lady, half hiding behind her companion; "are we among savages?"

"Was not that what you asked for?" said the journeyman baker, for such he was, who did not understand her movement in the least, and, accustomed to his own costume, never dreamed of its effect upon them.

"Yes, my friend, the Rue St. Claude," said the elder lady, hardly able to keep from laughing.

"Oh, it is not difficult to find; besides, I will conduct you there myself;" and, suiting the action to the words, he began to move his long bony legs, which terminated in immense wooden shoes.

"Oh, no!" cried the elder lady, who did not fancy such a guide; "pray do not disturb yourself. Tell us the way, and we shall easily find it."

"First street to the right," said he, drawing back again.

"Thanks," said the ladies, who ran on as fast as they could, that he might not hear the laughter which they could no longer restrain.

CHAPTER II
AN INTERIOR

If we do not calculate too much on the memory of our readers, they certainly know the Rue St. Claude, which joins at one end the boulevard, and at the other the Rue St. Louis; this was an important street in the first part of our story, when it was inhabited by Joseph Balsamo, his sibyl, Lorenza, and his master, Althotas. It was still a respectable street, though badly lighted, and by no means clean, but little known or frequented.

There was, however, at the corner of the boulevard a large house, with an aristocratic air; but this house, which might, from the number of its windows, have illuminated the whole street, had it been lighted up, was the darkest and most somber-looking of any. The door was never seen to open; and the windows were thick with dust, which seemed never disturbed. Sometimes an idler, attracted by curiosity, approached the gates and peeped through; all he could see, however, were masses of weeds growing between the stones of the courtyard, and green moss spreading itself over everything. Occasionally an enormous rat, sole inmate of those deserted domains, ran across the yard, on his way to his usual habitation in the cellars, which seemed, however, to be an excess of modesty, when he had the choice of so many fine sitting-rooms, where he need never fear the intrusion of a cat.

At times, one or two of the neighbors, passing the house, might stop to take a survey, and one would say to the other:

"Well, what do you see?"

"Why," he would reply, "I see the rat."

"Oh! let me look at him. How fat he has grown!"

"That is not to be wondered at; he is never disturbed; and there must be some good pickings in the house. M. de Balsamo disappeared so suddenly, that he must have left something behind."

"But you forget that the house was half burned down."

And they would pursue their way.

Opposite this ruin was a high narrow house inclosed within a garden wall. From the upper windows, a light was to be seen; the rest was shrouded in darkness. Either all the inhabitants were already asleep, or they were very economical of wood and candles, which certainly were frightfully dear this winter. It is, however, with the fifth story only that we have any business.

We must, in the first place, take a survey of the house, and, ascending the staircase, open the first door. This room is empty and dark, however, but it opens into another of which the furniture deserves our attention.

The doors were gaudily painted, and it contained easy chairs covered in white, with yellow velvet trimming, and a sofa to match; the cushions of which, however, were so full of the wrinkles of old age as scarcely to be cushions any longer. Two portraits hanging on the walls next attracted attention. A candle and a lamp—one placed on a stand, about three feet high, and the other on the chimney-piece—threw a constant light on them.

The first was a well-known portrait of Henry III., King of France and Poland; a cap on his head, surmounting his long pale face and heavy eyes; a pointed beard, and a ruff round his neck.

Under it was the inscription, traced in black letters, on a badly-gilded frame, "Henri de Valois."

The other portrait, of which the gilding was newer, and the painting more fresh and recent, represented a young lady with black eyes, a straight nose, and rather compressed lips, who appeared crushed under a tower of hair and ribbons, to which the cap of Henry III. was in the proportion of a mole-hill to a pyramid.

Under this portrait was inscribed, "Jeanne de Valois."

Glance at the fireless hearth, at the faded curtains, and then turn towards a little oak table in the corner; for there, leaning on her elbow, and writing the addresses of some letters, sits the original of this portrait.

A few steps off, in an attitude half curious, half respectful, stands a little old woman, apparently about sixty.

"Jeanne de Valois," says the inscription; but if this lady be indeed a Valois, one wonders however the portrait of Henry III., the sybarite king, the great voluptuary, could support the sight of so much poverty in a person not only of his race, but bearing his name.

In her person, however, this lady of the fifth story did no discredit to her portrait. She had white and delicate hands, which from time to time she rubbed together, as if to endeavor to put some warmth into them; her foot also, which was encased in a rather coquettish velvet slipper, was small and pretty.

The wind whistled through all the old doors, and penetrated the crevices of the shaking windows; and the old servant kept glancing sadly towards the empty grate. Her lady continued her occupation, talking aloud as she did so.

"Madame de Misery," she murmured; "first lady of the bedchamber to her majesty—I cannot expect more than six louis from her, for she has already given to me once." And she sighed. "Madame Patrick, lady's-maid to her majesty, two louis; M. d'Ormesson, an audience; M. de Calonne, some good advice, M. de Rohan, a visit; at least, we will try to induce him," said she, smiling at the thought. "Well, then, I think I may hope for eight louis within a week." Then, looking up, "Dame Clotilde," she said, "snuff this candle."

The old woman did as she was bid, and then resumed her place. This kind of inquisition seemed to annoy the young lady, for she said, "Pray go and look if you cannot find the end of a wax candle for me; this tallow is odious."

"There is none," replied the old woman.

"But just look."

"Where?"

"In the ante-chamber."

"It is so cold there."

"There is some one ringing," said the young lady.

"Madame is mistaken," replied the obstinate old woman.

"I thought I heard it, Dame Clotilde;" then, abandoning the attempt, she turned again to her calculations. "Eight louis! Three I owe for the rent, and five I have promised to M. de la Motte, to make him support his stay at Bar-sur-Aube. Pauvre diable, our marriage has not enriched him as yet—but patience;" and she smiled again, and looked at herself in the mirror that hung between the two portraits. "Well, then," she continued, "I still want one louis for going from Versailles to Paris and back again; living for a week, one louis; dress, and gifts to the porters of the houses where I go, four louis; but," said she, starting up, "some one is ringing!"

"No, madame," replied the old woman. "It is below, on the next floor."

"But I tell you it is not," said she angrily, as the bell rang yet louder.

Even the old woman could deny it no longer; so she hobbled off to open the door, while her mistress rapidly cleared away all the papers, and seated herself on the sofa, assuming the air of a person humble and resigned, although suffering.

It was, however, only her body that reposed; for her eyes, restless and unquiet, sought incessantly, first her mirror and then the door.

At last it opened, and she heard a young and sweet voice saying, "Is it here that Madame la Comtesse de la Motte lives?"

"Madame la Comtesse de la Motte Valois," replied Clotilde.

"It is the same person, my good woman; is she at home?"

"Yes, madame; she is too ill to go out."

During this colloquy, the pretended invalid saw reflected in the glass the figure of a lady talking to Clotilde, unquestionably belonging to the higher ranks. She then saw her turn round, and say to some one behind, "We can go in—it is here."

And the two ladies we have before seen asking the way prepared to enter the room.

"Whom shall I announce to the countess?" said Clotilde.

"Announce a Sister of Charity," said the elder lady.

"From Paris?"

"No; from Versailles."

Clotilde entered the room, and the strangers followed her.

Jeanne de Valois seemed to rise with difficulty from her seat to receive her visitors.

Clotilde placed chairs for them, and then unwillingly withdrew.

CHAPTER III
JEANNE DE LA MOTTE VALOIS

The first thought of Jeanne de la Motte was to examine the faces of her visitors, so as to gather what she could of their characters. The elder lady, who might have been, as we have said, about thirty-two years of age, was remarkably beautiful, although, at first sight, a great air of hauteur detracted slightly from the charm of her expression; her carriage was so proud, and her whole appearance so distingué that Jeanne could not doubt her nobility, even at a cursory glance.

She, however, seemed purposely to place herself as far as possible from the light, so as to be little seen.

Her companion appeared four or five years younger, and was not less beautiful. Her complexion was charming; her hair, drawn back from her temples, showed to advantage the perfect oval of her face; two large blue eyes, calm and serene; a well-formed mouth, indicating great frankness of disposition; a nose that rivaled the Venus de Medicis; such was the other face which presented itself to the gaze of Jeanne de Valois.

She inquired gently to what happy circumstance she owed the honor of their visit.

The elder lady signed to the younger, who thereupon said, "Madame, for I believe you are married——"

"I have the honor to be the wife of M. le Comte de la Motte, an excellent gentleman."

"Well, Madame la Comtesse, we are at the head of a charitable institution, and have heard concerning your condition things that interest us, and we consequently wished to have more precise details on the subject."

"Mesdames," replied Jeanne, "you see there the portrait of Henry III., that is to say, of the brother of my grandfather, for I am truly of the race of Valois, as you have doubtless been told." And she waited for the next question, looking at her visitors with a sort of proud humility.

"Madame," said the grave and sweet voice of the elder lady, "is it true, as we have also heard, that your mother was housekeeper at a place called Fontelle, near Bar-sur-Seine?"

Jeanne colored at this question, but replied, "It is true, madame; and," she went on, "as Marie Jossel, my mother, was possessed of rare beauty, my father fell in love with her, and married her, for it is by my father that I am nobly descended; he was a St. Rémy de Valois, direct descendant of the Valois who were on the throne."

"But how have you been reduced to this degree of poverty, madame?"

"Alas! that is easily told. You are not ignorant that after the accession of Henry IV., by which the crown passed from the house of Valois to that of Bourbon, there still remained many branches of the fallen family, obscure, doubtless, but incontestably springing from the same root as the four brothers who all perished so miserably."

The two ladies made a sign of assent.

"Then," continued Jeanne, "these remnants of the Valois, fearing, in spite of their obscurity, to be obnoxious to the reigning family, changed their name of Valois into that of St. Rémy, which they took from some property, and they may be traced under this name down to my father, who, seeing the monarchy so firmly established, and the old branch forgotten, thought he need no longer deprive himself of his illustrious name, and again called himself Valois, which name he bore in poverty and obscurity in a distant province, while no one at the court of France even knew of the existence of this descendant of their ancient kings."

Jeanne stopped at these words, which she had spoken with a simplicity and mildness which created a favorable impression.

"You have, doubtless, your proofs already arranged, madame," said the elder lady, with kindness.

"Oh, madame," she replied, with a bitter smile, "proofs are not wanting—my father arranged them, and left them to me as his sole legacy; but of what use are proofs of a truth which no one will recognize?"

"Your father is then dead?" asked the younger lady.

"Alas! yes."

"Did he die in the provinces?"

"No, madame."

"At Paris, then?"

"Yes."

"In this room?"

"No, madame; my father, Baron de Valois, great-nephew of the King Henry III., died of misery and hunger; and not even in this poor retreat, not in his own bed, poor as that was. No; my father died side by side with the suffering wretches in the Hôtel Dieu!"

The ladies uttered an exclamation of surprise and distress.

"From what you tell me, madame, you have experienced, it is evident, great misfortunes; above all, the death of your father."

"Oh, if you heard all the story of my life, madame, you would see that my father's death does not rank among its greatest misfortunes."

"How, madame! You regard as a minor evil the death of your father?" said the elder lady, with a frown.

"Yes, madame; and in so doing I speak only as a pious daughter, for my father was thereby delivered from all the ills which he experienced in this life, and which continue to assail his family. I experience, in the midst of the grief which his death causes me, a certain joy in knowing that the descendant of kings is no longer obliged to beg his bread."

"To beg his bread?"

"Yes, madame; I say it without shame, for in all our misfortunes there was no blame to my father or myself."

"But you do not speak of your mother?"

"Well, with the same frankness with which I told you just now that I blessed God for taking my father, I complain that He left me my mother."

The two ladies looked at each other, almost shuddering at these strange words.

"Would it be indiscreet, madame, to ask you for a more detailed account of your misfortunes?"

"The indiscretion, madame, would be in me, if I fatigued you with such a long catalogue of woes."

"Speak, madame," said the elder lady, so commandingly, that her companion looked at her, as if to warn her to be more guarded. Indeed, Madame de la Motte had been struck with this imperious accent, and stared at her with some astonishment.

"I listen, madame," she then said, in a more gentle tone; "if you will be good enough to inform us what we ask."

Her companion saw her shiver as she spoke, and fearing she felt cold, pushed towards her a rug, on which to place her feet, and which she had discovered under one of the chairs.

"Keep it yourself, my sister," said she, pushing it back again. "You are more delicate than I."

"Indeed, madame," said Jeanne, "it grieves me much to see you suffer from the cold; but wood is now so dear, and my stock was exhausted a week ago."

"You said, madame, that you were unhappy in having a mother," said the elder lady, returning to the subject.

"Yes, madame. Doubtless, such a blasphemy shocks you much, does it not?" said Jeanne; "but hear my explanation. I have already had the honor to tell you that my father made a mésalliance, and married his housekeeper. Marie Jossel, my mother, instead of feeling gratified and proud of the honor he had done her, began by ruining my father, which certainly was not difficult to a person determined to consult only her own pleasures. And having reduced him to sell all his remaining property, she induced him to go to Paris to claim the rights to which his name entitled him. My father was easily persuaded; perhaps he hoped in the justice of the king. He came then, having first turned all he possessed into money. He had, besides me, another daughter, and a son.

"His son, unhappy as myself, vegetates in the lowest ranks of the army; the daughter, my poor sister, was abandoned, on the evening of our departure, before the house of a neighboring farmer.

"The journey exhausted our little resources—my father wore himself out in fruitless appeals—we scarcely ever saw him—our house was wretched—and my mother, to whom a victim was necessary, vented her discontent and ill-humor upon me: she even reproached me with what I ate, and for the slightest fault I was unmercifully beaten. The neighbors, thinking to serve me, told my father of the treatment I experienced. He endeavored to protect me, but his interference only served to embitter her still more against me.

"At last my father fell ill, and was confined first to the house, and then to his bed. My mother banished me from his room on the pretext that I disturbed him. She made me now learn a sentence, which, child as I was, I shrank from saying; but she would drive me out into the street with blows, ordering me to repeat it to each passer-by, if I did not wish to be beaten to death."

"And what was this sentence?" asked the elder lady.

"It was this, madame: 'Have pity on a little orphan, who descends in a direct line from Henri de Valois.'"

"What a shame!" cried the ladies.

"But what effect did this produce on the people?" inquired Andrée.

"Some listened and pitied me, others were angry and menaced me; some kind people stopped and warned me that I ran a great risk from repeating such words; but I knew no other danger than that of disobeying my mother. The result was, however, as she hoped: I generally brought home a little money, which kept us for a time from starvation or the hospital; but this life became so odious to me, that at last, one day, instead of repeating my accustomed phrase, I sat on a doorstep all the time, and returned in the evening empty-handed. My mother beat me so that the next day I fell ill; then my poor father, deprived of all resources, was obliged to go to the Hôtel Dieu, where he died."

"Oh! what a horrible history," cried the ladies.

"What became of you after your father's death?" asked the elder lady.

"God took pity upon me a month after my father's death, my mother ran away with a soldier, abandoning my brother and me. We felt ourselves relieved by her departure, and lived on public charity, although we never begged for more than enough to eat. One day, I saw a carriage going slowly along the Faubourg Saint Marcel. There were four footmen behind, and a beautiful lady inside; I held out my hand to her for charity. She questioned me, and my reply and my name seemed to strike her with surprise. She asked for my address, and the next day made inquiries, and finding that I had told her the truth, she took charge of my brother and myself; she placed my brother in the army, and me with a dressmaker."

"Was not this lady Madame de Boulainvilliers?"

"It was."

"She is dead, I believe?"

"Yes; and her death deprived me of my only protector."

"Her husband still lives, and is rich."

"Ah, madame, it is to him that I owe my later misfortunes. I had grown tall, and, as he thought, pretty, and he wished to put a price upon his benefits which I refused to pay. Meanwhile, Madame de Boulainvilliers died, having first married me to a brave and loyal soldier, M. de la Motte, but, separated from him, I seemed more abandoned after her death than I had been after that of my father. This is my history, madame, which I have shortened as much as possible, in order not to weary you."

"Where, then, is your husband?" asked the elder lady.

"He is in garrison at Bar-sur-Aube; he serves in the gendarmerie, and is waiting, like myself, in hopes of better times."

"But you have laid your case before the court?"

"Undoubtedly."

"The name of Valois must have awakened some sympathy."

"I know not, madame, what sentiments it may have awakened, for I have received no answer to any of my petitions."

"You have seen neither the ministers, the king, nor the queen?"

"No one. Everywhere I have failed."

"You cannot now beg, however."

"No, madame; I have lost the habit; but I can die of hunger, like my poor father."

"You have no child?"

"No, madame; and my husband, by getting killed in the service of his king, will find for himself a glorious end to all our miseries."

"Can you, madame—I beg pardon if I seem intrusive—but can you bring forward the proofs of your genealogy?"

Jeanne rose, opened a drawer, and drew out some papers, which she presented to the lady, who rose to come nearer the light, that she might examine them; but seeing that Jeanne eagerly seized this opportunity to observe her more clearly than she had yet been able to do, she turned away as if the light hurt her eyes, turning her back to Madame de la Motte.

"But," said she, at last, "these are only copies."

"Oh! madame, I have the originals safe, and am ready to produce them."

"If any important occasion should present itself, I suppose?" said the lady, smiling.

"It is, doubtless, madame, an important occasion which procures me the honor of your visit, but these papers are so precious——"

"That you cannot show them to the first comer. I understand you."

"Oh, madame!" cried the countess; "you shall see them;" and opening a secret drawer above the other, she drew out the originals, which were carefully inclosed in an old portfolio, on which were the arms of the Valois.

The lady took them, and after examining them, said, "You are right; these are perfectly satisfactory, and you must hold yourself in readiness to produce them when called upon by proper authority."

"And what do you think I may expect, madame?" asked Jeanne.

"Doubtless a pension for yourself, and advancement for M. de la Motte, if he prove worthy of it."

"My husband is an honorable man, madame, and has never failed in his military duties."

"It is enough, madame," said the lady, drawing her hood still more over her face. She then put her hand in her pocket, and drew out first the same embroidered handkerchief with which we before saw her hiding her face when in the sledge, then a small roll about an inch in diameter, and three or four in length, which she placed on the chiffonier, saying, "The treasurer of our charity authorizes me, madame, to offer you this small assistance, until you shall obtain something better."

Madame de la Motte threw a rapid glance at the little roll. "Three-franc pieces," thought she, "and there must be nearly a hundred of them; what a boon from heaven."

While she was thus thinking, the two ladies moved quickly into the outer room, where Clotilde had fallen asleep in her chair.

The candle was burning out in the socket, and the smell which came from it made the ladies draw out their smelling-bottles. Jeanne woke Clotilde, who insisted on following them with the obnoxious candle-end.

"Au revoir, Madame la Comtesse," said they.

"Where may I have the honor of coming to thank you?" asked Jeanne.

"We will let you know," replied the elder lady, going quickly down the stairs.

Madame de la Motte ran back into her room, impatient to examine her rouleau, but her foot struck against something, and stooping to pick it up, she saw a small flat gold box.

She was some time before she could open it, but having at last found the spring, it flew open and disclosed the portrait of a lady possessing no small beauty. The coiffure was German, and she wore a collar like an order. An M and a T encircled by a laurel wreath ornamented the inside of the box. Madame de la Motte did not doubt, from the resemblance of the portrait to the lady who had just left her, that it was that of her mother, or some near relation.

She ran to the stairs to give it back to them; but hearing the street-door shut, she ran back, thinking to call them from the window, but arrived there only in time to see a cabriolet driving rapidly away. She was therefore obliged to keep the box for the present, and turned again to the little rouleau.

When she opened it, she uttered a cry of joy, "Double louis, fifty double louis, two thousand and four hundred francs!" and transported at the sight of more gold than she had ever seen before in her life, she remained with clasped hands and open lips. "A hundred louis," she repeated; "these ladies are then very rich. Oh! I will find them again."

CHAPTER IV
BELUS

Madame de la Motte was not wrong in thinking that the cabriolet which she saw driving off contained the two ladies who had just left her.

They had, in fact, found it waiting for them on their exit. It was lightly built, open and fashionable, with high wheels, and a place behind for a servant to stand. It was drawn by a magnificent bay horse of Irish breed, short-tailed, and plump, which was driven by the same man whom we have already heard addressed by the name of Weber. The horse had become so impatient with waiting, that it was with some difficulty that Weber kept him stationary.

When he saw the ladies, he said, "Madame, I intended to bring Scipio, who is gentle and easy to manage, but unluckily he received an injury last evening, and I was forced to bring Bélus, and he is rather unmanageable."

"Oh, Weber, I do not mind in the least," said the lady; "I am well used to driving, and not at all timid."

"I know how well madame drives, but the roads are so bad. Where are we to go?"

"To Versailles."

"By the boulevards then, madame?"

"No, Weber; it freezes hard, and the boulevards will be dreadful; the streets will be better."

He held the horse for the ladies to get in, then jumped up behind, and they set off at a rapid pace.

"Well, Andrée, what do you think of the countess?" asked the elder lady.

"I think, madame," she replied, "that Madame de la Motte is poor and unfortunate."

"She has good manners, has she not?"

"Yes, doubtless."

"You are somewhat cold about her, Andrée."

"I must confess, there is a look of cunning in her face that does not please me."

"Oh, you are always difficult to please, Andrée; to please you, one must have every good quality. Now, I find the little countess interesting and simple, both in her pride and in her humility."

"It is fortunate for her, madame, that she has succeeded in pleasing you."

"Take care!" cried the lady, at the same time endeavoring to check her horse, which nearly ran over a street-porter at the corner of the Rue St. Antoine.

"Gare!" shouted Weber, in the voice of the Stentor.

They heard the man growling and swearing, in which he was joined by several people near, but Bélus soon carried them away from the sound, and they quickly reached the Place Baudoyer.

From thence the skilful conductress continued her rapid course down the Rue de la Tisseranderie, a narrow unaristocratic street, always crowded. Thus, in spite of the reiterated warnings of herself and Weber, the numbers began to increase around them, many of whom cried fiercely, "Oh! the cabriolet! down with the cabriolet!"

Bélus, however, guided by the steady hand which held the reins, kept on his rapid course, and not the smallest accident had yet occurred.

But in spite of this skilful progress, the people seemed discontented at the rapid course of the cabriolet, which certainly required some care on their part to avoid, and the lady, perhaps half frightened at the murmurs, and knowing the present excited state of the people, only urged on her horse the faster to escape from them.

Thus they proceeded until they reached the Rue du Coq St. Honoré, and here had been raised one of the most beautiful of those monuments in snow of which we have spoken.

Round this a great crowd had collected, and they were obliged to stop until the people would make an opening for them to pass, which they did at last, but with great grumbling and discontent.

The next obstacle was at the gates of the Palais Royal, where, in a courtyard, which had been thrown open, were a host of beggars crowding round fires which had been lighted there, and receiving soup, which the servants of M. le Duc d'Orleans were distributing to them in earthen basins; and as in Paris a crowd collects to see everything, the number of the spectators of this scene far exceeded that of the actors.

Here, then, they were again obliged to stop, and to their dismay, began to hear distinctly from behind loud cries of "Down with the cabriolet! down with those that crush the poor!"

"Can it be that those cries are addressed to us?" said the elder lady to her companion.

"Indeed, madame, I fear so," she replied.

"Have we, do you think, run over any one?"

"I am sure you have not."

But still the cries seemed to increase. A crowd soon gathered round them, and some even seized Bélus by the reins, who thereupon began to stamp and foam most furiously.

"To the magistrate! to the magistrate!" cried several voices.

The two ladies looked at each other in terror. Curious heads began to peep under the apron of the cabriolet.

"Oh, they are women," cried some; "Opera girls, doubtless," said others, "who think they have a right to crush the poor because they receive ten thousand francs a month."

A general shout hailed these words, and they began again to cry, "To the magistrate!"

The younger lady shrank back trembling with fear; the other looked around her with wonderful resolution, though with frowning brows and compressed lips.

"Oh, madame," cried her companione, "for heaven's sake, take care!"

"Courage, Andrée, courage!" she replied.

"But they will recognize you, madame."

"Look through the windows, if Weber is still behind the cabriolet."

"He is trying to get down, but the mob surrounds him. Ah! here he comes."

"Weber," said the lady in German, "we will get out."

The man vigorously pushed aside those nearest the carriage, and opened the door. The ladies jumped out, and the crowd instantly seized on the horse and cabriolet, which would evidently soon be in pieces.

"What in heaven's name does it all mean? Do you understand it, Weber?" said the lady, still in German.

"Ma foi, no, madame," he replied, struggling to free a passage for them to pass.

"But they are not men, they are wild beasts," continued the lady; "with what do they possibly reproach me?"

She was answered by a voice, whose polite and gentlemanly tone contrasted strangely with the savage murmurs of the people, and which said in excellent German, "They reproach you, madame, with having braved the police order, which appeared this morning, and which prohibited all cabriolets, which are always dangerous, and fifty times more so in this frost, when people can hardly escape fast enough, from driving through the streets until the spring."

The lady turned, and saw she was addressed by a young officer, whose distinguished and pleasing air, and fine figure, could not but make a favorable impression.

"Oh, mon Dieu, monsieur," she said, "I was perfectly ignorant of this order."

"You are a foreigner, madame?" inquired the young officer.

"Yes, sir; but tell me what I must do? they are destroying my cabriolet."

"You must let them destroy it, and take advantage of that time to escape. The people are furious just now against all the rich, and on the pretext of your breaking this regulation would conduct you before the magistrate."

"Oh, never!" cried Andrée.

"Then," said the officer, laughing, "profit by the space which I shall make in the crowd, and vanish."

The ladies gathered from his manner that he shared the opinion of the people as to their station, but it was no time for explanations.

"Give us your arm to a cab-stand," said the elder lady, in a voice full of authority.

"I was going to make your horse rear, and thereby clear you a passage," said the young man, who did not much wish to take the charge of escorting them through the crowd; "the people will become yet more enraged, if they hear us speaking in a language unknown to them."

"Weber," cried the lady, in a firm voice, "make Bélus rear to disperse the crowd."

"And then, madame?"

"Remain till we are gone."

"But they will destroy the carriage."

"Let them; what does that matter? save Bélus if you can, but yourself above all."

"Yes, madame;" and a slight touch to the horse soon produced the desired effect of dispersing the nearest part of the crowd, and throwing down those who held by his reins.

"Your arm, sir!" again said the lady to the officer; "come on, petite," turning to Andrée.

"Let us go then, courageous woman," said the young man, giving his arm, with real admiration, to her who asked for it.

In a few minutes he had conducted them to a cab-stand, but the men were all asleep on their seats.

CHAPTER V
THE ROAD TO VERSAILLES

The ladies were free from the crowd for the present, but there was some danger that they might be followed and recognized, when the same tumult would doubtless be renewed and escape a second time be more difficult. The young officer knew this, and therefore hastened to awaken one of the half-frozen and sleepy men. So stupefied, however, did they seem, that he had great difficulty in rousing one of them. At last he took him by the collar and shook him roughly.

"Gently, gently!" cried the man, sitting up.

"Where do you wish to go, ladies?" asked the officer.

"To Versailles," said the elder lady, still speaking German.

"Oh, to Versailles!" repeated the coachman; "four miles and a half over this ice. No, I would rather not."

"We will pay well," said the lady.

This was repeated to the coachman in French by the young officer.

"But how much?" said the coachman; "you see it is not only going, I must come back again."

"A louis; is that enough?" asked the lady of the officer, who, turning to the coachman, said,—

"These ladies offer you a louis."

"Well, that will do, though I risk breaking my horses' legs."

"Why, you rascal, you know that if you were paid all the way there and back, it would be but twelve francs, and we offer you twenty-four."

"Oh, do not stay to bargain," cried the lady; "he shall have twenty louis if he will only set off at once."

"One is enough, madame."

"Come down, sir, and open the door."

"I will be paid first," said the man.

"You will!" said the officer fiercely.

"Oh! let us pay," said the lady, putting her hand in her pocket. She turned pale. "Oh! mon Dieu, I have lost my purse! Feel for yours, Andrée."

"Oh! madame, it is gone too."

They looked at each other in dismay, while the young officer watched their proceedings, and the coachman sat grinning, and priding himself on his caution.

The lady was about to offer her gold chain as a pledge, when the young officer drew out a louis, and offered it to the man, who thereupon got down and opened the door.

The ladies thanked him warmly and got in.

"And now, sir, drive these ladies carefully and honestly."

The ladies looked at each other in terror; they could not bear to see their protector leave them.

"Oh! madame," said Andrée, "do not let him go away."

"But why not? we will ask for his address, and return him his louis to-morrow, with a little note of thanks, which you shall write."

"But, madame, suppose the coachman should not keep faith with us, and should turn us out half way, what would become of us?"

"Oh! we will take his number."

"Yes, madame, I do not deny that you could have him punished afterwards; but meanwhile, you would not reach Versailles, and what would they think?"

"True," replied her companion.

The officer advanced to take leave.

"Monsieur," said Andrée, "one word more, if you please."

"At your orders, madame," he said politely, but somewhat stiffly.

"Monsieur, you cannot refuse us one more favor, after serving us so much?"

"What is it, madame?"

"We are afraid of the coachman, who seems so unwilling to go."

"You need not fear," replied he; "I have his number, and if he does not behave well, apply to me."

"To you, sir?" said Andrée in French, forgetting herself; "we do not even know your name."

"You speak French," exclaimed the young man, "and you have been condemning me all this time to blunder on in German!"

"Excuse us, sir," said the elder lady, coming to Andrée's rescue, "but you must see, that though not perhaps foreigners, we are strangers in Paris, and above all, out of our places in a hackney coach. You are sufficiently a man of the world to see that we are placed in an awkward position. I feel assured you are generous enough to believe the best of us, and to complete the service you have rendered, and above all, to ask us no questions."

"Madame," replied the officer, charmed with her noble, yet pleasing manner, "dispose of me as you will."

"Then, sir, have the kindness to get in, and accompany us to Versailles."

The officer instantly placed himself opposite to them, and directed the man to drive on.

After proceeding in silence for some little time, he began to feel himself surrounded with delicate and delicious perfumes, and gradually began to think better of the ladies' position. "They are," thought he, "ladies who have been detained late at some rendezvous, and are now anxious to regain Versailles, much frightened, and a little ashamed; still, two ladies, driving themselves in a cabriolet! However," recollected he, "there was a servant behind; but then again, no money on either of them, but probably the footman carried the purse; and the carriage was certainly a very elegant one, and the horse could not have been worth less than one hundred and fifty louis; therefore they must be rich, so that the accidental want of money proves nothing. But why speak a foreign language when they must be French? However, that at least shows a good education, and they speak both languages with perfect purity; besides, there is an air of distinction about them. The supplication of the younger one was touching, and the request of the other was noble and imposing; indeed, I begin to feel it dangerous to pass two or three hours in a carriage with two such pretty women, pretty and discreet also; for they do not speak, but wait for me to begin."

On their parts, the ladies were doubtless thinking of him, for just as he had arrived at these conclusions, the elder lady said to her companion, but this time in English:

"Really, this coachman crawls along; we shall never reach Versailles; I fear our poor companion must be terribly ennuyé."

"Particularly," answered Andrée, smiling, "as our conversation has not been very amusing."

"Do you not think he has a most distinguished air?"

"Yes, certainly."

"Besides, he wears the uniform of a naval officer, and all naval officers are of good family. He looks well in it, too, for he is very handsome."

Here the young man interrupted them. "Your pardon, ladies," said he, in excellent English, "but I must tell you that I understand English perfectly; I do not, however, know Spanish; therefore, if you can and like to speak in that language, you are safe from my understanding you."

"Oh, monsieur," replied the lady, laughing, "we had no harm to say of you, as you must have heard; therefore we will content ourselves with French for the remainder of the time."

"Thanks, madame, but if my presence be irksome to you— —"

"You cannot suppose that, sir, as it was we who begged you to accompany us."

"Exacted it, even," said Andrée.

"Oh, madame, you overwhelm me; pray pardon me my momentary hesitation; but Paris is so full of snares and deceptions."

"You then took us for— —"

"Monsieur took us for snares, that is all."

"Oh! ladies," said the young man, quite humiliated, "I assure you, I did not."

"But what is the matter? The coach stops."

"I will see, madame."

"Oh! I think we are overturning; pray take care, sir."

And Andrée, in her terror, laid her hand on the young man's shoulder.

He, yielding to an impulse, attempted to seize her little hand; but she had in a moment thrown herself back again in the carriage. He therefore got out, and found the coachman engaged in raising one of his horses, which had fallen on the ice.

The horse, with his aid, was soon on its legs again, and they pursued their way.

It seemed, however, that this little interruption had destroyed the intimacy which had begun to spring up, for after the ladies had asked and been told the cause of their detention, all relapsed into silence.

The young man, however, who had derived some pleasure from the touch of that little hand, thought he would at least have a foot in exchange; he therefore stretched out his, and endeavored to touch hers, which, was, however, quickly withdrawn; and when he did just touch that of the elder lady, she said, with great sang-froid, — —

"I fear, sir, I am dreadfully in your way."

He colored up to the ears, and felt thankful to the darkness, which prevented it from being seen. After this, he desisted, and remained perfectly still, fearing even to renew the conversation, lest he should seem impertinent to these ladies, to whom, at first, he had thought himself rather condescending in his politeness.

Still, in spite of himself, he felt more and more strongly attracted towards them, and an increasing interest in them. From time to time he heard them speak softly to each other, and he caught these words:

"So late an hour! what excuse for being out?"

At last the coach stopped again, but this time it was no accident, but simply that they had arrived at Versailles.

The young man thought the time had passed with marvelous quickness.

"We are at Versailles," said the coachman.

"Where must he stop, ladies?" asked the officer.

"At the Place d'Armes."

"At the Place d'Armes, coachman," said the officer; "go on.—I must say something to them," thought he, "or they will now think me a stupid, as they must before have thought me impertinent."

"Mesdames," said he, "you are at length arrived."

"Thanks to your generous assistance."

"What trouble we have given you," added Andrée.

"Oh, madame, do not speak of it!"

"Well, sir, we shall not forget; will you tell us your name?"

"My name?"

"Certainly, sir; you do not wish to make us a present of a louis, I hope."

"Oh, madame, if that is it," said the young man, rather piqued, "I yield; I am the Comte de Charney, and as madame has already remarked, a naval officer."

"Charney," repeated the elder lady, "I shall not forget."

"Yes, madame, Georges de Charney."

"And you live——?"

"Hôtel des Princes, Rue de Richelieu."

The coach stopped. The elder lady opened the door and jumped out quickly, holding out a hand to her companion.

"But pray, ladies," said he, preparing to follow them, "take my arm; you are not yet at your own home."

"Oh, sir, do not move."

"Not move?"

"No; pray remain in the coach."

"You cannot walk alone at this time of night; it is impossible."

"Now, you see," said the elder lady, gaily, "after almost refusing to oblige us, you wish to be too obliging."

"But, madame——"

"Sir, remain to the end a loyal and gallant cavalier; we thank you, M. de Charney, with all our hearts, and will not even ask your word——"

"To do what, madame?"

"To shut the door, and order the man to drive back to Paris, without even looking where we go, which you will do, will you not?"

"I will obey you, madame; coachman, back again." And he put a second louis into the man's hand, who joyfully set off on his return.

The young man sighed, as he took his place on the cushions which the unknown ladies had just occupied.

They remained motionless till the coach was out of sight, and then took their way towards the castle.

CHAPTER VI
LAURENT

At this moment our heroines heard the clock strike from the church of St. Louis.

"Oh, mon Dieu! a quarter to twelve," they cried, in terror.

"See, all the doors are shut," said Andrée.

"Oh, that is nothing; for, if they were open, we would not go in here. Let us go round by the reservoirs." And they turned to the right, where there was a private entrance.

When they arrived there, "The door is shut, Andrée," said the elder lady, rather uneasily.

"Let us knock, madame."

"No, we will call; Laurent must be waiting for me, for I told him perhaps I should return late."

"I will call," said Andrée, approaching the door.

"Who is there?" said a voice from inside.

"Oh, it is not Laurent!" said she, terrified.

"Is it not?" and the other lady advanced, and called softly, "Laurent."

No answer.

"Laurent?" again she called, louder.

"There is no Laurent here," replied the voice, rudely.

"But," said Andrée, "whether he be here or not, open the door."

"I cannot open it."

"But Laurent would have opened it immediately."

"I have my orders," was all the reply.

"Who are you, then?"

"Rather, who are you?"

Rude as the question was, it was no time to find fault, so they answered, "We are ladies of her majesty's suite, we lodge in the castle, and we wish to get home."

"Well, I, mesdames, am a Suisse of the Salischamade company, and I shall do just the contrary of Laurent, for I shall leave you at the door."

"Oh!" murmured the ladies, in terror and anger.

Then, making an effort over herself, the elder lady said, "My friend, I understand that you are obeying orders, and I do not quarrel with you for that—it is a soldier's duty; only do me the favor to call Laurent—he cannot be far distant."

"I cannot quit my post."

"Then send some one."

"I have no one to send."

"For pity's sake!"

"Oh, mon Dieu, sleep in the town, that is no great thing; if I were shut out of the barracks, I would soon find a bed."

"Listen," said the lady again; "you shall have twenty louis, if you open this door."

"And twelve years at the galleys: no, thank you. Forty-eight francs a year is not sufficient pay for that."

"I will get you made a sergeant."

"Yes, and he who gave me the order will have me shot."

"And who did give you the order?"

"The king."

"The king!" cried they; "oh, we are lost!"

"Is there no other door?"

"Oh! madame, if this one is closed, be sure all the others will be so also," said Andrée.

"You are right, Andrée. 'Tis a horrible trick of the king," she said, with a contempt almost menacing.

There was a sort of bank outside the door, which they sank down upon in despair. They could see the light under the door, and could hear the steps of the sentinel as he paced to and fro.

Within this little door was salvation; without, shame and scandal.

"Oh! to-morrow, to-morrow, when they will find out," murmured the elder lady.

"You will tell the truth, madame."

"But shall I be believed?"

"Oh! we can prove it; besides, the soldier will not stay all night; he will be relieved, and perhaps his successor will be more complacent."

"Yes, but the patrol will pass directly, and will find me here, waiting outside. It is infamous; I am suffocated with rage."

"Oh, take courage, madame! you, who are always so brave."

"It is a plot, Andrée, in order to ruin me. This door is never closed. Oh, I shall die!"

At this moment they heard a step approaching, and then the voice of a young man, singing gaily as he went along.

"That voice," cried the lady, "I know it, I am sure."

"Oh, yes, madame, he will save us."

A young man, wrapped up in a fur riding-coat, came quickly up, and without noticing them, knocked at the door, and called, "Laurent."

"Brother," said the elder lady, touching him on the shoulder.

"The queen," cried he, taking off his hat.

"Hush," said she.

"You are not alone?"

"No, I am with Mademoiselle Andrée de Taverney."

"Oh, good evening, mademoiselle."

"Good evening, monseigneur."

"Are you going out, madame?" asked he.

"No."

"Then you are going in."

"We wished to do so."

"Have you not called Laurent?"

"Yes, we have, but— —"

"But what?"

"You call Laurent, and you will see."

The young man, whom the reader has, perhaps, already recognized as the Comte d'Artois, approached and again called "Laurent."

"I warn you," answered from within the voice of the Suisse, "that if you torment me any more I will go and fetch my commanding officer."

"Who is this?" asked the count, turning round in astonishment to the queen.

"A Swiss who has been substituted for Laurent."

"By whom?"

"By the king."

"The king?"

"Yes, he told us so himself."

"And with orders?"

"Most strict, apparently."

"Diable! we must capitulate."

"What do you mean?" she asked.

"Offer him money."

"I have already done so, and he has refused it."

"Offer him promotion."

"I have offered that also, but he would not listen."

"Then there is but one way."

"What?"

"To make a noise."

"My dear Charles, you will compromise us."

"Not the least in the world; you keep in the background, I will knock like thunder, and shout like a madman; they will open at last, and you can slide in with me."

"Try, then."

The young prince began calling Laurent, knocking at the door and striking with his sword, till at last the Swiss said, "Ah, well! I will call my officer."

"Go and call him, that is just what I want."

They soon heard other steps approaching. The queen and Andrée kept close, ready to slip in if the door should open; then they heard the Swiss say, "It is a gentleman, lieutenant, who insists on coming in."

"Well, I suppose that is not astonishing, as we belong to the castle," said the count.

"It is no doubt a natural wish, but a forbidden one," replied the officer.

"Forbidden—by whom? morbleu!"

"By the king."

"But the king would not wish an officer of the castle to sleep outside."

"Sir, I am not the judge of that; I have only to obey orders."

"Come, lieutenant, open the door; we cannot talk through this oak."

"Sir, I repeat to you that my orders are to keep it shut; and if you are an officer, as you say, you know that I must obey."

"Lieutenant, you speak to the colonel of a regiment."

"Excuse me, then, colonel, but my orders are positive."

"But they cannot concern a prince. Come, sir, a prince cannot be kept out."

"My prince, I am in despair, but the king has ordered——"

"The king has ordered you to turn away his brother like a beggar or a robber? I am the Comte d'Artois, sir. Mordieu! you keep me here freezing at the door."

"Monseigneur, God is my witness that I would shed my blood for your royal highness. But the king gave me his orders in person, and confiding to me the charge of this door, ordered me not to open to any one, should it be even himself, after eleven o'clock. Therefore, monseigneur, I ask your pardon humbly for disobeying you, but I am a soldier, and were it her majesty the queen who asked admittance, I should be forced most unwillingly to refuse."

Having said this, the officer turned away and left the place.

"We are lost," said the queen.

"Do they know that you are out?" asked the count.

"Alas, I know not!"

"Perhaps, then, this order is leveled against me; the king knows I often go out at night, and stay late. Madame la Comtesse d'Artois must have heard something, and complained to him, and hence this tyrannical order."

"Ah, no, brother, I thank you for trying to reassure me, but I feel that it is against me these precautions are taken."

"Impossible, sister! the king has too much esteem— —"

"Meanwhile, I am left at the door, and to-morrow a frightful scandal will be the result. I know well I have an enemy near the king."

"It is possible; however, I have an idea."

"What? only be quick. If you can but save us from the ridicule of this position, it is all I care for."

"Oh, I will save you; I am not more foolish than he, for all his learning."

"Than whom?"

"Ah, pardieu, the Comte de Provence."

"Ah, then, you also know my enemy."

"Is he not the enemy of all that are young and beautiful, of all who are better than himself?"

"Count, I believe you know something about this order."

"Perhaps, but do not let us stop here. Come with me, dear sister."

"Where?"

"You shall see, somewhere where at least you will be warm, and en route I will tell you all I know about this. Take my arm, sister, and you the other, Madlle. de Taverney, and let us turn to the right."

"Well, but now go on," said the queen.

"This evening after the king's supper, he came to his cabinet. He had been talking all day to Count Haga, you had not been seen— —"

"No, at two o'clock I left to go to Paris."

"I know it. The king, allow me to tell you, dear sister, was thinking no more about you than about Haroun-al-Raschid, or his Vizier Giaffar, and was talking geography. I listened with some impatience, for I also wanted to go out; probably not with the same object as you."

"Where are we going?" interrupted the queen.

"Oh, close by; take care, there is a snow-heap. Madlle. de Taverney, if you leave my arm you will certainly fall. But to return to the king: he was thinking of nothing but latitude and longitude, when M. de Provence said to him, 'I should like to pay my respects to the queen.'

"'The queen sups at home,' replied the king.

"'Oh, I believed her at Paris.'

"'No, she is at home,' said the king, quietly.

"'I have just come from there, and been denied to her,' said M. de Provence.

"Then I saw the king frown. He dismissed us, and doubtless went to make inquiries. Louis is jealous by fits, you know; he must have asked to see you, and being refused, become suspicious."

"Yes, Madame de Misery had orders to do so."

"Then, to know whether you were out or not, he has given these strict orders."

"Oh, it is shameful treatment. Confess, is it not?"

"Indeed, I think so; but here we are."

"This house?"

"Does it displease you?"

"No, I do not say that—it is charming. But your servants?"

"Well!"

"If they see me."

"Come in, sister, and I will guarantee that no one sees you, not even whoever opens the door."

"Impossible!"

"We will try," said he, laughing; and laying his hand on one of the panels, the door flew open.

"Enter, I pray you," said he, "there is no one near."

The queen looked at Andrée, then, making up her mind, went in, and the door shut behind them.

She found herself in a vestibule, small, but ornamented in perfect taste. The floor was mosaic work, representing bouquets of flowers, while numerous rose-trees on marble brackets scented the air with a perfume equally delicious as rare at that time of the year.

It looked all so charming, that the ladies began to forget their fears and scruples.

"So far well," said the queen; "we have a shelter, at all events, and seemingly a very charming one; but you had better see to one thing—that is, to keep off your servants."

"Oh, nothing more easy;" and the prince, seizing a little bell which hung on one of the pillars, rang one clear stroke.

"Oh!" cried the queen, frightened, "is that the way to keep them off? I should have thought it would bring them."

"If I had rung again, it would have done so, but when I only ring once, they know they are not wanted."

"Oh, you are a man of precaution!" said the queen laughing.

"Now, dear sister, take the trouble to go up-stairs."

"Let us obey," said the queen, "the genius of this place appears not disagreeable;" and they went up, their steps making no sound on the thick Aubusson carpet.

At the top, the prince rang another bell, which gave them a fresh start of surprise, and their astonishment increased when they saw the doors open of themselves.

"Really, Andrée," said the queen, "I begin to tremble, do not you?"

"Oh, madame, I shall follow fearlessly wherever your majesty goes."

"Enter," said the prince, "for here is your apartment;" and he ushered them into a charming little room, furnished 'en buhl,' with a painted ceiling and walls, and a rosewood floor. It opened into a boudoir, fitted up with white cashmere, beautifully embroidered with groups of flowers, and hung with tapestry of exquisite workmanship. Beyond the boudoir was a bedroom, painted blue, hung with curtains of silk and lace, and with a sumptuous bed in an alcove. A fire burned on the hearth, and a dozen perfumed wax-lights in candelabra.

Such were the marvels which presented themselves to the eyes of the wondering ladies. No living being was to be seen; fire and lights seemed to have come without hands.

The queen stopped on the threshold of the bedroom, looking half afraid to enter.

"Sister," said the count, "these are my bachelor apartments; here I come alone."

"Always?" asked the queen.

"Doubtless," answered he.

"I understand now," said the queen, "why Madame la Comtesse is sometimes unquiet."

"Confess, however, that if she is unquiet to-night, it Will be without reason."

"To-night, I do not say, but other nights." Then, sitting down; "I am dreadfully tired," she said; "are not you, Andrée?"

"I can scarcely stand, and if your majesty permits——"

"Indeed you look ill, mademoiselle," said the count.

"You must go to bed," said the queen. "M. le Comte gives us up this room; do you not, Charles?"

"Entirely, madame."

"One moment, count. If you go away, how can we recall you?"

"You will not need me; you are mistress of this house."

"But there are other rooms."

"Certainly, there is a dining-room, which I advise you to visit."

"With a table ready spread, no doubt."

"Oh, yes, and Mademoiselle de Taverney, who seems to me to need it much, will find there jellies or chicken, and wine, and you, sister, plenty of those fruits you are so fond of."

"And no servants?"

"None."

"We will see; but how to return?"

"You must not think of returning to-night. At six o'clock the gates will be opened, go out a quarter before, you will find in these drawers mantles of all colors and all shapes, if you wish to disguise yourselves. Go therefore to the château, regain your rooms, go to bed, and all will be right."

"But you, what will you do?"

"Oh, I am going away."

"We turn you out, my poor brother!"

"It is better for me not to remain in the same house with you."

"But you must sleep somewhere."

"Do not fear; I have three other houses like this."

The queen laughed. "And he pretends Madame la Comtesse has no cause to be anxious; oh, I will tell her!"

"You dare not."

"It is true, we are dependent upon you. Then, to go away to-morrow morning without seeing any one?"

"You must ring once, as I did below, and the door will open."

"By itself?"

"By itself."

"Then good night, brother."

"Good night, sister." He bowed and disappeared.

CHAPTER VII
THE QUEEN'S BED-CHAMBER

The next day, or rather the same morning, for our last chapter brought us to two o'clock, the King Louis XVI., in a violet-colored morning dress, in some disorder, and with no powder in his hair, knocked at the door of the queen's ante-chamber.

It was opened by one of her women.

"The queen?" asked Louis, in a brusque manner.

"Her majesty is asleep, sire."

The king made a movement, as though to pass in but the woman did not move.

"Do you not see," he said, "that I wish to come in."

"But the queen is asleep, sire," again she said timidly.

"I told you to let me pass," answered the king, going in as he spoke.

When he reached the door of the bedroom, the king saw Madame de Misery, the first lady-in-waiting, who was sitting reading from her mass book.

She rose on seeing him. "Sire," she said, in a low voice, and with a profound reverence, "her majesty has not yet called for me."

"Really?" said the king, in an ironical tone.

"But, sire, it is only half-past six, and her majesty never rings before seven."

"And you are sure that her majesty is asleep in bed?"

"I cannot affirm that she is asleep, sire, but I can that she is in bed."

The king could contain himself no longer, but went straight to the door, which he opened with some noise. The room was in complete darkness, the shutters closed, and the curtains drawn. A night lamp burned on a bracket, but it only gave a dim and feeble light.

The king walked rapidly towards the bed.

"Oh, Madame de Misery," said the queen, "how noisy you are—you have disturbed me!"

The king remained stupefied. "It is not Madame de Misery," he murmured.

"What, is it you, sire?" said Marie Antoinette, raising herself up.

"Good morning, madame," said the king, in a surly tone.

"What good wind blows you here, sire? Madame de Misery, come and open the shutters."

She came in instantly, as usual, opened all the doors and windows, to let in light and fresh air.

"You sleep well, madame," said the king, seating himself, and casting scrutinizing glances round the room.

"Yes, sire, I read late, and had your majesty not disturbed me, might have slept for some time longer."

"How was it that you did not receive visitors yesterday?" asked the king.

"Whom do you mean?—M. de Provence," said the queen, with great presence of mind.

"Yes, exactly; he wished to pay his respects to you, and was refused."

"Well!"

"They said you were out."

"Did they say that?" asked the queen carelessly. "Madame de Misery——"

The lady appeared, bringing in with her a number of letters on a gold salver. "Did your majesty call?" she asked.

"Yes. Did they tell M. de Provence yesterday that I was out? Will you tell the king, for really I forget."

"Sire," said Madame de Misery, while the queen took her letters and began to read, "I told Monseigneur le Comte de Provence that her majesty did not receive."

"And by whose orders?"

"By the queen's, sire."

Meanwhile, the queen had opened one of the letters, and read these lines: "You returned from Paris yesterday, and entered the château at eight o'clock in the evening; Laurent saw you."

Madame de Misery left the room.

"Pardon, sire," said the queen, "but will you answer me one question?"

"What, madame?"

"Am I, or am I not, at liberty to see M. de Provence only when it pleases me?"

"Oh, perfectly at liberty, madame, but— —"

"Well, his conversation wearies me; besides, he does not love me, and I like him no better. I expected his visit, and went to bed at eight o'clock to avoid it. But you look disturbed, sire."

"I believed you to be in Paris yesterday."

"At what time?"

"At the time at which you pretend to have gone to bed."

"Doubtless, I went to Paris; but what of that?"

"All, madame, depends on what time you returned."

"Oh, you wish to know at what time exactly I returned?"

"Yes."

"It is easy. Madame de Misery— —"

The Lady reappeared.

"What time was it when I returned from Paris yesterday?"

"About eight o'clock, your majesty."

"I do not believe it," said the king, "you make a mistake, Madame de Misery."

The lady walked to the door, and called, "Madame Dural!"

"Yes, madame," replied a voice.

"At what time did her majesty return from Paris yesterday?"

"About eight o'clock, madame," replied the other.

"The king thinks we are mistaken."

Madame Dural put her head out of the window, and cried, "Laurent!"

"Who is Laurent?" asked the king.

"The porter at the gate where her majesty entered," said Madame de Misery.

"Laurent," said Madame Dural, "what time was it when her majesty came home last evening?"

"About eight o'clock," answered Laurent.

Madame de Misery then left the room, and the king and queen remained alone.

He felt ashamed of his suspicions.

The queen, however, only said coldly, "Well, sire, is there anything else you wish to know?"

"Oh, nothing!" cried he, taking her hands in his; "forgive me; I do not know what came into my head—my joy is as great as my repentance. You will not be angry, will you? I am in despair at having annoyed you."

The queen withdrew her hand, and said; "Sire, a queen of France must not tell a falsehood."

"What do you mean?"

"I mean that I did not return at eight o'clock last evening."

The king drew back in surprise.

"I mean," continued the queen in the same cold manner, "that I only returned at six o'clock this morning."

"Madame!"

"And that, but for the kindness of M. le Comte d'Artois, who gave me an asylum, and lodged me out of pity in one of his houses, I should have been left all night at the door of the château like a beggar."

"Ah! you had not then returned?" said the king, gloomily; "then I was right."

"Sire, you have not behaved towards me as a gentleman should."

"In what, madame?"

"In this—that if you wish to know whether I return late or early, you have no need to close the gates, with orders not to open them, but simply to come to me and ask, 'Madame, at what time did you return?' You have no more reason to doubt, sire. Your spies have been deceived, your precautions nullified, and your suspicions dissipated. I saw you ashamed of the part you had played, and I might have continued to triumph in my victory, but I think your proceedings shameful for a king, and unworthy of a gentleman; and I would not refuse myself the satisfaction of telling you so.

"It is useless, sire," she continued, seeing the king about to speak; "nothing can excuse your conduct towards me."

"On the contrary, madame," replied he, "nothing is more easy. Not a single person in the château suspected that you had not already returned; therefore no one could think that my orders referred to you. Probably they were attributed to the dissipations of M. le Comte d'Artois—for that I care nothing. Therefore, madame, appearances were saved, as far as you were concerned. I wished simply to give you a secret lesson, from which the amount of irritation you show leads me to hope you will profit. Therefore, I still think I was in the right, and do not repent what I have done."

The queen listened, and seemed to calm herself, by an effort, to prepare for the approaching contest. "Then, sire," she said, "you think you need no excuse for keeping at the door of your castle the daughter of Maria Theresa, your wife, and the mother of your children? No! it is in your eyes a pleasantry worthy of a king, and of which the morality doubles the value. It is nothing to you, to have forced the Queen of France to pass the night in this 'petite maison,' where the Comte d'Artois receives the ladies of the Opera and the 'femmes galantes' of your court. Oh no! that is nothing. A philosopher king is above all such considerations. Only, on this occasion, I have reason to thank heaven that my brother-in-law is a dissipated man, as his dissipation has saved me from disgrace, and his vices have sheltered my honor."

The king colored, and moved uneasily on his chair.

"Oh yes!" continued the queen, with a bitter laugh, "I know that you are a moral king, but your morality produces strange effects. You say that no one knew that I was out. Will you tell me that M. de Provence, your instigator, did not know it; or M. le Comte d'Artois—or my women? who, by my orders, told you falsehoods this morning; or Laurent—bought by M. d'Artois and by me? Let us continue this habit, sire; you, to set spies and Swiss guards; and I, to buy them over and cheat you; and in a month we will calculate together how much the dignity of the throne and our marriage has gained by it."

It was evident that her words had made a great impression on him to whom they were addressed.

"You know," said he, in an altered voice, "that I am always sincere, and willing to acknowledge if I have been wrong. Will you prove to me that you were right to go into Paris in sledges, accompanied by a gay party, which, in the present unhappy state of things, is likely to give offense? Will you prove to me, that you were right to disappear in Paris, like maskers at a ball, and only to reappear scandalously late at night, when every one else was asleep? You have spoken of the dignity of the throne, and of marriage; think you that it befits a queen, a wife, and a mother, to act thus?"

"I will reply in a few words, sire; for it seems to me, that such accusations merit nothing but contempt. I left Versailles in a sledge, because it is the quickest way of getting to Paris at present. I went with Madlle. de Taverney, whose reputation is certainly one of the purest in our court. I went to Paris, I repeat, to verify the fact that the King of France, the great upholder of morality—he who takes care of poor strangers, warms the beggars, and earns the gratitude of the people by his charities, leaves dying of hunger, exposed to every attack of vice and misery, one of his own family—one who is as much as himself a descendant of the kings who have reigned in France."

"What!" cried the king in surprise.

"I mounted," continued the queen, "into a garret, and there saw, without fire, almost without light, and without money, the granddaughter of a great prince, and I gave one hundred louis to this victim of royal forgetfulness and neglect. Then, as I was detained late there, and as the frost was severe, and horses go slowly over ice, particularly hackney-coach horses——"

"Hackney-coach horses!" cried the king. "You returned in a hackney-coach?"

"Yes, sire—No. 107."

"Oh, oh!" said the king, with every sign of vexation.

"Yes, and only too happy to get it," said the queen.

"Madame!" interrupted he, "you are full of noble feelings; but this impetuous generosity becomes a fault. Remember," continued he, "that I never suspected you of anything that was not perfectly pure and honest: it is only your mode of acting and adventurous spirit that displease me. You have, as usual, been doing good, but the way you set about it makes it injurious to yourself. This is what I reproach you with. You say that I have faults to repair—that I have failed in my duty to a member of my own family. Tell me who the unfortunate is, and he shall no longer have reason to complain."

"The name of Valois, sire, is sufficiently illustrious not to have escaped your memory."

"Ah!" cried Louis, with a shout of laughter, "I know now whom you mean. La petite Valois, is it not?—a countess of something or other."

"De la Motte, sire."

"Precisely, De la Motte; her husband is a gendarme."

"Yes, sire."

"And his wife is an intrigante. Oh! you need not trouble yourself about her: she is moving heaven and earth; she worries my ministers, she teases my aunts, and overwhelms me with supplications, memorials, and genealogies."

"And all this uselessly, sire."

"I must confess it."

"Is she, or is she not, a Valois?"

"I believe she is."

"Well, then, I ask an honorable pension for her and a regiment for her husband. In fact, a decent position for this branch of the royal family."

"An honorable pension? Mon Dieu! how you run on, madame. Do you know what a terrible hole this winter has made in my funds? A regiment for this little gendarme, who speculated in marrying a Valois? Why, I have no regiments to give, even to those who deserve them, or who can pay for them. An income befitting a Valois for these people? when we, monarch as we are, have not one befitting a rich gentleman. Why, M. d'Orleans has sent his horses and mules to England for sale, and has cut off a third of his establishment. I have put down my wolf-hounds, and given up many other things. We are all on the privation list, great and small."

"But these Valois must not die of hunger."

"Have you not just given them one hundred louis?"

"And what is that?"

"A royal gift."

"Then give such another."

"Yours will do for us both."

"No, I want a pension for them."

"No, I will not bind myself to anything fixed; they will not let me forget them, and I will give when I have money to spare. I do not think much of this little Valois."

Saying these words, Louis held out his hand to the queen, who, however, turned from him and said, "No, you are not good to me, and I am angry."

"You bear malice," said the king "and I——"

"Oh, you shut the gates against me; you come at half-past six to my room, and force open the door in a passion."

"I was not in a passion," said the king.

"You are not now, you mean."

"What will you give me if I prove that I was not, even when I came in?"

"Let me see the proof."

"Oh, it is very easy; I have it in my pocket."

"Bah!" said the queen; but adding, with curiosity, "You have brought something to give me, but I warn you I shall not believe you, unless you show it me at once."

Then, with a smile full of kindness, the king began searching in his pockets, with that slowness which makes the child doubly impatient for his toy, the animal for his food, and the woman for her present: at last he drew out a box of red morocco leather, artistically ornamented in gold.

"A jewel box!" cried the queen.

The king laid it on the bed.

She opened it impatiently, and then called out, "Oh, mon Dieu! how beautiful!"

The king smiled with delight. "Do you think so?" said he.

The queen could not answer—she was breathless with admiration. Then she drew out of the box a necklace of diamonds, so large, so pure, so glittering, and so even, that, with sparkling eyes, she cried again, "Oh! it is magnificent."

"Then you are content?" said the king.

"Enchanted, sire; you make me too happy."

"Really?"

"See this first row; the diamonds are as large as filberts, and so even, you could not tell one from the other; then how beautifully the gradation of the rows is managed; the jeweler who made this necklace is an artist."

"They are two."

"Then I wager it is Bœhmer and Bossange."

"You have guessed right."

"Indeed, no one but they would risk making such a thing."

"Madame, take care," said the king; "you will have to pay too dear for this necklace."

"Oh, sire!" cried the queen, all the delight fading from her countenance.

"You must pay the price of letting me be the first to put it on:" and he approached her, holding in his hands the two ends of the magnificent necklace, of which the clasp was one great diamond.

She stopped him, saying, "But, sire, is it very dear?"

"Have I not told you the price?"

"Ah, Louis, we must not jest. Put the necklace back again."

"You refuse to allow me to put it on?"

"Oh no, sire, if I were going to wear it."

"What?" said the king, surprised.

"No," she said; "no one shall see a necklace of this price round my neck."

"You will not wear it?"

"Never."

"You refuse me."

"I refuse to wear a million or a million and a half of francs round my neck, for this necklace must cost that."

"I do not deny it," said the king.

"Then I do refuse to wear such a necklace while the king's coffers are empty, when he is forced to stint his charities, and to say to the poor, 'God help you, for I have no more to give.'"

"Are you serious in saying this?"

"Listen, sire; M. de Sartines told me a short time since that with that sum we could build a ship of the line; and in truth, sire, the king has more need of a ship than the queen of a necklace."

"Oh!" cried the king, joyfully, and with his eyes full of tears, "what you do is sublime. Thanks, Antoinette; you are a good wife!" and he threw his arms round her neck and kissed her. "Oh! how France will bless you," continued he; "and it shall hear what you have done."

The queen sighed.

"You regret," said he: "it is not too late."

"No, sire; shut this case, and return it to the jewelers."

"But listen, first; I have arranged the terms of payment, and I have the money."

"No, I have decided. I will not have the necklace; but I want something else."

"Diable! then my 1,600,000 francs are gone, after all."

"What! it would have cost that?"

"Indeed it would."

"Reassure yourself; what I ask is much cheaper."

"What do you wish for?"

"To go to Paris once more."

"Oh! that is easy enough, and not dear."

"But wait— —"

"Diable!"

"To the Place Vendôme, to see M. Mesmer."

"Diable!" again said the king; but added: "Well, as you have denied yourself the necklace, I suppose I must let you go; but, on one condition."

"What?"

"You must be accompanied by a princess of the blood."

"Shall it be Madame de Lamballe?"

"Yes, if you like."

"I promise."

"Then I consent."

"Thanks, sire."

"And, now," said the king, "I shall order my ship of the line, and call it the 'Queen's Necklace.' You shall stand godmother, and then I will send it out to La Pérouse;" and, kissing his wife's hand, he went away quite joyful.

CHAPTER VIII
THE QUEEN'S PETITE LEVEE

No sooner was the king gone than the queen rose, and went to the window. The morning was lovely, and had the charming feeling of the commencement of spring, while the sun seemed almost warm. The wind had gone round to the west, and if it remained in that quarter this terrible winter was probably at an end.

The snow was beginning to drip from the trees, under the influence of this genial morning.

"If we wish to profit by the ice," cried the queen, "I believe we must make haste; for look, Madame de Misery, the spring seems to have begun. I much wish to make up a party on the Swiss lake, and will go to-day, for to-morrow it may be too late."

"Then at what hour will your majesty wish to dress?"

"Immediately; I will breakfast and then go."

"Are there any other orders, madame?"

"See if Madlle. de Taverney has risen, and tell her I wish to speak to her."

"She is already waiting for you in the boudoir, madame."

"Already?" said the queen, who knew at what time she had gone to bed.

"She has been there for twenty minutes, madame."

"Ask her to come in."

Andrée soon entered, dressed with her usual care, and smiling, though rather unquiet.

The queen's answering smile quite reassured her.

"Go, my good Misery, and send me Leonard."

When she was gone, "The king has been charming," said the queen to Andrée; "he has laughed, and is quite disarmed."

"But does he know, madame?"

"You understand, Andrée, that a woman does not tell falsehoods when she has done no wrong and is the Queen of France."

"Certainly, madame."

"Still, my dear Andrée, it seems we have been wrong— —"

"Doubtless, madame, but how?"

"Why, in pitying Madame de la Motte; the king dislikes her, but I confess she pleased me."

"Here is Leonard," said Madame de Misery, returning.

The queen seated herself before her silver-gilt toilet-table, and the celebrated hair-dresser commenced his operations.

She had the most beautiful hair in the world, and was fond of looking at it; Leonard knew this, and therefore with her was always tardy in his movements, that she might have time to admire it.

Marie Antoinette was looking beautiful that morning: she was pleased and happy.

Her hair finished, she turned again to Andrée.

"You have not been scolded," she said; "you are free: besides, they say every one is afraid of you, because, like Minerva, you are too wise."

"I, madame?"

"Yes, you; but, oh, mon Dieu! how happy you are to be unmarried, and, above all, to be content to be so."

Andrée blushed, and tried to smile.

"It is a vow that I have made," said she.

"And which you will keep, beautiful vestal?"

"I hope so."

"Apropos," said the queen, "I remember, that although unmarried, you have a master since yesterday morning."

"A master, madame?"

"Yes, your dear brother; what do you call him?—Philippe, is it not?"

"Yes, madame."

"Has he arrived?"

"He came yesterday."

"And you have not yet seen him? I took you away to Paris, selfish that I was; it was unpardonable."

"Oh, madame! I pardon you willingly, and Philippe also."

"Are you sure?"

"I answer for both of us."

"How is he?"

"As usual, beautiful and good, madame."

"How old is he now?"

"Thirty-two."

"Poor Philippe! do you know that it is fourteen years since I first met him! But I have not seen him now for nine or ten."

"Whenever your majesty pleases to receive him he will be but too happy to assure you that this long absence has not altered the sentiment of respectful devotion which he has ever felt for his queen."

"I will see him at once."

"In a quarter of an hour he will be at your majesty's feet."

Scarcely was Andrée gone, when the queen saw reflected in the glass an arch and laughing face. "My brother D'Artois," cried the queen; "how you frightened me!"

"Good morning, your majesty," said the young prince; "how did your majesty pass the night?"

"Very badly, brother."

"And the morning?"

"Very well."

"That is the most important; I guessed that all had gone right, for I have just met the king, and he was smiling most graciously."

The queen laughed, and he echoed it.

The queen had just cast off her dressing-gown of India muslin, and put on her morning dress, when the door opened and Andrée entered, leading by the hand a handsome man with a brown complexion, noble black eyes, profoundly imbued with melancholy, and a soldier-like carriage. He looked like one of Coypel's or Gainsborough's beautiful portraits.

He was dressed in a dark gray coat, embroidered in silver, a white cravat, and a dark waistcoat; and this rather somber style of dress seemed to suit the manly character of his beauty.

"Your majesty," said Andrée, "here is my brother."

Philippe bowed gravely.

The queen, who had until now been looking at his figure reflected in her mirror, turned round and saluted him. She was beautiful, with that royal beauty which made all around her not only partisans of the throne, but adorers of the woman. She possessed the power of beauty; and, if we may make use of the inversion, the beauty of power. Philippe, seeing her smile, and feeling those limpid eyes, at once soft and proud, fixed upon him, turned pale, and could hardly restrain his emotion.

"It appears, M. de Taverney," said she, "that you pay me your first visit; I thank you for it."

"Your majesty deigns to forget that it is I who should give thanks."

"How many years have passed since we last met, monsieur? Alas! the most beautiful part of our lives."

"For me, madame, but not for your majesty, to whom all days are alike charming."

"You were then pleased with America, M. de Taverney, as you remained there so long?"

"Madame," answered Philippe, "M. de la Fayette, when he left the New World, had need of an officer in whom he could place confidence to take the command of the French auxiliaries. He proposed me, therefore, to General Washington, who accepted me."

"It seems," said the queen, "that this new country sends us home many heroes."

"Your majesty does not mean that for me?" asked Philippe, laughing.

"Why not?" Then turning to the Comte d'Artois, "See, brother," she said; "has not M. de Taverney the look of a hero?"

Philippe, seeing himself thus introduced to the young prince, bowed low. He returned it, and said, "I am most happy to make the acquaintance of such a gentleman. What are your intentions in returning to France, sir?"

"Monseigneur," answered Philippe, "my sister is my first consideration; whatever she wishes, I shall do."

"But she has a father, I believe," said the count.

"Never mind him," said the queen, quickly, "I prefer Andrée under her brother's protection, and he under yours, count. You will take charge of M. de Taverney, will you not?"

The count bowed an assent.

"For, do you know," continued she, "that a very strong link binds me to M. de Taverney?"

"What do you mean, sister?"

"That he was the first Frenchman who presented himself to my eyes when I arrived in this country; and I had taken a very sincere vow to promote the happiness of the first Frenchman I should meet."

Philippe felt the blood rush to his face, and Andrée looked at him rather sadly.

The queen observed these looks of the brother and sister, and fancied she divined the cause. "Why," she thought, "should not Monsieur de Taverney have partaken the epidemic passion which pervaded all France for the dauphiness in 1774?" Marie Antoinette therefore attributed these looks to some confidence of this kind which the brother had made to the sister; and in consequence, she smiled still more upon him, and redoubled her kindness towards Andrée.

The queen was a true woman, and gloried in being loved.

It was an innocent coquetry, and the most generous souls have the most strongly these aspirations for the love of all who surround them.

Alas! a time is coming for thee, poor queen, when those smiles towards those who love thee, with which thou hast been reproached, thou shalt vainly bestow on those that love thee not!

The Comte d'Artois approached Philippe while the queen was talking to Andrée, and said, "Do you think Washington so very great a general?"

"Certainly a great man, monseigneur."

"And what effect did our French produce out there?"

"As much good as the English did harm."

"Ah, you are a partisan of the new ideas, my dear M. Philippe de Taverney; but have you reflected on one thing?"

"What, monseigneur? I assure you that out there, encamped in the fields, and in the savannahs on the borders of the great lakes, I had plenty of time for reflection."

"On this, that in making war out there, it was neither on the Indians nor on the English, but on us."

"Ah, monseigneur, I do not deny that that is possible."

"Therefore I do not admire so much these victories of M. de la Fayette and Washington. It is egotism, perhaps, but it is not egotism for myself alone."

"Oh, monseigneur!"

"But do you know why I will still support you with all my power?"

"Whatever be the reason, I shall be truly grateful."

"It is, because you are not one of those whose names have been blazoned forth. You have done your duty bravely, but you have not thrust yourself forward; you are not known in Paris."

The young prince then kissed the queen's hand, and bowing to Andrée, left the room.

Then the queen turned again to Philippe, saying, "Have you seen your father, sir?"

"No, madame."

"Why did you not go to see him first?"

"I had sent home my valet, and my luggage, but my father sent the servant back again, with orders to present myself first to you, or the king."

"It is a lovely morning," said the queen; "to-morrow the ice will begin to melt. Madame de Misery, order my sledge and send my chocolate in here."

"Will not your majesty take something to eat? You had no supper last night."

"You mistake, my good Misery, we had supper. Had we not, Andrée?"

"A very good one, madame."

"So I will only have my chocolate. Quick, Madame de Misery; this fine weather tempts me, and the Swiss lake will be full of company."

"Your majesty is going to skate?" asked Philippe.

"Ah, you will laugh at us, M. l'Américain; you, who have traversed lakes where there are more miles than we have feet here."

"Madame," replied Philippe, "here you amuse yourself with the cold, but there they die of it."

"Ah, here is my chocolate; Andrée, take a cup with me."

Andrée bowed, coloring with pleasure.

"You see, M. de Taverney, I am always the same, hating all etiquette, as in old times. Do you remember those old days? Are you changed since then, M. Philippe?"

"No, madame," replied the young man, "I am not changed—at least, not in heart."

"Well, I am glad to hear that, for it was a good one. A cup for M. de Taverney, Madame de Misery."

"Oh, madame!" cried Philippe, "you cannot mean it; such an honor for a poor obscure soldier like me."

"An old friend," said the queen; "this day seems to remind me of my youth; I seem again happy, free, proud and yet foolish. This day recalls to me that happy time at my dear Trianon, and all our frolics there, Andrée and I together. This day brings back to my memory my roses, my strawberries, and my birds, that I was so fond of, all, even to my good gardeners, whose happy faces often announced to me a new flower or a delicious fruit; and M. de Jussieu and that original old Rousseau, who is since dead. But come," continued she, herself pouring the chocolate into his cup, "you are a soldier, and accustomed to fire, so burn yourself gloriously with this chocolate, for I am in a hurry."

She laughed, but Philippe, taking it seriously, drank it off most heroically.

The queen saw him, and laughing still more, said, "You are indeed a perfect hero, M. de Taverney." She then rose, and her woman brought her bonnet, ermine mantle, and gloves.

Philippe took his hat under his arm, and followed her and Andrée out.

"M. de Taverney, I do not mean you to leave me," said the queen. "Come round to my right."

They went down the great staircase; the drums were beating, the clarions of the body-guard were playing, and this whole scene, and the enthusiasm everywhere shown towards that beautiful queen by whose side he was walking, completed the intoxication of the young man. The change was too sudden, after so many years of exile and regret, to such great joy and honor.

CHAPTER IX
THE SWISS LAKE

Every one knows this piece of water, which still goes by the same name. An avenue of linden trees skirts each bank, and these avenues were on this day thronged with pedestrians, of all ranks and ages, who had come to enjoy the sight of the sledges and the skating. The toilets of the ladies presented a brilliant spectacle of luxury and gaiety, their high coiffures, gay bonnets with the veils half down, fur mantles, and brilliant silks with deep flounces, were mingled with the orange or blue coats of the gentlemen.

Gay lackeys also, in blue and red, passed among the crowd, looking like poppies and cornflowers blown about by the wind.

Now and then a cry of admiration burst from the crowd, as St. George, the celebrated skater, executed some circle so perfect, that a mathematician could scarcely have found a fault in it.

While the banks of the lake were thus crowded, the ice itself presented a scene not less gay, and still more animated: sledges flew about in all directions. Several dogs, clothed in embroidered velvet, and with plumes of feathers on their heads, looking like fabulous animals, drew a sledge in which sat M. de Lauzun, who was wrapped up in a tiger skin. Here you might see a lady masked, doubtless on account of the cold, in some sledge of a quieter character, while a handsome skater, in a velvet riding-coat, hangs over the back, to assist and direct her progress; whatever they may be saying to each other is quite inaudible, amidst this busy hum of voices; but who can blame a rendezvous which takes place in the open air, and under the eyes of all Versailles? and whatever they may be saying matters to no one else: it is evident that in the midst of this crowd their life is an isolated one; they think only of each other.

All at once a general movement in the crowd announces that they have recognized the queen, who is approaching the lake. A general cry of "Vive la reine!" is heard, and all endeavor to approach as nearly as possible to the place where she has stationed herself. One person alone does not appear to share this feeling, for on her approach he disappears with all his suite as fast as possible in the opposite direction.

"Do you see," said the Comte d'Artois to the queen, whom he had hastened to join, "how my brother Provence flies from you?"

"He fears that I should reproach him."

"Oh, no; it is not that that makes him fly."

"It is his conscience, then."

"Not even that, sister."

"What then?"

"I will tell you. He had just heard that M. de Suffren, our glorious commander, will arrive this evening; and as the news is important, he wishes to leave you in ignorance of it."

"But is the Minister of Marine ignorant of this arrival?"

"Ah, mon Dieu, sister, have you not learned enough of ministers, during the fourteen years you have passed here, as dauphiness and queen, to know that they are always ignorant of precisely what they ought to know? However, I have told him about this, and he is deeply grateful."

"I should think so," said the queen.

"Yes, and I have need of his gratitude, for I want a loan."

"Oh," cried the queen, laughing, "how disinterested you are."

"Sister," said he, "you must want money; I offer you half of what I am going to receive."

"Oh no, brother, keep it for yourself; I thank you, but I want nothing just now."

"Diable! do not wait too long to claim my promise, because if you do, I may not be in a condition to fulfil it."

"In that case I must endeavor to find out some state secret for myself."

"Sister, you begin to look cold."

"Well, here is M. de Taverney returning with my sledge."

"Then you do not want me any longer?"

"No."

"Then send me away, I beg."

"Why? do you imagine you will be in my way?"

"No; it is I who want my liberty."

"Adieu, then."

"Au revoir, dear sister."

"Till when?"

"Till this evening."

"Is there anything to take place to-night, then?"

"Yes; this evening the minister will bring M. de Suffren to the jeu du roi."

"Very well, then, till this evening."

And the young prince, bowing with his habitual elegance, disappeared among the crowd.

Old Taverney, who was one of the nearest spectators of all this, had been watching his son eagerly, and felt almost chagrined at this conversation between the queen and her brother-in-law, as it interrupted the familiar intercourse which his son had before been enjoying; therefore, when the young man returned with the queen's sledge, and, seeing his father, whom he had not met for ten years, advanced towards him, he motioned him away, saying, "We will talk afterwards, when you have left the queen."

Philippe, therefore, returned to the queen, who was getting into the sledge with Andrée. Two attendants approached to push it, but she said, "No; I do not wish to go like that; you skate, M. de Taverney? Does he not, Andrée?"

"Philippe used to skate remarkably well," replied she.

"And now I dare say he rivals St. George," said the queen.

"I will do my best to justify your majesty's opinion," said he; and putting on his skates, he placed himself behind her sledge, and they commenced their course.

St. George, seeing the queen on the ice, began to execute his most skilful maneuvers, and finished off by going in circles round her sledge, making the most elegant bows each time he passed her.

Then Philippe, moved to emulation, began to push along the sledge with such wonderful rapidity that St. George found no little difficulty in keeping pace with it.

Several people, however, seeing the queen move at this marvelous rate, uttered cries of terror.

"If your majesty desires," said Philippe, "I will stop, or go slower."

"Oh no!" said she, with that enthusiasm which she carried into everything; "oh no! I am not at all afraid; quicker still, chevalier, if you can."

"Oh yes, madame, and you are quite safe; you may trust to me;" and his vigorous arm propelled them at a still increased pace. He emulated the circles of St. George, and flew round as fast with the sledge as could even that experienced skater without it.

Then, leaving these evolutions, he pushed the sledge straight before him, and with such force that he himself remained behind.

St. George, seeing this, made a tremendous effort to gain the sledge before him, but was distanced by Philippe, who once more seized it, turned it, and flew in a new direction.

The air now rang with such acclamations, that Philippe began to feel ashamed.

Then the queen, who had joined the applause with her hands, turned round and said to him, "And now, M. de Taverney, that you have gained the victory, stop, I beg, or you will kill me."

CHAPTER X
THE TEMPTER

Philippe, at this request of the queen, made a strong effort, and stopped the sledge abruptly.

"And now, rest yourself," said she, coming out of it all trembling. "Indeed, I never could have believed the delight of going so fast, but you have made me quite tremble;" and she took Philippe's arm to support herself, until a general murmur reminded her that she was once more committing a breach of etiquette.

As for Philippe, overwhelmed by this great honor, he felt more ashamed than if his sovereign had insulted him publicly; he lowered his eyes, and his heart beat as though it would burst.

The queen, however, withdrew her arm almost immediately, and asked for a seat. They brought her one.

"Thanks, M. de Taverney," said she; then, in a lower tone, "Mon Dieu, how disagreeable it is to be always surrounded by spying fools!"

A number of ladies and gentlemen soon crowded round her, and all looked with no little curiosity at Philippe, who, to hide his confusion, stooped to take off his skates, and then fell into the background.

After a short time, however, the queen said, "I shall take cold if I sit here, I must take another turn;" and she remounted her sledge.

Philippe waited, but in vain, for another order.

Twenty gentlemen soon presented themselves, but she said, "No, I thank you, I have my attendants;" and she moved slowly off, while Philippe remained alone.

He looked about for St. George, to console him for his defeat by some compliment, but he had received a message from his patron, the duke d'Orleans, and had left the place.

Philippe, therefore, rather tired, and half frightened at all that had passed, remained stationary, following with his eyes the queen's sledge, which was now at some distance, when he felt some one touch him; he turned round and saw his father.

The little old man, more shrunk than ever, enveloped in furs like a Laplander, had touched his son with his elbow, that he might not be obliged to take his hands out of the muff that hung from his neck.

"You do not embrace me, my son," said he.

"My dear father, I do it with all my heart."

"And now," said the old man, "go quickly;" and he pushed him away.

"Where do you wish me to go, sir?"

"Why, morbleu, over there."

"Where?"

"To the queen."

"No, I thank you, father."

"How? No, I thank you! are you mad? You will not go after the queen?"

"My dear father, it is impossible!"

"Impossible to join the queen, who is expecting you?"

"Who is expecting me!"

"Yes, who wishes for you."

"Wishes for me? Indeed, father," added he, coldly, "I think you forget yourself."

"It is astonishing!" said the old man, stamping his foot. "Where on earth do you spring from?"

"Monsieur," said his son, sadly, "you will make me conclude one of two things."

"What?"

"Either that you are laughing at me, or else, excuse me, that you are losing your senses."

The old man seized his son by the arm so energetically that he made him start. "Listen, M. Philippe," said he; "America is, I know, a country a long way from this, and where there is neither king nor queen."

"Nor subjects."

"Nor subjects, M. Philosopher; I do not deny it; that point does not interest me; but what does so is that I fear also to have to come to a conclusion——"

"What, father?"

"That you are a simpleton, my son; just trouble yourself to look over there."

"Well, sir!"

"Well, the queen looks back, and it is the third time she has done so; there! she turns again, and who do you think she is looking for but for you, M. Puritan?"

"Well, sir," said the young man; "if it were true, which it probably is not, that the queen was looking for——"

"Oh!" interrupted the old man, angrily, "this fellow is not of my blood; he cannot be a Taverney. Sir, I repeat to you that the queen is looking for you."

"You have good sight, sir," said his son, dryly.

"Come," said the old man, more gently, and trying to moderate his impatience, "trust my experience: are you, or are you not, a man?"

Philippe made no reply.

His father ground his teeth with anger, to see himself opposed by this steadfast will; but making one more effort, "Philippe, my son," said he, still more gently, "listen to me."

"It seems to me, sir, that I have been doing nothing else for the last quarter of an hour."

"Oh," thought the old man, "I will draw you down from your stilts. I will find out your weak side." Then aloud, "You have overlooked one thing, Philippe."

"What, sir?"

"When you left for America, there was a king, but no queen, if it were not the Dubarry; hardly a respectable sovereign. You come back and see a queen, and you think you must be very respectful."

"Doubtless."

"Poor child!" said his father, laughing.

"How, sir? You blame me for respecting the monarchy—you, a Taverney Maison-Rouge, one of the best names in France."

"I do not speak of the monarchy, but only of the queen."

"And you make a difference?"

"Pardieu, I should think so. What is royalty? a crown that is unapproachable. But what is a queen? a woman, and she, on the contrary, is very approachable."

Philippe made a gesture of disgust.

"You do not believe me," continued the old man, almost fiercely; "well, ask M. de Coigny, ask M. de Lauzun, or M. de Vaudreuil."

"Silence, father!" cried Philippe; "or for these three blasphemies, not being able to strike you three blows with my sword, I shall strike them on myself."

The old man stepped back, murmuring, "Mon Dieu, what a stupid animal! Good evening, son; you rejoice me; I thought I was the father, the old man, but now I think it is I who must be the young Apollo, and you the old man;" and he turned away.

Philippe stopped him: "You did not speak seriously, did you, father? It is impossible that a gentleman of good blood like you should give ear to these calumnies, spread by the enemies, not only of the queen, but of the throne."

"He will not believe, the double mule!" said the old man.

"You speak to me as you would speak before God?"

"Yes, truly."

"Before God, whom you approach every day?"

"It seems to me, my son," replied he, "that I am a gentleman, and that you may believe my word."

"It is, then, your opinion that the queen has had lovers?"

"Certainly."

"Those whom you have named?"

"And others, for what I know. Ask all the town and the court. One must be just returned from America to be ignorant of all they say."

"And who say this, sir? some vile pamphleteers!"

"Oh! do you, then, take me for an editor?"

"No, and there is the mischief, when men like you repeat such calumnies, which, without that, would melt away like the unwholesome vapors which sometimes obscure the most brilliant sunshine; but people like you, repeating them, give them a terrible stability. Oh! monsieur, for mercy's sake do not repeat such things."

"I do repeat them, however."

"And why do you repeat them?" cried Philippe, fiercely.

"Oh!" said the old man with his satanic laugh, "to prove to you that I was not wrong when I said, 'Philippe, the queen looks back; she is looking for you. Philippe, the queen wishes for you; run to her.'"

"Oh! father, hold your tongue, or you will drive me mad."

"Really, Philippe, I do not understand you. Is it a crime to love? It shows that one has a heart; and in the eyes of this woman, in her voice, in everything, can you not read her heart? She loves; is it you? or is it another? I know not, but believe in my own experience: at this moment she loves, or is beginning to love, some one. But you are a philosopher, a Puritan, a Quaker, an American; you do not love; well, then, let her look; let her turn again and again; despise her, Philippe, I should say Joseph de Taverney."

The old man hurried away, satisfied with the effect he had produced, and fled like the serpent who was the first tempter into crime.

Philippe remained alone, his heart swelling and his blood boiling. He remained fixed in his place for about half an hour, when the queen, having finished her tour, returned to where he stood, and called out to him:

"You must be rested now, M. de Taverney; come, then, for there is no one like you to guide a queen royally."

Philippe ran to her, giddy, and hardly knowing what he did. He placed his hand on the back of the sledge, but started as though he had burned his fingers; the queen had thrown herself negligently back in the sledge, and the fingers of the young man touched the locks of Marie Antoinette.

CHAPTER XI
M. DE SUFFREN

Contrary to the usual habits of a court, the secret had been faithfully confined to Louis XVI. and the Comte d'Artois. No one knew at what time or hour M. de Suffren would arrive.

The king had announced his jeu du roi for the evening; and at seven o'clock he entered, with ten princes and princesses of his family. The queen came holding the princess royal, now about seven years old, by the hand. The assembly was numerous and brilliant. The Comte d'Artois approached the queen, and said, "Look around you, madame."

"Well?"

"What do you see?"

The queen looked all around, and then said, "I see nothing but happy and friendly faces."

"Rather, then, whom do you not see?"

"Oh! I understand; I wonder if he is always going to run away from me."

"Oh no! only this is a good joke; M. de Provence has gone to wait at the barrier for M. de Suffren."

"Well, I do not see why you laugh at that; he has been the most cunning, after all, and will be the first to receive and pay his compliments to this gentleman."

"Come, dear sister," replied the young prince, laughing, "you have a very mean opinion of our diplomacy. M. de Provence has gone to meet him at Fontainebleau; but we have sent some one to meet him at Villejuif, so that my brother will wait by himself at Fontainebleau, while our messenger will conduct M. de Suffren straight to Versailles, without passing through Paris at all."

"That is excellently imagined."

"It is not bad, I flatter myself; but it is your turn to play."

The king had noticed that M. d'Artois was making the queen laugh, and guessing what it was about, gave them a significant glance, to show that he shared their amusement.

The saloon where they played was full of persons of the highest rank—M. de Condé, M. de Penthièvre, M. de Tremouille, etc. The news of the arrival of M. de Suffren had, as we have said, been kept quiet, but there had been a kind of vague rumor that some one was expected, and all were somewhat preoccupied and watchful. Even the king, who was in the habit of playing six-franc pieces in order to moderate the play of the court, played gold without thinking of it.

The queen, however, to all appearances entered, as usual, eagerly into the game.

Philippe, who, with his sister, was admitted to the party, in vain endeavored to shake from his mind his father's words. He asked himself if indeed this old man, who had seen so much of courts, was not right; and if his own ideas were indeed those of a Puritan, and belonging to another land. This queen, so charming, so beautiful, and so friendly towards him, was she indeed only a terrible coquette, anxious to add one lover more to her list, as the entomologist transfixes a new insect or butterfly, without thinking of the tortures of the poor creature whose heart he is piercing? "Coigny, Vaudreuil," repeated he to himself, "they loved the queen, and were loved by her. Oh, why does this calumny haunt me so, or why will not some ray of light discover to me the heart of this woman?"

Then Philippe turned his eyes to the other end of the table, where, by a strange chance, these gentlemen were sitting side by side, and both seemingly equally forgetful of, and insensible to, the queen; and he thought that it was impossible that these men could have loved and be so calm, or that they could have been loved and seem so forgetful. From them he turned to look at Marie Antoinette herself and interrogated that pure forehead, that haughty mouth, and beautiful face; and the answer they all seemed to give him was: calumnies, all calumnies, these rumors, originating only in the hates and jealousies of a court.

While he was coming to these conclusions the clock struck a quarter to eight, and at that moment a great noise of footsteps and the sound of many voices were heard on the staircase. The king, hearing it, signed to the queen, and they both rose and broke up the game. She then passed into the great reception-hall, and the king followed her.

An aide-de-camp of M. de Castries, Minister of Marine, approached the king and said something in a low tone, when M. de Castries himself entered, and said aloud, "Will your majesty receive M. de Suffren, who has arrived from Toulon?"

At this name a general movement took place in the assembly.

"Yes, sir," said the king, "with great pleasure;" and M. de Castries left the room.

To explain this interest for M. de Suffren, and why king, queen, princes, and ministers contended who should be the first to receive him, a few words will suffice.

Suffren is a name essentially French, like Turenne or Jean Bart. Since the last war with England, M. de Suffren had fought seven great naval battles without sustaining a defeat. He had taken Trincomalee and Gondeleur, scoured the seas, and taught the Nabob Hyder Ali that France was the first Power in Europe. He had carried into his profession all the skill of an able diplomatist, all the bravery and all the tactics of a soldier, and all the prudence of a wise ruler. Hardy, indefatigable, and proud when the honor of the French nation was in question, he had harassed the English, by land and by sea, till even these fierce islanders were afraid of him.

But after the battle, in which he risked his life like the meanest sailor, he ever showed himself humane, generous, and compassionate. He was now about fifty-six years of age, stout and short, but with an eye of fire and a noble carriage, and, like a man accustomed to surmount all difficulties, he had dressed in his traveling-carriage.

He wore a blue coat embroidered with gold, a red waistcoat, and blue trousers.

All the guards through whom he had passed, when he was named to them by M. de Castries, had saluted him as they would have done a king.

"M. de Suffren," said the king when he entered, "welcome to Versailles; you bring glory with you."

M. de Suffren bent his knee to the king, who, however, raised him and embraced him cordially; then, turning to the queen, "Madame," said he, "here is M. de Suffren, the victor of Trincomalee and Gondeleur, and the terror of the English."

"Monsieur," said the queen, "I wish you to know that you have not fired a shot for the glory of France but my heart has beaten with admiration and gratitude."

When she ceased, the Comte d'Artois approached with his son, the Duc d'Angoulême.

"My son," said he, "you see a hero; look at him well, for it is a rare sight."

"Monseigneur," replied the young prince, "I have read about the great men in Plutarch, but I could not see them; I thank you for showing me M. de Suffren."

The king now took the arm of M. de Suffren, in order to lead him to his study, and talk to him of his travels; but he made a respectful resistance.

"Sire," said he, "will your majesty permit me——"

"Oh! whatever you wish, sir."

"Then, sire, one of my officers has committed so grave a fault against discipline, that I thought your majesty ought to be sole judge of the offense."

"Oh, M. de Suffren, I had hoped your first request would have been a favor, and not a punishment."

"Your majesty, as I have had the honor to say, shall judge what ought to be done. In the last battle the officer of whom I speak was on board *La Sévère*."

"Oh, the ship that struck her flag!" cried the king, frowning.

"Yes, sire. The captain of *La Sévère* had indeed struck his flag, and already Sir Hugh, the English admiral, had despatched a boat to take possession of his prize, when the lieutenant in command of the guns of the middle deck, perceiving that the firing above had ceased, and having received orders to stop his own fire, went on deck, saw the flag lowered, and the captain ready to surrender. At this sight, sir, all his French blood revolted, he took the flag which lay there, and, seizing a hammer, ordered the men to recommence the fire, while he nailed it to the mast. It was by this action, sire, that *La Sévère* was preserved to your majesty."

"A splendid action!" cried the king and queen simultaneously.

"Yes, sire—yes, madame, but a grave fault against discipline. The order had been given by the captain, and the lieutenant ought to have obeyed. I, however, ask for the pardon of the officer, and the more so as he is my own nephew."

"Your nephew!" cried the king; "and you have never mentioned him!"

"Not to you, sire; but I made my report to the ministers, begging them to say nothing about it until I had obtained his pardon from your majesty."

"It is granted," said the king. "I promise beforehand my protection to all who may violate discipline in such a cause. You must present this officer to me, M. de Suffren."

M. de Suffren turned. "Approach, M. de Charny," he said.

The queen started at the sound of this name, which she had so recently heard. A young officer advanced from the crowd, and presented himself before the king.

The queen and Andrée looked anxiously at each other; but M. de Charny bowed before the king almost without raising his eyes, and, after kissing his hand, retired again, without seeming to have observed the queen.

"Come now, M. de Suffren," said the king, "and let us converse; I am impatient to hear all your adventures." But before leaving the room he turned to the queen and said. "Apropos, madame, I am going to have built, as you know, a ship of one hundred guns, and I think of changing the name we had destined for it, and of calling it instead——"

"Oh yes!" cried Marie Antoinette, catching his thought, "we will call it *Le Suffren*, and I will still stand sponsor."

"Vive le roi! vive la reine!" cried all.

"And vive M. de Suffren!" added the king, and then left the room with him.

CHAPTER XII
M. DE CHARNY

M. de Suffren had requested his nephew to wait his return, and he therefore remained in the group as before.

The queen, speaking low to Andrée, and glancing towards him, said: "It is he, there is no doubt."

"Mon Dieu! yes, madame, it is he indeed."

At this moment the door opened, and a gentleman dressed in the robes of a cardinal, and followed by a long train of officers and prelates, entered the room.

The queen immediately recognized M. de Rohan, and turned away her head, without taking the trouble to hide the frown which overspread her face.

He crossed the room without stopping to speak to any one, and, coming straight up to her, bowed to her more as a man of the world bows to a lady than as a subject to a queen, and then addressed some rather high-flown compliments to her; but she scarcely looked at him, and, after murmuring a few cold words in reply, began to talk to Madame de Lamballe.

The cardinal did not seem to notice this chilling reception, but bowed again, and retired without appearing in the least disconcerted.

He then turned to the king's aunts, from whom he met with a reception as cordial as the queen's had been the reverse. The Cardinal Louis de Rohan was a man in the prime of life, and of an imposing figure and noble bearing; his eyes shone with intelligence, his mouth was well cut and handsome, and his hands were beautiful. A premature baldness indicated either a man of pleasure or a studious one—and he was both. He was a man no little sought after by the ladies, and was noted for his magnificent style of living; indeed, he had found the way to feel himself poor with an income of 1,600,000 francs.

The king liked him for his learning, but the queen hated him. The reasons for this hate were twofold: first, when ambassador to Vienna, he had written to Louis XV. letters so full of sarcasm on Maria Theresa, that her daughter had never forgiven him; and he had also written letters opposing her marriage, which had been read aloud by Louis XV. at a supper at Madame Dubarry's. The embassy at Vienna had been taken from M. de Breteuil and given to M. de Rohan; the former gentleman, not strong enough to revenge himself alone, had procured copies of these letters, which he had laid before the dauphiness, thus making her the eternal enemy of M. de Rohan.

This hatred rendered the cardinal's position at court not a little uncomfortable. Every time he presented himself before the queen, he met with the same discouraging reception. In spite of this, he neglected no occasion of being near her, for which he had frequent opportunities, as he was chaplain to the court; and he never complained of the treatment he received. A circle of friends, among whom the Baron de Planta was the most intimate, helped to console him for these royal rebuffs; not to speak of the ladies of the court, who by no means imitated the severity of the queen towards him.

When he was gone, Marie Antoinette recovered her serenity, and said to Madame de Lamballe:

"Do you not think that this action of the nephew of M. de Suffren is one of the most remarkable of the war? What is his name, by the bye?"

"M. de Charny, I believe," replied the princess. "Was it not?" she said, turning to Andrée.

"Yes, your highness."

"M. de Charny shall describe it to us himself," said the queen. "Is he still here? Let him be sought for."

An officer who stood near hastened to obey her, and immediately returned with M. de Charny, and the circle round the queen made way for him to approach.

He was a young man, about eight-and-twenty, tall and well made; his face, animated and yet sweet, took a character of singular energy when he spoke, and dilated his large blue eyes; and he was, strange to say, for one who had been fighting in India, as fair as Philippe was dark.

When he had approached the place where the queen sat, with Madlle. de Taverney standing near her, he did not betray his surprise in any way, although it must have been great, in recognizing the ladies of the evening before. He did not look up until she addressed him, saying:

"M. de Charny, these ladies experience the natural desire, which I share with them, to hear from yourself all the details of this action of your ship."

"Madame," replied the young officer, "I beg your majesty to spare me the recital, not from modesty, but from humanity. What I did as lieutenant, a dozen other officers doubtless wished to do, only I was the first to put it in execution; and it is not worthy being made the subject of a narration to your majesty. Besides, the captain of *La Sévère* is a brave officer, who on that day lost his presence of mind. Alas, madame, we all know that the most courageous are not always equally brave. He wanted but ten minutes to recover himself; my determination not to surrender gave him the breathing time, his natural courage returned to him, and he showed himself the bravest of us all. Therefore I beg your majesty not to exaggerate the merit of my action, and thereby crush this deserving officer, who deplores incessantly the failing of a few moments."

"Right!" said the queen, touched by these generous words; "you are a true gentleman, M. de Charny, and such I already know you to be."

The young man colored crimson, and looked almost frightened at Andrée, fearing what the queen's rash generosity might lead her to say.

"For," continued the intrepid queen, "I must tell you all, that this is not the first time I have heard of M. de Charny, who deserves to be known and admired by all ladies; and to show you that he is as indulgent to our sex as he is merciless to his enemies, I will relate a little history of him which does him the greatest honor."

"Oh, madame!" stammered the young man, who felt as if he would have given a year of his life to be back in the West Indies.

"This, then, is it," continued the queen, to her eager listeners: "two ladies, whom I know, were detained out late and became embarrassed in a crowd; they ran a great risk, a real danger awaited them; M. de Charny happily passed by at the moment: he dispersed the crowd, and, although they were unknown to him, and it was impossible to recognize their rank, took them under his protection, and escorted them a long way, ten miles from Paris, I believe."

"Oh! your majesty exaggerates," said M. de Charny, laughing, and now quite reassured.

"Well, we will call it five," said the Count d'Artois, suddenly joining in the conversation.

"Let it be five, then, brother," said the queen; "but the most admirable part of the story is, that M. de Charny did not seek even to know the names of these ladies whom he had served, but left them at the place where they wished to stop, and went away without even looking back, so that they escaped from his protection without even a moment's disquietude."

All expressed their admiration.

"A knight of the round table could not have acted better," her majesty went on; "and so, M. de Charny, as the king will doubtless take upon himself to reward M. de Suffren, I, for my part, wish to do something for the nephew of this great man."

As she spoke, she held out her hand to him, and Charny, pale with joy, pressed his lips to this beautiful hand, while Philippe looked on from an obscure corner, pale with an opposite emotion.

The voice of M. d'Artois interrupted this scene, saying loudly, "Ah, Provence! you come too late! you have missed a fine sight, the reception of M. de Suffren. Really, it was one that a Frenchman can never forget. How the devil did it happen that you were not here—you who are generally the punctual man par excellence?"

M. de Provence bit his lips with vexation, and whispered to M. de Favras, his captain of the guards, "How does it come to pass that he is here?"

"Ah! monseigneur, I have been asking myself that question for the last hour, and have not yet found an answer."

CHAPTER XIII
THE ONE HUNDRED LOUIS OF THE QUEEN

Now we have introduced the principal characters of this history to our readers, and have taken them both into the "petite maison" of the Comte d'Artois and into the king's palace at Versailles, we will return to that house in the Rue St. Claude where we saw the queen enter incognito with Mademoiselle Andrée de Taverney.

We left Madame de la Motte counting over and delighted with her fifty double louis; next to the pleasure of having them, she knew no greater than that of displaying them, and having no one else, she called Dame Clotilde, who was still in the ante-chamber.

When she entered, "Come and look here!" said her mistress.

"Oh, madame!" cried the old woman, clasping her hands in astonishment.

"You were uneasy about your wages," said the countess.

"Oh, madame! I never said that; I only asked madame if she could pay me, as I had received nothing for three months."

"Do you think there is enough there to pay you?"

"Oh! madame, if I had all that, I should be rich for the rest of my life. But in what will madame spend all that?"

"In everything."

"The first thing, I think, madame, will be to furnish the kitchen, for you will have good dinners cooked now."

"Listen!" said Madame de la Motte; "someone knocks."

"I did not hear it," said the old woman.

"But I tell you that I did; so go at once." She hastily gathered up her money, and put it into a drawer, murmuring, "Oh! if Providence will but send me another such a visitor." Then she heard the steps of a man below, but could not distinguish what he said. Soon however, the door opened, and Clotilde came in with a letter.

The countess examined it attentively, and asked, "Was this brought by a servant?"

"Yes, madame."

"In livery?"

"No, madame."

"I know these arms, surely," said Jeanne to herself. "Who can it be from? but the letter will soon show for itself;" and opening it, she read: "Madame, the person to whom you wrote will see you to-morrow evening, if it be agreeable to you to remain at home for that purpose;" and that was all. "I have written to so many people," thought the countess. "Is this a man or a woman? The writing is no guide, nor is the style; it might come from either. Who is it that uses these arms? Oh! I remember now—the arms of the Rohans. Yes, I wrote to M. de Guémenée, and to M. de Rohan; it is one of them: but the shield is not quartered—it is therefore the cardinal. Ah! Monsieur de Rohan, the man of gallantry, the fine gentleman, and the ambitious one; he will come to see Jeanne de la Motte, if it be agreeable to her. Oh, yes! M. de Rohan, it is very agreeable. A charitable lady who gives a hundred louis may be received in a garret, freeze in my cold room, and suffer on my hard chair; but a clerical prince, a lady's man, that is quite another thing. We must have luxury to greet him."

Then, turning to Clotilde, who was getting her bed ready, she said: "Be sure to call me early to-morrow morning;" and when she did retire to rest, so absorbed was she in her expectations and plans, that it was nearly three o'clock before she fell asleep; nevertheless, she was quite ready when Dame Clotilde called her according to her directions early in the morning, and had finished her toilet by eight o'clock, although this day it consisted of an elegant silk dress, and her hair was elaborately dressed.

She sent Clotilde for a coach, and ordered the man to drive to the Place Royale, where, under one of the arcades, was the shop of M. Fingret, an upholsterer and decorator, and who had furniture always ready for sale or hire.

She entered his immense show-rooms, of which the walls were hung with different tapestries, and the ceiling completely hidden by the number of chandeliers and lamps that hung from it. On the ground were furniture, carpets, and cornices of every fashion and description.

CHAPTER XIV
M. FINGRET

Madame de la Motte, looking at all this, began to perceive how much she wanted. She wanted a drawing-room to hold sofas and lounging-chairs; a dining-room for tables and sideboards; and a boudoir for Persian curtains, screens, and knick-knacks; above all, she wanted the money to buy all these things. But in Paris, whatever you cannot afford to buy, you can hire; and Madame de la Motte set her heart on a set of furniture covered in yellow silk, with gilt nails, which she thought would be very becoming to her dark complexion. But this furniture she felt sure would never go into her rooms on the fifth story; it would be necessary to hire the third, which was composed of an ante-chamber, a dining-room, small drawing-room, and bedroom, so that she might, she thought, receive on this third story the visits of the cardinal, and on the fifth those of ladies of charity—that is to say, receive in luxury those who give from ostentation, and in poverty those who only desire to give when it is needed.

The countess, having made all these reflections, turned to where M. Fingret himself stood, with his hat in his hand, waiting for her commands.

"Madame?" said he in a tone of interrogation, advancing towards her.

"Madame la Comtesse de la Motte Valois," said Jeanne.

At this high-sounding name M. Fingret bowed low, and said: "But there is nothing in this room worthy Madame la Comtesse's inspection. If madame will take the trouble to step into the next one, she will see what is new and beautiful."

Jeanne colored. All this had seemed so splendid to her, too splendid even to hope to possess it; and this high opinion of M. Fingret's concerning her perplexed her not a little. She regretted that she had not announced herself as a simple bourgeoise; but it was necessary to speak, so she said, "I do not wish for new furniture."

"Madame has doubtless some friend's apartments to furnish?"

"Just so," she replied.

"Will madame, then, choose?" said M. Fingret, who did not care whether he sold new or old, as he gained equally by both.

"This set," said Jeanne, pointing to the yellow silk one.

"That is such a small set, madame."

"Oh, the rooms are small."

"It is nearly new, as madame may see."

"But the price?"

"Eight hundred francs."

The price made the countess tremble; and how was she to confess that a countess was content with second-hand things, and then could not afford to pay eight hundred francs for them? She therefore thought the best thing was to appear angry, and said: "Who thinks of buying, sir? Who do you think would buy such old things? I only want to hire."

Fingret made a grimace; his customer began gradually to lose her value in his eyes. She did not want to buy new things, only to hire old ones, "You wish it for a year?" he asked.

"No, only for a month. It is for some one coming from the country."

"It will be one hundred francs a month."

"You jest, surely, monsieur; why, in eight months I should have paid the full price of it."

"Granted, Madame la Comtesse."

"Well, is not that too bad?"

"I shall have the expense of doing it up again when you return it."

Madame de la Motte reflected. "One hundred francs a month is very dear, certainly; but either I can return it at the end of that time and say it is too dear, or I shall then perhaps be in a situation to buy."

"I will take it," she said, "with curtains to match."

"Yes, madame."

"And carpets."

"Here they are."

"What can you give me for another room?"

"These oak chairs, this table with twisted legs, and green damask curtains."

"And for a bedroom?"

"A large and handsome bed, a counterpane of velvet embroidered in rose-color and silver, an excellent couch, and blue curtains."

"And for my dressing-room?"

"A toilet-table hung with Mechlin lace; chest of drawers with marqueterie; sofa and chairs of tapestry. The whole came from the bedroom of Madame de Pompadour at Choisy."

"All this for what price?"

"For a month?"

"Yes."

"Four hundred francs."

"Come, Monsieur Fingret, do not take me for a grisette who is dazzled by your fine descriptions. Please to reflect that you are asking at the rate of four thousand eight hundred francs a year, and for that I can take a whole furnished house. You disgust me with the Place Royale."

"I am very sorry, madame."

"Prove it, then; I will only give half that price." Jeanne pronounced these words with so much authority that the merchant began again to think she might be worth conciliating.

"So be it, then, madame."

"And on one condition, M. Fingret."

"What, madame?"

"That everything be arranged in its proper place by three o'clock."

"But consider, madame, it is now ten."

"Can you do it or not?"

"Where must they go to?"

"Rue St. Claude."

"Close by?"

"Precisely."

The upholsterer opened a door, and called, "Sylvain! Landry! Rémy!"

Three men answered to the call.

"The carts and the trucks instantly. Rémy, you shall take this yellow furniture; Sylvain, you take that for the dining-room; and you, Landry, that for the bedroom. Here is the bill, madame; shall I receipt it?"

"Here are six double louis," she said, "and you can give the change to these men if the order is completed in time;" and, having given her address, she reentered her coach.

On her return she engaged the third floor, and in a few hours all was in order.

The lodgings thus transformed, the windows cleaned, and the fires lighted, Jeanne went again to her toilet, which she made as recherché as possible, and then took a last look at all the delights around her. Nothing had been forgotten: there were gilded branches from the walls for wax-lights, and glass lusters on each side of the mirror; Jeanne had also added flowers, to complete the embellishment of the paradise in which she intended to receive his eminence. She took care even to leave the door of the bedroom a little open, through which the light of a bright fire gave a glimpse of the luxuries within.

All these preparations completed, she seated herself in a chair by the fire, with a book in her hand, listening eagerly to the sound of every carriage that passed; but nine, ten, and eleven o'clock struck, and no one came. Still she did not despair; it was not too late for a gallant prelate, who had probably been first to some supper, and would come to her from there. But at last twelve struck; no one appeared, the lights were burning low, and the old servant, after many lamentations over her new cap, had fallen asleep in her chair.

At half-past twelve Jeanne rose furious from her chair, looked out of window for the hundredth time, and, seeing no one near, undressed herself and went to bed, refusing supper, or to answer any of the remarks made to her by Clotilde; and on her sumptuous bed, under her beautiful curtains, she experienced no better rest than she had on the previous night. At last, however, her anger began a little to abate, and she commenced framing excuses for the cardinal. He had so much to occupy him, he must have been detained, and, most potent of all, he had not yet seen her. She would not have been so easily consoled if he had broken the promise of a second visit.

CHAPTER XV
THE CARDINAL DE ROHAN

The next evening Jeanne, not discouraged, renewed all her preparations of the night before; and on this occasion she had no time to grow impatient, for at seven o'clock a carriage drove up to the door, from which a gentleman got out. At the sound of the door-bell Jeanne's heart beat so loud that you might almost have heard it; however, she composed herself as well as she could, and in a few minutes Clotilde opened the door, and announced the person who had written the day before yesterday.

"Let him come in," said Jeanne; and a gentleman dressed in silk and velvet, and with a lofty carriage, entered the room.

Jeanne made a step forward, and said: "To whom have I the honor of speaking?"

"I am the Cardinal de Rohan," he replied; at which Madame de la Motte, feigning to be overwhelmed with the honor, courtesied, as though he were a king. Then she advanced an armchair for him, and placed herself in another.

The cardinal laid his hat on the table, and, looking at Jeanne, began: "It is, then, true, mademoiselle——"

"Madame," interrupted Jeanne.

"Pardon me; I forgot."

"My husband is called De la Motte, monseigneur."

"Oh, yes; a gendarme, is he not?"

"Yes, sir."

"And you, madame, are a Valois?"

"I am, monseigneur."

"A great name," said the cardinal, "but rare—believed extinct."

"Not extinct, sir, since I bear it, and as I have a brother, Baron de Valois."

"Recognized?"

"That has nothing to do with it. Recognized or unrecognized, rich or poor, he is still Baron de Valois."

"Madame, explain to me this descent; it interests me; I love heraldry."

Jeanne repeated all that the reader already knows.

The cardinal listened and looked. He did not believe either her story or her merit; but she was poor and pretty.

"So that," he said carelessly, when she had finished, "you have really been unfortunate."

"I do not complain, monseigneur."

"Indeed, I had heard a most exaggerated account of the difficulties of your position; this lodging is commodious and well furnished."

"For a grisette, no doubt," replied Jeanne.

"What! do you call these rooms fit for a grisette?"

"I do not think you can call them fit for a princess," replied Jeanne.

"And you are a princess?" said he, in an ironical tone.

"I was born a Valois, monseigneur, as you were a Rohan," said Jeanne, with so much dignity that he felt a little touched by it.

"Madame," said he, "I forgot that my first words should have been an apology. I wrote to you that I would come yesterday, but I had to go to Versailles to assist at the reception of M. de Suffren."

"Monseigneur does me too much honor in remembering me to-day; and my husband will more than ever regret the exile to which poverty compels him, since it prevents him from sharing this favor with me."

"You live alone, madame?" asked the cardinal.

"Absolutely alone. I should be out of place in all society but that from which my poverty debars me."

"The genealogists do not contest your claim?"

"No; but what good does it do me?"

"Madame," continued the cardinal, "I shall be glad to know in what I can serve you."

"In nothing, monseigneur," she said.

"How! in nothing? Pray be frank."

"I cannot be more frank than I am."

"You were complaining just now."

"Certainly, I complain."

"Well, then?"

"Well, then, monseigneur, I see that you wish to bestow charity on me."

"Oh, madame!"

"Yes, sir, I have taken charity, but I will do so no more. I have borne great humiliation."

"Madame, you are wrong, there is no humiliation in misfortune."

"Not even with the name I bear? Would you beg, M. de Rohan?"

"I do not speak of myself," said he, with an embarrassment mingled with hauteur.

"Monseigneur, I only know two ways of begging: in a carriage, or at a church door in velvet or in rags. Well, just now, I did not expect the honor of this visit; I thought you had forgotten me."

"Oh, you knew, then, that it was I who wrote?"

"Were not your arms on the seal?"

"However, you feigned not to know me."

"Because you did not do me the honor to announce yourself."

"This pride pleases me," said the cardinal.

"I had then," continued Jeanne, "despairing of seeing you, taken the resolution of throwing off all this flimsy parade, which covers my real poverty, and of going in rags, like other mendicants, to beg my bread from the passers-by."

"You are not at the end of your resources, I trust, madame?"

Jeanne did not reply.

"You have some property, even if it be mortgaged? Some family jewels? This, for example," and he pointed to a box, with which the delicate fingers of the lady had been playing. "A singular box, upon my word! Will you permit me to look? Oh, a portrait!" he continued, with a look of great surprise. "Do you know the original of this portrait?" asked Jeanne.

"It is that of Maria Theresa."

"Of Maria Theresa?"

"Yes, the Empress of Austria."

"Really!" cried Jeanne. "Are you sure, monseigneur?"

"Where did you get it?" he asked.

"From a lady who came the day before yesterday."

"To see you?"

"Yes."

The cardinal examined the box with minute attention.

"There were two ladies," continued Jeanne.

"And one of them gave you this box?" said he, with evident suspicion.

"No; she dropped it here."

The cardinal remained thoughtful for some time, and then said, "What was the name of this lady? I beg pardon for being inquisitive."

"Indeed, it is a somewhat strange question."

"Indiscreet, perhaps, but not strange."

"Yes, very strange; for if I had known her name, I should have returned it long before this."

"Then, you know not who she is?"

"I only know she is the head of some charitable house."

"In Paris?"

"No; in Versailles."

"From Versailles; the head of a charitable house!"

"Monseigneur, I accept charity from ladies; that does not so much humiliate a poor woman; and this lady, who had heard of my wants, left a hundred louis on my table when she went away."

"A hundred louis!" said the cardinal in surprise; then, fearing to offend, he added, "I am not astonished, madame, that they should give you such a sum. You merit, on the contrary, all the solicitude of charitable people, and your name makes it a duty to help you. It is only the title of the Sister of Charity that surprised me, they are not in the habit of giving such donations. Could you describe this lady to me?"

"Not easily, sir."

"How so, since she came here?"

"Yes, but she probably did not wish to be recognized, for she hid her face as much as possible in her hood, and was besides, enveloped in furs."

"Well, but you saw something?"

"My impressions were, that she had blue eyes, and a small mouth, though the lips were rather thick."

"Tall or short?"

"Of middle height."

"Her hands?"

"Perfect."

"Her throat?"

"Long and slender."

"Her expression?"

"Severe and noble. But you, perhaps, know this lady, monseigneur?"

"Why should you think so, madame?"

"From the manner in which you question me; besides, there is a sympathy between the doers of good works."

"No, madame, I do not know her."

"But, sir, if you had some suspicion."

"How should I?"

"Oh, from this portrait, perhaps."

"Yes, certainly, the portrait," said the cardinal, rather uneasily.

"Well, sir, this portrait you still believe to be that of Maria Theresa?"

"I believe so, certainly."

"Then you think— —?"

"That you have received a visit from some German lady who has founded one of these houses!" But it was evident that the cardinal doubted, and he was pondering how this box, which he had seen a hundred times in the hands of the queen, came into the possession of this woman. Had the queen really been to see her? If she had been, was she indeed unknown to Jeanne? Or, if not, why did she try to hide the knowledge from him. If the queen had really been there, it was no longer a poor woman he had to deal with, but a princess succored by a queen, who bestowed her gifts in person.

Jeanne saw that the cardinal was thoughtful, and even suspicious of her. She felt uneasy, and knew not what to say.

At last, however, he broke the silence by saying, "And the other lady?"

"Oh, I could see her perfectly; she is tall and beautiful, with a determined expression, and a brilliant complexion."

"And the other lady did not name her?"

"Yes, once; but by her Christian name."

"What was it?"

"Andrée."

"Andrée!" repeated the cardinal, with a start.

This name put an end to all his doubts. It was known that the queen had gone to Paris on that day with Mademoiselle de Taverney. It was evident, also, that Jeanne had no intention of deceiving him; she was telling all she knew. Still, he would try one more proof.

"Countess," he said, "one thing astonishes me, that you have not addressed yourself to the king."

"But, sir, I have sent him twenty petitions."

"Without result?"

"Yes."

"Well, then, the princes of the blood; M. le Duc d'Orleans is charitable, and often likes to do what the king refuses."

"I have tried him, equally fruitlessly."

"That astonishes me."

"Oh, when one is poor, and not supported by any one——"

"There is still the Comte d'Artois; sometimes dissipated men do more generous actions than charitable ones."

"It is the same story with him."

"But the princesses, the aunts of the king, Madame Elizabeth particularly, would refuse assistance to no one."

"It is true, monseigneur, her royal highness, to whom I wrote, promised to receive me; but, I know not why, after having received my husband, I could never get any more notice from her."

"It is strange, certainly," said the cardinal; then, as if the thought had just struck him, he cried, "Ah! mon Dieu! but we are forgetting the person to whom you should have addressed yourself first of all."

"Whom do you mean?"

"To the dispenser of all favors, she who never refuses help where it is deserved—to the queen. Have you seen her?"

"No," answered Jeanne.

"You have never presented your petition to the queen?"

"Never."

"You have not tried to obtain an audience of her?"

"I have tried, but failed."

"Have you tried to throw yourself in her way, that she might remark you?"

"No, monseigneur."

"But that is very strange."

"I have only been twice to Versailles, and then saw but two persons there; one was Doctor Louis, who had attended my poor father at the Hôtel Dieu, and the other was M. le Baron de Taverney, to whom I had an introduction."

"What did M. de Taverney say to you? He might have brought you to the queen."

"He told me that I was very foolish to bring forward as a claim to the benevolence of the king a relationship which would be sure to displease him, as nobody likes poor relations."

"I recognize the egotistical and rude old baron. Well," continued he, "I will conduct you myself to Versailles, and will open the doors for you."

"Oh, monseigneur, how good you are," cried Jeanne, overwhelmed with joy.

The cardinal approached her, and said, "It is impossible but that before long all must interest themselves in you."

"Alas! monseigneur," said Jeanne, with a sigh, "do you think so?"

"I am sure of it."

"I fear you flatter me," she said, looking earnestly at him, for she could hardly believe in his sudden change of manner, he had been so cold and suspicious at first.

This look had no small effect on the cardinal; he began to think he had never met a woman prettier or more attractive. "Ah, ma foi!" said he to himself, with the eternally scheming spirit of a man used to diplomacy, "it would be too extraordinary and too fortunate if I have met at once an honest woman with the attractions of a scheming one, and found in this poverty an able coadjutrix to my desires."

"Monseigneur, the silence you keep every now and then disquiets me."

"Why so, countess?"

"Because a man like you only fails in politeness to two kinds of women."

"Mon Dieu! countess, you frighten me. What are you about to say?" and he took her hand.

"I repeat it," said she, "with women that you love too much, or with women whom you do not esteem enough to be polite to."

"Countess, you make me blush. Have I, then, failed in politeness towards you?"

"Rather so, monseigneur; and yet you cannot love me too much, and I have given you no cause to despise me."

"Oh, countess, you speak as if you were angry with me."

"No, monseigneur; you have not yet merited my anger."

"And I never will, madame. From this day, in which I have had the pleasure of making your acquaintance, my solicitude for you will not cease."

"Oh, sir, do not speak to me of your protection."

"Oh, mon Dieu! I should humiliate myself, not you, in mentioning such a thing;" and he pressed her hand, which he continued to hold, to his lips.

She tried to withdraw it; but he said, "Only politeness, madame," and she let it remain.

"To know," said she, "that I shall occupy a place, however small, in the mind of a man so eminent and so busy, would console me for a year."

"Let us hope the consolation will last longer than that, countess."

"Well, perhaps so, monseigneur; I have confidence in you, because I feel that you are capable of appreciating a mind like mine, adventurous, brave, and pure, in spite of my poverty, and of the enemies which my position has made me. Your eminence will, I am sure, discover all the good that is in me, and be indulgent to all the rest."

"We, are, then, warm friends, madame;" and he advanced towards her, but his arms were a little more extended than the occasion required. She avoided him, and said, laughing:

"It must be a friendship among three, cardinal."

"Among three?"

"Doubtless, for there exists an exile, a poor gendarme, who is called M. de la Motte."

"Oh, countess, what a deplorably good memory you have!"

"I must speak to you of him, that you may not forget him."

"Do you know why I do not speak of him, countess?"

"No; pray tell me."

"Because he will speak enough for himself: husbands never let themselves be forgotten. We shall hear that M. le Comte de la Motte found it good, or found it bad, that the Cardinal de Rohan came two, three, or four times a week to visit his wife."

"Ah! but will you come so often, monseigneur?"

"Without that, where would be our friendship? Four times! I should have said six or seven."

Jeanne laughed, "I should not indeed wonder in that case if people did talk of it."

"Oh! but we can easily prevent them."

"How?"

"Quite easily. The people know me——"

"Certainly, monseigneur."

"But you they have the misfortune not to know."

"Well?"

"Therefore, if you would——"

"What, sir?"

"Come out instead of me."

"Come to your hotel, monseigneur?"

"You would go to see a minister."

"Oh! a minister is not a man."

"You are adorable, countess. But I did not speak of my hotel; I have a house——"

"Oh! a petite maison?"

"No; a house of yours."

"A house of mine, cardinal! Indeed, I did not know it."

"To-morrow, at ten o'clock, you shall have the address."

The countess blushed; the cardinal took her hand again, and imprinted another kiss upon it, at once bold, respectful, and tender. They then bowed to each other.

"Light monseigneur down," said the countess; and he went away.

"Well," thought she, "I have made a great step in the world."

"Come," said the cardinal to himself as he drove off, "I think I have killed two birds with one stone; this woman has too much talent not to catch the queen as she has caught me?"

CHAPTER XVI
MESMER AND ST. MARTIN

The fashionable study in Paris at this time, and that which engrossed most of those who had no business to attend to, was Mesmerism—a mysterious science, badly defined by its discoverers, who did not wish to render it too plain to the eyes of the people. Dr. Mesmer, who had given to it his own name, was then in Paris, as we have already heard from Marie Antoinette.

This Doctor Mesmer deserves a few words from us, as his name was then in all mouths.

He had brought this science from Germany, the land of mysteries, in 1777. He had previously made his début there, by a theory on the influence of the planets. He had endeavored to establish that these celestial bodies, through the same power by which they attract each other, exercised an influence over living bodies, and particularly over the nervous system, by means of a subtle fluid with which the air is impregnated. But this first theory was too abstract: one must, to understand it, be initiated into all the sciences of Galileo or Newton; and it would have been necessary, for this to have become popular, that the nobility should have been transformed into a body of savants. He therefore abandoned this system, and took up that of the loadstone, which was then attracting great attention, people fancying that this wonderful power was efficacious in curing illnesses.

Unhappily for him, however, he found a rival in this already established in Vienna; therefore he once more announced that he abandoned mineral magnetism, and intended to effect his cures through animal magnetism.

This, although a new name, was not in reality a new science; it was as old as the Greeks and Egyptians, and had been preserved in traditions, and revived every now and then by the sorcerers of the thirteenth, fourteenth, and fifteenth centuries, many of whom had paid for their knowledge with their lives. Urbain Grandier was nothing but an animal magnetizer; and Joseph Balsamo we have seen practising it. Mesmer only condensed this knowledge into a science, and gave it a name. He then communicated his system to the scientific academies of Paris, London, and Berlin. The two first did not answer him, and the third said that he was mad. He came to France, and took out of the hands of Dr. Storck, and of the oculist Wenzel, a young girl seventeen years old, who had a complaint of the liver and gutta serena, and after three months of his treatment, restored her health and her sight.

This cure convinced many people, and among them a doctor called Deslon, who, from his enemy, became his pupil. From this time his reputation gradually increased; the academy declared itself against him, but the court for him. At last the government offered him, in the king's name, an income for life of twenty thousand francs to give lectures in public, and ten thousand more to instruct three persons, who should be chosen by them, in his system.

Mesmer, however, indignant at the royal parsimony, refused, and set out for the Spa waters with one of his patients; but while he was gone, Deslon, his pupil, possessor of the secret which he had refused to sell for thirty thousand francs a year, opened a public establishment for the treatment of patients. Mesmer was furious, and exhausted himself in complaints and menaces. One of his patients, however, M. de Bergasse, conceived the idea of forming a company. They raised a capital of 340,000 francs, on the condition that the secret should be revealed to the shareholders. It was a fortunate time: the people, having no great public events to interest them, entered eagerly into every new amusement and occupation; and this mysterious theory possessed no little attraction, professing, as it did, to cure invalids, restore mind to the fools, and amuse the wise.

Everywhere Mesmer was talked of. What had he done? On whom had he performed these miracles? To what great lord had he restored sight? To what lady worn out with dissipation had he renovated the nerves? To what young girl had he shown the future in a magnetic trance? The future! that word of ever-entrancing interest and curiosity.

Voltaire was dead; there was no one left to make France laugh, except perhaps Beaumarchais, who was still more bitter than his master; Rousseau was dead, and with him the sect of religious philosophers. War had generally occupied strongly the minds of the French people, but now the only war in which they were engaged was in America, where the people fought for what they called independence, and what the French called liberty; and even this distant war in another land, and affecting another people, was on the point of termination. Therefore they felt more interest just now in M. Mesmer, who was near, than in Washington or Lord Cornwallis, who were so far off. Mesmer's only rival in the public interest was St. Martin, the professor of spiritualism, as Mesmer was of materialism, and who professed to cure souls, as he did bodies.

Imagine an atheist with a religion more attractive than religion itself; a republican full of politeness and interest for kings; a gentleman of the privileged classes tender and solicitous for the people, endowed with the most startling eloquence, attacking all the received religions of the earth.

Imagine Epicurus in white powder, embroidered coat, and silk stockings, not content with endeavoring to overturn a religion in which he did not believe, but also attacking all existing governments, and promulgating the theory that all men are equal, or, to use his own words, that all intelligent beings are kings.

Imagine the effect of all this in society as it then was, without fixed principles or steady guides, and how it was all assisting to light the fire with which France not long after began to consume herself.

CHAPTER XVII
THE BUCKET

We have endeavored to give an idea in the last chapter of the interest and enthusiasm which drew such crowds of the people to see M. Mesmer perform publicly his wonderful experiments.

The king, as we know, had given permission to the queen to go and see what all Paris was talking of, accompanied by one of the princesses. It was two days after the visit of M. de Rohan to the countess. The weather was fine, and the thaw was complete, and hundreds of sweepers were employed in cleaning away the snow from the streets. The clear blue sky was just beginning to be illumined by its first stars, when Madame de la Motte, elegantly dressed, and presenting every appearance of opulence, arrived in a coach, which Clotilde had carefully chosen as the best looking at the Place Vendôme, and stopped before a brilliantly-lighted house.

It was that of Doctor Mesmer. Numbers of other carriages were waiting at the door, and a crowd of people had collected to see the patients arrive and depart, who seemed to derive much pleasure when they saw some rich invalid, enveloped in furs and satins, carried in by footmen, from the evident proof it afforded that God made men healthy or unhealthy, without reference to their purses or their genealogies. A universal murmur would arise when they recognized some duke paralyzed in an arm or leg; or some marshal whose feet refused their office, less in consequence of military fatigues and marches than from halts made with the ladies of the Opera, or of the Comédie Italienne. Sometimes it was a lady carried in by her servants with drooping head and languid eye, who, weakened by late hours and an irregular life, came to demand from Doctor Mesmer the health she had vainly sought to regain elsewhere.

Many of these ladies were as well known as the gentlemen, but a great many escaped the public gaze, especially on this evening, by wearing masks; for there was a ball at the Opera that night, and many of them intended to drive straight there when they left the doctor's house.

Through this crowd Madame de la Motte walked erect and firm, also with a mask on, and elicited only the exclamation, "This one does not look ill, at all events."

Ever since the cardinal's visit, the attention with which he had examined the box and portrait had been on Jeanne's mind; and she could not but feel that all his graciousness commenced after seeing it, and she therefore felt proportionate curiosity to learn more about it.

First she had gone to Versailles to inquire at all the houses of charity about German ladies; but there were there, perhaps, a hundred and fifty or two hundred, and all Jeanne's inquiries about the two ladies who had visited her had proved fruitless. In vain she repeated that one of them was called Andrée; no one knew a German lady of that name, which indeed was not German. Baffled in this, she determined to try elsewhere, and having heard much of M. Mesmer, and the wonderful secrets revealed through him, determined upon going there. Many were the stories of this kind in circulation. Madame de Duras had recovered a child who had been lost; Madame de Chantoué, an English dog, not much bigger than her fist, for which she would have given all the children in the world; and M. de Vaudreuil a lock of hair, which he would have bought back with half his fortune. All these revelations had been made by clairvoyants after the magnetic operations of Doctor Mesmer.

Those who came to see him, after traversing the ante-chambers, were admitted into a large room, from which the darkened and hermetically closed windows excluded light and air. In the middle of this room, under a luster which gave but a feeble light, was a vast unornamented tank, filled with water impregnated with sulphur, and to the cover of which was fastened an iron ring; attached to this ring was a long chain, the object of which we shall presently see.

All the patients were seated round the room, men and women indiscriminately; then a valet, taking the chain, wound it round the limbs of the patients, so that they might all feel, at the same time, the effects of the electricity contained in the tank; they were then directed to touch each other in some way, either by the shoulder, the elbow, or the feet, and each was to take in his hand a bar of iron, which was also connected with the tank, and to place it to the heart, head, or whatever was the seat of the malady. When they were all ready, a soft and pleasing strain of music, executed by invisible performers, was heard. Among the most eager of the crowd, on the evening of which we speak, was a young, distinguished-looking, and beautiful woman, with a graceful figure, and rather showily dressed, who pressed the iron to her heart with wonderful energy, rolling her beautiful eyes, and beginning to show, in the trembling of her hands, the first effects of the electric fluid.

As she constantly threw back her head, resting it on the cushions of her chair, all around could see perfectly her pale but beautiful face, and her white throat. Many seemed to look at her with great astonishment, and a general whispering commenced among those who surrounded her.

Madame de la Motte was one of the most curious of the party; and of all she saw around her, nothing attracted her attention so much as this young lady, and after gazing earnestly at her for some time, she at last murmured, "Oh! it is she, there is no doubt. It is the lady who came to see me the other day." And convinced that she was not mistaken, she advanced towards her, congratulating herself that chance had effected for her what she had so long been vainly trying to accomplish; but at this moment the young lady closed her eyes, contracted her mouth, and began to beat the air feebly with her hands, which hands, however, did not seem to Jeanne the white and beautiful ones she had seen in her room a few days before.

The patients now began to grow excited under the influence of the fluid. Men and women began to utter sighs, and even cries, moving convulsively their heads, arms, and legs. Then a man suddenly made his appearance; no one had seen him enter; you might have fancied he came out of the tank. He was dressed in a lilac robe, and held in his hand a long wand, which he several times dipped into the mysterious tank; then he made a sign, the doors opened, and twenty robust servants entered, and seizing such of the patients as began to totter on their seats, carried them into an adjoining room.

While this was going on Madame de la Motte heard a man who had approached near to the young lady before-mentioned, and who was in a perfect paroxysm of excitement, say in a loud voice, "It is surely she!" Jeanne was about to ask him who she was, when her attention was drawn to two ladies who were just entering, followed by a man, who, though disguised as a bourgeois, had still the appearance of a servant.

The tournure of one of these ladies struck Jeanne so forcibly that she made a step towards them, when a cry from the young woman near her startled every one. The same man whom Jeanne had heard speak before now called out, "But look, gentlemen, it is the queen."

"The queen!" cried many voices, in surprise. "The queen here! The queen in that state! Impossible!"

"But look," said he again; "do you know the queen, or not?"

"Indeed," said many, "the resemblance is incredible."

"Monsieur," said Jeanne to the speaker, who was a stout man, with quick observant eyes, "did you say the queen?"

"Oh! madame, there is no doubt of it."

"And where is she?"

"Why, that young lady that you see there, on the violet cushions, and in such a state that she cannot moderate her transports, is the queen."

"But on what do you found such an idea, monsieur?"

"Simply because it is the queen." And he left Jeanne to go and spread his news among the rest.

She turned from the almost revolting spectacle, and going near to the door, found herself face to face with the two ladies she had seen enter. Scarcely had she seen the elder one than she uttered a cry of surprise.

"What is the matter?" asked the lady.

Jeanne took off her mask, and asked, "Do you recognize me, madame?"

The lady made, but quickly suppressed, a movement of surprise, and said, "No, madame."

"Well, madame, I recognize you, and will give you a proof;" and she drew the box from her pocket, saying, "you left this at my house."

"But supposing this to be true, what makes you so agitated?"

"I am agitated by the danger that your majesty is incurring here."

"Explain yourself."

"Not before you have put on this mask;" and she offered hers to the queen, who, however, did not take it.

"I beg your majesty; there is not an instant to lose."

The queen put on the mask. "And now, pray come away," added Jeanne.

"But why?" said the queen.

"Your majesty has not been seen by any one?"

"I believe not."

"So much the better."

The queen mechanically moved to the door, but said again, "Will you explain yourself?"

"Will not your majesty believe your humble servant for the present, that you were running a great risk?"

"But what risk?"

"I will have the honor to tell your majesty whenever you will grant me an hour's audience; but it would take too long now;" and seeing that the queen looked displeased, "Pray, madame," said she, turning to the Princess Lamballe, "join your petitions to mine that the queen should leave this place immediately."

"I think we had better, madame," said the princess.

"Well, then, I will," answered the queen; then, turning to Madame de la Motte, "You ask for an audience?" she said.

"I beg for that honor, that I may explain this conduct to your majesty."

"Well, bring this box with you, and you shall be admitted; Laurent, the porter, shall have orders to do so." Then going into the street, she called in German, "Kommen sie da, Weber."

A carriage immediately drove up, they got in, and were immediately out of sight.

When they were gone, Madame de la Motte said to herself, "I have done right in this—for the rest, I must consider."

CHAPTER XVIII
MADEMOISELLE OLIVA

During this time, the man who had pointed out the fictitious queen to the people touched on the shoulder another man who stood near him, in a shabby dress, and said. "For you, who are a journalist, here is a fine subject for an article."

"How so?" replied the man.

"Shall I tell you?"

"Certainly."

"The danger of being governed by a king who is governed by a queen who indulges in such paroxysms as these."

The journalist laughed. "But the Bastile?" he said.

"Pooh, nonsense! I do not mean you to write it out plainly. Who can interfere with you if you relate the history of Prince Silou and the Princess Etteniotna, Queen of Narfec? What do you say to that?"

"It is an admirable idea!" said the journalist.

"And I do not doubt that a pamphlet called 'The Paroxysms of the Princess Etteniotna at the house of the Fakeer Remsem' would have a great success."

"I believe it also."

"Then go and do it."

The journalist pressed the hand of the unknown. "Shall I send you some copies, sir? I will with pleasure if you will give me your name."

"Certainly; the idea pleases me. What is the usual circulation of your journal?"

"Two thousand."

"Then do me a favor: take these fifty louis, and publish six thousand."

"Oh, sir, you overwhelm me. May I not know the name of such a generous patron of literature?"

"You shall know, when I call for one thousand copies—at two francs each, are they not? Will they be ready in a week?"

"I will work night and day, monsieur."

"Let it be amusing."

"It shall make all Paris die with laughing, except one person."

"Who will weep over it. Apropos, date the publication from London."

"Sir, I am your humble servant." And the journalist took his leave, with his fifty louis in his pocket, highly delighted.

The unknown again turned to look at the young woman, who had now subsided into a state of exhaustion, and looked beautiful as she lay there. "Really," he said to himself, "the resemblance is frightful. God had his motives in creating it, and has no doubt condemned her to whom the resemblance is so strong."

While he made these reflections, she rose slowly from the midst of the cushions, assisting herself with the arm of an attendant, and began to arrange her somewhat disordered toilet, and then traversed the rooms, confronting boldly the looks of the people. She was somewhat astonished, however, when she found herself saluted with deep and respectful bows by a group which had already been assembled by the indefatigable stranger, who kept whispering, "Never mind, gentlemen, never mind, she is still the Queen of France; let us salute her." She next entered the courtyard, and looked about for a coach or chair, but, seeing none, was about to set off on foot, when a footman approached and said, "Shall I call madame's carriage?"

"I have none," she replied.

"Madame came in a coach?"

"Yes."

"From the Rue Dauphine?"

"Yes."

"I will take madame home."

"Do so, then," said she, although somewhat surprised at the offer.

The man made a sign, and a carriage drove up. He opened the door for her, and then said to the coachman, "To the Rue Dauphine." They set off, and the young woman, who much approved of this mode of transit, regretted she had not further to go. They soon stopped, however; the footman handed her out, and immediately drove off again.

"Really," said she to herself, "this is an agreeable adventure; it is very gallant of M. Mesmer. Oh, I am very tired, and he must have foreseen that. He is a great doctor."

Saying these words, she mounted to the second story, and knocked at a door, which was quickly opened by an old woman.

"Is supper ready, mother?"

"Yes, and growing cold."

"Has he come?"

"No, not yet, but the gentleman has."

"What gentleman?"

"He who was to speak to you this evening."

"To me?"

"Yes."

This colloquy took place in a kind of ante-chamber opening into her room, which was furnished with old curtains of yellow silk, chairs of green Utrecht velvet, not very new, and an old yellow sofa.

She opened the door, and, going in, saw a man seated on the sofa whom she did not know in the least, although we do, for it was the same man whom we have seen taking so much interest in her at Mesmer's.

She had not time to question him, for he began immediately: "I know all that you are going to ask, and will tell you without asking. You are Mademoiselle Oliva, are you not?"

"Yes, sir."

"A charming person, highly nervous, and much taken by the system of M. Mesmer."

"I have just left there."

"All this, however, your beautiful eyes are saying plainly, does not explain what brings me here."

"You are right, sir."

"Will you not do me the favor to sit down, or I shall be obliged to get up also, and that is an uncomfortable way of talking."

"Really, sir, you have very extraordinary manners."

"Mademoiselle, I saw you just now at M. Mesmer's, and found you to be all I could wish."

"Sir!"

"Do not alarm yourself, mademoiselle. I do not tell you that I found you charming—that would seem like a declaration of love, and I have no such intention. I know that you are accustomed to have yourself called beautiful, but I, who also think so, have other things to talk to you about."

"Really, sir, the manner in which you speak to me— —"

"Do not get angry before you have heard me. Is there any one that can overhear us?"

"No, sir, no one. But still— —"

"Then, if no one can hear, we can converse at our ease. What do you say to a little partnership between us?"

"Really, sir— —"

"Do not misunderstand; I do not say 'liaison'—I say partnership; I am not talking of love, but of business."

"What kind of business?" said Oliva, with growing curiosity.

"What do you do all day?"

"Why, I do nothing, or, at least, as little as possible."

"You have no occupation—so much the better. Do you like walking?"

"Very much."

"To see sights, and go to balls?"

"Excessively."

"To live well?"

"Above all things."

"If I gave you twenty-five louis a month, would you refuse me?"

"Sir!"

"My dear Mademoiselle Oliva, now you are beginning to doubt me again, and it was agreed that you were to listen quietly. I will say fifty louis if you like."

"I like fifty louis better than twenty-five, but what I like better than either is to be able to choose my own lover."

"Morbleu! but I have already told you that I do not desire to be your lover. Set your mind at ease about that."

"Then what am I to do to earn my fifty louis?"

"You must receive me at your house, and always be glad to see me. Walk out with me whenever I desire it, and come to me whenever I send for you."

"But I have a lover, sir."

"Well, dismiss him."

"Oh, Beausire cannot be sent away like that!"

"I will help you."

"No; I love him."

"Oh!"

"A little."

"That is just a little too much."

"I cannot help it."

"Then he may stop."

"You are very obliging."

"Well—but do my conditions suit you?"

"Yes, if you have told me all."

"I believe I have said all I wish to say now."

"On your honor?"

"On my honor."

"Very well."

"Then that is settled; and here is the first month in advance."

He held out the money, and, as she still seemed to hesitate a little, slipped it himself into her pocket.

Scarcely had he done so, when a knock at the door made Oliva run to the window. "Good God!" she cried; "escape quickly; here he is!"

"Who?"

"Beausire, my lover. Be quick, sir!"

"Nonsense!"

"He will half murder you."

"Bah!"

"Do you hear how he knocks?"

"Well, open the door." And he sat down again on the sofa, saying to himself, "I must see this fellow, and judge what he is like."

The knocks became louder, and mingled with oaths.

"Go, mother, and open the door," cried Oliva. "As for you, sir, if any harm happens to you, it is your own fault."

CHAPTER XIX
MONSIEUR BEAUSIRE

Oliva ran to meet a man, who came in swearing furiously, and in a frightful passion.

"Come, Beausire," said she, apparently not at all frightened.

"Let me alone!" cried he, shaking her off brutally. "Ah! I see, it was because there is a man here that the door was not opened!" And as the visitor remained perfectly still, he advanced furiously towards him, saying, "Will you answer me, sir?"

"What do you want to know, my dear M. Beausire?"

"What are you doing here, and who are you?"

"I am a very quiet man, and I was simply talking to madame."

"That was all," said Oliva.

"Will you hold your tongue?" bawled Beausire.

"Now," said the visitor, "do not be so rude to madame, who has done nothing to deserve it; and if you are in a bad temper——"

"Yes, I am."

"He must have lost at cards," murmured Oliva.

"I am cleaned out, mort de diable!" cried Beausire. "But you, sir, will do me the favor to leave this room."

"But, M. Beausire——"

"Diable! if you do not go immediately it will be the worse for you."

"You did not tell me, mademoiselle, that he was troubled with these fits. Good heavens! what ferocity!"

Beausire, exasperated, drew his sword, and roared, "If you do not move, I will pin you to the sofa!"

"Really, it is impossible to be more disagreeable," said the visitor, also drawing a small sword, which they had not before seen.

Oliva uttered piercing shrieks.

"Oh, mademoiselle, pray be quiet," said he, "or two things will happen: first, you will stun M. Beausire, and he will get killed; secondly, the watch will come up and carry you straight off to St. Lazare."

Oliva ceased her cries.

The scene that ensued was curious. Beausire, furious with rage, was making wild and unskilful passes at his adversary, who, still seated on the sofa, parried them with the utmost ease, laughing immoderately all the time.

Beausire began to grow tired and also frightened, for he felt that if this man, who was now content to stand on the defensive, were to attack him in his turn, he should be done for in a moment. Suddenly, however, by a skilful movement, the stranger sent Beausire's sword flying across the room; it went through an open window, and fell into the street.

"Oh, M. Beausire," said he, "you should take more care; if your sword falls on any one, it will kill him."

Beausire ran down at his utmost speed to fetch his sword, and meanwhile, Oliva, seizing the hand of the victor, said:

"Oh, sir, you are very brave; but as soon as you are gone, Beausire will beat me."

"Then I will remain."

"Oh, no; when he beats me, I beat him in return, and I always get the best of it, because I am not obliged to take any care; so if you would but go, sir— —"

"But, my dear, if I go now, I shall meet M. Beausire on the stairs; probably the combat will recommence, and as I shall not feel inclined to stand on the staircase, I shall have to kill M. Beausire."

"Mon Dieu! it is true."

"Well, then, to avoid that I will remain here."

"No, sir, I entreat; go up to the next story, and as soon as he returns to this room I will lock the door and take the key, and you can walk away while we fight it out."

"You are a charming girl. Au revoir!"

"Till when?"

"To-night, if you please."

"To-night! are you mad?"

"Not at all; but there is a ball at the Opera to-night."

"But it is now midnight."

"That does not matter."

"I should want a domino."

"Beausire will fetch it when you have beaten him."

"You are right," said Oliva, laughing.

"And here are ten louis to buy it with."

"Adieu! and thanks." And she pushed him out, saying, "Quick! he is coming back."

"But if by chance he should beat you, how will you let me know?"

She reflected a moment. "You have a servant?"

"Yes."

"Send him here, and let him wait under the window till I let a note fall."

"I will. Adieu!" And he went up-stairs.

Oliva drowned the sound of his footsteps by calling loudly to Beausire, "Are you coming back, madman?" for he did not seem in much hurry to reencounter his formidable adversary. At last, however, he came up. Oliva was standing outside the door; she pushed him in, locked it, and put the key in her pocket.

Before the stranger left the house, he heard the noise of the combat begin, and both voices loud and furious. "There is no doubt," said he to himself, "that this woman knows how to take care of herself." His carriage was waiting for him at the corner of the street, but before getting in he spoke to the footman, who thereupon stationed himself within view of Mademoiselle Oliva's windows.

CHAPTER XX
GOLD

We must now return to the interior of the room. Beausire was much surprised to see Oliva lock the door, and still more so not to see his adversary. He began to feel triumphant, for if he was hiding from him he must, he thought, be afraid of him. He therefore began to search for him; but Oliva talked so loud and fast that he advanced towards her to try and stop her, but was received with a box on the ear, which he returned in kind. Oliva replied by throwing a china vase at his head, and his answer was a blow with a cane. She, furious, flew at him and seized him by the throat, and he, trying to free himself, tore her dress.

Then, with a cry, she pushed him from her with such force that he fell in the middle of the room.

He began to get tired of this, so he said, without commencing another attack, "You are a wicked creature; you ruin me."

"On the contrary, it is you who ruin me."

"Oh, I ruin her!—she who has nothing!"

"Say that I have nothing now, say that you have eaten, and drank, and played away all that I had."

"You reproach me with my poverty."

"Yes, for it comes from your vices."

"Do not talk of vices; it only remained for you to take a lover."

"And what do you call all those wretches who sit by you in the tennis-court, where you play?"

"I play to live."

"And nicely you succeed; we should die of hunger from your industry."

"And you, with yours, are obliged to cry if you get your dress torn, because you have nothing to buy another with."

"I do better than you, at all events;" and, putting her hand in her pocket, she drew out some gold and threw it across the room.

When Beausire saw this, he remained stupefied.

"Louis!" cried he at last.

She took out some more, and threw them in his face.

"Oh!" cried he, "Oliva has become rich!"

"This is what my industry brings in," said she, pushing him with her foot as he kneeled down to pick up the gold.

"Sixteen, seventeen, eighteen," counted he, joyfully.

"Miserable wretch!" said Oliva.

"Nineteen, twenty, twenty-one, twenty-two."

"Coward!"

"Twenty-three, twenty-four, twenty-five."

"Infamous wretch!"

He got up. "And so, mademoiselle, you have been saving money when you kept me without necessaries. You let me go about in an old hat, darned stockings, and patched clothes, while you had all this money! Where does it come from! From the sale of my things?"

"Scoundrel!" murmured Oliva, looking at him with contempt.

"But I pardon your avarice," continued he.

"You would have killed me just now," said Oliva.

"Then I should have been right; now I should be wrong to do it."

"Why, if you please?"

"Because now you contribute to our ménage."

"You are a base wretch.'"

"My little Oliva!"

"Give me back my money."

"Oh, my darling!"

"If you do not, I will pass your own sword through your body!"

"Oliva!"

"Will you give it?"

"Oh, you would not take it away?"

"Ah, coward! you beg, you solicit for the fruits of my bad conduct—that is what they call a man! I have always despised you."

"I gave to you when I could, Nicole."

"Do not call me Nicole."

"Pardon, then, Oliva. But is it not true?"

"Fine presents, certainly: some silver buckles, six louis d'or, two silk dresses, and three embroidered handkerchiefs."

"It is a great deal for a soldier."

"Hold your tongue! The buckles you stole from some one else, the louis d'or you borrowed and never returned, the silk dresses——"

"Oliva! Oliva!"

"Give me back my money."

"What shall I give you instead?"

"Double the quantity."

THE QUEEN'S NECKLACE

Dumas, Vol. Eight

"Well," said the rogue, gravely, "I will go to the Rue de Bussy and play with it, and bring you back, not the double, but the quintuple;" and he made two steps to the door.

She caught him by the coat.

"There," said he, "you have torn my coat."

"Never mind; you shall have a new one."

"That will be six louis, Oliva. Luckily, at the Rue de Bussy they are not particular about dress."

Oliva seized hold of the other tail, and tore it right off.

Beausire became furious.

"Mort de tous les diables!" cried he, "you will make me kill you at last! You are tearing me to bits! Now I cannot go out."

"On the contrary, you must go out immediately."

"Without a coat?"

"Put on your great-coat."

"It is all in holes."

"Then do not put it on; but you must go out."

"I will not."

She took out of her pocket another handful of gold, and put it into his hands.

Beausire kneeled at her feet and cried, "Order, and I will obey!"

"Go quickly to the Capucin, Rue de Seine, where they sell dominoes for the bal masque, and buy me one complete, mask and all."

"Good."

"And one for yourself—black, but mine white; and I only give you twenty minutes to do it in."

"Are we going to the ball?"

"Yes, if you are obedient."

"Oh, always."

"Go, then, and show your zeal."

"I run; but the money?"

"You have twenty-five louis, that you picked up."

"Oh, Oliva, I thought you meant to give me those."

"You shall have more another time, but if I give you them now, you will stop and play."

"She is right," said he to himself; "that is just what I intended to do;" and he set off.

As soon as he was gone, Oliva wrote rapidly these words: "The peace is signed, and the ball decided on; at two o'clock we shall be at the Opera. I shall wear a white domino, with a blue ribbon on my left shoulder." Then, rolling this round a bit of the broken vase, she went to the window and threw it out.

The valet picked it up, and made off immediately.

In less than half an hour M. Beausire returned, followed by two men, bringing, at the cost of eighteen louis, two beautiful dominoes, such as were only turned out at the Capucin, makers to her majesty and the maids of honor.

CHAPTER XXI
LA PETITE MAISON

We left Madame de la Motte at M. Mesmer's door, watching the queen's carriage as it drove off. Then she went home; for she also intended to put on a domino, and indulge herself by going to the Opera. But a contretemps awaited her: a man was waiting at her door with a note from the Cardinal de Rohan. She opened it, and read as follows:

> "Madame la Comtesse, you have doubtless not forgotten that we have business together; even if you have a short memory, I never forget what has pleased me. I shall have the honor to wait for you where my messenger will conduct you, if you please to come."

Jeanne, although rather vexed, immediately reentered the coach, and told the footman to get on the box with the coachman. Ten minutes sufficed to bring her to the entrance of the Faubourg St. Antoine, where, in a hollow and completely hidden by great trees, was one of those pretty houses built in the time of Louis XV., with all the taste of the sixteenth, with the comfort of the eighteenth, century.

"Oh, oh! a petite maison!" said she to herself. "It is very natural on the part of M. de Rohan, but very humiliating for Valois. But, patience."

She was led from room to room till she came to a small dining-room, fitted up with exquisite taste. There she found the cardinal waiting for her. He was looking over some pamphlets, but rose immediately on seeing her.

"Ah, here you are. Thanks, Madame la Comtesse," and he approached to kiss her hand; but she drew back with a reproachful and indignant air.

"What is the matter, madame?" he asked.

"You are, doubtless, not accustomed, monseigneur, to receive such a greeting from the women whom your eminence is in the habit of summoning here."

"Oh! madame."

"We are in your petite maison, are we not, sir?" continued she, looking disdainfully around her.

"But, madame— —"

"I had hoped that your eminence would have deigned to remember in what rank I was born. I had hoped that you would have been pleased to consider, that if God has made me poor, He has at least left me the pride of my race."

"Come, come, countess, I took you for a woman of intellect."

"You call a woman of intellect, it appears, monseigneur, every one who is indifferent to, and laughs at, everything, even dishonor. To these women, pardon me, your eminence, I have been in the habit of giving a different name."

"No, countess, you deceive yourself; I call a woman of intellect one who listens when you speak to her, and does not speak before having listened."

"I listen, then."

"I had to speak to you of serious matters, countess."

"Therefore you receive me in a dining-room."

"Why, would you have preferred my receiving you in a boudoir?"

"The distinction is nice," said she.

"I think so, countess."

"Then I am simply to sup with you?"

"Nothing else."

"I trust your eminence is persuaded that I feel the honor as I ought."

"You are quizzing, countess."

"No, I only laugh; would you rather I were angry? You are difficult to please, monseigneur."

"Oh; you are charming when you laugh, and I ask nothing better than to see you always doing so; but at this moment you are not laughing; oh, no! there is anger in that smile which shows your beautiful teeth."

"Not the least in the world, monseigneur."

"That is good."

"And I hope you will sup well."

"I shall sup well, and you?"

"Oh, I am not hungry."

"How, madame, you refuse to sup with me—you send me away?"

"I do not understand you, monseigneur."

"Listen, dear countess; if you were less in a passion, I would tell you that it is useless to behave like this—you are always equally charming; but as at each compliment I fear to be dismissed, I abstain."

"You fear to be dismissed? Really, I beg pardon of your eminence, but you become unintelligible."

"It is, however, quite clear, what I say. The other day, when I came to see you, you complained that you were lodged unsuitably to your rank. I thought, therefore, that to restore you to your proper place would be like restoring air to the bird whom the experimenter has placed under his air-pump. Consequently, beautiful countess, that you might receive me with pleasure, and that I, on my part, might visit you without compromising either you or myself——" He stopped and looked at her.

"Well!" she said.

"I hoped that you would deign to accept this small residence; you observe, I do not call it 'petite maison.'"

"Accept! you give me this house, monseigneur?" said Jeanne, her heart beating with eagerness.

"A very small gift, countess; but if I had offered you more, you would have refused."

"Oh, monseigneur, it is impossible for me to accept this."

"Impossible, why? Do not say that word to me, for I do not believe in it. The house belongs to you, the keys are here on this silver plate; do you find out another humiliation in this?"

"No, but——"

"Then accept."

"Monseigneur, I have told you."

"How, madame? you write to the ministers for a pension, you accept a hundred louis from an unknown lady——"

"Oh, monseigneur, it is different."

"Come, I have waited for you in your dining-room. I have not yet seen the boudoir, nor the drawing-room, nor the bedrooms, for I suppose there are all these."

"Oh, monseigneur, forgive me; you force me to confess that you the most delicate of men," and she blushed with the pleasure she had been so long restraining. But checking herself, she sat down and said, "Now, will your eminence give me my supper?"

The cardinal took off his cloak, and sat down also.

Supper was served in a few moments. Jeanne put on her mask before the servants came in.

"It is I who ought to wear a mask," said the cardinal, "for you are at home, among your own people."

Jeanne laughed, but did not take hers off. In spite of her pleasure and surprise, she made a good supper. The cardinal was a man of much talent, and from his great knowledge of the world and of women, he was a man difficult to contend with, and he thought that this country girl, full of pretension, but who, in spite of her pride, could not conceal her greediness, would be an easy conquest, worth undertaking on account of her beauty, and of a something piquant about her, very pleasing to a man "blasé" like him. He therefore never took pains to be much on his guard with her; and she, more cunning than he thought, saw through his opinion of her, and tried to strengthen it by playing the provincial coquette, and appearing silly, that her adversary might be in reality weak in his over-confidence.

The cardinal thought her completely dazzled by the present he had made her—and so, indeed, she was; but he forgot that he himself was below the mark of the ambition of a woman like Jeanne.

"Come," said he, pouring out for her a glass of cyprus wine, "as you have signed your contract with me, you will not be unfriendly any more, countess."

"Oh no!"

"You will receive me here sometimes without repugnance?"

"I shall never be so ungrateful as to forget whose house this really is."

"Not mine."

"Oh yes, monseigneur."

"Do not contradict me, I advise you, or I shall begin to impose conditions."

"You take care on your part——"

"Of what?"

"Why, I am at home here, you know, and if your conditions are unreasonable, I shall call my servants——"

The cardinal laughed.

"Ah, you laugh, sir; you think if I call they will not come."

"Oh, you quite mistake, countess. I am nothing here, only your guest. Apropos," continued he, as if it had just entered his head, "have you heard anything more of the ladies who came to see you?"

"The ladies of the portrait?" said Jeanne, who, now knowing the queen, saw through the artifice.

"Yes, the ladies of the portrait."

"Monseigneur, you know them as well and even better than I do, I feel sure."

"Oh, countess, you do me wrong. Did you not express a wish to learn who they were?"

"Certainly; it is natural to desire to know your benefactors."

"Well, if knew, I should have told you."

"M. le Cardinal, you do know them."

"No."

"If you repeat that 'no,' I shall have to call you a liar."

"I shall know how to avenge that insult."

"How?"

"With a kiss."

"You know the portrait of Maria Theresa?"

"Certainly, but what of that?"

"That, having recognized this portrait, you must have had some suspicion of the person to whom it belonged."

"And why?"

"Because it was natural to think that the portrait of a mother would only be in the hands of her daughter."

"The queen!" cried the cardinal, with so truthful a tone of surprise that it duped even Jeanne. "Do you really think the queen came to see you?"

"And you did not suspect it?"

"Mon Dieu, no! how should I? I, who speak to you, am neither son, daughter, nor even relation of Maria Theresa, yet I have a portrait of her about me at this moment. Look," said he—and he drew out a snuff-box and showed it to her; "therefore you see that if I, who am in no way related to the imperial house, carry about such a portrait, another might do the same, and yet be a stranger."

Jeanne was silent—she had nothing to answer.

"Then it is your opinion," he went on, "that you have had a visit from the queen, Marie Antoinette."

"The queen and another lady."

"Madame de Polignac?"

"I do not know."

"Perhaps Madame de Lamballe?"

"A young lady, very beautiful and very serious."

"Oh, perhaps Mademoiselle de Taverney."

"It is possible; I do not know her."

"Well, if her majesty has really come to visit you, you are sure of her protection. It is a great step towards your fortune."

"I believe it, monseigneur."

"And her majesty was generous to you?"

"She gave me a hundred louis."

"And she is not rich, particularly now."

"That doubles my gratitude."

"Did she show much interest in you?"

"Very great."

"Then all goes well," said the prelate; "there only remains one thing now—to penetrate to Versailles."

The countess smiled.

"Ah, countess, it is not so easy."

She smiled again, more significantly than before.

"Really, you provincials," said he, "doubt nothing; because you have seen Versailles with the doors open, and stairs to go up, you think any one may open these doors and ascend these stairs. Have you seen the monsters of brass, of marble, and of lead, which adorn the park and the terraces?"

"Yes."

"Griffins, gorgons, ghouls, and other ferocious beasts. Well, you will find ten times as many, and more wicked, living animals between you and the favor of sovereigns."

"Your eminence will aid me to pass through the ranks of these monsters."

"I will try, but it will be difficult. And if you pronounce my name, if you discover your talisman, it will lose all its power."

"Happily, then, I am guarded by the immediate protection of the queen, and I shall enter Versailles with a good key."

"What key, countess?"

"Ah, Monsieur le Cardinal, that is my secret—or rather it is not, for if it were mine, I should feel bound to tell it to my generous protector."

"There is, then, an obstacle, countess?"

"Alas! yes, monseigneur. It is not my secret, and I must keep it. Let it suffice you to know that to-morrow I shall go to Versailles; that I shall be received, and, I have every reason to hope, well received."

The cardinal looked at her with wonder. "Ah, countess," said he, laughing, "I shall see if you will get in."

"You will push your curiosity so far as to follow me?"

"Exactly."

"Very well."

"Really, countess, you are a living enigma."

"One of those monsters who inhabit Versailles."

"Oh, you believe me a man of taste, do you not?"

"Certainly, monseigneur."

"Well, here I am at your knees, and I take your hand and kiss it. Should I do that if I thought you a monster?"

"I beg you, sir, to remember," said Jeanne coldly, "that I am neither a grisette nor an opera girl; that I am my own mistress, feeling myself the equal of any man in this kingdom. Therefore I shall take freely and spontaneously, when it shall please me, the man who will have gained my affections. Therefore, monseigneur, respect me a little, and, in me, the nobility to which we both belong."

The cardinal rose. "I see," said he, "you wish me to love you seriously."

"I do not say that; but I wish to be able to love you. When that day comes—if it does comes—you will easily find it out, believe me. If you do not, I will let you know it; for I feel young enough and attractive enough not to mind making the first advances, nor to fear a repulse."

"Countess, if it depends upon me, you shall love me."

"We shall see."

"You have already a friendship for me, have you not?"

"More than that."

"Oh! then we are at least half way. And you are a woman that I should adore, if— —" He stopped and sighed.

"Well," said she, "if— —"

"If you would permit it."

"Perhaps I shall, when I shall be independent of your assistance, and you can no longer suspect that I encourage you from interested motives."

"Then you forbid me to pay my court now?"

"Not at all; but there are other ways besides kneeling and kissing hands."

"Well, countess, let us hear; what will you permit?"

"All that is compatible with my tastes and duties."

"Oh, that is vague indeed."

"Stop! I was going to add—my caprices."

"I am lost!"

"You draw back?"

"No," said the cardinal, "I do not."

"Well, then, I want a proof."

"Speak."

"I want to go to the ball at the Opera."

"Well, countess, that only concerns yourself. Are you not free as air to go where you wish?"

"Ah, but you have not heard all. I want you to go with me."

"I to the Opera, countess!" said he, with a start of horror.

"See already how much your desire to please me is worth."

"A cardinal cannot go to a ball at the Opera, countess. It is as if I proposed to you to go into a public-house."

"Then a cardinal does not dance, I suppose?"

"Oh no!"

"But I have read that M. le Cardinal de Richelieu danced a saraband."

"Yes, before Anne of Austria."

"Before a queen," repeated Jeanne. "Perhaps you would do as much for a queen?"

The cardinal could not help blushing, dissembler as he was.

"Is it not natural," she continued, "that I should feel hurt when, after all your protestations, you will not do as much for me as you would for a queen?—especially when I only ask you to go concealed in a domino and a mask; besides, a man like you, who may do anything with impunity!"

The cardinal yielded to her flattery and her blandishments. Taking her hand, he said, "For you I will do anything, even the impossible."

"Thanks, monseigneur; you are really amiable. But now you have consented, I will let you off."

"No, no! he who does the work can alone claim the reward. Countess, I will attend you, but in a domino."

"We shall pass through the Rue St. Denis, close to the Opera," said the countess. "I will go in masked, buy a domino and a mask for you, and you can put them on in the carriage."

"That will do delightfully."

"Oh, monseigneur, you are very good! But, now I think of it, perhaps at the Hôtel Rohan you might find a domino more to your taste than the one I should buy."

"Now, countess, that is unpardonable malice. Believe me if I go to the Opera, I shall be as surprised to find myself there as you were to find yourself supping tête-à-tête with a man not your husband."

Jeanne had nothing to reply to this. Soon a carriage without arms drove up; they both got in, and drove off at a rapid pace.

CHAPTER XXII
SOME WORDS ABOUT THE OPERA

The Opera, that temple of pleasure at Paris, was burned in the month of June, 1781. Twenty persons had perished in the ruins; and as it was the second time within eighteen years that this had happened, it created a prejudice against the place where it then stood, in the Palais Royal, and the king had ordered its removal to a less central spot. The place chosen was La Porte St. Martin.

The king, vexed to see Paris deprived for so long of its Opera, became as sorrowful as if the arrivals of grain had ceased, or bread had risen to more than seven sous the quartern loaf. It was melancholy to see the nobility, the army, and the citizens without their after-dinner amusement; and to see the promenades thronged with the unemployed divinities, from the chorus-singers to the prima donnas.

An architect was then introduced to the king, full of new plans, who promised so perfect a ventilation, that even in case of fire no one could be smothered. He would make eight doors for exit, besides five large windows placed so low that any one could jump out of them. In the place of the beautiful hall of Moreau he was to erect a building with ninety-six feet of frontage towards the boulevard, ornamented with eight caryatides on pillars forming three entrance-doors, a bas-relief above the capitals, and a gallery with three windows. The stage was to be thirty-six feet wide, the theater seventy-two feet deep and eighty across, from one wall to the other. He asked only seventy-five days and nights before he opened it to the public.

This appeared to all a mere gasconade, and was much laughed at. The king, however, concluded the agreement with him. Lenoir set to work, and kept his word. But the public feared that a building so quickly erected could not be safe, and when it opened no one would go.

Even the few courageous ones who did go to the first representation of "Adéle de Ponthieu" made their wills first. The architect was in despair. He came to the king to consult him as to what was to be done.

It was just after the birth of the dauphin; all Paris was full of joy. The king advised him to announce a gratuitous performance in honor of the event, and give a ball after. Doubtless plenty would come, and if the theater stood, its safety was established.

"Thanks, sire," said the architect.

"But reflect, first," said the king, "if there be a crowd, are you sure of your building?"

"Sire, I am sure, and shall go there myself."

"I will go to the second representation," said the king.

The architect followed this advice. They played "Adéle de Ponthieu" to three thousand spectators, who afterwards danced. After this there could be no more fear. It was three years afterwards that Madame de la Motte and the cardinal went to the ball.

CHAPTER XXIII
THE BALL AT THE OPERA

The ball was at its height when they glided in quietly, and were soon lost in the crowd. A couple had taken refuge from the pressure under the queen's box; one of them wore a white domino and the other a black one. They were talking with great animation. "I tell you, Oliva," said the black domino, "that I am sure you are expecting some one. Your head is no longer a head, but a weather cock, and turns round to look after every newcomer."

"Well, is it astonishing that I should look at the people, when that is what I came here for?"

"Oh, that is what you came for!"

"Well, sir, and for what do people generally come?"

"A thousand things."

"Men perhaps, but women only for one—to see and be seen by as many people as possible."

"Mademoiselle Oliva!"

"Oh, do not speak in that big voice, it does so frighten me; and above all, do not call me by name; it is bad taste to let every one here know who you are."

The black domino made an angry gesture; it was interrupted by a blue domino who approached them.

"Come, monsieur," said he, "let madame amuse herself; it is not every night one comes to a ball at the Opera."

"Meddle with your own affairs," replied Beausire, rudely.

"Monsieur, learn once for all that a little courtesy is never out of place."

"I do not know you," he replied, "and do not want to have anything to do with you."

"No, you do not know me; but I know you, M. Beausire."

At hearing his name thus pronounced, Beausire visibly trembled.

"Oh, do not be afraid, M. Beausire; I am not what you take me for."

"Pardieu! sir, do you guess thoughts, as well as names?"

"Why not?"

"Then tell me what I thought. I have never seen a sorcerer, and should find it amusing."

"Oh, what you ask is not difficult enough to entitle me to that name."

"Never mind—tell."

"Well, then! you took me for an agent of M. de Crosne."

"M. de Crosne!" he repeated.

"Yes; the lieutenant of police."

"Sir!"

"Softly, M. de Beausire, you really look as if you were feeling for your sword."

"And so I was, sir."

"Good heavens! what a warlike disposition; but I think, dear M. Beausire, you left your sword at home, and you did well. But to speak of something else, will you relinquish to me madame for a time?"

"Give you up madame?"

"Yes, sir; that is not uncommon, I believe, at a ball at the Opera."

"Certainly not, when it suits the gentleman."

"It suffices sometimes that it should please the lady."

"Do you ask it for a long time?"

"Really, M. Beausire, you are too curious. Perhaps for ten minutes—perhaps for an hour—perhaps for all the evening."

"You are laughing at me, sir."

"Come, reply; will you or not?"

"No, sir."

"Come, come, do not be ill-tempered, you who were so gentle just now."

"Just now?"

"Yes; at the Rue Dauphine."

Oliva laughed.

"Hold your tongue, madame," said Beausire.

"Yes," continued the blue domino, "where you were on the point of killing this poor lady, but stopped at the sight of some louis."

"Oh, I see; you and she have an understanding together."

"How can you say such a thing?" cried Oliva.

"And if it were so," said the stranger, "it is all for your benefit."

"For my benefit! that would be curious."

"I will prove to you that your presence here is as hurtful as your absence would be profitable. You are a member of a certain academy, not the Académie Française, but in the Rue du Pôt au Fer, in the second story, is it not, my dear M. Beausire?"

"Hush!" said Beausire.

The blue domino drew out his watch, which was studded with diamonds that made Beausire's eyes water to look at them. "Well!" continued he, "in a quarter of an hour they are going to discuss there a little project, by which, they hope to secure 2,000,000 francs among the twelve members, of whom you are one, M. Beausire."

"And you must be another; if you are not——"

"Pray go on."

"A member of the police."

"Oh, M. Beausire, I thought you had more sense. If I were of the police, I should have taken you long ago, for some little affairs less honorable than this speculation."

"So, sir, you wish to send me to the Rue du Pôt au Fer: but I know why—that I may be arrested there: I am not such a fool."

"Now, you are one. If I wanted to arrest you, I had only to do it, and I am rid of you at once; but gentleness and persuasion are my maxims."

"Oh, I know now," said Beausire, "you are the man that was on the sofa two hours ago."

"What sofa?"

"Never mind; you have induced me to go, and if you are sending a gallant man into harm, you will pay for it some day."

"Be tranquil," said the blue domino, laughing; "by sending you there, I give you 100,000 francs at least, for you know the rule of this society is, that whoever is absent loses his share."

"Well, then, good-by!" said Beausire, and vanished.

The blue domino took possession of Oliva's arm, left at liberty by Beausire.

"Now!" said she, "I have let you manage poor Beausire at your ease, but I warn you, you will find me not so easy to talk over; therefore, find something pretty to say to me, or——"

"I know nothing prettier than your own history, dear Mademoiselle Nicole," said he, pressing the pretty round arm of the little woman, who uttered a cry at hearing herself so addressed; but, recovering herself with marvelous quickness, said:

"Oh, mon Dieu! what a name! Is it I whom you call Nicole? If so, you are wrong, for that is not my name."

"At present I know that you call yourself Oliva, but we will talk afterwards of Oliva; at present I want to speak of Nicole. Have you forgotten the time when you bore that name? I do not believe it, my dear child, for the name that one bears as a young girl is ever the one enshrined in the heart, although one may have been forced to take another to hide the first. Poor Oliva, happy Nicole!"

"Why do you say 'Poor Oliva'? do you not think me happy?"

"It would be difficult to be happy with a man like Beausire."

Oliva sighed and said, "Indeed I am not."

"You love him, however."

"A little."

"If you do not love him much, leave him."

"No."

"Why not?"

"Because I should no sooner have done so than I should regret it."

"Do you think so?"

"I am afraid I should."

"What could you have to regret in a drunkard; a gambler, a man who beats you, and a black-leg, who will one day come to the gallows?"

"You would not understand me if I told you."

"Try."

"I should regret the excitement he keeps me in."

"I ought to have guessed it; that comes of passing your youth with such silent people."

"You know about my youth?"

"Perfectly."

Oliva laughed and shook her head.

"You doubt it?"

"Really I do."

"Then we will talk a little about it, Mademoiselle Nicole."

"Very well; but I warn you, I will tell nothing."

"I do not wish it. I do not mean your childhood. I begin from the time when you first perceived that you had a heart capable of love."

"Love for whom?"

"For Gilbert."

At this name Oliva trembled.

"Ah, mon Dieu!" she cried. "How do you know?" Then with, a sigh said, "Oh, sir! you have pronounced a name indeed fertile in remembrances. You knew Gilbert?"

"Yes; since I speak to you of him."

"Alas!"

"A charming lad, upon my word. You loved him?"

"He was handsome. No, perhaps not; but I thought him so; he was full of mind, my equal in birth, but Gilbert thought no woman his equal."

"Not even Mademoiselle de Ta——"

"Oh, I know whom you mean, sir. You are well instructed. Yes, Gilbert loved higher than the poor Nicole: you are possessed of terrible secrets, sir; tell me, if you can," she continued, looking earnestly at him, "what has become of him?"

"You should know best."

"Why, in heaven's name?"

"Because if he followed you from Taverney to Paris, you followed him from Paris to Trianon."

"Yes, that is true, but that is ten years ago; and I wished to know what had passed since the time I ran away, and since he disappeared. When Gilbert loved Mademoiselle de——"

"Do not pronounce names aloud," said he.

"Well, then, when he loved her so much that each tree at Trianon was witness to his love——"

"You loved him no more."

"On the contrary, I loved him more than ever; and this love was my ruin. I am beautiful, proud, and, when I please, insolent; and would lay my head on the scaffold rather than confess myself despised."

"You have a heart, Nicole?"

"I had then," she said, sighing.

"This conversation makes you sad."

"No, it does me good to speak of my youth. But tell me why Gilbert fled from Trianon."

"Do you wish me to confirm a suspicion, or to tell you something you do not know."

"Something I do not know."

"Well, I cannot tell you this. Have you not heard that he is dead?"

"Yes, I have, but——"

"Well, he is dead."

"Dead!" said Nicole, with an air of doubt. Then, with a sudden start, "Grant me one favor!" she cried.

"As many as you like."

"I saw you two hours ago; for it was you, was it not?"

"Certainly."

"You did not, then, try to disguise yourself?"

"Not at all."

"But I was stupid; I saw you, but I did not observe you."

"I do not understand."

"Do you know what I want?"

"No."

"Take off your mask."

"Here! impossible!"

"Oh, you cannot fear other people seeing you. Here, behind this column, you will be quite hidden. You fear that I should recognize you."

"You!"

"And that I should cry, 'It is you—it is Gilbert!'"

"What folly!"

"Take off your mask."

"Yes, on one condition—that you will take off yours, if I ask it."

"Agreed." The unknown took off his immediately.

Oliva looked earnestly at him, then sighed, and said:

"Alas! no, it is not Gilbert."

"And who am I?"

"Oh, I do not care, as you are not he."

"And if it had been Gilbert?" said he, as he put on his mask again.

"Ah! if it had been," cried she passionately, "and he had said to me, 'Nicole, do you remember Taverney Maison-Rouge?' then there would have been no longer a Beausire in the world for me."

"But I have told you, my dear child, that Gilbert is dead."

"Ah! perhaps, then, it is for the best," said Oliva, with a sigh.

"Yes; he would never have loved you, beautiful as you are."

"Do you, then, think he despised me?"

"No; he rather feared you."

"That is possible."

"Then you think it better he is dead?"

"Do not repeat my words; in your mouth they wound me."

"But it is better for Mademoiselle Oliva. You observe, I abandon Nicole, and speak to Oliva. You have before you a future, happy, rich, and brilliant."

"Do you think so?"

"Yes, if you make up your mind to do anything to arrive at this end."

"I promise you."

"But you must give up sighing, as you were doing just now."

"Very well. I sighed for Gilbert, and as he is dead, and there are not two Gilberts in the world, I shall sigh no more. But enough of him."

"Yes; we will speak of yourself. Why did you run away with Beausire?"

"Because I wished to quit Trianon, and I was obliged to go with some one; I could no longer remain a 'pis aller,' rejected by Gilbert."

"You have, then, been faithful for ten years through pride? You have paid dearly for it."

Oliva laughed.

"Oh, I know what you are laughing at. To hear a man, who pretends to know everything, accuse you of having been ten years faithful, when you think you have not rendered yourself worthy of such a ridiculous reproach. However, I know all about you. I know that you went to Portugal with Beausire, where you remained two years; that you then left him, and went to the Indies with the captain of a frigate, who hid you in his cabin, and who left you at Chandernagor when he returned to Europe. I know that you had two millions of rupees to spend in the house of a nabob who kept you shut up; that you escaped through the window on the shoulders of a slave. Then, rich—for you had carried away two beautiful pearl bracelets, two diamonds, and three large rubies—you came back to France. When landing at Brest, your evil genius made you encounter Beausire on the quay, who recognized you immediately, bronzed and altered as you were, while you almost fainted at the sight of him."

"Oh, mon Dieu!" cried Oliva, "who are you, then, who know all this?"

"I know, further, that Beausire carried you off again, persuaded you that he loved you, sold your jewels, and reduced you to poverty. Still, you say you love him, and, as love is the root of all happiness, of course you ought to be happy."

Oliva hung her head, and covered her eyes with her hands, but two large tears might be seen forcing their way through her fingers—liquid pearls, more precious, though not so marketable, as those Beausire had sold.

"And this woman," at last she said, "whom you describe as so proud and so happy, you have bought to-day for fifty louis."

"I am aware it is too little, mademoiselle."

"No, sir; on the contrary, I am surprised that a woman like me should be worth so much."

"You are worth more than that, as I will show you; but just now I want all your attention."

"Then I will be silent."

"No; talk, on the contrary, of anything, it does not matter what, so that we seem occupied."

"You are very odd."

"Take hold of my arm, and let us walk."

They walked on among the various groups. In a minute or two, Oliva asked a question.

"Talk as much as you like, only do not ask questions at present," said her companion, "for I cannot answer now; only, as you speak, disguise your voice, hold your head up, and scratch your neck with your fan."

She obeyed.

In a minute, they passed a highly perfumed group, in the center of which a very elegant-looking man was talking fast to three companions, who were listening respectfully.

"Who is that young man in that beautiful gray domino?" asked Oliva.

"M. le Comte d'Artois; but pray do not speak just now!" At this moment two other dominoes passed them, and stood in a place near, which was rather free from people.

"Lean on this pillar, countess," said one of them in a low voice, but which was overheard by the blue domino, who started at its sound.

Then a yellow domino, passing through the crowd, came up to the blue one, and said, "It is he."

"Very good," replied the other, and the yellow domino vanished.

"Now, then," said Oliva's companion, turning to her, "we will begin to enjoy ourselves a little."

"I hope so, for you have twice made me sad: first by taking away Beausire, and then by speaking of Gilbert."

"I will be both Gilbert and Beausire to you," said the unknown.

"Oh!" sighed Oliva.

"I do not ask you to love me, remember; I only ask you to accept the life I offer you—that is, the accomplishment of all your desires, provided occasionally you give way to mine. Just now I have one."

"What?"

"That black domino that you see there is a German of my acquaintance, who refused to come to the ball with me, saying he was not well; and now he is here, and a lady with him."

"Who is she?"

"I do not know. We will approach them; I will pretend that you are a German, and you must not speak, for fear of being found out. Now, pretend to point him out to me with the end of your fan."

"Like that?"

"Yes; very well. Now whisper to me."

Oliva obeyed with a docility which charmed her companion.

The black domino, who had his back turned to them, did not see all this; but his companion did. "Take care, monseigneur," said she; "there are two masks watching us."

"Oh, do not be afraid, countess; they cannot recognize us. Do not mind them; but let me assure you that never form was so enchanting as yours, never eyes so brilliant, never——"

"Hush! the spies approach."

"Spies!" said the cardinal, uneasily. "Disguise your voice if they make you speak, and I will do the same."

Oliva and her blue domino indeed approached; he came up to the cardinal, and said, "Mask——"

"What do you want?" said the cardinal, in a voice as unlike his natural one as he could make it.

"The lady who accompanies me desires me to ask you some questions."

"Ask," said M. de Rohan.

"Are they very indiscreet?" said Madame de la Motte.

"So indiscreet that you shall not hear them;" and he pretended to whisper to Oliva, who made a sign in answer. Then, in irreproachable German, he said to the cardinal, "Monseigneur, are you in love with the lady who accompanies you?"

The cardinal trembled.

"Did you say monseigneur?" he asked.

"Yes."

"You deceive yourself; I am not the person you think."

"Oh, M. le Cardinal, do not deny it; it is useless. If even I did not know you, the lady who accompanies me assures me she knows you perfectly." And he again whispered to Oliva, "Make a sign for 'yes.' Do so each time I press your arm."

She did so.

"You astonish me!" said the cardinal. "Who is this lady?"

"Oh, monseigneur, I thought you would have known; she soon knew you. It is true that jealousy— —"

"Madame is jealous of me!" cried the cardinal.

"We do not say that," replied the unknown, rather haughtily.

"What are you talking about?" asked Madame de la Motte, who did not like this conversation in German.

"Oh, nothing, nothing!"

"Madame," said the cardinal to Oliva, "one word from you, and I promise to recognize you instantly."

Oliva, who saw him speaking to her, but did not understand a word, whispered to her companion.

All this mystery piqued the cardinal.

"One single German word," he said, "could not much compromise madame."

The blue domino again pretended to take her orders, and then said: "M. le Cardinal, these are the words of madame, 'He whose thoughts are not ever on the alert, he whose imagination does not perpetually suggest the presence of the loved one, does not love, however much he may pretend it.'"

The cardinal appeared struck with these words; all his attitude expressed surprise, respect and devotion.

"It is impossible!" he murmured in French.

"What is impossible?" asked Madame de la Motte, who seized eagerly on these few words she could understand.

"Nothing, madame, nothing!"

"Really, cardinal, you are making me play but a sorry part," said she, withdrawing her arm angrily.

He did not even seem to notice it, so great was his preoccupation with the German lady.

"Madame," said he to her, "these words that your companion has repeated to me in your name are some German lines which I read in a house which is perhaps known to you."

The blue domino pressed Oliva's arm, who thereupon bowed an assent.

"That house," said the cardinal, hesitatingly, "is it not called Schoenbrunn?"

She again made a gesture of assent.

"They were written on a table of cherry-wood, with a gold bodkin, by an august hand."

"Yes," bowed Oliva again.

The cardinal stopped, he tottered, and leaned against a pillar for support. Madame de la Motte stood by, watching this strange scene. Then the cardinal, touching the blue domino, said: "This is the conclusion of the quotation—'But he who sees everywhere the loved object, who recognizes her by a flower, by a perfume, through the thickest veils, he can still be silent—his voice is in his heart—and if one other understands him, he is happy.'"

"Oh, they are speaking German here," said a young voice from an approaching group; "let us listen. Do you speak German, marshal?"

"No, monseigneur."

"You, Charny?"

"Yes, your highness."

"Here is M. le Comte d'Artois," said Oliva softly to her companion.

A crowd followed them, and many were passing round.

"Take care, gentlemen!" said the blue domino.

"Monsieur," replied the prince, "the people are pushing us."

At this moment some invisible hand pulled Oliva's hood from behind, and her mask fell. She replaced it as quickly as possible, with a half-terrified cry, which was echoed by one of affected disquiet from her companion.

Several others around looked no little bewildered.

The cardinal nearly fainted, and Madame de la Motte supported him. The pressure of the crowd separated the Comte d'Artois and his party from them. Then the blue domino approached the cardinal, and said:

"This is indeed an irreparable misfortune; this lady's honor is at your mercy."

"Oh, monsieur!" murmured the cardinal, who was much agitated.

"Let us go quickly," said the blue domino to Oliva; and they moved away.

"Now I know," said Madame de la Motte to herself, "what the cardinal meant was impossible: he took this woman for the queen. But what an effect it has had on him?"

"Would you like to leave the ball?" asked M. de Rohan, in a feeble voice.

"As you please, monseigneur," replied Jeanne.

"I do not find much interest here, do you?"

"None at all."

They pushed their way through the crowd. The cardinal, who was tall, looked all around him, to try and see again the vision which had disappeared; but blue, white, and gray dominoes were everywhere, and he could distinguish no one. They had been some time in the carriage, and he had not yet spoken to Jeanne.

CHAPTER XXIV
THE EXAMINATION

At last Jeanne said, "Where is this carriage taking me to, cardinal?"

"Back to your own house, countess."

"My house—in the faubourg?"

"Yes, countess. A very small house to contain so many charms."

They soon stopped. Jeanne alighted, and he was preparing to follow her, but she stopped him, and said, "It is very late, cardinal."

"Adieu, then," said he; and he drove away, absorbed with the scene at the ball.

Jeanne entered alone into her new house. Six lackeys waited for her in the hall, and she looked at them as calmly as though she had been used to it all her life.

"Where are my femmes de chambre?" said she.

One of the men advanced respectfully.

"Two women wait for madame in her room."

"Call them." The valet obeyed.

"Where do you usually sleep?" said Jeanne to them, when they entered.

"We have no place as yet," said one of them; "we can sleep wherever madame pleases."

"Where are the keys?"

"Here, madame."

"Well, for this night you shall sleep out of the house."

The women looked at her in surprise.

"You have some place to go to?" said Jeanne.

"Certainly, madame; but it is late. Still, if madame wishes——"

"And these men can accompany you," she continued, dismissing the valets also, who seemed rather pleased.

"When shall we return?" asked one of them.

"To-morrow at noon."

They seemed more astonished than ever, but Jeanne looked so imperious that they did not speak.

"Is there any one else here?" she asked.

"No one, madame. It is impossible for madame to remain like this; surely you must have some one here."

"I want no one."

"The house might take fire; madame might be ill."

"Go, all of you," said Jeanne; "and take this," added she, giving them money from her purse.

They all thanked her, and disappeared, saying to each other that they had found a strange mistress.

Jeanne then locked the doors and said triumphantly, "Now I am alone here, in my own house." She now commenced an examination, admiring each thing individually. The ground-floor contained a bath-room, dining-room, three drawing-rooms, and two morning-rooms. The furniture of these rooms was handsome, though not new. It pleased Jeanne better than if it had been furnished expressly for her. All the rich antiques disdained by fashionable ladies, the marvelous pieces of carved ebony, the glass lusters, the gothic clocks; chefs-d'œuvre of carving and enamel, the screens with embroidered Chinese figures, and the immense vases, threw Jeanne into indescribable raptures. Here on a chimney-piece two gilded tritons were bearing branches of coral, upon which were hung jeweled fruits. In another place, on a gilded console table, was an enormous elephant, with sapphires hanging from his ears, supporting a tower filled with little bottles of scent. Books in gilt bindings were on rosewood shelves. One room was hung with Gobelin tapestry, and furnished in gray and gold; another, paneled in paintings by Vernet. The small rooms contained pictures. The whole was evidently the collection of years.

Jeanne examined it all with delight. Then, as her domino was inconvenient, she went into her room to put on a dressing-gown of wadded silk; and, secure of meeting no one, she wandered from room to room, continuing her examination, till at last, her light nearly exhausted, she returned to her bedroom, which was hung with embroidered blue satin.

She had seen everything, and admired everything: there only remained herself to be admired; and she thought, as she undressed before the long mirror, that she was not the object least worthy of admiration in the place. At last, wearied out with pleasurable excitement, she went to bed, and soon sank to sleep.

CHAPTER XXV
THE ACADEMY OF M. BEAUSIRE

Beausire had followed the advice of the blue domino, and repaired to the place of meeting in the Rue du Pôt au Fer. He was frightened by the apparent exclusion which his companions had seemed to meditate, in not communicating their plans to him; and he knew none of them to be particularly scrupulous. He had acquired the reputation among them of a man to be feared; it was not wonderful, as he had been a soldier, and worn a uniform. He knew how to draw his sword, and he had a habit of looking very fierce at the slightest word that displeased him—all things which appear rather terrifying to those of doubtful courage, especially when they have reason to shun the éclat of a duel and the curiosity of the police.

Beausire counted, therefore, on revenging himself by frightening them a little. It was a long way, but Beausire had money in his pocket; so he took a coach, promised the driver an extra franc to go fast, and, to make up for the absence of his sword, he assumed as fierce a look as he could on entering the room.

It was a large hall, full of tables, at which were seated about twenty players, drinking beer or syrups, and smiling now and then on some highly rouged women who sat near them. They were playing faro at the principal table, but the stakes were low, and the excitement small in proportion.

On the entrance of the domino, all the women smiled on him, half in raillery, and half in coquetry, for M. Beausire was a favorite among them. However, he advanced in silence to the table without noticing any one.

One of the players, who was a good-humored looking fellow, said to him, "Corbleu, chevalier, you come from the ball looking out of sorts."

"Is your domino uncomfortable?" said another.

"No, it is not my domino," replied Beausire, gruffly.

"Oh!" said the banker, "he has been unfaithful to us; he has been playing somewhere else and lost."

"It is not I who am unfaithful to my friends; I am incapable of it. I leave that to others."

"What do you mean, dear chevalier?"

"I know what I mean," replied he; "I thought I had friends here."

"Certainly," replied several voices.

"Well, I was deceived."

"How?"

"You plan things without me."

Several of the members began to protest it was not true.

"I know better," said Beausire; "and these false friends shall be punished." He put his hand to his side to feel for his sword, but, as it was not there, he only shook his pocket, and the gold rattled.

"Oh, oh!" said the banker, "M. Beausire has not lost. Come, will you not play?"

"Thanks," said Beausire; "I will keep what I have got."

"Only one louis," said one of the women, caressingly.

"I do not play for miserable louis," said he. "We play for millions here to-night—yes, gentlemen, millions."

He had worked himself up into a great state of excitement, and was losing sight of all prudence, when a blow from behind made him turn, and he saw by him a great dark figure, stiff and upright, and with two shining black eyes. He met Beausire's furious glance with a ceremonious bow.

"The Portuguese!" said Beausire.

"The Portuguese!" echoed the ladies, who abandoned Beausire to crowd round the newcomer, he being their especial pet, as he was in the habit of bringing them sweetmeats, sometimes wrapped up in notes of forty or fifty francs. This man was one of the twelve associates.

He was used as a bait at their society. It was agreed that he should lose a hundred louis a week as an inducement to allure strangers to play. He was, therefore, considered a useful man. He was also an agreeable one, and was held in much consideration.

Beausire became silent on seeing him.

The Portuguese took his place at the table, and put down twenty louis, which he soon lost, thereby making some of those who had been stripped before forget their losses.

All the money received by the banker was dropped into a well under the table, and he was forbidden to wear long sleeves, lest he should conceal any within them, although the other members generally took the liberty of searching both sleeves and pockets before they left.

Several now put on their great-coats and took leave—some happy enough to escort the ladies.

A few, however, after making a feint to go, returned into another room; and here the twelve associates soon found themselves united.

"Now we will have an explanation," said Beausire.

"Do not speak so loud," said the Portuguese in good French. Then they examined the doors and windows to make certain that all was secure, drew the curtain close, and seated themselves.

"I have a communication to make," said the Portuguese; "it was lucky, however, I arrived when I did, for M. Beausire was seized this evening with a most imprudent flow of eloquence."

Beausire tried to speak.

"Silence," said the Portuguese; "let us not waste words: you know my ideas beforehand very well; you are a man of talent, and may have guessed it, but I think 'amour propre' should never overcome self-interest."

"I do not understand."

"M. Beausire hoped to be the first to make this proposition."

"What proposition?" cried the rest.

"Concerning the two million francs," said Beausire.

"Two million francs!" cried they.

"First," said the Portuguese, "you exaggerate; it is not as much as that."

"We do not know what you are talking of," said the banker.

"But are not the less all ears," said another.

The Portuguese drank off a large glass of Orgeat, and then began: "The necklace is not worth more than 1,500,000 francs."

"Oh, then it concerns a necklace?" said Beausire.

"Yes, did you not mean the same thing?"

"Perhaps."

"Now he is going to be discreet after his former folly," said the Portuguese; "but time presses, for the ambassador will arrive in eight days."

"This matter becomes complicated," said the banker; "a necklace! 1,500,000 francs! and an ambassador! Pray explain."

"In a few words," said the Portuguese; "MM. Bœhmer and Bossange offered to the queen a necklace worth that sum. She refused it, and now they do not know what to do with it, for none but a royal fortune could buy it. Well, I have found the royal personage who will buy this necklace, and obtain the custody of it from MM. Bœhmer and Bossange; and that is my gracious sovereign the Queen of Portugal."

"We understand it less than ever," said the associates.

"And I not at all," thought Beausire; then he said aloud, "Explain yourself clearly, dear M. Manoël; our private differences should give place to the public interests. I acknowledge you the author of the idea, and renounce all right to its paternity. Therefore speak on."

"Willingly," said Manoël, drinking a second glass of Orgeat; "the embassy is vacant just now; the new ambassador, M. de Souza, will not arrive for a week. Well, he may arrive sooner."

They all looked stupefied but Beausire, who said, "Do you not see some ambassador, whether true or false?"

"Exactly," said Manoël; "and the ambassador who arrives may desire to buy this necklace for the Queen of Portugal, and treat accordingly with MM. Bœhmer and Bossange; that is all."

"But," said the banker, "they would not allow such a necklace to pass into the hands of M. de Souza himself without good security."

"Oh, I have thought of all that; the ambassador's house is vacant, with the exception of the chancellor, who is a Frenchman, and speaks bad Portuguese, and who is therefore delighted when the Portuguese speak French to him, as he does not then betray himself; but who likes to speak Portuguese to the French, as it sounds grand. Well, we will present ourselves to this chancellor with all the appearances of a new legation."

"Appearances are something," said Beausire: "but the credentials are much more."

"We will have them," replied Manoël.

"No one can deny that Don Manoël is an invaluable man," said Beausire.

"Well, our appearances, and the credentials having convinced the chancellor of our identity, we will establish ourselves at the house."

"That is pretty bold," said Beausire.

"It is necessary, and quite easy," said Manoël; "the chancellor will be convinced, and if he should afterwards become less credulous, we will dismiss him. I believe an ambassador has the right to change his chancellor."

"Certainly."

"Then, when we are masters of the hotel, our first operation will be to wait on MM. Bœhmer and Bossange."

"But you forget one thing," said Beausire; "our first act should be to ask an audience of the king, and then we should break down. The famous Riza Bey, who was presented to Louis XIV. as ambassador from the Shah of Persia, spoke Persian at least, and there were no savants here capable of knowing how well; but we should be found out at once. We should be told directly that our Portuguese was remarkably French, and we should be sent to the Bastile."

"We will escape this danger by remaining quietly at home."

"Then M. Bœhmer will not believe in our ambassadorship."

"M. Bœhmer will be told that we are sent merely to buy the necklace. We will show him our order to do this, as we shall before have shown it to the chancellor, only we must try to avoid showing it to the ministers, for they are suspicious, and might find a host of little flaws."

"Oh yes," cried they all, "let us avoid the ministers."

"But if MM. Bœhmer and Bossange require money on account?" asked Beausire.

"That would complicate the affair, certainly."

"For," continued Beausire, "it is usual for an ambassador to have letters of credit, at least, if not ready money; and here we should fail."

"You find plenty of reasons why it should fail," said Manoël, "but nothing to make it succeed."

"It is because I wish it to succeed that I speak of the difficulties. But stop—a thought strikes me: in every ambassador's house there is a strong box."

"Yes; but it may be empty."

"Well! if it be, we must ask MM. Bœhmer and Bossange who are their correspondents at Lisbon, and we will sign and stamp for them letters of credit for the sum demanded."

"That will do," said Manoël, "I was engrossed with the grand idea, but had not sufficiently considered the details."

"Now, let us think of arranging the parts," said Beausire. "Don Manoël will be ambassador."

"Certainly," they all said.

"And M. Beausire my secretary and interpreter," said Manoël.

"Why so?" said Beausire, rather uneasily.

"I am M. de Souza, and must not speak a word of French; for I know that that gentleman speaks nothing but Portuguese, and very little of that. You, on the contrary, M. Beausire, who have traveled, and have acquired French habits, who speak Portuguese also — —"

"Very badly," said Beausire.

"Quite enough to deceive a Parisian; and then, you know, the most useful agents will have the largest shares."

"Assuredly," said the others.

"Well! it is agreed; I am secretary and interpreter. Then as to the money?"

"It shall be divided into twelve parts; but I as ambassador and author of the scheme shall have a share and a half; M. Beausire the same, as interpreter, and because he partly shared my idea; and also a share and a half to him who sells the jewels."

"So far, then, it is settled! we will arrange the minor details to-morrow, for it is very late," said Beausire, who was thinking of Oliva, left at the ball with the blue domino, towards whom, in spite of his readiness in giving away louis d'or, he did not feel very friendly.

"No, no; we will finish at once," said the others. "What is to be prepared?"

"A traveling carriage, with the arms of M. de Souza," said Beausire.

"That would take too long to paint and to dry," said Manoël.

"Then we must say that the ambassador's carriage broke down on the way, and he was forced to use that of the secretary: I must have a carriage, and my arms will do for that. Besides, we will have plenty of bruises and injuries on the carriage, and especially round the arms, and no one will think of them."

"But the rest of the embassy?"

"We will arrive in the evening; it is the best time to make a début, and you shall all follow next day, when we have prepared the way."

"Very well."

"But every ambassador, besides a secretary, must have a valet de chambre. You, captain," said Don Manoël, addressing one of the gang, "shall take this part."

The captain bowed.

"And the money for the purchases?" said Manoël. "I have nothing."

"I have a little," said Beausire, "but it belongs to my mistress. What have we in our fund?"

"Your keys, gentlemen," said the banker.

Each drew out a key, which opened one of twelve locks in the table; so that none of these honest associates could open it without all the others. They went to look.

"One hundred and ninety-eight louis, besides the reserve fund," said the banker.

"Give them to M. Beausire and me. It is not too much," said Manoël.

"Give us two-thirds, and leave the rest," said Beausire, with a generosity which won all their hearts.

Don Manoël and Beausire received, therefore, one hundred and thirty-two louis and sixty-six remained for the others.

They then separated, having fixed a rendezvous for the next day.

Beausire rolled up his domino under his arm, and hastened to the Rue Dauphine, where he hoped to find Oliva in possession of some new louis d'or.

CHAPTER XXVI
THE AMBASSADOR

On the evening of the next day a traveling-carriage passed through the Barrière d'Enfer, so covered with dust and scratches that no one could discern the arms. The four horses that drew it went at a rapid pace, until it arrived before an hotel of handsome appearance, in the Rue de la Jussienne, at the door of which two men, one of whom was in full dress, were waiting. The carriage entered the courtyard of the hotel, and one of the persons waiting approached the door, and commenced speaking in bad Portuguese.

"Who are you?" said a voice from the inside, speaking the language perfectly.

"The unworthy chancellor of the embassy, your excellency."

"Very well. Mon Dieu! how badly you speak our language, my dear chancellor! But where are we to go?"

"This way, monseigneur."

"This is a poor reception," said Don Manoël, as he got out of the carriage, leaning on the arms of his secretary and valet.

"Your excellency must pardon me," said the chancellor, "but the courier announcing your arrival only reached the hotel at two o'clock to-day. I was absent on some business, and when I returned, found your excellency's letter; I have only had time to have the rooms opened and lighted."

"Very good."

"It gives me great pleasure to see the illustrious person of our ambassador."

"We desire to keep as quiet as possible," said Don Manoël, "until we receive further orders, from Lisbon. But pray show me to my room, for I am dying with fatigue; my secretary will give you all necessary directions."

The chancellor bowed respectfully to Beausire, who returned it, and then said, "We will speak French, sir; I think it will be better for both of us."

"Yes," murmured the chancellor, "I shall be more at my ease; for I confess that my pronunciation— —"

"So I hear," interrupted Beausire.

"I will take the liberty to say to you, sir, as you seem so amiable, that I trust M. de Souza will not be annoyed at my speaking such bad Portuguese."

"Oh, not at all, as you speak French."

"French!" cried the chancellor; "I was born in the Rue St. Honoré."

"Oh, that will do," said Beausire. "Your name is Ducorneau, is it not?"

"Yes, monsieur; rather a lucky one, as it has a Spanish termination. It is very flattering to me that monsieur knew my name."

"Oh, you are well known; so well that we did not bring a chancellor from Lisbon with us."

"I am very grateful, monsieur; but I think M. de Souza is ringing."

"Let us go and see."

They found Manoël attired in a magnificent dressing-gown. Several boxes and dressing-cases, of rich appearance, were already unpacked and lying about.

"Enter," said he to the chancellor.

"Will his excellency be angry if I answer in French?" said Ducorneau, in a low voice, to Beausire.

"Oh, no; I am sure of it."

M. Ducorneau, therefore, paid the compliments in French.

"Oh, it is very convenient that you speak French so well, M. Ducorno," said the ambassador.

"He takes me for a Portuguese," thought the chancellor, with joy.

"Now," said Manoël, "can I have supper?"

"Certainly, your excellency. The Palais Royal is only two steps from here, and I know an excellent restaurant, from which your excellency can have a good supper in a very short time."

"Order it in your own name, if you please, M. Ducorno."

"And if your excellency will permit me, I will add to it some bottles of capital wine."

"Oh, our chancellor keeps a good cellar, then?" said Beausire, jokingly.

"It is my only luxury," replied he. And now, by the wax-lights, they could remark his rather red nose and puffed cheeks.

"Very well, M. Ducorno; bring your wine, and sup with us."

"Such an honor— —"

"Oh, no etiquette to-night; I am only a traveler. I shall not begin to be ambassador till to-morrow; then we will talk of business."

"Monseigneur will permit me to arrange my toilet."

"Oh, you are superb already," said Beausire.

"Yes, but this is a reception dress, and not a gala one."

"Remain as you are, monsieur, and give the time to expediting our supper."

Ducorneau, delighted, left the room to fulfil his orders. Then the three rogues, left together, began to discuss their affairs.

"Does this chancellor sleep here?" said Manoël.

"No; the fellow has a good cellar, and, I doubt not, a snug lodging somewhere or other. He is an old bachelor."

"There is a Suisse."

"We must get rid of him; and there are a few valets, whom we must replace to-morrow with our own friends."

"Who is in the kitchen department?"

"No one. The old ambassador did not live here; he had a house in the town."

"What about the strong-box?"

"Oh, on that point we must consult the chancellor; it is a delicate matter."

"I charge myself with it," said Beausire; "we are already capital friends."

"Hush! here he comes."

Ducorneau entered, quite out of breath. He had ordered the supper, and fetched six bottles of wine from his cellar, and was looking quite radiant at the thoughts of the coming repast.

"Will your excellency descend to the dining-room?"

"No, we will sup up here."

"Here is the wine, then," said Ducorneau.

"It sparkles like rubies," said Beausire, holding it to the light.

"Sit down, M. Ducorneau; my valet will wait upon us. What day did the last despatches arrive?"

"Immediately after the departure of your excellency's predecessor."

"Are the affairs of the embassy in good order?"

"Oh yes, monseigneur."

"No money difficulties? no debts?"

"Not that I know of."

"Because, if there are, we must begin by paying them."

"Oh, your excellency will have nothing of that sort to do. All the accounts were paid up three weeks ago; and the day after the departure of the late ambassador one hundred thousand francs arrived here."

"One hundred thousand francs?" said Beausire.

"Yes, in gold."

"So," said Beausire, "the box contains——"

"100,380 francs, monsieur."

"It is not much," said Manoël, coldly; "but, happily, her majesty has placed funds at my disposal. I told you," continued he, turning to Beausire, "that I thought we should need it at Paris."

"Your excellency took wise precautions," said Beausire, respectfully.

From the time of this important communication the hilarity of the party went on increasing. A good supper, consisting of salmon, crabs, and sweets, contributed to their satisfaction. Ducorneau, quite at his ease, ate enough for ten, and did not fail, either, in demonstrating that a Parisian could do honor to port and sherry.

CHAPTER XXVII
MESSRS. BŒHMER AND BOSSANGE

M. Ducorneau blessed heaven repeatedly for sending an ambassador who preferred his speaking French to Portuguese, and liked Portuguese wines better than French ones. At last, Manoël expressed a wish to go to bed; Ducorneau rose and left the room, although, it must be confessed, he found some difficulty in the operation.

It was now the turn of the valet to have supper, which he did with great good-will.

The next day the hotel assumed an air of business; all the bureaux were opened, and everything indicated life in the recently deserted place.

The report soon spread in the neighborhood that some great personages had arrived from Portugal during the night. This, although what was wanted to give them credit, could not but inspire the conspirators with some alarm; for the police had quick ears and Argus eyes. Still, they thought that by audacity, combined with prudence, they might easily keep them from becoming suspicious, until they had had time to complete their business.

Two carriages containing the other nine associates arrived, as agreed upon, and they were soon installed in their different departments.

Beausire induced Ducorneau himself to dismiss the porter, on the ground that he did not speak Portuguese. They were, therefore, in a good situation to keep off all unwelcome visitors.

About noon, Don Manoël, gaily dressed, got into a carriage, which they had hired for five hundred francs a month, and set out, with his secretary, for the residence of MM. Bœhmer and Bossange.

Their servant knocked at the door, which was secured with immense locks, and studded with great nails, like that of a prison. A servant opened it. "His Excellency the Ambassador of Portugal desires to speak to MM. Bœhmer and Bossange."

They got out, and M. Bœhmer came to them in a few moments, and received them with a profusion of polite speeches, but, seeing that the ambassador did not deign even a smile in reply, looked somewhat disconcerted.

"His excellency does not speak or understand French, sir, and you must communicate to him through me, if you do not speak Portuguese," said Beausire.

"No, monsieur, I do not."

Manoël then spoke in Portuguese to Beausire, who, turning to M. Bœhmer, said:

"His excellency M. le Comte de Souza, ambassador from the Queen of Portugal, desires me to ask you if you have not in your possession a beautiful diamond necklace?"

Bœhmer looked at him scrutinizingly.

"A beautiful diamond necklace!" repeated he.

"The one which you offered to the Queen of France, and which our gracious queen has heard of."

"Monsieur," said Bœhmer, "is an officer of the ambassador's?"

"His secretary, monsieur."

Don Manoël was seated with the air of a great man, looking carelessly at the pictures which hung round the room.

"M. Bœhmer," said Beausire abruptly, "do you not understand what I am saying to you?"

"Yes, sir," answered Bœhmer, rather startled by the manner of the secretary.

"Because I see his excellency is becoming impatient."

"Excuse me, sir," said Bœhmer, coloring, "but I dare not show the necklace, except in my partner's presence."

"Well, sir, call your partner."

Don Manoël approached Beausire, and began again talking to him in Portuguese.

"His excellency says," interpreted he, "that he has already waited ten minutes, and that he is not accustomed to be kept waiting."

Bœhmer bowed, and rang the bell. A minute afterwards M. Bossange entered.

Bœhmer explained the matter to him, who, after looking scrutinizingly at the Portuguese, left the room with a key given him by his partner, and soon returned with a case in one hand; the other was hidden under his coat, but they distinctly saw the shining barrel of a pistol.

"However well we may look," said Manoël gravely, in Portuguese, to his companion, "these gentlemen seem to take us for pickpockets rather than ambassadors."

M. Bossange advanced, and put the case into the hands of Manoël. He opened it, and then cried angrily to his secretary:

"Monsieur, tell these gentlemen that they tire my patience! I ask for a diamond necklace, and they bring me paste. Tell them I will complain to the ministers, and will have them thrown into the Bastile, impertinent people, who play tricks upon an ambassador." And he threw down the case in such a passion that they did not need an interpretation of his speech, but began explaining most humbly that in France it was usual to show only the models of diamonds, so as not to tempt people to robbery, were they so inclined.

Manoël, with an indignant gesture, walked towards the door.

"His excellency desires me to tell you," said Beausire, "that he is sorry that people like MM. Bœhmer and Bossange, jewelers to the queen, should not know better how to distinguish an ambassador from a rogue, and that he will return to his hotel."

The jewelers began to utter most respectful protestations, but Manoël walked on, and Beausire followed him.

"To the ambassador's hotel, Rue de la Jussienne," said Beausire to the footman.

"A lost business," groaned the valet, as they set off.

"On the contrary, a safe one; in an hour these men will follow us."

CHAPTER XXVIII
THE AMBASSADOR'S HOTEL

On returning to their hotel, these gentlemen found Ducorneau dining quietly in his bureau. Beausire desired him, when he had finished, to go up and see the ambassador, and added:

"You will see, my dear chancellor, that M. de Souza is not an ordinary man."

"I see that already."

"His excellency," continued Beausire, "wishes to take a distinguished position in Paris, and this residence will be insupportable to him. He will require a private house."

"That will complicate the diplomatic business," said Ducorneau; "we shall have to go so often to obtain his signature."

"His excellency will give you a carriage, M. Ducorneau."

"A carriage for me!"

"Certainly; every chancellor of a great ambassador should have a carriage. But we will talk of that afterwards. His excellency wishes to know where the strong-box is."

"Up-stairs, close to his own room."

"So far from you?"

"For greater safety, sir. Robbers would find greater difficulty in penetrating there, than here on the ground-floor."

"Robbers!" said Beausire, disdainfully, "for such a little sum?"

"One hundred thousand francs!" said Ducorneau. "It is easy to see M. de Souza is rich, but there is not more kept in any ambassador's house in Europe."

"Shall we examine it now?" said Beausire. "I am rather in a hurry to attend to my own business."

"Immediately, monsieur."

They went up and the money was found all right.

Ducorneau gave his key to Beausire, who kept it for some time, pretending to admire its ingenious construction, while he cleverly took the impression of it in wax. Then he gave it back, saying, "Keep it, M. Ducorneau; it is better in your hands than in mine. Let us now go to the ambassador."

They found Don Manoël drinking chocolate, and apparently much occupied with a paper covered with ciphers.

"Do you understand the ciphers used in the late correspondence?" said he to the chancellor.

"No, your excellency."

"I should wish you to learn it; it will save me a great deal of trouble. What about the box?" said he to Beausire.

"Perfectly correct, like everything else with which M. Ducorneau has any connection."

"Well, sit down, M. Ducorneau; I want you to give me some information. Do you know any honest jewelers in Paris?"

"There are MM. Bœhmer and Bossange, jewelers to the queen."

"But they are precisely the people I do not wish to employ. I have just quitted them, never to return."

"Have they had the misfortune to displease your excellency?"

"Seriously, M. Ducorneau."

"Oh, if I dared speak."

"You may."

"I would ask how these people, who bear so high a name— —"

"They are perfect Jews, M. Ducorneau, and their bad behavior will make them lose a million or two. I was sent by her gracious majesty to make an offer to them for a diamond necklace."

"Oh! the famous necklace which had been ordered by the late king for Madame Dubarry?"

"You are a valuable man, sir—you know everything. Well, now, I shall not buy it."

"Shall I interfere?"

"M. Ducorneau!"

"Oh, only as a diplomatic affair."

"If you knew them at all."

"Bossange is a distant relation of mine."

At this moment a valet opened the door, and announced MM. Bœhmer and Bossange. Don Manoël rose quickly, and said in any angry tone, "Send those people away!"

The valet made a step forward. "No; you do it," said he to his secretary.

"I beg you to allow me," said Ducorneau; and he advanced to meet them.

"There! this affair is destined to fail," said Manoël.

"No; Ducorneau will arrange it."

"I am convinced he will embroil it. You said at the jewelers that I did not understand French, and Ducorneau will let out that I do."

"I will go," said Beausire.

"Perhaps that is equally dangerous."

"Oh, no; only leave me to act."

Beausire went down. Ducorneau had found the jewelers much more disposed to politeness and confidence since entering the hotel; also, on seeing an old friend, Bossange was delighted.

"You here!" said he; and he approached to embrace him.

"Ah! you are very amiable to-day, my rich cousin," said Ducorneau.

"Oh," said Bossange, "if we have been a little separated, forgive, and render me a service."

"I came to do it."

"Thanks. You are, then, attached to the embassy?"

"Yes."

"I want advice."

"On what?"

"On this embassy."

"I am the chancellor."

"That is well; but about the ambassador?"

"I come to you, on his behalf, to tell you that he begs you to leave his hotel as quickly as possible."

The two jewelers looked at each other, disconcerted.

"Because," continued Ducorneau, "it seems you have been uncivil to him."

"But listen— —"

"It is useless," said Beausire, who suddenly appeared; "his excellency told you to dismiss them—do it."

"But, monsieur— —"

"I cannot listen," said Beausire.

The chancellor took his relation by the shoulder, and pushed him out, saying, "You have spoiled your fortune."

"Mon Dieu! how susceptible these foreigners are!"

"When one is called Souza, and has nine hundred thousand francs a year, one has a right to be anything," said Ducorneau.

"Ah!" sighed Bossange, "I told you, Bœhmer, you were too stiff about it."

"Well," replied the obstinate German, "at least, if we do not get his money, he will not get our necklace."

Ducorneau laughed. "You do not understand either a Portuguese or an ambassador, bourgeois that you are. I will tell you what they are: one ambassador, M. de Potemkin, bought every year for his queen, on the first of January, a basket of cherries which cost one hundred thousand crowns— one thousand francs a cherry. Well, M. de Souza will buy up the mines of Brazil till he finds a diamond as big as all yours put together. If it cost him twenty years of his income, what does he care?—he has no children."

And he was going to shut the door, when Bossange said:

"Arrange this affair, and you shall have— —"

"I am incorruptible," said he, and closed the door.

That evening the ambassador received this letter:

> "Monseigneur,—A man who waits for your orders, and desires to present you our respectful excuses, is at the door of your hotel, and at a word from your excellency he will place in the hands of one of your people the necklace of which you did us the honor to speak. Deign to receive, monseigneur, the assurances of our most profound respect.
>
> "Bœhmer and Bossange."

"Well," said Manoël, on reading this note, "the necklace is ours."

"Not so," said Beausire; "it will only be ours when we have bought it. We must buy it; but remember, your excellency does not know French."

"Yes, I know; but this chancellor?"

"Oh, I will send him away on some diplomatic mission."

"You are wrong; he will be our security with these men."

"But he will say that you know French."

"No, he will not; I will tell him not to do so."

"Very well, then; we will have up the man."

The man was introduced: it was Bœhmer himself, who made many bows and excuses, and offered the necklace for examination.

"Sit down," said Beausire; "his excellency pardons you."

"Oh, how much trouble to sell!" sighed Bœhmer.

"How much trouble to steal!" thought Beausire.

CHAPTER XXIX
THE BARGAIN

Then the ambassador consented to examine the necklace in detail. M. Bœhmer showed each individual beauty.

"On the whole," said Beausire, interpreting for Manoël, "his excellency sees nothing to complain of in the necklace, but there are ten of the diamonds rather spotted."

"Oh!" said Bœhmer.

"His excellency," interrupted Beausire, "understands diamonds perfectly. The Portuguese nobility play with the diamonds of Brazil, as children do here with glass beads."

"Whatever it may be, however," said Bœhmer, "this necklace is the finest collection of diamonds in all Europe."

"That is true," said Manoël.

Then Beausire went on: "Well, M. Bœhmer, her majesty the Queen of Portugal has heard of this necklace, and has given M. de Souza a commission to buy it, if he approved of the diamonds, which he does. Now, what is the price?"

"1,600,000 francs."

Beausire repeated this to the ambassador.

"It is 100,000 francs too much," replied Manoël.

"Monseigneur," replied the jeweler, "one cannot fix the exact price of the diamonds on a thing like this. It has been necessary, in making this collection, to undertake voyages, and make searches and inquiries which no one would believe but myself."

"100,000 francs too dear," repeated Manoël.

"And if his excellency says this," said Beausire, "it must be his firm conviction, for he never bargains."

Bœhmer was shaken. Nothing reassures a suspicious merchant so much as a customer who beats down the price. However, he said, after a minute's thought, "I cannot consent to a deduction which will make all the difference of loss or profit to myself and my partner."

Don Manoël, after hearing this translated, rose, and Beausire returned the case to the jeweler.

"I will, however, speak to M. Bossange about it," contained Bœhmer. "I am to understand that his excellency offers 1,500,000 francs for the necklace."

"Yes, he never draws back from what he has said."

"But, monsieur, you understand that I must consult with my partner."

"Certainly, M. Bœhmer."

"Certainly," repeated Don Manoël, after hearing this translated; "but I must have a speedy answer."

"Well, monseigneur, if my partner will accept the price, I will."

"Good."

"It then only remains, excepting the consent of M. Bossange, to settle the mode of payment."

"There will be no difficulty about that," said Beausire. "How do you wish to be paid?"

"Oh," said Bœhmer, laughing, "if ready money be possible— —"

"What do you call ready money?" said Beausire coldly.

"Oh, I know no one has a million and a half of francs ready to pay down," said Bœhmer, sighing.

"Certainly not."

"Still, I cannot consent to dispense with some ready money."

"That is but reasonable." Then, turning to Manoël: "How much will your excellency pay down to M. Bœhmer?"

"100,000 francs." Beausire repeated this.

"And when the remainder?" asked Bœhmer.

"When we shall have had time to send to Lisbon."

"Oh!" said Bœhmer, "we have a correspondent there, and by writing to him— —"

"Yes," said Beausire, laughing ironically, "write to him, and ask if M. de Souza is solvent, and if her majesty be good for 1,400,000 francs."

"We cannot, sir, let this necklace leave France forever without informing the queen; and our respect and loyalty demand that we should once more give her the refusal of it."

"It is just," said Manoël, with dignity. "I should wish a Portuguese merchant to act in the same way."

"I am very happy that monseigneur approves of my conduct. Then all is settled, subject only to the consent of M. Bossange, and the reiterated refusal of her majesty. I ask three days to settle these two points."

"On one side," said Beausire, "100,000 francs down, the necklace to be placed in my hands, who will accompany you to Lisbon, to the honor of your correspondents, who are also our bankers. The whole of the money to be paid in three months."

"Yes, monseigneur," said Bœhmer, bowing.

Manoël returned it, and the jeweler took leave.

When they were alone, Manoël said angrily to Beausire, "Please to explain what the devil you mean by this journey to Portugal? Are you mad? Why not have the jewels here in exchange for our money?"

"You think yourself too really ambassador," replied Beausire; "you are not yet quite M. de Souza to this jeweler."

"If he had not thought so he would not have treated."

"Agreed; but every man in possession of 1,500,000 francs holds himself above all the ambassadors in the world; and every one who gives that value in exchange for pieces of paper wishes first to know what the papers are worth."

"Then you mean to go to Portugal—you, who cannot speak Portuguese properly? I tell you, you are mad."

"Not at all; you shall go yourself, if you like."

"Thank you," said Don Manoël. "There are reasons why I would rather not return to Portugal."

"Well, I tell you, M. Bœhmer would never give up the diamonds for mere papers."

"Papers signed Souza?"

"I said you thought yourself a real Souza."

"Better say at once that we have failed," said Manoël.

"Not at all. Come here, captain," said Beausire to the valet; "you know what we are talking of?"

"Yes."

"You have listened to everything?"

"Certainly."

"Very well; do you think I have committed a folly?"

"I think you perfectly right."

"Explain why."

"M. Bœhmer would, on the other plan, have been incessantly watching us, and all connected with us. Now, with the money and the diamonds both in his hands, he can have no suspicion, but will set out quietly for Portugal, which, however, he will never reach. Is it not so, M. Beausire?"

"Ah, you are a lad of discernment!"

"Explain your plan," said Manoël.

"About fifty leagues from here," said Beausire, "this clever fellow here will come and present two pistols at the heads of our postilions, will steal from us all we have, including the diamonds, and will leave M. Bœhmer half dead with blows."

"Oh, I did not understand exactly that," said the valet. "I thought you would embark for Portugal."

"And then— —"

"M. Bœhmer, like all Germans, will like the sea, and walk on the deck. One day he may slip and fall over, and the necklace will be supposed to have perished with him."

"Oh, I understand," said Manoël.

"That is lucky at last."

"Only," replied Manoël, "for stealing diamonds one is simply sent to the Bastile, but for murder one is hanged."

"But for stealing diamonds one may be taken; for a little push to M. Bœhmer we should never even be suspected."

"Well, we will settle all this afterwards," said Beausire.

"At present let us conduct our business in style, so that they may say, 'If he was not really ambassador, at least he seemed like one.'"

CHAPTER XXX
THE JOURNALIST'S HOUSE

It was the day after the agreement with M. Bœhmer, and three days after the ball at the Opera. In the Rue Montorgueil, at the end of a courtyard, was a high and narrow house. The ground floor was a kind of shop, and here lived a tolerably well-known journalist. The other stories were occupied by quiet people, who lived there for cheapness. M. Reteau, the journalist, published his paper weekly. It was issued on the day of which we speak; and when M. Reteau rose at eight o'clock, his servant brought him a copy, still wet from the press. He hastened to peruse it, with the care which a tender father bestows on the virtues or failings of his offspring. When he had finished it:

"Aldegonde," said he to the old woman, "this is a capital number; have you read it?"

"Not yet; my soup is not finished."

"It is excellent," repeated the journalist.

"Yes," said she; "but do you know what they say of it in the printing-office?"

"What?"

"That you will certainly be sent to the Bastile."

"Aldegonde," replied Reteau, calmly, "make me a good soup, and do not meddle with literature."

"Always the same," said she, "rash and imprudent."

"I will buy you some buckles with what I make to-day. Have many copies been sold yet?"

"No, and I fear my buckles will be but poor. Do you remember the number against M. de Broglie? We sold one hundred before ten o'clock; therefore this cannot be as good."

"Do you know the difference, Aldegonde? Now, instead of attacking an individual, I attack a body; and instead of a soldier, I attack a queen."

"The queen! Oh, then there is no fear; the numbers will sell, and I shall have my buckles."

"Some one rings," said Reteau.

The old woman ran to the shop, and returned a minute after, triumphant.

"One thousand copies!" said she, "there is an order!"

"In whose name?" asked Reteau, quickly.

"I do not know."

"But I want to know; run and ask."

"Oh, there is plenty of time; they cannot count a thousand copies in a minute."

"Yes, but be quick; ask the servant—is it a servant?"

"It is a porter."

"Well, ask him where he is to take them to."

Aldegonde went, and the man replied that he was to take them to the Rue Neuve St. Gilles, to the house of the Count de Cagliostro.

The journalist jumped with delight, and ran to assist in counting off the numbers.

They were not long gone when there was another ring.

"Perhaps that is for another thousand copies," cried Aldegonde. "As it is against the Austrian, every one will join in the chorus."

"Hush, hush, Aldegonde! do not speak so loud, but go and see who it is."

Aldegonde opened the door to a man, who asked if he could speak to the editor of the paper.

"What do you want to say to him?" asked Aldegonde, rather suspiciously.

The man rattled some money in his pocket, and said:

"I come to pay for the thousand copies sent for by M. le Comte de Cagliostro."

"Oh, come in!"

A young and handsome man, who had advanced just behind him, stopped him as he was about to shut the door, and followed him in.

Aldegonde ran to her master. "Come," said she, "here is the money for the thousand copies."

He went directly, and the man, taking out a small bag, paid down one hundred six-franc pieces.

Reteau counted them and gave a receipt, smiling graciously on the man, and said, "Tell the Count de Cagliostro that I shall always be at his orders, and that I can keep a secret."

"There is no need," replied the man; "M. de Cagliostro is independent. He does not believe in magnetism, and wishes to make people laugh at M. Mesmer—that is all."

"Good!" replied another voice; "we will see if we cannot turn the laugh against M. de Cagliostro;" and M. Reteau, turning, saw before him the young man we mentioned.

His glance was menacing; he had his left hand on the hilt of his sword, and a stick in his right.

"What can I do for you, sir?" said Reteau, trembling.

"You are M. Reteau?" asked the young man.

"Yes, sir."

"Journalist, and author of this article?" said the visitor, drawing the new number from his pocket.

"Not exactly the author, but the publisher," said Reteau.

"Very well, that comes to the same thing; for if you had not the audacity to write it, you have had the baseness to give it publicity. I say baseness, for, as I am a gentleman, I wish to keep within bounds even with you. If I expressed all I think, I should say that he who wrote this article is infamous, and that he who published it is a villain!"

"Monsieur!" said Reteau, growing pale.

"Now listen," continued the young man; "you have received one payment in money, now you shall have another in caning."

"Oh!" cried Reteau, "we will see about that."

"Yes, we will see," said the young man, advancing towards him; but Reteau was used to these sort of affairs, and knew the conveniences of his own house. Turning quickly round, he gained a door which shut after him, and which opened into a passage leading to a gate, through which there was an exit into the Rue Vieux Augustins. Once there, he was safe; for in this gate the key was always left, and he could lock it behind him.

But this day was an unlucky one for the poor journalist, for, just as he was about to turn the key, he saw coming towards him another young man, who, in his agitation, appeared to him like a perfect Hercules. He would have retreated, but he was now between two fires, as his first opponent had by this time discovered him, and was advancing upon him.

"Monsieur, let me pass, if you please," said Reteau to the young man who guarded the gate.

"Monsieur," cried the one who followed him, "stop the fellow, I beg!"

"Do not be afraid, M. de Charny; he shall not pass."

"M. de Taverney!" cried Charny; for it was really he who was the first comer.

Both these young men, on reading the article that morning, had conceived the same idea, because they were animated with the same sentiments, and, unknown to each other, had hastened to put it in practise. Each, however, felt a kind of displeasure at seeing the other, divining a rival in the man who had the same idea as himself. Thus it was that with a rather disturbed manner Charny had called out, "You, M. de Taverney!"

"Even so," replied the other, in the same way; "but it seems I am come too late, and can only look on, unless you will be kind enough to open the gate."

"Oh!" cried Reteau, "do you want to murder me, gentlemen?"

"No," said Charny, "we do not want to murder you; but first we will ask a few questions, then we will see the end. You permit me to speak, M. de Taverney?"

"Certainly, sir; you have the precedence, having arrived first."

Charny bowed; then, turning to Reteau, said:

"You confess, then, that you have published against the queen the playful little tale, as you call it, which appeared this morning in your paper?"

"Monsieur, it is not against the queen."

"Good! it only wanted that."

"You are very patient, sir!" cried Philippe, who was boiling with rage outside the gate.

"Oh, be easy, sir," replied Charny; "he shall lose nothing by waiting."

"Yes," murmured Philippe; "but I also am waiting."

Charny turned again to Reteau. "Etteniotna is Antoinette transposed — oh, do not lie, sir, or instead of beating, or simply killing you, I shall burn you alive! But tell me if you are the sole author of this?"

"I am not an informer," said Reteau.

"Very well; that means that you have an accomplice; and, first, the man who bought a thousand copies of this infamy, the Count de Cagliostro; but he shall pay for his share, when you have paid for yours."

"Monsieur, I do not accuse him," said Reteau, who feared that he should encounter the anger of Cagliostro after he had done with these two.

Charny raised his cane.

"Oh, if I had a sword!" cried Reteau.

"M. Philippe, will you lend your sword to this man?"

"No, M. de Charny, I cannot lend my sword to a man like that; but I will lend you my cane, if yours does not suffice."

"Corbleu! a cane!" cried Reteau. "Do you know that I am a gentleman?"

"Then lend me your sword, M. de Taverney; he shall have mine, and I will never touch it again!" cried Charny.

Philippe unsheathed his sword, and passed it through the railings.

"Now," said Charny, throwing down his sword at the feet of Reteau, "you call yourself a gentleman, and you write such infamies against the Queen of France; pick up that sword, and let us see what kind of a gentleman you are."

But Reteau did not stir; he seemed as afraid of the sword at his feet as he had been of the uplifted cane.

"Morbleu!" cried Philippe, "open the gate to me!"

"Pardon, monsieur," said Charny, "but you acknowledged my right to be first."

"Then be quick, for I am in a hurry to begin."

"I wished to try other methods before resorting to this, for I am not much more fond of inflicting a caning than M. Reteau is of receiving one; but as he prefers it to fighting, he shall be satisfied;" and a cry from Reteau soon announced that Charny had begun.

The noise soon attracted old Aldegonde, who joined her voice to her master's.

Charny minded one no more than the other; at last, however, he stopped, tired with his work.

"Now have you finished, sir?" said Philippe.

"Yes."

"Then pray return me my sword, and let me in."

"Oh, no, monsieur!" implored Reteau, who hoped for a protector in the man who had finished with him.

"I cannot leave monsieur outside the door," said Charny.

"Oh, it is a murder!" cried Reteau. "Kill me right off, and have done with it!"

"Be easy," said Charny; "I do not think monsieur will touch you."

"You are right," said Philippe; "you have been beaten—let it suffice; but there are the remaining numbers, which must be destroyed."

"Oh yes!" cried Charny. "You see, two heads are better than one; I should have forgotten that. But how did you happen to come to this gate, M. de Taverney?"

"I made some inquiries in the neighborhood about this fellow, and hearing that he had this mode of escape, I thought by coming in here, and locking the gate after me, I should cut off his retreat, and make sure of him. The same idea of vengeance struck you, only more in a hurry, you came straight to his house without any inquiries, and he would have escaped you if I had not luckily been here."

"I am rejoiced that you were, M. de Taverney. Now, fellow, lead us to your press."

"It is not here," said Reteau.

"A lie!" said Charny.

"No, no," cried Philippe, "we do not want the press; the numbers are all printed and here, except those sold to M. de Cagliostro."

"Then he shall burn them before our eyes!"

And they pushed Reteau into his shop.

CHAPTER XXXI
HOW TWO FRIENDS BECAME ENEMIES

Aldegonde, however, had gone to fetch the guard; but before she returned they had had time to light a fire with the first numbers, and were throwing them in, one after another, as quickly as possible, when the guard appeared, followed by a crowd of ragged men, women, and boys.

Happily, Philippe and Charny knew Reteau's secret exit, so when they caught sight of the guard they made their escape through it, carrying the key with them.

Then Reteau began crying "Murder!" while Aldegonde, seeing the flames through the window, cried "Fire!"

The soldiers arrived, but finding the young men gone, and the house not on fire, went away again, leaving Reteau to bathe his bruises. But the crowd lingered about all day, hoping to see a renewal of the fun.

When Taverney and Charny found themselves in the Rue Vieux Augustins, "Monsieur," said Charny, "now we have finished that business, can I be of any use to you?"

"Thanks, sir, I was about to ask you the same question."

"Thank you, but I have private business which will probably keep me in Paris all day."

"Permit me, then, to take leave of you; I am happy to have met you."

"And I you, sir;" and the two young men bowed, but it was easy to see that all this courtesy went no further than the lips.

Philippe went towards the boulevards, while Charny turned to the river; each turned two or three times till he thought himself quite out of sight, but after walking for some time Charny entered the Rue Neuve St. Gilles, and there once more found himself face to face with Philippe.

Each had again the same idea of demanding satisfaction from the Count de Cagliostro. They could not now doubt each other's intentions, so Philippe said:

"I left you the seller, leave me the buyer; I left you the cane, leave me the sword."

"Sir," replied Charny, "you left it to me simply because I came first, and for no other reason."

"Well," replied Taverney, "here we arrive both together, and I will make no concession."

"I did not ask you for any, sir; only I will defend my right."

"And that, according to you, M. de Charny, is to make M. de Cagliostro burn his thousand copies."

"Remember, sir, that it was my idea to burn the others."

"Then I will have these torn."

"Monsieur, I am sorry to tell you that I wish to have the first turn with M. de Cagliostro."

"All that I can agree to, sir, is to take our chance. I will throw up a louis, and whoever guesses right shall be first."

"Thanks, sir, but I am not generally lucky, and should probably lose," and he stepped towards the door.

Charny stopped him.

"Stay, sir, we will soon understand each other."

"Well, sir?" answered Philippe, turning back.

"Then, before asking satisfaction of M. de Cagliostro, suppose we take a turn in the Bois de Boulogne: it will be out of our way, but perhaps we can settle our dispute there. One of us will probably be left behind, and the other be uninterrupted."

"Really, monsieur," said Philippe, "you echo my own thoughts—where shall we meet?"

"Well, if my society be not insupportable to you, we need not part. I ordered my carriage to wait for me in the Place Royale, close by here."

"Then you will give me a seat?" said Philippe.

"With the greatest pleasure;" and they walked together to the carriage, and getting in, set off for the Champs Elysées.

First, however, Charny wrote a few words on his tablets, and gave them to the footman to take to his hotel.

In less than half an hour they reached the Bois de Boulogne. The weather was lovely, and the air delightful, although the power of the sun was already felt: the fresh leaves were appearing on the trees, and the violets filled the place with their perfume.

"It is a fine day for our promenade, is it not, M. de Taverney?" said Charny.

"Beautiful, sir."

"You may go," said Charny to his coachman.

"Are you not wrong, sir, to send away your carriage?—one of us may need it."

"No, sir," replied Charny; "in this affair secrecy before everything, and once in the knowledge of a servant, we risk it being talked of all over Paris to-morrow."

"As you please, but do you think the fellow does not know what he came here for? These people know well what brings two gentlemen to the Bois de Boulogne, and even if he did not feel sure now, he will perhaps afterwards see one of us wounded, and will have no doubts left then. Is it not then better to keep him here to take back either who shall need him, than to be left, or leave me here, wounded and alone?"

"You are right, monsieur," replied Charny; and, turning to the coachman, he said, "No, stop, Dauphin; you shall wait here."

Dauphin remained accordingly, and as he perfectly guessed what was coming, he arranged his position, so as to see through the still leafless trees all that passed.

They walked on a little way, then Philippe said, "I think, M. de Charny, this is a good place."

"Excellent, monsieur," said Charny, and added: "Chevalier, if it were any one but you, I would say one word of courtesy, and we were friends again; but to you, coming from America, where they fight so well, I cannot."

"And I, sir, to you, who the other evening gained the admiration of an entire court by a glorious feat of arms, can only say, M. le Comte, do me the honor to draw your sword."

"Monsieur," said Charny, "I believe we have neither of us touched on the real cause of quarrel."

"I do not understand you, comte."

"Oh! you understand me perfectly, sir; and you blush while you deny it."

"Defend yourself," cried Philippe; their swords crossed. Philippe soon perceived that he was superior to his adversary, and therefore became as calm as though he had been only fencing, and was satisfied with defending himself without attacking.

"You spare me, sir," said Charny; "may I ask why?"

Philippe went on as before; Charny grew warm, and wished to provoke him from this sang froid, therefore he said:

"I told you, sir, that we had not touched on the real cause of the quarrel."

Philippe did not reply.

"The true cause," continued Charny, "why you sought a quarrel, for it was you who sought it, was, that you were jealous of me."

Still Philippe remained silent.

"What is your intention?" again said Charny. "Do you wish to tire my arm? that is a calculation unworthy of you. Kill me if you can, but do not dally thus."

"Yes, sir," replied Philippe at last, "your reproach is just; the quarrel did begin with me, and I was wrong."

"That is not the question now. You have your sword in your hand; use it for something more than mere defense."

"Monsieur," said Philippe, "I have the honor to tell you once more I was wrong, and that I apologize."

But Charny was by this time too excited to appreciate the generosity of his adversary. "Oh!" said he, "I understand; you wish to play the magnanimous with me; that is it, is it not, chevalier? You wish to relate to the ladies this evening how you brought me here, and then spared my life."

"Count," said Philippe, "I fear you are losing your senses."

"You wish to kill M. de Cagliostro to please the queen; and, for the same reason, you wish to turn me into ridicule."

"Ah! this is too much," cried Philippe, "and proves to me that you have not as generous a heart as I thought."

"Pierce it then," cried Charny, exposing himself as Philippe made another pass.

The sword glanced along his ribs, and the blood flowed rapidly.

"At last," cried Charny, "I am wounded. Now I may kill you if I can."

"Decidedly," said Philippe, "you are mad. You will not kill me—you will only be disabled without cause, and without profit; for no one will ever know for what you have fought;" and as Charny made another pass, he dexterously sent his sword flying from his hand; then, seizing it, he broke it across his foot. "M. de Charny," said he, "you did not require to prove to me that you were brave; you must therefore detest me very much when you fight with such fury."

Charny did not reply, but grew visibly pale, and then tottered.

Philippe advanced to support him, but he repulsed him, saying, "I can reach my carriage."

"At least take this handkerchief to stop the blood."

"Willingly."

"And my arm, sir; at the least obstacle you met you would fall, and give yourself unnecessary pain."

"The sword has only penetrated the skin. I hope soon to be well."

"So much the better, sir; but I warn you, that you will find it difficult to make me your adversary again."

Charny tried to reply, but the words died on his lips. He staggered, and Philippe had but just time to catch him in his arms, and bear him half fainting to his carriage.

Dauphin, who had seen what had passed, advanced to meet him, and they put Charny in.

"Drive slowly," said Philippe, who then took his way back to Paris, murmuring to himself, with a sigh, "She will pity him."

CHAPTER XXXII
THE HOUSE IN THE RUE ST. GILLES

Philippe jumped into the first coach he saw, and told the man to drive to the Rue St. Gilles, where he stopped at the house of M. de Cagliostro.

A large carriage, with two good horses, was standing in the courtyard; the coachman was asleep, wrapped in a greatcoat of fox-skins, and two footmen walked up and down before the door.

"Does the Count Cagliostro live here?" asked Philippe.

"He is just going out."

"The more reason to be quick, for I wish to speak to him first. Announce the Chevalier Philippe de Taverney;" and he followed the men up-stairs.

"Ask him to walk in," said, from within, a voice at once manly and gentle.

"Excuse me, sir," said the chevalier to a man whom we have already seen, first at the table of M. de Richelieu, then at the exhibition of M. Mesmer, in Oliva's room, and with her at the Opera ball.

"For what, sir?" replied he.

"Because I prevent you from going out."

"You would have needed an excuse had you been much later, for I was waiting for you."

"For me?"

"Yes, I was forewarned of your visit."

"Of my visit?"

"Yes; two hours ago. It is about that time, is it not, since you were coming here before, when an interruption caused you to postpone the execution of your project?"

Philippe began to experience the same strange sensation with which this man inspired every one.

"Sit down, M. de Taverney," continued he; "this armchair was placed for you."

"A truce to pleasantry, sir," said Philippe, in a voice which he vainly tried to render calm.

"I do not jest, sir."

"Then a truce to charlatanism. If you are a sorcerer, I did not come to make trial of your skill; but if you are, so much the better, for you must know what I am come to say to you."

"Oh, yes, you are come to seek a quarrel."

"You know that? perhaps you also know why?"

"On account of the queen. Now, sir, I am ready to listen;" and these last words were no longer pronounced in the courteous tones of a host, but in the hard and dry ones of an adversary.

"Sir, there exists a certain publication."

"There are many publications," said Cagliostro.

"Well, this publication to-day was written against the queen."

Cagliostro did not reply.

"You know what I refer to, count?"

"Yes, sir."

"You have bought one thousand copies of it?"

"I do not deny it."

"Luckily, they have not reached your hands."

"What makes you think so, sir?"

"Because I met the porter, paid him, and sent him with them to my house; and my servant, instructed by me, will destroy them."

"You should always finish yourself the work you commence, sir. Are you sure these thousand copies are at your house?"

"Certainly."

"You deceive yourself, sir; they are here. Ah, you thought that I, sorcerer that I am, would let myself be foiled in that way. You thought it a brilliant idea to buy off my messenger. Well, I have a steward, and you see it is natural for the steward of a sorcerer to be one also. He divined that you would go to the journalist, and that you would meet my messenger, whom he afterwards followed, and threatened to make him give back the gold you had given him, if he did not follow his original instructions, instead of taking them to you. But I see you doubt."

"I do."

"Look, then, and you will believe;" and, opening an oak cabinet, he showed the astonished chevalier the thousand copies lying there.

Philippe approached the count in a menacing attitude, but he did not stir. "Sir," said Philippe, "you appear a man of courage; I call upon you to give me immediate satisfaction."

"Satisfaction for what?"

"For the insult to the queen, of which you render yourself an accomplice while you keep one number of this vile paper."

"Monsieur," said Cagliostro, "you are in error; I like novelties, scandalous reports, and other amusing things, and collect them, that I may remember at a later day what I should otherwise forget."

"A man of honor, sir, does not collect infamies."

"But, if I do not think this an infamy?"

"You will allow at least that it is a lie."

"You deceive yourself, sir. The queen was at M. Mesmer's."

"It is false, sir."

"You mean to tell me I lie?"

"I do."

"Well, I will reply in a few words—I saw her there."

"You saw her!"

"As plainly as I now see you."

Philippe looked full at Cagliostro. "I still say, sir, that you lie."

Cagliostro shrugged his shoulders, as though he were talking to a madman.

"Do you not hear me, sir?" said Philippe.

"Every word."

"And do you not know what giving the lie deserves?"

"Yes, sir; there is a French proverb which says it merits a box on the ears."

"Well, sir, I am astonished that your hand has not been already raised to give it, as you are a French gentleman, and know the proverb."

"Although a French gentleman, I am a man, and love my brother."

"Then you refuse me satisfaction?"

"I only pay what I owe."

"Then you will compel me to take satisfaction in another manner."

"How?"

"I exact that you burn the numbers before my eyes, or I will proceed with you as with the journalist."

"Oh! a beating," said Cagliostro, laughing.

"Neither more nor less, sir. Doubtless you can call your servants."

"Oh, I shall not call my servants; it is my own business. I am stronger than you, and if you approach me with your cane, I shall take you in my arms and throw you across the room, and shall repeat this as often as you repeat your attempt."

"Well, M. Hercules, I accept the challenge," said Philippe, throwing himself furiously upon Cagliostro, who, seizing him round the neck and waist with a grasp of iron, threw him on a pile of cushions, which lay some way off, and then remained standing as coolly as ever.

Philippe rose as pale as death. "Sir," said he, in a hoarse voice, "you are in fact stronger than I am, but your logic is not as strong as your arm; and you forgot, when you treated me thus, that you gave me the right to say, 'Defend yourself, count, or I will kill you.'"

Cagliostro did not move.

"Draw your sword, I tell you, sir, or you are a dead man."

"You are not yet sufficiently near for me to treat you as before, and I will not expose myself to be killed by you, like poor Gilbert."

"Gilbert!" cried Philippe, reeling back. "Did you say Gilbert?"

"Happily you have no gun this time, only a sword."

"Monsieur," cried Philippe, "you have pronounced a name——"

"Which has awakened a terrible echo in your remembrance, has it not? A name that you never thought to hear again, for you were alone with the poor boy, in the grotto of Açores, when you assassinated him."

"Oh!" said Philippe, "will you not draw?"

"If you knew," said Cagliostro, "how easily I could make your sword fly from your hand!"

"With your sword?"

"Yes, with my sword, if I wished."

"Then try."

"No, I have a still surer method."

"For the last time, defend yourself," said Philippe, advancing towards him.

Then the count took from his pocket a little bottle, which he uncorked, and threw the contents in Philippe's face. Scarcely had it touched him, when he reeled, let his sword drop, and fell senseless.

Cagliostro picked him up, put him on a sofa, waited for his senses to return, and then said, "At your age, chevalier, we should have done with follies; cease, therefore, to act like a foolish boy, and listen to me."

Philippe made an effort to shake off the torpor which still held possession of him, and murmured, "Oh, sir, do you call these the weapons of a gentleman?"

Cagliostro shrugged his shoulders. "You repeat forever the same word," he said; "when we of the nobility have opened our mouths wide enough to utter the word gentleman, we think we have said everything. What do you call the weapons of a gentleman? Is it your sword, which served you so badly against me, or is it your gun, which served you so well against Gilbert? What makes some men superior to others? Do you think that it is that high-sounding word gentleman? No; it is first reason, then strength, most of all, science. Well, I have used all these against you. With my reason I braved your insults, with my strength I conquered yours, and with my science I extinguished at once your moral and physical powers. Now I wish to show you that you have committed two faults in coming here with menaces in your mouth. Will you listen to me?"

"You have overpowered me," replied Philippe; "I can scarcely move. You have made yourself master of my muscles and of my mind, and then you ask me if I will listen!"

Then Cagliostro took down from the chimney-piece another little gold phial. "Smell this, chevalier," said he.

Philippe obeyed, and it seemed to him that the cloud which hung over him dispersed. "Oh, I revive!" he cried.

"And you feel free and strong?"

"Yes."

"With your full powers and memory of the past?"

"Yes."

"Then this memory gives me an advantage over you."

"No," said Philippe, "for I acted in defense of a vital and sacred principle."

"What do you mean?"

"I defended the monarchy."

"You defended the monarchy!—you, who went to America to defend a republic. Ah, mon Dieu! be frank; it is not the monarchy you defend."

Philippe colored.

"To love those who disdain you," continued Cagliostro, "who deceive and forget you, is the attribute of great souls. It is the law of the Scriptures to return good for evil. You are a Christian, M. de Taverney."

"Monsieur," cried Philippe, "not a word more; if I did not defend the monarchy, I defended the queen, that is to say, an innocent woman, and to be respected even if she were not so, for it is a divine law not to attack the weak."

"The weak! the queen—you call a feeble being her to whom twenty-eight million human beings bow the knee!"

"Monsieur, they calumniate her."

"How do you know?"

"I believe it."

"Well, I believe the contrary; we have each the right to think as we please."

"But you act like an evil genius."

"Who tells you so?" cried Cagliostro, with sparkling eyes. "How, have you the temerity to assume that you are right, and that I am wrong? You defend royalty; well, I defend the people. You say, render to Cæsar the things which are Cæsar's; and I say, render to God the things that are God's. Republican of America, I recall you to the love of the people, to the love of equality. You trample on the people to kiss the hands of a queen; I would throw down a queen to elevate a people. I do not disturb you in your adoration; leave me in peace at my work. You say to me, die, for you have offended the object of my worship; and I say to you, who combat mine, live, for I feel myself so strong in my principles, that neither you nor any one else can retard my progress for an instant."

"Sir, you frighten me," said Philippe; "you show me the danger in which our monarchy is."

"Then be prudent, and shun the opening gulf."

"You know," replied Philippe, "that I would sooner entomb myself in it, than see those whom I defend in danger."

"Well, I have warned you."

"And I," said Philippe, "I, who am but a feeble individual, will use against you the arms of the weak. I implore you, with tearful eyes and joined hands, to be merciful towards those whom you pursue. I ask you to spare me the remorse of knowing you were acting against this poor queen, and not preventing you. I beg you to destroy this publication, which would make a woman shed tears. I ask you, by the love which you have guessed, or I swear that with this sword, which has proved so powerless against you, I will pierce myself before your eyes!"

"Ah!" murmured Cagliostro, "why are they not all like you? Then I would join them, and they should not perish."

"Monsieur, monsieur, I pray you to reply to me!"

"See, then," said Cagliostro, "if all the thousand numbers be there, and burn them yourself."

Philippe ran to the cabinet, took them out, and threw them on the fire. "Adieu, monsieur!" then he said; "a hundred thanks for the favor you have granted me."

"I owed the brother," said Cagliostro, when he had gone, "some compensation for all I made the sister endure."

Then he called for his carriage.

CHAPTER XXXIII
THE HEAD OF THE TAVERNEY FAMILY

While this was passing in the Rue St. Gilles, the elder M. Taverney was walking in his garden, followed by two footmen, who carried a chair, with which they approached him every five minutes, that he might rest. While doing so, a servant came to announce the chevalier.

"My son," said the old man, "come, Philippe, you arrive àpropos—my heart is full of happy thoughts; but how solemn you look!"

"Do I, sir?"

"You know already the results of that affair?"

"What affair?"

The old man looked to see that no one was listening, then said, "I speak of the ball."

"I do not understand."

"Oh, the ball at the Opera."

Philippe colored.

"Sit down," continued his father; "I want to talk to you. It seems that you, so timid and delicate at first, now compromise her too much."

"Whom do you mean, sir?"

"Pardieu! do you think I am ignorant of your escapade, both together at the Opera ball? It was pretty."

"Sir, I protest——"

"Oh, do not be angry; I only mean to warn you for your good. You are not careful enough; you were seen there with her." "I was seen?"

"Pardieu! had you, or not, a blue domino?"

Philippe was about to explain that he had not, and did not know what his father meant, but he thought to himself, "It is of no use to explain to him; he never believes me. Besides, I wish to learn more."

"You see," continued the old man, triumphantly, "you were recognized. Indeed, M. de Richelieu, who was at the ball in spite of his eighty-four years, wondered who the blue domino could be with whom the queen was walking, and he could only suspect you, for he knew all the others."

"And pray how does he say he recognized the queen?"

"Not very difficult, when she took her mask off. Such audacity as that surpasses all imagination; she must really be mad about you. But take care, chevalier; you have jealous rivals to fear; it is an envied post to be favorite of the queen, when the queen is the real king. Pardon my moralizing, but I do not wish that the breath of chance should blow down what you have reared so skilfully."

Philippe rose; the conversation was hateful to him, but a kind of savage curiosity impelled him to hear everything.

"We are already envied," continued the old man; "that is natural, but we have not yet attained the height to which we shall rise. To you will belong the glory of raising our name; and now you are progressing so well, only be prudent, or you will fail after all. Soon, however, you must ask for some high post, and obtain for me a lord-lieutenancy not too far from Paris. Then you can have a peerage, and become a duke and lieutenant-general. In two years, if I am still alive — —"

"Enough, enough!" groaned Philippe.

"Oh, if you are satisfied with that, I am not. You have a whole life before you; I, perhaps, only a few months. However, I do not complain; God gave me two children, and if my daughter has been useless in repairing our fortunes, you will make up for it. I see in you the great Taverney, and you inspire me with respect, for your conduct has been admirable; you show no jealousy, but leave the field apparently open to every one, while you really hold it alone."

"I do not understand you," replied Philippe.

"Oh, no modesty; it was exactly the conduct of M. Potemkin, who astonished the world with his fortunes. He saw that Catherine loved variety in her amours; that, if left free, she would fly from flower to flower, returning always to the sweetest and most beautiful; but that, if pursued, she would fly right away. He took his part, therefore; he even introduced new favorites to his sovereign, to weary her out with their number; but through and after the quickly succeeding reigns of the twelve Cæsars, as they were ironically called, Potemkin in reality was supreme."

"What incomprehensible infamies!" murmured poor Philippe. But the old man went on:

"According to his system, however, you have been still a little wrong. He never abandoned his surveillance, and you are too lax in this."

Philippe replied only by shrugging his shoulders. He really began to think his father was crazy.

"Ah! you thought I did not see your game. You are already providing a successor, for you have divined that there is no stability in the queen's amours, and in the event of her changing, you wish not to be quite thrown aside; therefore you make friends with M. de Charny, who might otherwise, when his turn comes, exile you, as you now might MM. de Coigny, Vaudreuil, and others."

Philippe, with an angry flush, said:

"Once more, enough; I am ashamed to have listened so long. Those who say that the Queen of France is a Messalina are criminal calumniators."

"I tell you," said the old man, "no one can hear, and I approve your plan. M. de Charny will repay your kindness some day."

"Your logic is admirable, sir; and M. de Charny is so much my favorite that I have just passed my sword through his ribs."

"What!" cried the old man, somewhat frightened at his son's flashing eyes, "you have not been fighting?"

"Yes, sir; that is my method of conciliating my successors. And he turned to go away.

"Philippe, you jest."

"I do not, sir."

The old man rose, and tottered off to the house.

"Quick," said he to the servant; "let a man on horseback go at once and ask after M. de Charny, who has been wounded, and let him be sure to say he comes from me." Then he murmured to himself, "Mine is still the only head in the family."

CHAPTER XXXIV
THE STANZAS OF M. DE PROVENCE

While these events were passing in Paris and in Versailles, the king, tranquil as usual, sat in his study, surrounded by maps and plans, and traced new paths for the vessels of La Pérouse.

A slight knock at his door roused him from his study, and a voice said, "May I come in, brother?"

"The Comte de Provence," growled the king, discontentedly. "Enter."

A short person came in.

"You did not expect me, brother?" he said.

"No, indeed."

"Do I disturb you?"

"Have you anything particular to say?"

"Such a strange report——"

"Oh, some scandal?"

"Yes, brother."

"Which has amused you?"

"Because it is so strange."

"Something against me?"

"Should I laugh if it were?"

"Then against the queen?"

"Sire, imagine that I was told quite seriously that the queen slept out the other night."

"That would be very sad if it were true," replied the king.

"But it is not true, is it?"

"No."

"Nor that the queen was seen waiting outside the gate at the reservoirs?"

"No."

"The day, you know, that you ordered the gates to be shut at eleven o'clock?"

"I do not remember."

"Well, brother, they pretend that the queen was seen arm-in-arm with M. d'Artois at half-past twelve that night."

"Where?"

"Going to a house which he possesses behind the stables. Has not your majesty heard this report?"

"Yes, you took care of that."

"How, sire?—what have I done?"

"Some verses which were printed in the *Mercury*."

"Some verses!" said the count, growing red.

"Oh, yes; you are a favorite of the Muses."

"Not I, sire."

"Oh, do not deny it; I have the manuscript in your writing! Now, if you had informed yourself of what the queen really did that day, instead of writing these lines against her, and consequently against me, you would have written an ode in her favor. Perhaps the subject does not inspire you; but I should have liked a bad ode better than a good satire."

"Sire, you overwhelm me; but I trust you will believe I was deceived, and did not mean harm."

"Perhaps."

"Besides, I did not say I believed it; and then, a few verses are nothing. Now, a pamphlet like one I have just seen——"

"A pamphlet?"

"Yes, sire; and I want an order for the Bastile for the author of it."

The king rose. "Let me see it," he said.

"I do not know if I ought."

"Certainly you ought. Have you got it with you?"

"Yes, sire;" and he drew from his pocket "The History of the Queen Etteniotna," one of the fatal numbers which had escaped from Philippe and Charny.

The king glanced over it rapidly. "Infamous!" he cried.

"You see, sire, they pretend the queen went to M. Mesmer's."

"Well, she did go."

"She went?"

"Authorized by me."

"Oh, sire!"

"That is nothing against her; I gave my consent."

"Did your majesty intend that she should experimentalize on herself?"

The king stamped with rage as the count said this; he was reading one of the most insulting passages—the history of her contortions, voluptuous disorder, and the attention she had excited.

"Impossible!" he cried, growing pale; and he rang the bell. "Oh, the police shall deal with this! Fetch M. de Crosne."

"Sire, it is his day for coming here, and he is now waiting."

"Let him come in."

"Shall I go, brother?" said the count.

"No; remain. If the queen be guilty, you are one of the family, and must know it; if innocent, you, who have suspected her, must hear it."

M. de Crosne entered, and bowed, saying, "The report is ready, sire."

"First, sir," said the king, "explain how you allow such infamous publications against the queen."

"Etteniotna?" asked M. de Crosne.

"Yes."

"Well, sire, it is a man called Reteau."

"You know his name, and have not arrested him!"

"Sire, nothing is more easy. I have an order already prepared in my portfolio."

"Then why is it not done?"

M. de Crosne looked at the count.

"I see, M. de Crosne wishes me to leave," said he.

"No," replied the king, "remain. And you, M. de Crosne, speak freely."

"Well, sire, I wished first to consult your majesty whether you would not rather give him some money, and send him away to be hanged elsewhere."

"Why?"

"Because, sire, if these men tell lies, the people are glad enough to see them whipped, or even hanged; but if they chance upon a truth— —"

"A truth! It is true that the queen went to M. Mesmer's, but I gave her permission."

"Oh, sire!" cried M. de Crosne.

His tone of sincerity struck the king more than anything M. de Provence had said; and he answered, "I suppose, sir, that was no harm."

"No, sire; but her majesty has compromised herself."

"M. de Crosne, what have your police told you?"

"Sire, many things, which, with all possible respect for her majesty, agree in many points with this pamphlet."

"Let me hear."

"That the queen went in a common dress, in the middle of this crowd, and alone."

"Alone!" cried the king.

"Yes, sire."

"You are deceived, M. de Crosne."

"I do not think so, sire."

"You have bad reporters, sir."

"So exact, that I can give your majesty a description of her dress, of all her movements, of her cries— —"

"Her cries!"

"Even her sighs were observed, sire."

"It is impossible she could have so far forgotten what is due to me and to herself."

"Oh, yes," said the Comte de Provence; "her majesty is surely incapable— —"

Louis XVI. interrupted him. "Sir," said he, to M. de Crosne, "you maintain what you have said?"

"Unhappily, yes, sire."

"I will examine into it further," said the king, passing his handkerchief over his forehead, on which the drops hung from anxiety and vexation. "I did permit the queen to go, but I ordered her to take with her a person safe, irreproachable, and even holy."

"Ah," said M. de Crosne, "if she had but done so——"

"Yes," said the count; "if a lady like Madame de Lamballe for instance——"

"It was precisely she whom the queen promised to take."

"Unhappily, sire, she did not do so."

"Well," said the king, with agitation; "if she has disobeyed me so openly I ought to punish, and I will punish; only some doubts still remain on my mind; these doubts you do not share; that is natural; you are not the king, husband, and friend of her whom they accuse. However, I will proceed to clear the affair up." He rang. "Let some one see," said he to the person who came, "where Madame de Lamballe is."

"Sire, she is walking in the garden with her majesty and another lady."

"Beg her to come to me. Now, gentlemen, in ten minutes we shall know the truth."

All were silent.

M. de Crosne was really sad, and the count put on an affectation of it which might have solemnized Momus himself.

CHAPTER XXXV
THE PRINCESS DE LAMBALLE

The Princesse de Lamballe entered beautiful and calm. Her hair drawn back from her noble forehead, her dark penciled eyebrows, her clear blue eyes and beautiful lips, and her unrivaled figure, formed a lovely tout ensemble. She seemed always surrounded by an atmosphere of virtue and grace.

The king looked at her with a troubled expression, dreading what he was about to hear; then bowing, said, "Sit down, princess."

"What does your majesty desire?" asked she, in a sweet voice.

"Some information, princess: what day did you last go with the queen to Paris?"

"Wednesday, sire."

"Pardon me, cousin," said Louis XVI.; "but I wish to know the exact truth."

"You will never hear anything else from me, sire."

"What did you go there for?"

"I went to M. Mesmer's, Place Vendôme."

The two witnesses trembled. The king colored with delight.

"Alone?" asked the king.

"No, sire; with the queen."

"With the queen?" cried Louis, seizing her hand.

"Yes, sire."

M. de Provence and M. de Crosne looked stupefied.

"Your majesty had authorized the queen to go; at least, so she told me," continued the princess.

"It was true, cousin: gentlemen, I breathe again; Madame de Lamballe never tells a falsehood."

"Never, sire."

"Oh, never, sire," said M. de Crosne, with perfect sincerity. "But will you permit me, sire?"

"Certainly, monsieur; question, search as much as you please; I place the princess at your disposal."

Madame de Lamballe smiled. "I am ready," she said.

"Madame," said the lieutenant of police, "have the goodness to tell his majesty what you did there, and how the queen was dressed."

"She had on a dress of gray taffeta, a mantle of embroidered muslin, an ermine muff, and a rose-colored velvet bonnet, trimmed with black."

M. de Crosne looked astonished. It was a totally different dress from that which he had had described to him. The Comte de Provence bit his lips with vexation, and the king rubbed his hands.

"What did you do on entering?" asked he.

"Sire, you are right to say on entering, for we had hardly entered the room— —"

"Together?"

"Yes, sire; and we could scarcely have been seen, for every one was occupied with the experiments going on, when a lady approached the queen, and, offering her a mask, implored her to turn back."

"And you stopped?"

"Yes, sire."

"You never went through the rooms?" asked M. de Crosne.

"No, monsieur."

"And you never quitted the queen?" asked the king.

"Not for a moment, sire. Her majesty never left my arm."

"Now!" cried the king, "what do you say, M. de Crosne? and you, brother?"

"It is extraordinary, quite supernatural," said the count, who affected a gaiety which could not conceal his disappointment.

"There is nothing supernatural," said M. de Crosne, who felt real remorse: "what Madame de Lamballe says is undoubtedly true; therefore my informants must have been mistaken."

"Do you speak seriously, sir?" asked the count.

"Perfectly, monseigneur. Her majesty did what Madame de Lamballe states, and nothing more, I feel convinced; my agents were, somehow or other, deceived. As for this journalist, I will immediately send the order for his imprisonment."

Madame de Lamballe looked from one to the other with an expression of innocent curiosity.

"One moment," said the king; "you spoke of a lady who came to stop you; tell us who she was?"

"Her majesty seemed to know her, sire."

"Because, cousin, I must speak to this person; then we shall learn the key to this mystery."

"That is my opinion also, sire," said M. de Crosne.

"Did the queen tell you that she knew this person?" said the count.

"She told me so, monseigneur."

"My brother means to say that you probably know her name."

"Madame de la Motte Valois."

"That intriguer!" cried the king.

"Diable!" said the count; "she will be difficult to interrogate: she is cunning."

"We will be as cunning as she," said M. de Crosne.

"I do not like such people about the queen," said Louis; "she is so good that all the beggars crowd round her."

"Madame de la Motte is a true Valois," said the princess.

"However that may be, I will not see her here. I prefer depriving myself of the pleasure of hearing the queen's innocence confirmed, to doing that."

"But you must see her, sire," said the queen, entering at that moment, pale with anger, beautiful with a noble indignation. "It is not now for you to say, 'I do, or I do not wish to see her.' She is a witness from whom the intelligence of my accusers," said she, looking at her brother-in-law, "and the justice of my judges," turning to the king and M. de Crosne, "must draw the truth. I, the accused, demand that she be heard."

"Madame," said the king, "we will not do Madame de la Motte the honor of sending for her to give evidence either for or against you. I cannot stake your honor against the veracity of this woman."

"You need not send for her, she is here."

"Here!" cried the king.

"Sire, you know I went to see her one day; that day of which so many things were said," and she looked again at the Comte de Provence, who felt ready to sink through the ground; "and I then dropped at her house a box, containing a portrait, which she was to return to me to-day, and she is here."

"No, no," said the king; "I am satisfied, and do not wish to see her."

"But I am not satisfied, and shall bring her in. Besides, why this repugnance? What has she done? If there be anything, tell me; you, M. de Crosne? you know everything."

"I know nothing against this lady," replied he.

"Really?"

"Certainly not; she is poor, and perhaps ambitious, but that is all."

"If there be no more than that against her, the king can surely admit her."

"I do not know why," said Louis; "but I have a presentiment that this woman will be the cause of misfortune to me."

"Oh! sire, that is superstition; pray fetch her, Madame de Lamballe."

Five minutes after, Jeanne, with a timid air, although with a distinguished appearance, entered the room.

Louis XVI., strong in his antipathies, had turned his back towards her, and was leaning his head on his hands, seeming to take no longer a part in the conversation. The Comte de Provence cast on her a look which, had her modesty been real, would have increased her confusion; but it required much more than that to trouble Jeanne.

"Madame," said the queen, "have the goodness to tell the king exactly what passed the other day at M. Mesmer's."

Jeanne did not speak.

"It requires no consideration," continued the queen; "we want nothing but the simple truth."

Jeanne understood immediately that the queen had need of her, and knew that she could clear her in a moment by speaking the simple truth; but she felt inclined to keep her secret.

"Sire," said she, "I went to see M. Mesmer from curiosity, like the rest of the world. The spectacle appeared to me rather a coarse one; I turned and suddenly saw her majesty entering, whom I had already had the honor of seeing, but without knowing her till her generosity revealed her rank. It seemed to me that her majesty was out of place in this room, where much suffering and many ridiculous exhibitions were going on. I beg pardon for having taken it on myself to judge; it was a woman's instinct, but I humbly beg pardon if I passed the bounds of proper respect." She seemed overcome with emotion as she concluded.

Every one but the king was pleased.

Madame de Lamballe thought her conduct delicate, and herself timid, intelligent, and good.

The queen thanked her by a look.

"Well," she said, "you have heard, sire."

He did not move, but said, "I did not need her testimony."

"I was told to speak," said Jeanne timidly, "and I obeyed."

"It is enough," answered he; "when the queen says a thing she needs no witnesses to confirm her; and when she has my approbation, and she has it, she need care for that of no one else."

He cast an overwhelming look on his brother, and kissing the hands of the queen and the princess, and begging pardon of the latter for having disturbed her for nothing, made a very slight bow to Jeanne.

The ladies then left the room.

"Brother," said Louis to the count, "now I will detain you no longer; I have work to do with M. de Crosne. You have heard your sister's complete justification, and it is easy to see you are as pleased as myself. Pray sit down, M. de Crosne."

CHAPTER XXXVI
THE QUEEN

The queen, after leaving the king, felt deeply the danger she had been so nearly incurring. She was therefore pleased with Jeanne, who had been the means of preventing it, and said to her, with a gracious smile:

"It is really fortunate, madame, that you prevented my prolonging my stay at M. Mesmer's, for only think, they have taken advantage of my being there to say that I was under the influence of the magnetism."

"But," said Madame de Lamballe, "it is very strange that the police should have been so deceived, and have affirmed that they saw the queen in the inner room."

"It is strange," said the queen; "and M. de Crosne is an honest man, and would not willingly injure me; but his agents may have been bought. I have enemies, dear Lamballe. Still there must have been some foundation for this tale. This infamous libel represents me as intoxicated, and overcome to such a degree by the magnetic fluid, that I lost all control over myself, and all womanly reserve. Did any such scene take place, Madame la Comtesse? Was there any one who behaved like this?"

Jeanne colored; the secret once told, she lost all the fatal influence which she could now exercise over the queen's destiny; therefore she again resolved to keep silent on this point.

"Madame," said she, "there was a woman much agitated who attracted great attention by her contortions and cries."

"Probably some actress or loose character."

"Possibly, madame."

"Countess, you replied very well to the king, and I will not forget you. How have you advanced in your own affairs?"

At this moment Madame de Misery came in, to say that Mademoiselle de Taverney wished to know if her majesty would receive her.

"Assuredly," said the queen. "How ceremonious you always are, Andrée; why do you stand so much upon etiquette?"

"Your majesty is too good to me."

Madame de Lamballe now availed herself of Andrée's entrance to take leave.

"Well, Andrée," the queen then said, "here is this lady whom we went to see the other day."

"I recognize madame," said Andrée, bowing.

"Do you know what they have been saying of me?"

"Yes, madame; M. de Provence has been repeating the story."

"Oh! no doubt; therefore we will leave that subject. Countess, we were speaking of you—who protects you now?"

"You, madame," replied Jeanne, boldly, "since you permit me to come and kiss your hand. Few people," she continued, "dared to protect me when I was in obscurity; now that I have been seen with your majesty, every one will be anxious to do so."

"Then," said the queen, "no one has been either brave enough or corrupt enough to protect you for yourself?"

"I had first Madame de Boulainvilliers, a brave protector; then her husband, a corrupt one; but since my marriage no one. Oh yes, I forget one brave man—a generous prince."

"Prince, countess! who is it?"

"Monsieur the Cardinal de Rohan."

"My enemy," said the queen, smiling.

"Your enemy! Oh, madame!"

"It seems you are astonished that a queen should have an enemy. It is evident you have not lived at court."

"But, madame, he adores you. The devotion of the cardinal equals his respect for you."

"Oh, doubtless," said the queen, with a hearty laugh; "that is why he is my enemy."

Jeanne looked surprised.

"And you are his protégée," continued the queen; "tell me all about it."

"It is very simple; his eminence has assisted me in the most generous, yet the most considerate, manner."

"Good; Prince Louis is generous; no one can deny that. But do you not think, Andrée, that M. le Cardinal also adores this pretty countess a little?

Come, countess, tell us." And Marie Antoinette laughed again in her frank, joyous manner.

"All this gaiety must be put on," thought Jeanne. So she answered, in a grave tone, "Madame, I have the honor to affirm to your majesty that M. de Rohan— —"

"Well, since you are his friend, ask him what he did with some hair of mine which he bribed a certain hair-dresser to steal; and which trick cost the poor man dear, for he lost my custom."

"Your majesty surprises me; M. de Rohan did that?"

"Oh, yes; all his adoration, you know. After having hated me at Vienna, and having employed every means to try and prevent my marriage, he at last began to perceive that I was a woman, and his queen, and that he had offended me forever. Then this dear prince began to fear for his future, and, like all of his profession, who seem most fond of those whom they most fear, and as he knew me young and believed me foolish and vain, he turned—he became a professed admirer, and began with sighs and glances. He adores me, does he not, Andrée?"

"Madame!"

"Oh! Andrée will not compromise herself, but I say what I please; at least I may have that advantage from being a queen. So it is a settled thing that the cardinal adores me, and you may tell him, countess, that he has my permission."

Jeanne, instead of seeing in all this only the angry disdain of a noble character, which she was incapable of appreciating, thought it all pique against M. de Rohan, hiding another feeling for him, and therefore began to defend him with all her eloquence.

The queen listened.

"Good! she listens," thought Jeanne, and did not again understand that she listened through generosity, and through pleasure at anything so novel as to hear any person defend one of whom the sovereign chose to speak ill, and felt pleased with her, thinking she saw a heart where none was placed.

All at once a joyous voice was heard near, and the queen said, "Here is the Comte d'Artois."

When he entered, the queen introduced the countess to him.

"Pray do not let me send you away, Madame la Comtesse," said he, as Jeanne made a move to depart.

The queen also requested her to stay. "You have returned from the wolf-hunt, then?" she said.

"Yes, sister, and have had good sport; I have killed seven. I am not sure," continued he, laughing, "but they say so. However, do you know I have gained seven hundred francs?"

"How?"

"Why, they pay a hundred francs a head for these beasts. It is dear, but I would give two hundred of them just now for the head of a certain journalist."

"Ah! you know the story?"

"M. de Provence told me."

"He is indefatigable. But tell me how he related it."

"So as to make you whiter than snow, or Venus Aphroditus. It seems you came out of it gloriously; you are fortunate."

"Oh, you call that fortunate. Do you hear him, Andrée?"

"Yes, for you might have gone alone, without Madame de Lamballe; and you might not have had Madame de la Motte there to stop your entrance."

"Ah! you know that too?"

"Oh yes; the count told everything. Then you might not have had Madame de la Motte at hand to give her testimony. You will tell me, doubtless, that virtue and innocence are like the violet which does not require to be seen in order to be recognized; but still I say you are fortunate."

"Badly proved."

"I will prove it still better. Saved so well from the unlucky scrape of the cabriolet, saved from this affair, and then the ball," whispered he in her ear.

"What ball?"

"The ball at the Opera."

"What do you mean?"

"I mean the ball at the Opera; but I beg pardon, I should not have mentioned it."

"Really, brother, you puzzle me; I know nothing about the ball at the Opera."

The words "ball" and "Opera" caught Jeanne's ear, and she listened intently.

"I am dumb," said the prince.

"But, count, I insist on knowing what it means."

"Oh, pray allow me to let it drop."

"Do you want to disoblige me?"

"No, sister; but I have said quite enough for you to understand."

"You have told me nothing."

"Oh, sister, it is needless with me."

"But really I am in earnest."

"You wish me to speak?"

"Immediately."

"Not here," said he, looking at the others.

"Yes, here; there cannot be too many at such an explanation."

"Then you mean to say you were not at the last ball?"

"I!" cried the queen, "at the ball at the Opera?"

"Hush, I beg."

"No, I will not hush; I will speak it aloud. You say I was at the ball?"

"Certainly I do."

"Perhaps you saw me?" she said ironically.

"Yes, I did."

"Me?"

"Yes, you."

"Oh, it is too much! Why did you not speak to me?"

"Ma foi! I was just going to do so, when the crowd separated us."

"You are mad!"

"I should not have spoken of it. I have been very foolish."

The queen rose, and walked up and down the room in great agitation.

Andrée trembled with fear and disquietude, and Jeanne could hardly keep from laughing.

Then the queen stopped, and said:

"My friend, do not jest any more; you see, I am so passionate that I have lost my temper already. Tell me at once that you were joking with me."

"I will, if you please, sister."

"Be serious, Charles. You have invented all this, have you not?"

He winked at the ladies, and said, "Oh, yes, of course."

"You do not understand me, brother!" cried the queen vehemently. "Say yes or no. Do not tell falsehoods; I only want the truth!"

"Well, then, sister," said he, in a low voice, "I have told the truth, but I am sorry I spoke."

"You saw me there?"

"As plain as I see you now; and you saw me."

The queen uttered a cry, and, running up to Andrée and Jeanne, cried, "Ladies, M. le Comte d'Artois affirms that he saw me at the ball at the Opera; let him prove it."

"Well," said he, "I was with M. de Richelieu and others, when your mask fell off."

"My mask!"

"I was about to say, 'This is too rash, sister,' but the gentleman with you drew you away so quickly."

"Oh, mon Dieu! you will drive me mad! What gentleman?"

"The blue domino."

The queen passed her hand over her eyes.

"What day was this?" she asked.

"Saturday. The next day I set off to hunt, before you were up."

"What time do you say you saw me?"

"Between two and three."

"Decidedly one of us is mad!"

"Oh, it is I. It is all a mistake. Do not be so afraid; there is no harm done. At first I thought you were with the king; but the blue domino spoke German, and he does not."

"Well, brother, on Saturday I went to bed at eleven."

The count bowed, with an incredulous smile.

The queen rang. "Madame de Misery shall tell you."

"Why do you not call Laurent also?" said he, laughing.

"Oh!" cried the queen in a rage, "not to be believed!"

"My dear sister, if I believed you, others would not."

"What others?"

"Those who saw you as well as myself."

"Who were they?"

"M. Philippe de Taverney, for instance."

"My brother?" cried Andrée.

"Yes; shall we ask him?"

"Immediately."

"Mon Dieu!" murmured Andrée, "my brother a witness!"

"Yes; I wish it;" and she went to seek him at his father's.

He was just leaving, after the scene we have described with his father, when the messenger met him. He came quickly, and Marie Antoinette turned to him at once.

"Sir," said she, "are you capable of speaking the truth?"

"Incapable of anything else, madame."

"Well, then, say frankly, have you seen me at any public place within the last week?"

"Yes, madame."

All hearts beat so that you might have heard them.

"Where?" said the queen, in a terrible voice.

Philippe was silent.

"Oh, no concealment, sir! My brother says you saw me at the ball of the Opera."

"I did, madame."

The queen sank on a sofa; then, rising furiously, she said:

"It is impossible, for I was not there! Take care, M. de Taverney!"

"Your majesty," said Andrée, pale with anger, "if my brother says he saw you, he did see you."

"You also!" cried Marie Antoinette; "it only remains now for you to have seen me. Pardieu! my enemies overwhelm me."

"When I saw that the blue domino was not the king," said the Comte d'Artois, "I believed him to be that nephew of M. de Suffren whom you received so well here the other night."

The queen colored.

"Did it not look something like his tournure, M. de Taverney?" continued the count.

"I did not remark, monseigneur," said he, in a choking voice.

"But I soon found out that it was not he; for suddenly I saw him before me, and he was close by you when your mask fell off."

"So he saw me too?"

"If he were not blind, he did."

The queen rang.

"What are you about to do?"

"Send for him also, and ask. I will drain this cup to the dregs!"

"I do not think he can come," said Philippe.

"Why?"

"Because I believe he is not well."

"Oh, he must come, monsieur! I am not well either, but I would go to the end of the world barefoot to prove——"

All at once Andrée, who was near the window, uttered an exclamation.

"What is it?" cried the queen.

"Oh, nothing; only here comes M. de Charny."

The queen, in her excitement, ran to the window, opened it, and cried, "M. de Charny!"

He, full of astonishment, hastened to enter.

CHAPTER XXXVII
AN ALIBI

M. de Charny entered, a little pale, but upright, and not apparently suffering.

"Take care, sister," said the Comte d'Artois; "what is the use of asking so many people?"

"Brother, I will ask the whole world, till I meet some one who will tell you you are deceived."

Charny and Philippe bowed courteously to each other, and Philippe said in a low voice, "You are surely mad to come out wounded; one would say you wished to die."

"One does not die from the scratch of a thorn in the Bois de Boulogne," replied Charny.

The queen approached, and put an end to this conversation. "M. de Charny," said she, "these gentlemen say that you were at the ball at the Opera?"

"Yes, your majesty."

"Tell us what you saw there."

"Does your majesty mean whom I saw there?"

"Precisely; and no complaisant reserve, M. de Charny."

"Must I say, madame?"

The cheeks of the queen assumed once more that deadly paleness, which had many times that morning alternated with a burning red.

"Did you see me?" she asked.

"Yes, your majesty, at the moment when your mask unhappily fell off."

Marie Antoinette clasped her hands.

"Monsieur," said she, almost sobbing, "look at me well; are you sure of what you say?"

"Madame, your features are engraved in the hearts of your subjects; to see your majesty once is to see you forever."

"But, monsieur," said she, "I assure you I was not at the ball at the Opera."

"Oh, madame," said the young man, bowing low, "has not your majesty the right to go where you please?"

"I do not ask you to find excuses for me; I only ask you to believe."

"I will believe all your majesty wishes me to believe," cried he.

"Sister, sister, it is too much," murmured the count.

"No one believes me!" cried she, throwing herself on the sofa, with tears in her eyes.

"Sister, pardon me," said the count tenderly, "you are surrounded by devoted friends; this secret, which terrifies you so, we alone know. It is confined to our hearts, and no one shall drag it from us while we have life."

"This secret! oh, I want nothing but to prove the truth."

"Madame," said Andrée, "some one approaches."

The king was announced.

"The king! oh, so much the better. He is my only friend; he would not believe me guilty even if he thought he saw me."

The king entered with an air of calmness, in strange contrast to the disturbed countenances of those present.

"Sire," said the queen, "you come àpropos; there is yet another calumny, another insult to combat."

"What is it?" said Louis, advancing.

"An infamous report. Aid me, sire, for now it is no longer my enemies that accuse me, but my friends."

"Your friends!"

"Yes, sire; M. le Comte d'Artois, M. de Taverney, and M. de Charny affirm that they saw me at the ball at the Opera."

"At the ball at the Opera!" cried the king.

A terrible silence ensued.

Madame de la Motte saw the mortal paleness of the queen, the terrible disquietude of the king and of all the others, and with one word she could have put an end to all this, and saved the queen, not only now, but in the future, from much distress. But she said to herself that it was too late; that they would see, if she spoke now, that she had deceived them before when the simple truth would have been of such advantage to the queen, and she should forfeit her newly-acquired favor. So she remained silent.

The king repeated, with an air of anguish, "At the ball at the Opera! Does M. de Provence know this?"

"But, sire, it is not true. M. le Comte d'Artois is deceived; M. de Taverney is deceived; M. de Charny, you are deceived, one may be mistaken."

All bowed.

"Come," continued she, "call all my people, ask every one. You say it was Saturday?"

"Yes, sister."

"Well, what did I do on Saturday? Let some one tell me, for I think I am going mad, and shall begin at last to believe that I did go to this infamous ball. But, gentlemen, if I had been there I would have confessed it."

At this moment the king approached her, every cloud gone from his brow. "Well, Marie," said he, "if it was Saturday, there is no need to call your women, or only to ask them at what hour I came to your room. I believe it was past eleven."

"Oh!" cried the queen, joyfully, "you are right, sire." And she threw herself into his arms; then, blushing and confused, she hid her face on his shoulder, while he kissed her tenderly.

"Well," said the Comte d'Artois, full of both surprise and joy, "I will certainly buy spectacles. But on my word, I would not have lost this scene for a million of money. Would you, gentlemen?"

Philippe was leaning against the wainscot as pale as death. Charny wiped the burning drops from his forehead.

"Therefore, gentlemen," said the king, turning towards them, "I know it to be impossible that the queen was that night at the ball at the Opera. Believe it or not, as you please. The queen I am sure is content that I know her to be innocent."

"Well," said M. d'Artois, "Provence may say what he pleases, but I defy his wife to prove an alibi in the same way, if she should be accused of passing the night out."

"Charles!"

"Pardon, sire, now I will take my leave."

"Well, I will go with you." And once more kissing the queen's hand, they left the room.

"M. de Taverney," said the queen severely, when they were gone, "do you not accompany M. d'Artois?"

Philippe started, all the blood rushed to his head, and he had hardly strength to bow and leave the room.

Andrée was to be pitied also. She knew that Philippe would have given the world to have taken M. de Charny away with him, but she felt as though she could not follow to comfort him, leaving Charny alone with the queen, or only with Madame de la Motte, who, she instinctively felt, was worse than no one. But why this feeling? She could not love Charny; that, she told herself, was impossible. So slight and recent an acquaintance, and she who had vowed to love no one. Why then did she suffer so much when Charny addressed words of such respectful devotion to the queen? Was not this jealousy? "Yes," she thought, but only jealousy that this woman should draw all hearts towards her, while the whole world of gallantry and love passed her coldly by. It was no attraction to be a living problem, ever cold and reserved like Andrée; they felt it, turned from her beauty and her intellect, and contented themselves with mere politeness. Andrée felt this deeply; but on the night when they first met Charny, he showed towards her nothing of this coldness or reserve; she was to him as interesting as any other beautiful woman, and she felt cheered and warmed by it. But now the queen absorbed his every look and thought, and left her lonely again; therefore she did not follow her brother, although she suffered in his sufferings, and almost idolized him. She did not, however, attempt to mingle in the conversation, but sat down by the fire almost with her back to the queen and Charny, while Madame de la Motte stood in one of the deep windows, nearly out of sight, although she could observe all that passed.

The Queen remained silent for some minutes, then she said, almost to herself, "Would any one believe that such things pass here?" Then, turning to Charny, said, "We hear, sir, of the dangers of the sea and of the fury of tempests, but you have doubtless encountered all their assaults, and you are still safe and honored."

"Madame——"

"Then the English, our enemies, have attacked you with their guns and their power, but still you are safe; and on account of the enemies you have conquered, the king felicitates and admires you, and the people bless and love you; therefore, blessed are such enemies who menace us only with death. Our enemies do not endanger existence, it is true, but they add years to our lives; they make us bow the head, fearing, though innocent, to meet, as I have done, the double attacks of friends and enemies. And then, sir, if you knew how hard it is to be hated!"

Andrée listened anxiously for his reply, but he only leaned against the wall, and grew pale.

The queen looked at him, and said, "It is too hot here; Madame de la Motte, open the window; monsieur is accustomed to the fresh sea-breezes; he would stifle in our boudoirs."

"It is not that, madame; but I am on duty at two o'clock, and unless your majesty wishes me to remain— —"

"Oh! no, monsieur; we know what duty is. You are free," said the queen, in a tone of slight pique.

Charny bowed, and disappeared like a man in haste; but in a minute they heard from the ante-chamber the sound of a groan, and people hurrying forward. The queen, who was near the door, opened it, and uttered an exclamation; and was going out, when Andrée rose quickly, saying, "Oh no! madame."

Then they saw through the open door the guards assisting M. de Charny, who had fainted. The queen closed the door, and sat down again, pensive and thoughtful. At last, she said, "It is an odd thing, but I do not believe M. de Charny was convinced!"

"Oh, madame! in spite of the king's word—impossible!"

"He may have thought the king said it for his own sake."

"My brother was not so incredulous," said Andrée.

"It would be very wrong," continued the queen, not heeding her; "he could not have as noble a heart as I thought. But, after all, why should he believe? He thought he saw me. They all thought so. There is something in all this; something which I must clear up. Andrée, I must find out what it all means."

"Your majesty is right; you must investigate it."

"For," continued the queen, "people said they saw me at M. Mesmer's."

"But your majesty was there," said Madame de la Motte.

"Yes; but I did not do what they insist they saw me do. And they saw me at the Opera, and I was not there. Oh!" cried she, "at last I guess the truth."

"The truth!" stammered the countess.

"Oh! I hope so," said Andrée.

"Send for M. de Crosne," said the queen, joyously.

CHAPTER XXXVIII
M. DE CROSNE

M. de Crosne had felt himself in no slight degree embarrassed since his interview with the king and queen. It was no light matter to have the care of the interests of a crown and of the fame of a queen; and he feared that he was about to encounter all the weight of a woman's anger and a queen's indignation. He knew, however, that he had but done his duty, and he entered, therefore, tranquilly, with a smile on his face.

"Now, M. de Crosne," said the queen, "it is our turn for an explanation."

"I am at your majesty's orders."

"You ought to know the cause of all that has happened to me, sir."

M. de Crosne looked round him rather frightened.

"Never mind these ladies," said the queen; "you know them both; you know every one."

"Nearly," said the magistrate; "and I know the effects, but not the cause, of what has happened to your majesty."

"Then I must enlighten you, although it is a disagreeable task. I might tell you in private, but my thoughts and words are always open as the day; all the world may know them. I attribute the attacks that have been made upon me to the misconduct of some one who resembles me, and who goes everywhere; and thus your agents have made these mistakes."

"A resemblance!" cried M. de Crosne, too much occupied with the idea to observe the unquiet look which Jeanne could not for a moment prevent appearing.

"Well, sir, do you think this impossible; or do you prefer to think that I am deceiving you?"

"Oh no, madame! but surely, however strong a resemblance may be, there must be some points of difference to prevent people being so deceived."

"It seems not, sir; some are deceived."

"Oh! and I remember," said Andrée, "when we lived at Taverney Maison Rouge, we had a servant who very strongly——"

"Resembled me?"

"Most wonderfully, your majesty."

"And what became of her?"

"We did not then know the great generosity of your majesty's mind, and my father feared that this resemblance might be disagreeable to you; and when we were at Trianon we kept her out of sight."

"You see, M. de Crosne. Ah! this interests you."

"Much, madame."

"Afterwards, dear Andrée?"

"Madame, this girl, who was of an ambitious disposition and troublesome temper, grew tired of this quiet life, and had doubtless made bad acquaintances, for one night when I went to bed I was surprised not to see her; we sought her in vain, she had disappeared."

"Did she steal anything?"

"Nothing, madame."

"You did not know all this, M. de Crosne?"

"No, madame."

"Thus, then, there is a woman whose resemblance to me is striking, and you do not know her. I fear your police is badly organized."

"No, madame; a police magistrate is but a man, and though the vulgar may rate his power as something almost superhuman, your majesty is more reasonable."

"Still, sir, when a man has secured all possible powers for penetrating secrets, when he pays agents and spies, and to such an extent as to know every movement I make, he might prevent this sort of thing."

"Madame, when your majesty passed the night out, I knew it, the day you went to see madame at the Rue St. Claude; therefore my police is not bad. When you went to M. Mesmer's, my agents saw you. When you went to the Opera——"

The queen started.

"Pardon me, madame, if I saw you; but if your own brother-in-law mistook you, surely an agent at a crown a day may be pardoned for having done so. They thought they saw you, and reported accordingly; therefore my police is not bad. They also knew this affair of the journalist, so well punished by M. de Charny."

"M. de Charny!" cried the queen and Andrée in a breath.

"Yes, madame: his blows are yet fresh on the shoulders of the journalist."

"M. de Charny committed himself with this fellow!"

"I know it by my calumniated police, madame; and also, which was more difficult, the duel which followed."

"A duel! M. de Charny fought?"

"With the journalist?" asked Andrée.

"No, madame; the journalist was too well beaten to give M. de Charny the sword-thrust which made him faint here just now."

"Wounded!" cried the queen; "how and when? He was here just now."

"Oh!" said Andrée, "I saw that he suffered."

"What do you say?" cried the queen, almost angrily; "you saw that he suffered, and did not mention it!"

Andrée did not reply.

Jeanne, who wished to make a friend of her, came to her aid, saying, "I also, madame, saw that M. de Charny had difficulty in standing up while your majesty spoke to him."

"Monsieur," said the queen again to M. de Crosne, "with whom and why did M. de Charny fight?"

"With a gentleman who — — But really, madame, it is useless now. The two adversaries are friends again, for they spoke just now in your majesty's presence."

"In my presence!"

"Yes, madame; the conqueror left about twenty minutes ago."

"M. de Taverney!" cried the queen.

"My brother!" murmured Andrée.

"I believe," said M. de Crosne, "that it was he with whom M. de Charny fought."

The queen made an angry gesture. "It is not right," she said; "these are American manners brought to Versailles. It is not because one has fought under M. Lafayette and Washington that my court should be disgraced by such proceedings. Andrée, did you know your brother had fought?"

"Not till this moment, madame."

"Why did he fight?"

"If my brother fought," said Andrée, "it was in your majesty's service."

"That is to say, that M. de Charny fought against me."

"Your majesty, I spoke only of my brother, and of no one else."

The queen tried hard to remain calm. She walked once or twice up and down the room, and then said, "M. de Crosne, you have convinced me: I was much disturbed by these rumors and accusations; your police is efficient, but I beg you not to forget to investigate this resemblance of which I have spoken. Adieu!" and she held out her hand to him with her own peculiar grace.

Andrée made a movement to depart. The queen gave her a careless adieu.

Jeanne also prepared to leave, when Madame de Misery entered.

"Madame," said she to the queen, "did your majesty appoint this hour to receive MM. Bœhmer and Bossange?"

"Oh, yes, it is true; let them come in. Remain a little longer, Madame de la Motte; I want the king to make a full peace with you." Perhaps she wished to pique Andrée by this favor to a newcomer, but Andrée did not seem to heed.

"All these Taverneys are made of iron," thought the queen. "Ah, gentlemen, what do you bring me now? you know I have no money."

CHAPTER XXXIX
THE TEMPTRESS

Madame de la Motte remained, therefore, as before.

"Madame," replied M. Bœhmer, "we do not come to offer anything to your majesty, we should fear to be indiscreet; but we come to fulfil a duty, and that has emboldened us— —"

"A duty?"

"Concerning the necklace which your majesty did not deign to take."

"Oh! then, the necklace has come again," said Marie Antoinette, laughing. "It was really beautiful, M. Bœhmer."

"So beautiful," said Bossange, "that your majesty alone was worthy to wear it."

"My consolation is," said the queen, with a sigh which did not escape Jeanne, "that it cost a million and a half. Was not that the price, M. Bœhmer?"

"Yes, your majesty."

"And in these times," continued the queen, "there is no sovereign that can give such a sum for a necklace; so that although I cannot wear it, no one else can: and once broken up, I should care nothing about it."

"That is an error of your majesty's; the necklace is sold."

"Sold!" cried the queen. "To whom?"

"Ah! madame, that is a state secret."

"Oh!" said the queen, "I think I am safe. A state secret means that there is nothing to tell."

"With your majesty," continued Bœhmer, as gravely as ever, "we do not act as with others. The necklace is sold, but in the most secret manner, and an ambassador— —"

"I really think he believes it himself!" interrupted the queen, laughing again. "Come, M. Bœhmer, tell me at least the country he comes from, or, at all events, the first letter of his name."

"Madame, it is the ambassador from Portugal," said Bœhmer, in a low voice, that Madame de la Motte might not hear.

"The ambassador from Portugal!" said the queen. "There is none here, M. Bœhmer."

"He came expressly for this, madame."

"Do you imagine so?"

"Yes, madame."

"What is his name?"

"M. de Souza."

The queen did not reply for a few minutes, and then said, "Well, so much the better for the Queen of Portugal. Let us speak of it no more."

"But allow us one moment, madame," said Bœhmer.

"Have you ever seen those diamonds?" said the queen to Jeanne.

"No, madame."

"They are beautiful. It is a pity these gentlemen have not brought them."

"Here they are," said Bœhmer, opening the case.

"Come, countess, you are a woman, and these will please you."

Jeanne uttered a cry of admiration when she saw them, and said, "They are indeed beautiful."

"1,500,000 francs, which you hold in the palm of your hand," said the queen.

"Monsieur was right," said Jeanne, "when he said that no one was worthy to wear these diamonds but your majesty."

"However, my majesty will not wear them."

"We could not let them leave France without expressing our regret to your majesty. It is a necklace which is now known all over Europe, and we wished to know definitively that your majesty really refused it before we parted with it."

"My refusal has been made public," said the queen, "and has been too much applauded for me to repent of it."

"Oh, madame!" said Bœhmer, "if the people found it admirable that your majesty preferred a ship of war to a necklace, the nobility at least would not think it surprising if you bought the necklace after all."

"Do not speak of it any more," said Marie Antoinette, casting at the same time a longing look at the casket.

Jeanne sighed, "Ah, you sigh, countess; in my place you would act differently."

"I do not know, madame."

"Have you looked enough?"

"Oh no! I could look forever."

"Let her look, gentlemen; that takes nothing from the value. Unfortunately, they are still worth 1,500,000 francs."

"Oh," thought Jeanne, "she is regretting it." And she said, "On your neck, madame, they would make all women die with jealousy, were they as beautiful as Cleopatra or Venus." And, approaching, she clasped it round her neck. "Ah, your majesty is beautiful so!"

The queen turned to the mirror. It was really splendid; every one must have admired. Marie Antoinette forgot herself for a time in admiration; then, seized with fear, she tried to take it off.

"It has touched your majesty's neck; it ought not to belong to any one else," said Bœhmer.

"Impossible!" said the queen, firmly. "Gentlemen, I have amused myself with these jewels; to do more would be a fault."

"We will return to-morrow," said Bœhmer.

"No; I must pay sooner or later; and, besides, doubtless you want your money. You will get it soon."

"Yes, your majesty," said the merchant, a man of business again.

"Take the necklace back," said the queen; "put it away immediately."

"Your majesty forgets that such a thing is equal to money itself."

"And that in a hundred years it will be worth as much as it is now," said Jeanne.

"Give me 1,500,000 francs," said the queen, "and we shall see."

"Oh, if I had them!"

MM. Bœhmer and Bossange took as long as possible to put back the necklace, but the queen did not speak.

At last they said, "Your majesty refuses them?"

"Yes, oh yes!" And they quitted the room.

Marie Antoinette remained sitting, looking rather gloomy, and beating with her foot in an impatient manner; at last she said, "Countess, it seems the king will not return; we must defer our supplication till another time."

Jeanne bowed respectfully.

"But I will not forget you," added the queen.

"She is regretting and desiring," thought Jeanne, as she left; "and yet she is a queen."

CHAPTER XL
TWO AMBITIONS THAT WISH TO PASS FOR TWO LOVES

When Jeanne returned to her pretty little house in the faubourg, it was still early; so she took a pen and wrote a few rapid lines, enclosed them in a perfumed envelope, and rang the bell. "Take this letter to Monseigneur the Cardinal de Rohan," said she.

In five minutes the man returned.

"Well," said Madame de la Motte, impatiently, "why are you not gone?"

"Just as I left the house, madame, his eminence came to the door. I told him I was about to go to his hotel with a letter from you; he read it, and is now waiting to come in."

"Let him enter," said the countess.

Jeanne had been thinking all the way home of the beautiful necklace, and wishing it was hers. It would be a fortune in itself.

The cardinal entered. He also was full of desires and ambitions, which he wished to hide under the mask of love.

"Ah, dear Jeanne," said he, "you have really become so necessary to me that I have been gloomy all day knowing you to be so far off. But you have returned from Versailles?"

"As you see, monseigneur."

"And content?"

"Enchanted."

"The queen received you, then?"

"I was introduced immediately on my arrival."

"You were fortunate. I suppose, from your triumphant air, that she spoke to you."

"I passed three hours in her majesty's cabinet."

"Three hours! You are really an enchantress whom no one can resist. But perhaps you exaggerate. Three hours!" he repeated; "how many things a clever woman like you might say in three hours!"

"Oh, I assure you, monseigneur, that I did not waste my time."

"I dare say that in the whole three hours you did not once think of me."

"Ungrateful man!"

"Really!" cried the cardinal.

"I did more than think of you; I spoke of you."

"Spoke of me! to whom?" asked the prelate, in a voice from which all his power over himself could not banish some emotion.

"To whom should it be but to the queen?"

"Ah, dear countess, tell me about it. I interest myself so much in all that concerns you, that I should like to hear the most minute details."

Jeanne smiled. She knew what interested the cardinal as well as he did himself. Then she related to him all the circumstances which had so fortunately made her, from a stranger, almost the friend and confidant of the queen.

Scarcely had she finished, when the servant entered to announce supper.

Jeanne invited the cardinal to accompany her.

He gave her his arm, and they went in together.

During supper, the cardinal continued to drink in long draughts of love and hope from the recitals which Jeanne kept making to him from time to time. He remarked also, with surprise, that, instead of making herself sought like a woman that knows that you have need of her, she had thrown off all her former pride, and only seemed anxious to please him. She did the honors of her table as if she had all her life mixed in the highest circles; there was neither awkwardness nor embarrassment.

"Countess," said he at length, "there are two women in you."

"How so?"

"One of yesterday, and another of to-day."

"And which does your excellency prefer?"

"I do not know, but at least the one of this evening is a Circe—a something irresistible."

"And which you will not attempt to resist, I hope, prince as you are."

The cardinal imprinted a long kiss on her hand.

CHAPTER XLI
FACES UNDER THEIR MASKS

Two hours had elapsed, and the conversation still continued. The cardinal was now the slave, and Jeanne was triumphant. Two men often deceive each other as they shake hands, a man and a woman as they kiss; but here, each only deceived the other because they wished to be deceived: each had an end to gain, and for that end intimacy was necessary.

The cardinal now did not demonstrate his impatience, but always managed to bring back the conversation to Versailles, and to the honors which awaited the queen's new favorite.

"She is generous," said he, "and spares nothing towards those she loves. She has the rare talent of giving a little to every one, and a great deal to a few."

"You think, then, she is rich?"

"She makes resources with a word or a smile; no minister, except perhaps Turgot, ever refused her anything."

"Well," said Madame de la Motte, "I have seen her poorer than you think."

"What do you mean?"

"Are those rich who are obliged to impose privations on themselves?"

"Privations! What do you mean, dear countess?"

"I will tell you what I saw—I saw the queen suffer. Do you know what a woman's desire is, my dear prince?"

"No, countess; but I should like you to tell me."

"Well, the queen has a desire, which she cannot satisfy."

"For what?"

"For a diamond necklace."

"Oh, I know what you mean—the diamonds of MM. Bœhmer and Bossange."

"Precisely."

"That is an old story, countess."

"Old or new, it is a real vexation for a queen not to be able to buy what was intended for a simple favorite. Fifteen more days added to the life of Louis XV., and Jeanne Vaubernier would have had what Marie Antoinette cannot buy."

"My dear countess, you mistake; the queen could have had it, and she refused it; the king offered them to her."

And he recounted the history of the ship of war.

"Well," said she, "after all, what does that prove?"

"That she did not want them, it seems to me."

Jeanne shrugged her shoulders.

"You know women and courts, and believe that? The queen wanted to do a popular act, and she has done it."

"Good!" said the cardinal; "that is how you believe in the royal virtues. Ah, skeptic, St. Thomas was credulous, compared to you!"

"Skeptic or not, I can assure you of one thing—that the queen had no sooner refused it than she earnestly desired to have it."

"You imagine all this, my dear countess; for if the queen has one quality more than another, it is disinterestedness. She does not care for gold or jewels, and likes a simple flower as well as a diamond."

"I do not know that; I only know she wishes for this necklace."

"Prove it, countess."

"It is easy. I saw the necklace, and touched it."

"Where?"

"At Versailles, when the jewelers brought it for the last time to try and tempt the queen."

"And it is beautiful?"

"Marvelous! I, who am a woman, think that one might lose sleep and appetite in wishing for it."

"Alas! why have I not a vessel to give the king?"

"A vessel!"

"Yes, for in return he would give me the necklace, and then you could eat and sleep in peace."

"You laugh."

"No, really."

"Well, I will tell you something that will astonish you. I would not have the necklace."

"So much the better, countess, for I could not give it to you."

"Neither you nor any one—that is what the queen feels."

"But I tell you that the king offered it to her."

"And I tell you that women like best those presents that come from people from whom they are not forced to accept them."

"I do not understand you."

"Well, never mind; and, after all, what does it matter to you, since you cannot have it?"

"Oh, if I were king and you were queen, I would force you to have it."

"Well, without being king, oblige the queen to have it, and see if she is angry, as you suppose she would be."

The cardinal looked at her with wonder.

"You are sure," said he, "that you are not deceived, and that the queen wishes for it?"

"Intensely. Listen, dear prince. Did you tell me, or where did I hear it, that you would like to be minister?"

"You may have heard me say so, countess."

"Well, I will bet that the queen would make that man a minister who would place the necklace on her toilet within a week."

"Oh, countess!"

"I say what I think. Would you rather I kept silent?"

"Certainly not."

"However, it does not concern you, after all. It is absurd to suppose that you would throw away a million and a half on a royal caprice; that would be paying too dearly for the portfolio, which you ought to have for nothing, so think no more of what I have said."

The cardinal continued silent and thoughtful.

"Ah, you despise me now!" continued she; "you think I judge the queen by myself. So I do; I thought she wanted these diamonds because she sighed as she looked at them, and because in her place I should have coveted them."

"You are an adorable woman, countess! You have, by a wonderful combination, softness of mind and strength of heart; sometimes you are so little of a woman that I am frightened; at others, so charmingly so, that I bless Heaven and you for it. And now we will talk of business no more."

"So be it," thought Jeanne; "but I believe the bait has taken, nevertheless."

Indeed, although the cardinal said, "Speak of it no more," in a few minutes he asked, "Does not Bœhmer live somewhere on the Quai de la Ferraille, near the Pont Neuf?"

"Yes, you are right; I saw the name on the door as I drove along."

Jeanne was not mistaken—the fish had taken the hook; and the next morning the cardinal drove to M. Bœhmer. He intended to preserve his incognito, but they knew him, and called him "Monseigneur" directly.

"Well, gentlemen," said he, "if you know me, keep my secret from others."

"Monseigneur may rely upon us. What can we do for your eminence?"

"I come to buy the necklace which you showed her majesty."

"Really we are in despair, but it is too late."

"How so?"

"It is sold."

"Impossible, as you offered it only yesterday to the queen."

"Who again refused it, so our other bargain held good."

"And with whom was this bargain?"

"It is secret, monseigneur."

"Too many secrets, M. Bœhmer," said he, rising; "but I should have thought that a French jeweler would prefer selling these beautiful stones in France. You prefer Portugal—very well."

"Monseigneur knows that!" cried the jeweler.

"Well, is that astonishing?"

"No one knew it but the queen."

"And if that were so?" said M. de Rohan without contradicting a supposition that flattered him.

"Ah! that would change matters."

"Why so, sir?"

"May I speak freely?"

"Certainly."

"The queen wishes for the necklace."

"You think so?"

"I am sure of it."

"Then why did she not buy it?"

"Because she had already refused the king, and she thought it would look capricious to buy it now."

"But the king wished her to have it."

"Yes, but he thanked her for refusing; therefore I think she wishes to have it without seeming to buy it."

"Well, you are wrong, sir."

"I am sorry for it, monseigneur. It would have been our only excuse for breaking our word to the Portuguese ambassador."

The cardinal reflected for a moment. "Then, sir, let us suppose that the queen wishes for your necklace."

"Oh! in that case, monseigneur, we would break through anything, that she should have it."

"What is the price?"

"1,500,000 francs."

"How do you want payment?"

"The Portuguese was to give 100,000 francs down, and I was to take the necklace myself to Lisbon, where the balance was to be paid."

"Well, the 100,000 francs down you shall have; that is reasonable. As for the rest——"

"Your eminence wishes for time? With such a guarantee, we should not object; only credit implies a loss. The interest of our money must be considered."

"Well, call it 1,600,000 francs, and divide the time of payment into three periods, making a year."

"That would be a loss to us, sir."

"Oh! nonsense; if I paid you the whole amount to-morrow, you would hardly know what to do with it."

"There are two of us, monseigneur."

"Well, you will receive 500,000 francs every four months. That ought to satisfy you."

"Monseigneur forgets that these diamonds do not belong to us; if they did, we should be rich enough to wait; they belong to a dozen different creditors. We got some from Hamburg, some from Naples, one at Buenos Ayres, and one at Moscow. All these people wait for the sale of the necklace to be paid. The profit that we make is all that will be ours; and we have already had it two years on hand."

M. de Rohan interrupted him. "After all," said he, "I have not seen the necklace."

"True, monseigneur; here it is."

"It is really superb," cried the cardinal; "it is a bargain?"

"Yes, monseigneur. I must go to the ambassador and excuse myself."

"I did not think there was a Portuguese ambassador just now."

"M. de Souza arrived incognito."

"To buy this necklace?"

"Yes, monseigneur."

"Oh! poor Souza, I know him well," said he, laughing.

"With whom am I to conclude the transaction?" asked M. Bœhmer.

"With myself; you will see no one else. To-morrow I will bring the 100,000 francs, and will sign the agreement. And as you are a man of secrets, M. Bœhmer, remember that you now possess an important one."

"Monseigneur, I feel it, and will merit your confidence and the queen's."

M. de Rohan went away happy, like all men who ruin themselves in a transport of passion.

The next day M. Bœhmer went to the hotel of the Portuguese ambassador. At the moment he knocked at the door, M. Beausire was going through some accounts with M. Ducorneau, while Don Manoël was taking over some new plan with the valet, his associate.

M. Ducorneau was charmed to find an ambassador so free from national prejudice as to have formed his whole establishment of Frenchmen. Thus his conversation was full of praises of him.

"The Souzas, you see," replied Beausire, "are not of the old school of Portuguese. They are great travelers, very rich, who might be kings if they liked."

"And do they not?"

"Why should they? With a certain number of millions, and the name of a prince, one is better than a king."

"Ah, Portugal will soon become great with such men at its head. But when is the presentation to take place? It is most anxiously looked for. The people around begin to talk of it, and to collect about the doors of the hotel, as though they were of glass, and they could see through."

"Do you mean the people of the neighborhood?" asked Beausire.

"And others; for, the mission of M. de Souza being a secret one, you may be sure the police would soon interest themselves about it; and look," continued Ducorneau, leading Beausire to the window, "do you see that man in the brown surtout, how he looks at the house?"

"Yes, he does indeed. Who do you take him to be?"

"Probably a spy of M. de Crosne. However, between ourselves, M. de Crosne is not equal to M. Sartines. Did you know him?"

"No."

"Ah! he would have found out all about you long ago, in spite of all your precautions."

A bell rang. "His excellency rings!" said Beausire, who was beginning to feel embarrassed by the conversation, and opening the door quickly, he nearly knocked down two of the clerks who were listening.

CHAPTER XLII
IN WHICH M. DUCORNEAU UNDERSTANDS NOTHING OF WHAT IS PASSING

Don Manoël was less yellow than usual, that is to say, he was more red. He had just been having a fierce altercation with his valet, and they were still disputing when Beausire entered.

"Come, M. Beausire, and set us right," said the valet.

"About what?"

"This 100,000 francs. It is the property of the association, is it not?"

"Certainly."

"Ah, M. Beausire agrees with me."

"Wait," said Don Manoël.

"Well, then," continued the valet, "the chest ought not to be kept close to the ambassador's room."

"Why not?" asked Beausire.

"M. Manoël ought to give us each a key to it."

"Not so," said Manoël; "do you suspect me of wishing to rob the association? I may equally suspect you, when you ask for a key."

"But," said the valet, "we have all equal rights."

"Really, monsieur, if you wish to make us all equal, we ought to have played the ambassador in turn. It would have been less plausible in the eyes of the public, but it would have satisfied you."

"And besides," said Beausire, "M. Manoël has the incontestable privilege of the inventor."

"Oh," replied the valet, "the thing once started, there are no more privileges. I do not speak for myself only; all our comrades think the same."

"They are wrong," said both Manoël and Beausire.

"I was wrong myself to take the opinion of M. Beausire; of course the secretary supports the ambassador."

"Monsieur," replied Beausire, "you are a knave, whose ears I would slit, if it had not already been done too often. You insult me by saying that I have an understanding with Manoël."

"And me also," said Manoël.

"And I demand satisfaction," added Beausire.

"Oh, I am no fighter."

"So I see," said Beausire, seizing hold of him.

"Help! help!" cried the valet, attacked at once by both of them. But just then they heard a bell ring.

"Leave him, and let him open the door," said Manoël.

"Our comrades shall hear all this," replied the valet.

"Tell them what you please; we will answer for our conduct."

"M. Bœhmer!" cried the porter from below.

"Well, we shall have no more contests about the 100,000 francs," said Manoël; "for they will disappear with M. Bœhmer."

M. Bœhmer entered, followed by Bossange. Both looked humble and embarrassed. Bœhmer began, and explained that political reasons would prevent their fulfilling their contract.

Manoël cried out angrily; Beausire looked fierce.

Manoël said "that the bargain was completed, and the money ready."

Bœhmer persisted.

Manoël, always through Beausire, replied, "that his Government had been apprised of the conclusion of the bargain, and that it was an insult to his queen to break it off."

M. Bœhmer was very sorry, but it was impossible to act otherwise.

Beausire, in Manoël's name, refused to accept the retractation, and abused M. Bœhmer as a man without faith, and ended by saying, "You have found some one to pay more for it."

The jewelers colored.

Beausire saw that he was right, and feigned to consult his ambassador. "Well," said he at length, "if another will give you more for your diamonds, we would do the same, rather than have this affront offered to our queen. Will you take 50,000 francs more?"

Bœhmer shook his head.

"100,000, or even 150,000," continued Beausire, willing to offer anything rather than lose the booty.

The jewelers looked dazzled for a moment, consulted together, and then said, "No, monsieur, it is useless to tempt us. A will more powerful than our own compels us to decline. You understand, no doubt, that it is not we who refuse. We only obey the orders of one greater than any of us."

Beausire and Manoël saw that it was useless to say more, and tried to look and speak indifferently on the matter.

Meanwhile the valet had been listening attentively, and just then making an unlucky movement, stumbled against the door. Beausire ran to the ante-chamber. "What on earth are you about?" cried he.

"Monsieur, I bring the morning despatches."

"Good," said Beausire, taking them from him, "now go."

They were letters from Portugal, generally very insignificant, but which, passing through their hands before going to Ducorneau, often gave them useful information about the affairs of the embassy.

The jewelers, hearing the word despatches, rose to leave like men who had received their congé.

"Well," said Manoël, when they were gone, "we are completely beaten. Only 100,000 francs, a poor spoil; we shall have but 8,000 each."

"It is not worth the trouble. But it might be 50,000 each."

"Good," replied Manoël, "but the valet will never leave us now he knows the affair has failed."

"Oh, I know how we will manage him. He will return immediately, and claim his share and that of his comrades, and we shall have the whole house on our hands. Well, I will call him first to a secret conference; then leave me to act."

"I think I understand," said Manoël.

Neither, however, would leave his friend alone with the chest while he went to call him.

Manoël said "that his dignity as ambassador prevented him from taking such a step."

"You are not ambassador to him," said Beausire; "however, I will call through the window."

The valet, who was just beginning a conversation with the porter, hearing himself called, came up.

Beausire said to him, with a smiling air, "I suppose you were telling this business to the porter?"

"Oh, no."

"Are you sure?"

"I swear!"

"For if you were, you were committing a great folly, and have lost a great deal of money."

"How so?"

"Why, at present only we three know the secret, and could divide the 100,000 francs between us, as they all now think we have given it to M. Bœhmer."

"Morbleu!" cried the valet, "it is true: 33,300 francs each."

"Then you accept?"

"I should think so."

"I said you were a rogue," said Beausire, in a thundering voice; "come, Don Manoël, help me to seize this man, and give him up to our associates."

"Pardon! pardon!" cried the unfortunate, "I did but jest."

"Shut him up until we can devise his punishment."

The man began to cry out.

"Take care," said Beausire, "that Ducorneau does not hear us."

"If you do not leave me alone," said the valet, "I will denounce you all."

"And I will strangle you," said Don Manoël, trying to push him into a neighboring closet.

"Send away Ducorneau somewhere, Beausire, while I finish this fellow."

When he had locked him up, he returned to the room. Beausire was not there; Don Manoël felt tempted. He was alone, and Beausire might be some little time; he could open the chest, take out all the bank-notes, and be off in two minutes. He ran to the room where it was: the door was locked. "Ah," thought he, "Beausire distrusted me, and locked the door before he went." He forced back the lock with his sword, and then uttered a terrible cry. The chest was opened and empty. Beausire had got, as we know, a second key; he had forestalled Manoël.

Manoël ran down like a madman; the porter was singing at the door — he asked if Beausire had passed.

"Yes, some ten minutes ago."

Manoël became furious, summoned them all, and ran to release the unfortunate valet. But when he told his story, Manoël was accused of being an accomplice of Beausire, and they all turned against him.

M. Ducorneau felt ready to faint, when he entered and saw the men preparing to hang M. de Souza. "Hang M. de Souza!" cried he. "It is high treason."

At last they threw him into a cellar, fearing his cries would arouse the neighborhood.

At that moment loud knocks at the door disturbed them,—they looked at each other in dismay. The knocks were repeated, and some one cried, "Open in the name of the Portuguese ambassador."

On hearing this, each made his escape in terror, as he best could, scrambling over walls and roofs. The true ambassador could only enter by the help of the police.

They found and arrested M. Ducorneau, who slept that night in the Châtelet.

Thus ended the adventure of the sham embassy from the Portugal.

CHAPTER XLIII
ILLUSIONS AND REALITIES

Beausire, on leaving the house, ran as fast as possible down the Rue Coquillière, then into the Rue St. Honoré, and took everywhere the most intricate and improbable turnings he could think of, and continued this until he became quite exhausted. Then, thinking himself tolerably safe, he sat down in the corn market, on a sack, to recover his breath. "Ah!" thought he, "now I have made my fortune; I will be an honest man for the future, and I will make Oliva an honest woman. She is beautiful, and she will not mind leading a retired life with me in some province, where we shall live like lords. She is very good; she has but two faults, idleness and pride, and as I shall satisfy her on both these points, she will be perfect." He then began to reflect on what he should do next. They would seek him, of course, and most likely divide into different parties, and some would probably go first to his own house. Here lay his great difficulty, for there they would find Oliva, and they might ill-treat her. They might even take her as a hostage, speculating on his love for her. What should he do? Love carried the day; he ran off again like lightning, took a coach, and drove to the Pont Neuf. He then looked cautiously down the Rue Dauphine to reconnoiter, and he saw two men, who seemed also looking anxiously down the street. He thought they were police spies, but that was nothing uncommon in that part of the town; so, bending his back, and walking lamely, for disguise, he went on till he nearly reached his house. Suddenly he thought he saw the coat of a gendarme in the courtyard; then he saw one at the window of Oliva's room. He felt ready to drop, but he thought his best plan was to walk quietly on; he had that courage, and passed the house. Heavens! what a sight! the yard was full of soldiers, and among them a police commissioner. Beausire's rapid glance showed him what he thought disappointed faces. He thought that M. de Crosne had somehow begun to suspect him, and, sending to take him, had found only Oliva.

"I cannot help her now," thought he; "I should only lose my money and destroy us both. No, let me place that in safety, and then I will see what can be done." He therefore ran off again, taking his way almost mechanically towards the Luxembourg; but as he turned the corner of the Rue St. Germain, he was almost knocked down by a handsome carriage which was driving towards the Rue Dauphine, and, raising his head to swear at the coachman, he thought he saw Oliva inside, talking with much animation to a handsome man who sat by her. He gave a cry of surprise, and would have run after it, but he could not again encounter the Rue Dauphine. He felt bewildered, for he had before settled that Oliva had been arrested in her own house, and he fancied his brain must be turning when he believed he saw her in the carriage. But he started off again and took refuge in a small cabaret at the Luxembourg, where the hostess was an old friend. There he gradually began to recover again his courage and hope. He thought the police would not find him, and that his money was safe. He remembered also that Oliva had committed no crime, and that the time was passed when people were kept prisoners for nothing. He also thought that his money would soon obtain her release, even if she were sent to prison, and he would then set off with her for Switzerland. Such were his dreams and projects as he sat sipping his wine.

CHAPTER XLIV
OLIVA BEGINS TO ASK WHAT THEY WANT OF HER

If M. Beausire had trusted to his eyesight, which was excellent, instead of trusting his imagination, he would have spared himself much regret and many mistakes. It was, in fact, Oliva who sat in the carriage by the side of a man, whom he would also have recognized if he had looked a little longer. She had gone that morning, as usual, to take a walk in the gardens of the Luxembourg, where she had met the strange friend whose acquaintance she had made the day of the ball at the Opera.

It was just as she was about to return that he appeared before her, and said, "Where are you going?"

"Home, monsieur."

"Just what the people want who are there waiting for you."

"Waiting for me? No one is there for me."

"Oh, yes, a dozen visitors at least."

"A whole regiment, perhaps?" said Oliva, laughing.

"Perhaps, had it been possible to send a whole regiment, they would have done so."

"You astonish me!"

"You would be far more astonished if I let you go."

"Why?"

"Because you would be arrested."

"I! arrested?"

"Assuredly. The twelve gentlemen who wait for you are sent by M. de Crosne."

Oliva trembled. Some people are always fearful on certain points. But she said:

"I have done nothing; why should they arrest me?"

"For some intrigue, perhaps."

"I have none."

"But you have had."

"Oh, perhaps."

"Well, perhaps they are wrong to wish to arrest you, but the fact is that they do desire to do so. Will you still go home?"

"You deceive me," said Oliva; "if you know anything, tell me at once. Is it not Beausire they want?"

"Perhaps; he may have a conscience less clear than yours."

"Poor fellow!"

"Pity him, if you like; but if he is taken, there is no need for you to be taken too."

"What interest have you in protecting me?" asked she. "It is not natural for a man like you."

"I would not lose time if I were you; they are very likely to seek you here, finding you do not return."

"How should they know I am here?"

"Are you not always here? My carriage is close by, if you will come with me. But I see you doubt still."

"Yes."

"Well, we will commit an imprudence to convince you. We will drive past your house, and when you have seen these gentlemen there, I think you will better appreciate my good offices."

He led her to the carriage, and drove to the Rue Dauphine, at the corner of which they passed Beausire. Had Oliva seen him, doubtless she would have abandoned everything to fly with him and share his fate, whatever it might be; but Cagliostro, who did see him, took care to engage her attention by showing her the crowd, which was already in sight, and which was waiting to see what the police would do.

When Oliva could distinguish the soldiers who filled her house, she threw herself into the arms of her protector in despair. "Save me! save me!" she cried.

He pressed her hand. "I promise you."

"But they will find me out anywhere."

"Not where I shall take you; they will not seek you at my house."

"Oh!" cried she, frightened, "am I to go home with you?"

"You are foolish," said he; "I am not your lover, and do not wish to become so. If you prefer a prison, you are free to choose."

"No," replied she, "I trust myself to you, take me where you please."

He conducted her to the Rue Neuve St. Gilles, into a small room on the second floor.

"How triste!" said she; "here, without liberty, and without even a garden to walk in."

"You are right," said he; "besides, my people would see you here at last."

"And would betray me, perhaps."

"No fear of that. But I will look out for another abode for you; I do not mean you to remain here."

Oliva was consoled; besides, she found amusing books and easy-chairs.

He left her, saying, "If you want me, ring; I will come directly if I am at home."

"Ah!" cried she, "get me some news of Beausire."

"Before everything." Then, as he went down, he said to himself, "It will be a profanation to lodge her in that house in the Rue St. Claude; but it is important that no one should see her, and there no one will. So I will extinguish the last spark of my old light."

CHAPTER XLV
THE DESERTED HOUSE

When Cagliostro arrived at the deserted house in the Rue St. Claude, with which our readers are already acquainted, it was getting dark, and but few people were to be seen in the streets.

Cagliostro drew a key from his pocket, and applied it to the lock; but the door was swollen with the damp, and stiff with age, and it required all his strength to open it. The courtyard was overgrown with moss, the steps crumbling away; all looked desolate and deserted. He entered the hall, and lighted a lamp which he had brought with him. He felt a strange agitation as he approached the door which he had so often entered to visit Lorenza. A slight noise made his heart beat quickly; he turned, and saw an adder gliding down the staircase; it disappeared in a hole near the bottom.

He entered the room; it was empty, but in the grate still lay some ashes, the remains of the furniture which had adorned it, and which he had burned there. Among it several pieces of gold and silver still sparkled. As he turned, he saw something glittering on the floor; he picked it up. It was one of those silver arrows with which the Italian women were in the habit of confining their hair. He pressed it to his lips, and a tear stood in his eyes as he murmured, "Lorenza!" It was but for a moment; then he opened the window and threw it out, saying to himself, "Adieu! this last souvenir, which would soften me. This house is about to be profaned—another woman will ascend the staircase, and perhaps even into this room, where Lorenza's last sigh still vibrates; but to serve my end the sacrifice shall be made. I must, however, have some alterations made."

He then wrote on his tablets the following words: "To M. Lenoir, my architect,—Clean out the court and vestibule, restore the coach-house and stable, and demolish the interior of the pavilion. To be done in eight days."

"Now, let us see," said he to himself, "if we can perfectly distinguish the window of the countess. It is infallible," said he, after looking out; "the women must see each other."

The next day fifty workmen had invaded the house and commenced the projected alterations, which were completed within the given time. Some of the passers-by saw a large rat hung up by the tail.

CHAPTER XLVI
JEANNE THE PROTECTRESS

M. le Cardinal de Rohan received, two days after his visit to M. Bœhmer, the following note:

"His Eminence the Cardinal de Rohan knows, doubtless, where he will sup this evening."

"From the little countess," said he; "I will go."

Among the footmen given to her by the cardinal, Jeanne had distinguished one, black-haired and dark-eyed, and, as she thought, active and intelligent. She set this man to watch the cardinal, and learned from him that he had been twice to M. Bœhmer's. Therefore she concluded the necklace was bought, and yet he had not communicated it to her. She frowned at the thought, and wrote the note which we have seen.

M. de Rohan sent before him a basket of Tokay and other rarities, just as if he was going to sup with La Guimard or Mademoiselle Dangeville. Jeanne determined not to use any of it at supper.

"When they were alone, she said to him:

"Really, monseigneur, one thing afflicts me."

"What, countess?"

"To see, not only that you no longer love me, but that you never have loved me."

"Oh, countess! how can you say so?"

"Do not make excuses, monseigneur; it would be lost time."

"Oh, countess!"

"Do not be uneasy; I am quite indifferent about it now."

"Whether I love you or not?"

"Yes, because I do not love you."

"That is not flattering."

"Indeed, we are not exchanging compliments, but facts. We have never loved each other."

"Oh, as for myself, I cannot allow that; I have a great affection for you, countess."

"Come, monseigneur, let us esteem each other enough to speak the truth, and that is, that there is between us a much stronger bond than love — that is, interest."

"Oh, countess, what a shame!"

"Monseigneur, if you are ashamed, I am not."

"Well, countess, supposing ourselves interested, how can we serve each other?"

"First, monseigneur, I wish to ask you a question. Why have you failed in confidence towards me?"

"I! How so, pray?"

"Will you deny that, after skilfully drawing from me the details — which, I confess, I was not unwilling to give you — concerning the desire of a certain great lady for a certain thing, you have taken means to gratify that desire without telling me?"

"Countess, you are a real enigma, a sphinx."

"Oh, no enigma, cardinal; I speak of the queen, and of the diamonds which you bought yesterday of MM. Bœhmer and Bossange."

"Countess!" cried he, growing pale.

"Oh, do not look so frightened," continued she. "Did you not conclude your bargain yesterday?"

He did not speak, but looked uncomfortable, and half angry. She took his hand.

"Pardon, prince," she said, "but I wished to show you your mistake about me; you believe me foolish and spiteful."

"Oh, countess, now I understand you perfectly. I expected to find you a pretty woman and a clever one, but you are better than this. Listen to me: you have, you say, been willing to become my friend without loving me?"

"I repeat it," replied she.

"Then you had some object?"

"Assuredly. Do you wish me to tell it to you?"

"No; I understand it. You wished to make my fortune; that once done, you are sure that my first care would be for yours. Am I right?"

"Yes, monseigneur; but I have not pursued my plans with any repugnance—the road has been a pleasant one."

"You are an amiable woman, countess, and it is a pleasure to discuss business with you. You have guessed rightly that I have a respectful attachment towards a certain person."

"I saw it at the Opera ball," she said.

"I know well that this affection will never be returned."

"Oh, a queen is only a woman, and you are surely equal to Cardinal Mazarin."

"He was a very handsome man," said M. de Rohan, laughing.

"And an excellent minister," said Jeanne.

"Countess, it is superfluous trouble to talk to you; you guess and know everything. Yes, I do wish to become prime minister. Everything entitles me to it—my birth, my knowledge of business, my standing with foreign courts, and the affection which is felt for me by the French people."

"There is but one obstacle," said Jeanne.

"An antipathy."

"Yes, of the queen's; and the king always ends by liking what she likes, and hating what she hates."

"And she hates me? Be frank, countess."

"Well, monseigneur, she does not love you."

"Then I am lost! Of what use is the necklace?"

"You deceive yourself, prince."

"It is bought."

"At least, it will show the queen that you love her. You know, monseigneur, we have agreed to call things by their right names."

"Then you say you do not despair of seeing me one day prime minister?"

"I am sure of it."

"And what are your own ambitions?"

"I will tell you, prince, when you are in a position to satisfy them."

"We will hope for that day."

"Now let us sup."

"I am not hungry."

"Then let us talk."

"I have nothing more to say."

"Then go."

"How! is that what you call our alliance? Do you send me away?"

"Yes, monseigneur."

"Well, countess, I will not deceive myself again about you." Before leaving, however, he turned, and said, "What must I do now, countess?"

"Nothing; wait for me to act. I will go to Versailles."

"When?"

"To-morrow."

"And when shall I hear from you?"

"Immediately."

"Then I abandon myself to your protection; au revoir, countess."

CHAPTER XLVII
JEANNE PROTECTED

Mistress of such a secret, rich in such a future, and supported by such a friend, Jeanne felt herself strong against the world. To appear at court, no longer as a suppliant, as the poor mendicant, drawn from poverty by Madame de Boulainvilliers, but as a Valois, with an income of 100,000 francs; to be called the favorite of the queen, and consequently governing the king and state through her.—Such was the panorama that floated before the eyes of Jeanne.

She went to Versailles. She had no audience promised, but she trusted to her good fortune, and as the queen had received her so well before, all the officials were anxious to serve her. Therefore, one of the doorkeepers said aloud, as the queen came from chapel, to one of her gentlemen, "Monsieur, what am I to do? Here is Madame la Comtesse de la Motte Valois asking admission, and she has no letter of audience."

The queen heard and turned round. "Did you say Madame de la Motte Valois was here?" she asked.

"Your majesty, the doorkeeper says so."

"I will receive her; bring her to the bath-room."

The man told Jeanne what he had done. She drew out her purse; but he said, "Will Madame la Comtesse allow this debt to accumulate? Some day she can pay me with interest."

"You are right, my friend; I thank you."

Marie Antoinette looked serious when Jeanne entered.

"She supposes I am come again to beg," thought Jeanne.

"Madame," said the queen, "I have not yet had an opportunity to speak to the king."

"Oh, your majesty has already done too much for me; I ask nothing more. I came— —" she hesitated.

"Is it something urgent, that you did not wait to ask for an audience?"

"Urgent! Yes, madame; but not for myself."

"For me, then?" and the queen conducted her into the bath-room, where her women were waiting for her. Once in the bath, she sent them away.

"Now, countess."

"Madame," said Jeanne, "I am much embarrassed."

"Why so?"

"Your majesty knows the kindness I have received from M. de Rohan."

The queen frowned. "Well, madame?"

"Yesterday his eminence came to see me, and spoke to me as usual of your majesty's goodness and kindness."

"What does he want?"

"I expressed to him all my sense of your generosity, which constantly empties your purse, and told him that I felt almost guilty in thinking of your majesty's gift to myself, and remembering that were it not for such liberality your majesty need not have been forced to deny yourself the beautiful necklace which became you so well. When I related this circumstance to M. de Rohan, I saw him grow pale and the tears came into his eyes. Indeed, madame, his fine face, full of admiration for, and emotion caused by, your noble conduct, is ever before my eyes."

"Well, countess, if he has impressed you so deeply, I advise you not to let him see it. M. de Rohan is a worldly prelate, and gathers the sheep as much for himself as for his Lord."

"Oh, madame!"

"It is not I who say it: that is his reputation; he almost glories in it; his trophies are numerous, and some of them have made no little scandal."

"Well, madame, I am sure he thought then of no one but your majesty."

The queen laughed.

"Your majesty's modesty will not allow you to listen to praises."

"Not from the cardinal—I suspect them all."

"It is not my part," replied Jeanne, respectfully, "to defend any one who has incurred your majesty's displeasure."

"M. de Rohan has offended me, but I am a queen and a Christian, and do not wish to dwell on offenses."

Jeanne was silent.

"You think differently to me on this subject?"

"Completely, your majesty."

"You would not speak so if you knew what he has done against me; but as you have so great a friendship for him, I will not attack him again before you. You have not, then, forgotten the diamonds?"

"Oh, madame, I have thought of them night and day. They will look so well on your majesty."

"What do you mean? They are sold to the Portuguese ambassador."

Jeanne shook her head.

"Not sold!" cried the queen.

"Yes, madame, but to M. de Rohan."

"Oh," said the queen, becoming suddenly cold again.

"Oh! your majesty," cried Jeanne; "do not be ungenerous towards him. It was the impulse of a generous heart that your majesty should understand and sympathize with. When he heard my account he cried,—'What! the queen refuse herself such a thing, and perhaps see it one day worn by one of her subjects!' And when I told him that it was bought for the Queen of Portugal, he was more indignant than ever. He cried, 'It is no longer a simple question of pleasure for the queen, but of the dignity of the French crown. I know the spirit of foreign courts; they will laugh at our queen because they happen to have more money to spare: and I will never suffer this.' And he left me abruptly. An hour after I heard that he had bought the necklace."

"For 1,500,000 francs?"

"1,600,000, madame."

"With what intention?"

"That at least if your majesty would not have them no one else should."

"Are you sure it is not for some mistress?"

"I am sure he would rather break it to pieces than see it on any other neck than your own."

Marie Antoinette reflected, and her expressive countenance showed clearly every thought that passed through her mind. At last she said:

"What M. de Rohan has done is a noble trait of a delicate devotion, and you will thank him for me."

"Oh yes, madame."

"You will add, that he has proved to me his friendship, and that I accept it, but not his gift."

"But, madame— —"

"No, but as a loan. He has advanced his money and his credit to please me, and I will repay him. Bœhmer has asked for money down?"

"Yes, madame."

"How much?"

"100,000 francs."

"That is my quarter's allowance from the king. I received it this morning; it is in advance, but still I have it." She rang the bell. Her woman came and wrapped her in warm sheets, and then she dressed herself. Once more alone in her bedroom with Jeanne, she said:

"Open that drawer, and you will see a portfolio."

"Here it is, madame."

"It holds the 100,000 francs—count them."

Jeanne obeyed.

"Take them to the cardinal with my thanks; each quarter I will pay the same. In this manner I shall have the necklace which pleased me so much, and if it embarrasses me to pay it, at least it will not hurt the king; and I shall have gained the knowledge that I have a friend who has guessed my wishes." Then, after a pause, "You will add, countess, that M. de Rohan will be welcome at Versailles to receive my thanks."

Jeanne went away full of joy and delight.

CHAPTER XLVIII
THE QUEEN'S PORTFOLIO

The cardinal was at home when Madame de la Motte came to his hotel. She had herself announced, and was immediately admitted.

"You come from Versailles?" said he.

"Yes."

"Well?"

"Well, monseigneur, what do you expect?"

"Ah, countess, you say that with an air that frightens me."

"You wished me to see the queen, and I have seen her; and that I should speak to her of you whom she has always so much disliked."

"And you did?"

"Yes, and her majesty listened."

"Say no more, countess, I see she will not overcome her repugnance."

"Oh! as to that, I spoke of the necklace."

"And did you dare to say that I wished——"

"To buy it for her? Yes."

"Oh, countess, you are sublime; and she listened?"

"Yes, but she refused."

"Oh, I am lost."

"Refused to accept it as a gift, but not as a loan."

"I lend to the queen! countess, it is impossible."

"It is more than giving, is it not?"

"A thousand times."

"So I thought."

The cardinal rose and came towards her. "Do not deceive me," he said.

"One does not play with the affections of a man like you, monseigneur."

"Then it is true?"

"The exact truth."

"I have a secret with the queen!" and he pressed Jeanne's hand.

"I like that clasp of the hand," she said, "it is like one man to another."

"It is that of a happy man to a protecting angel."

"Monseigneur, do not exaggerate."

"Oh, my joy! my gratitude! impossible."

"But lending a million and a half to the queen is not all you wish for? Buckingham would have asked for more."

"Buckingham believed what I dare not even dream of."

"The queen sends you word that she will see you with pleasure at Versailles."

The cardinal looked as pale as a youth who gives his first kiss of love.

"Ah," thought she, "it is still more serious than I imagined. I can get what I please from him, for he acts really not from ambition but from love."

He quickly recovered himself, however: "My friend," said he, "how does the queen mean to act about this loan she talks of?"

"Ah, you think she has no money. But she will pay you as she would have paid Bœhmer. Only if she had paid him all Paris must have known it, which she would not have liked, after the credit she has had for her refusal of it. You are a cashier for her, and a solvent one if she becomes embarrassed. She is happy and she pays. Ask no more."

"She pays?"

"Yes, she knows you have debts; and when I told her you had advanced 100,000 francs——"

"You told her?"

"Yes; why not?" Jeanne put her hand in her pocket, and drew out the portfolio. "The queen sends you this with thanks; it is all right, for I have counted it."

"Who cares for that? But the portfolio?"

"Well, it is not handsome."

"It pleases me, nevertheless."

"You have good taste."

"Ah, you quiz me."

"You have the same taste as the queen, at all events."

"Then it was hers?"

"Do you wish for it?"

"I cannot deprive you of it."

"Take it."

"Oh, countess, you are a precious friend; but while you have worked for me, I have not forgotten you."

Jeanne looked surprised.

"Yes," said he, "my banker came to propose to me some plan of a marsh to drain, which must be profitable. I took two hundred shares, and fifty of them are for you."

"Oh, monseigneur!"

"He soon returned, he had realized already on them cent. per cent. He gave me 100,000 francs, and here is your share, dear countess;" and from the pocket-book she had just given him he slid 25,000 francs into her hand.

"Thanks, monseigneur. What gratifies me most is, that you thought of me."

"I shall ever do so," said he, kissing her hand.

"And I of you, at Versailles."

CHAPTER XLIX
IN WHICH WE FIND DR. LOUIS

Perhaps our readers, remembering in what a position we left M. de Charny, will not dislike to return with us to that little ante-chamber at Versailles into which this brave seaman, who feared neither men nor elements, had fled, lest he should show his weakness to the queen. Once arrived there, he felt it impossible to go further; he stretched out his arms, and was only saved from falling to the ground by the aid of those around. He then fainted, and was totally ignorant that the queen had seen him, and would have run to his assistance had Andrée not prevented her, more even from a feeling of jealousy than from regard for appearances. Immediately after the king entered, and seeing a man lying supported by two guards, who, unaccustomed to see men faint, scarcely knew what to do, advanced, saying, "Some one is ill here."

At his voice the men started and let their burden fall.

"Oh!" cried the king, "it is M. de Charny. Place him on this couch, gentlemen." Then they brought him restoratives, and sent for a doctor.

The king waited to hear the result. The doctor's first care was to open the waistcoat and shirt of the young man to give him air, and then he saw the wound.

"A wound!" cried the king.

"Yes," said M. de Charny, faintly, "an old wound, which has reopened;" and he pressed the hand of the doctor to make him understand.

But this was not a court doctor, who understands everything; so, willing to show his knowledge, "Old, sir! this wound is not twenty-four hours old."

Charny raised himself at this, and said, "Do you teach me, sir, when I received my wound?" Then, turning round, he cried, "The king!" and hastened to button his waistcoat.

"Yes, M. de Charny, who fortunately arrived in time to procure you assistance."

"A mere scratch, sire," stammered Charny, "an old wound."

"Old or new," replied Louis, "it has shown me the blood of a brave man."

"Whom a couple of hours in bed will quite restore," continued Charny, trying to rise; but his strength failed him, his head swam, and he sank back again.

"He is very ill," said the king.

"Yes, sire," said the doctor, with importance, "but I can cure him."

The king understood well that M. de Charny wished to hide some secret from him, and determined to respect it. "I do not wish," said he, "that M. de Charny should run the risk of being moved; we will take care of him here. Let M. de Suffren be called, this gentleman recompensed, and my own physician, Dr. Louis, be sent for."

While one officer went to execute these orders, two others carried Charny into a room at the end of the gallery. Dr. Louis and M. de Suffren soon arrived. The latter understood nothing of his nephew's illness. "It is strange," said he; "do you know, doctor, I never knew my nephew ill before."

"That proves nothing," replied the doctor.

"The air of Versailles must be bad for him."

"It is his wound," said one of the officers.

"His wound!" cried M. de Suffren; "he never was wounded in his life."

"Oh, excuse me," said the officer, opening the shirt, covered with blood, "but I thought— —"

"Well," said the doctor, who began to see the state of the case, "do not let us lose time disputing over the cause, but see what can be done to cure him."

"Is it dangerous, doctor?" asked M. de Suffren, with anxiety.

"Not at all," replied he.

M. de Suffren took his leave, and left Charny with the doctor. Fever commenced, and before long he was delirious. Three hours after the doctor called a servant, and told him to take Charny in his arms, who uttered doleful cries. "Roll the sheet over his head," said the doctor.

"But," said the man, "he struggles so much that I must ask assistance from one of the guards."

"Are you afraid of a sick man, sir? If he is too heavy for you, you are not strong enough for me. I must send you back to Auvergne." This threat had its effect. Charny, crying, fighting, and gesticulating, was carried by the man through the guards.

Some of the officers questioned the doctor.

"Oh! gentlemen," said he, "this gallery is too far off for me; I must have him in my own rooms."

"But I assure you, doctor, we would all have looked after him here. We all love M. de Suffren."

"Oh yes, I know your sort of care! The sick man is thirsty, and you give him something to drink, and kill him."

"Now there remains but one danger," said the doctor to himself, as he followed Charny, "that the king should want to visit him, and if he hear him— — Diable! I must speak to the queen." The good doctor, therefore, having bathed the head and face of his patient with cold water, and seen him safe in bed, went out and locked the door on him, leaving his servant to look after him. He went towards the queen's apartments, and met Madame de Misery, who had just been despatched to ask after the patient.

"Come with me," he said.

"But, doctor, the queen waits for intelligence."

"I am going to her."

"The queen wishes— —"

"The queen shall know all she wishes. I will take care of that."

CHAPTER L
ÆGRI SOMNIA

The queen was expecting the return of Madame de Misery. The doctor entered with his accustomed familiarity. "Madame," he said, "the patient in whom your majesty and the king are interested is as well as any one can be who has a fever."

"Is it a slight wound?" asked the queen.

"Slight or not, he is in a fever."

"Poor fellow!—a bad fever?"

"Terrible!"

"You frighten me; dear doctor; you, who are generally so cheering. Besides, you look about you, as though you had a secret to tell."

"So I have."

"About the fever?"

"Yes."

"To tell me?"

"Yes."

"Speak, then, for I am curious."

"I wait for you to question me, madame."

"Well, how does the fever go on?"

"No; ask me why I have taken him away from the guard's gallery, where the king left him, to my own room."

"Well, I ask. Indeed it is strange."

"Then, madame, I did so, because it is not an ordinary fever."

The queen looked surprised. "What do you mean?"

"M. de Charny is delirious already, and in his delirium he says a number of things rather delicate for the gentlemen of the guard to hear."

"Doctor!"

"Oh, madame! you should not question me, if you do not wish to hear my answers."

"Well, then, dear doctor, is he an atheist? Does he blaspheme?"

"Oh, no! he is on the contrary a devotee."

The queen assumed a look of sang-froid. "M. de Charny," she said, "interests me. He is the nephew of M. de Suffren, and has besides rendered me personal services. I wish to be a friend to him. Tell me, therefore, the exact truth."

"But I cannot tell you, madame. If your majesty wishes to know, the only way is to hear him yourself."

"But if he says such strange things?"

"Things which your majesty ought to hear."

"But," said the queen, "I cannot move a step here, without some charitable spy watching me."

"I will answer for your security. Come through my private way, and I will lock the door after us."

"I trust to you, then, dear doctor." And she followed him, burning with curiosity.

When they reached the second door the doctor put his ear to the keyhole.

"Is your patient in there, doctor?"

"No, madame, or you would have heard him at the end of the corridor. Even here you can hear his voice."

"He groans."

"No, he speaks loud and distinct."

"But I cannot go in to him."

"I do not mean you to do so. I only wish you to listen in the adjoining room, where you will hear without being seen." They went on, and the doctor entered the sick-room alone.

Charny, still dressed in his uniform, was making fruitless efforts to rise, and was repeating to himself his interview with the German lady in the coach. "German!" he cried—"German! Queen of France!"

"Do you hear, madame?"

"It is frightful," continued Charny, "to love an angel, a woman—to love her madly—to be willing to give your life for her; and when you come near her, to find her only a queen—of velvet and of gold, of metal and of silk, and no heart."

"Oh! oh!" cried the doctor again.

"I love a married woman!" Charny went on, "and with that wild love which, makes me forget everything else. Well, I will say to her, there remain for us still some happy days on this earth. Come, my beloved, and we will live the life of the blessed, if we love each other. Afterwards there will be death—better than a life like this. Let us love at least."

"Not badly reasoned for a man in a fever," said the doctor.

"But her children!" cried Charny suddenly, with fury; "she will not leave her children. Oh! we will carry them away also. Surely I can carry her, she is so light, and her children too." Then he gave a terrible cry: "But they are the children of a king!"

The doctor left his patient and approached the queen.

"You are right, doctor," said she; "this young man would incur a terrible danger if he were overheard."

"Listen again," said the doctor.

"Oh, no more."

But just then Charny said, in a gentler voice:

"Marie, I feel that you love me, but I will say nothing about it. Marie, I felt the touch of your foot in the coach; your hand touched mine, but I will never tell; I will keep this secret with my life. My blood may all flow away, Marie, but my secret shall not escape with it. My enemy steeped his sword in my blood, but if he has guessed my secret, yours is safe. Fear nothing, Marie, I do not even ask you if you love me; you blushed, that is enough."

"Oh!" thought the doctor; "this sounds less like delirium than like memory."

"I have heard enough," cried the queen, rising and trembling violently; and she tried to go.

The doctor stopped her. "Madame," said he, "what do you wish?"

"Nothing, doctor, nothing."

"But if the king ask to see my patient?"

"Oh! that would be dreadful!"

"What shall I say?"

"Doctor, I cannot think; this dreadful spectacle has confused me."

"I think you have caught his fever," said the doctor, feeling her pulse. She drew away her hand, and escaped.

CHAPTER LI
ANDRÉE

The doctor remained thoughtful, then said to himself,—"There are other difficulties here besides those I can contend with by science." He bathed again the temples of his patient, who for the time began to grow calmer.

All at once the doctor heard the rustling of a dress outside. "Can it be the queen returned?" thought he; and opening the door softly, he saw before him the motionless figure of a woman, looking like a statue of despair. It was almost dark; he advanced suddenly along the corridor to the place where the figure was standing. On seeing him, she uttered a cry.

"Who is there?" asked Doctor Louis.

"I, doctor!" replied a sweet and sorrowful voice—a voice that he knew but could not immediately recognize. "I, Andrée de Taverney," continued she.

"Oh, mon Dieu! what is the matter?" cried the doctor; "is she ill?"

"She! who?"

The doctor felt that he had committed an imprudence.

"Excuse me, but I saw a lady going away just now, perhaps it was you."

"Oh, yes, there has been a lady here before me, has there not?" asked Andrée, in a tone of emotion.

"My dear child," replied the doctor, "of whom do you speak? what do you want to know?"

"Doctor," answered Andrée, in a sorrowful voice, "you always speak the truth, do not deceive me now; I am sure there was a woman here before me."

"Doubtless. Why should I deceive you? Madame de Misery was here."

"It was Madame de Misery who came?"

"Certainly; what makes you doubt? What inexplicable beings women are."

"Dear doctor."

"Well, but to the point. Is she worse?"

"Who?"

"Pardieu, the queen."

"The queen!"

"Yes, the queen, for whom Madame de Misery came to fetch me, and who was troubled with her palpitations. If you come from her, tell me, and we will go back together."

"No, doctor, I do not come from the queen, and was even ignorant that she was suffering. But pardon me, doctor, I scarcely know what I an saying." In fact, she seemed on the point of fainting.

The doctor supported her. She rallied by a strong effort. "Doctor," she said, "you know I am nervous in the dark; I lost my way in these intricate passages, and have grown frightened and foolish."

"And why the devil should you be wandering about these dark passages, since you came for nothing?"

"I did not say I came for nothing, only that no one sent me."

"Well, if you have anything to say to me, come away from here, for I am tired of standing."

"Oh, I shall not be ten minutes; can any one hear us?"

"No one."

"Not even your patient in there?"

"Oh, no fear of his hearing anything."

Andrée clasped her hands. "Oh, mon Dieu!" she cried, "he is, then, very ill?"

"Indeed he is not well. But tell me quickly what brings you here, for I cannot wait."

"Well, doctor, we have spoken of it; I came to ask after him."

Doctor Louis received this confession with a solemn silence, which Andrée took for a reproach.

"You may excuse this step, doctor," she said, "as he was wounded in a duel with my brother."

"Your brother! I was ignorant of that."

"But now that you know it, you understand why I inquire after him."

"Oh, certainly, my child," said the good doctor, enchanted to find an excuse for being indulgent; "I could not know this."

"A duel between two gentlemen is a thing of everyday occurrence, doctor."

"Certainly; the only thing that could make it of importance would be that they have fought about a lady!"

"About a lady!"

"About yourself, for example."

Andrée sighed.

"Oh, doctor! they did not fight about me."

"Then," said the doctor, "is it your brother that has sent you for news of M. de Charny?"

"Oh, yes, my brother, doctor."

Dr. Louis looked at her scrutinizingly.

"I will find out the truth," thought he. Then he said, "Well, I will tell you the truth, that your brother may make his arrangements accordingly; you understand."

"No, doctor."

"Why, a duel is never a very agreeable thing to the king, and if it makes a scandal, he often banishes or imprisons the actors; but when death ensues, he is always inflexible. Therefore counsel your brother to hide for a time."

"Then," cried Andrée, "M. de Charny is—dangerously ill?"

"My dear young lady, if he is not out of danger by this time to-morrow, if before that time I cannot quell the fever that devours him, M. de Charny is a dead man."

Andrée bit her lips till the blood came, and clenched her hands till the nails stuck into the flesh, to stifle the cry that was ready to burst from her. Having conquered herself, she said, "My brother will not fly; he wounded M. de Charny in fair fight, and if he has killed him, he will take his chance."

The doctor was deceived. She did not come on her own account, he thought.

"How does the queen take it?" he asked.

"The queen? I know not. What is it to her?"

"But she likes your brother."

"Well, he is safe; and perhaps she will defend him if he is accused."

"Then, mademoiselle, you have learned what you wished. Let your brother fly, or not, as he pleases; that is your affair. Mine is to do the best to-night for the wounded man; without which, death will infallibly carry him off. Adieu."

Andrée fled back to her room, locked herself in, and falling on her knees by the side of her bed, "My God!" cried she, with a torrent of burning tears, "you will not leave this young man to die who has done no wrong, and who is so loved in this world. Oh! save him, that I may see a God of mercy, and not of vengeance." Her strength gave way, and she fell senseless on the floor. When her senses returned to her, her first muttered words were, "I love him! oh, I love him!"

CHAPTER LII
DELIRIUM

M. De Charny conquered the fever. The next day the report was favorable. Once out of danger, Doctor Louis ceased to take so much interest in him; and after the lapse of a week, as he had not forgotten all that had passed in his delirium, he wished to have him removed from Versailles: but Charny, at the first hint of this, rebelled, and said angrily, "that his majesty had given him shelter there, and that no one had a right to disturb him."

The doctor, who was not patient with intractable convalescents, ordered four men to come in and move him; but Charny caught hold of his bed with one hand, and struck furiously with the other at every one who approached; and with the effort, the wound reopened, the fever returned, and he began to cry out that the doctor wished to deprive him of the visions that he had in his sleep, but that it was all in vain; for that she who sent them to him was of too high rank to mind the doctor.

Then the doctor, frightened, sent the men away, and dressed the wound again; but as the delirium returned stronger than ever, he determined to go once more to the queen.

Marie Antoinette received him with a smile; she expected to hear that the patient was cured, but on hearing that he was very ill, she cried:

"Why, yesterday you said he was going on so well!"

"It was not true, madame."

"And why did you deceive me? Is there, then, danger?"

"Yes, madame, to himself and others; but the evil is moral, not physical. The wound in itself is nothing; but, madame, M. de Charny is fast becoming a monomaniac, and this I cannot cure. Madame, you will have ruined this young man."

"I, doctor! Am I the cause, if he is mad?"

"If you are not now, you soon will be."

"What must I do, then? Command me, doctor."

"This young man must be cured either with kindness or coercion. The woman whose name he evokes every instant must kill or cure him."

"Doctor, you exaggerate. Can you kill a man with a hard word, or cure a madman with a smile?"

"If your majesty be incredulous, I have only to pay my respects, and take leave."

"No, doctor; tell me what you wish."

"Madame, if you desire to free this palace from his cries, and from scandal, you must act."

"You wish me to come and see him?"

"Yes."

"Then I will call some one—Mademoiselle de Taverney, for example—and you have all ready to receive us. But it is a dreadful responsibility to run the risk of kill or cure, as you say."

"It is what I have to do every day. Come, madame, all is ready."

The queen sighed, and followed the doctor, without waiting for Andrée, who was not to be found.

It was eleven o'clock in the morning, and Charny was asleep, after the troubled night he had gone through. The queen, attired in an elegant morning dress, entered the corridor. The doctor advised her to present herself suddenly, determined to produce a crisis, either for good or ill; but at the door they found a woman standing, who had not time to assume her usual unmoved tranquillity, but showed an agitated countenance, and trembled before them.

"Andrée!" cried the queen.

"Yes, your majesty; you are here too!"

"I sent for you, but they could not find you."

Andrée, anxious to hide her feelings, even at the price of a falsehood, said, "I heard your majesty had asked for me, and came after you."

"How did you know I was here?"

"They said you were gone with Doctor Louis, so I guessed it."

"Well guessed," replied the queen, who was little suspicious, and forgot immediately her first surprise.

She went on, leaving Andrée with the doctor.

Andrée, seeing her disappear, gave a look full of anger and grief. The doctor said to her:

"Do you think she will succeed?"

"Succeed in what?"

"In getting this poor fellow removed, who will die here."

"Will he live elsewhere?" asked Andrée, surprised.

"I believe so."

"Oh, then, may she succeed!"

CHAPTER LIII
CONVALESCENCE

The queen walked straight up to where Charny lay, dressed, on a couch. He raised his head, wakened by her entrance.

"The queen!" cried he, trying to rise.

"Yes, sir, the queen," she replied, "who knows how you strive to lose both reason and life; the queen, whom you offend both dreaming and waking; the queen, who cares for your honor and your safety, and therefore comes to you. Is it possible," continued she, "that a gentleman, formerly renowned like you for his loyalty and honor, should become such an enemy as you have been to the reputation of a woman? What will my enemies do, if you set them the example of treason?"

"Treason!" stammered Charny.

"Yes, sir. Either you are a madman, and must be forcibly prevented from doing harm; or you are a traitor, and must be punished."

"Oh, madame, do not call me a traitor! From the mouth of a king, such an accusation would precede death; from the mouth of a woman, it is dishonor. Queen, kill me, or spare me!"

"Are you in your right mind, M. de Charny?" said the queen, in a moved voice.

"Yes, madame."

"Do you remember your wrongs towards me, and towards the king?"

"Mon Dieu!" he murmured.

"For you too easily forget, you gentlemen, that the king is the husband of the woman whom you insult, by raising your eyes to her—that he is the father of your future master, the dauphin; you forget, also, that he is a greater and better man than any of you—a man whom I esteem and love."

"Oh!" murmured Charny, with a groan, and seemed ready to faint.

This cry pierced the queen's heart; she thought he was about to die, and was going to call for assistance; but, after an instant's reflection, she went on: "Let us converse quietly, and be a man. Doctor Louis has vainly tried to cure you; your wound, which was nothing, has been rendered dangerous through your own extravagances. When will you cease to present to the good doctor the spectacle of a scandalous folly which disquiets him? When will you leave the castle?"

"Madame," replied Charny, "your majesty sends me away; I go, I go!" And he rose with a violent effort, as though he would have fled that instant, but, unable to stand, fell almost into the arms of the queen, who had risen to stop him.

She replaced him on the sofa; a bloody foam rose to his lips. "Ah, so much the better!" cried he; "I die, killed by you!" The queen forgot everything but his danger; she supported his drooping head on her shoulders, and pressed her cold hands to his forehead and heart. Her touch seemed to revive him as if by magic—he lived again; then she wished to fly, but he caught hold of her dress, saying:

"Madame, in the name of the respect which I feel for you——"

"Adieu, adieu!" cried the queen.

"Oh, madame, pardon me!"

"I do pardon you."

"Madame, one last look."

"M. de Charny," said the queen, trembling, "if you are not the basest of men, to-morrow you will be dead, or have left this castle."

He threw himself at her feet; she opened the door, and rushed away.

Andrée saw for an instant the young man on his knees before her, and felt struck with both hate and despair. She thought, as she saw the queen return, that God had given too much to this woman in adding to her throne and her beauty this half-hour with M. de Charny.

The doctor, occupied only with the success of the negotiation, said, "Well, madame, what will he do?"

"He will leave," replied the queen; and, passing them quickly, she returned to her apartment.

The doctor went to his patient, and Andrée to her room.

Doctor Louis found Charny a changed man, declaring himself perfectly strong, asking the doctor how he should be moved, and when he should be quite well, with so much energy that the doctor feared it was too much, and that he must relapse after it. He was, however, so reasonable as to feel the necessity of explaining this sudden change. "The queen has done me more good by making me ashamed of myself," he said, "than you, dear doctor, with all your science. She has vanquished me by an appeal to my amour propre."

"So much the better," said the doctor.

"Yes. I remember that a Spaniard—they are all boasters—told me one day, to prove the force of his will, that it sufficed for him in a duel which he had fought, and in which he had been wounded, to will that the blood should not flow in the presence of his adversary in order to retain it. I laughed at him. However, I now feel something like it myself; I think that if my fever and delirium wished to return, I could chase them away, saying, Fever and delirium, I forbid you to appear!"

"We know such things are possible," replied the doctor. "Allow me to congratulate you, for you are cured morally."

"Oh yes."

"Well, the physical cure will soon follow. Once sound in mind, you will be sound in body within a week."

"Thanks, doctor."

"And, to begin, you must leave this place."

"I am ready immediately."

"Oh, we will not be rash; we will wait till this evening. Where will you go?"

"Anywhere—to the end of the world if you like."

"That is too far for a first journey; we will content ourselves with Versailles. I have a house there where you shall go to-night."

Accordingly, that evening the four valets, who had been so rudely repulsed before, carried him to his carriage. The king had been hunting all day; Charny felt somewhat uneasy at leaving without apprizing him; but the doctor promised to make his excuses.

Andrée, concealed behind her curtains, saw the carriage drive off.

"If he resumes his desire to die," thought the doctor, "at least it will not be in my rooms, and under my care."

Charny arrived safely, however, and the next day the doctor found him so well, that he told him he thought he would require him no longer.

He received a visit from his uncle, and from an officer sent by the king to inquire after him. At the end of a week he could ride slowly on horseback: then the doctor advised him to go for a time to his estates in Picardy to regain strength. He accordingly took leave of the king, charged M. de Suffren with his adieus to the queen, who was ill that evening, and set off for his château at Boursonnes.

CHAPTER LIV
TWO BLEEDING HEARTS

On the day following the queen's visit to M. de Charny, Madlle. de Taverney entered the royal bedroom as usual at the hour of the petite toilette. The queen was just laughing over a note from Madame de la Motte. Andrée, paler than usual, looked cold and grave: the queen, however, being occupied, did not notice it, but merely turning her head, said in her usual friendly tone, "Bon jour, petite." At last, however, Andrée's silence struck her, and looking up she saw her sad expression and said, "Mon Dieu! Andrée, what is the matter? Has any misfortune happened to you?"

"Yes, madame, a great one."

"What is it?"

"I am going to leave your majesty."

"Leave me!"

"Yes, madame."

"Where are you going? and what is the cause of this sudden departure?"

"Madame, I am not happy in my affections; in my family affections, I mean," added Andrée, blushing.

"I do not understand you—you seemed happy yesterday."

"No, madame," replied Andrée, firmly. "Yesterday was one of the unhappy days of my life."

"Explain yourself."

"It would but fatigue your majesty, and the details are not worthy of your hearing. Suffice it to say, that I have no satisfaction in my family—that I have no good to expect in this world. I come, therefore, to beg your majesty's permission to retire into a convent."

The queen rose, and although with some effort to her pride, took Andrée's hand, and said: "What is the meaning of this foolish resolution? Have you not to-day, like yesterday, a father and a brother? and were they different yesterday from to-day? Tell me your difficulties. Am I no longer your protectress and mother?"

Andrée, trembling, and bowing low, said, "Madame, your kindness penetrates my heart, but does not shake my resolution. I have resolved to quit the court. I have need of solitude. Do not force me to give up the vocation to which I feel called."

"Since yesterday?"

"I beg your majesty not to make me speak on this point."

"Be free, then," said the queen, rather bitterly; "only I have always shown you sufficient confidence for you to have placed some in me. But it is useless to question one who will not speak. Keep your secrets, and I trust you will be happier away than you have been here. Remember one thing, however, that my friendship does not expire with people's caprices, and that I shall ever look on you as a friend. Now, go, Andrée; you are at liberty. But where are you going to?"

"To the convent of St. Denis, madame."

"Well, mademoiselle, I consider you guilty towards me of ingratitude and forgetfulness."

Andrée, however, left the room and the castle without giving any of those explanations which the good heart of the queen expected, and without in any way softening or humbling herself. When she arrived at home, she found Philippe in the garden—the brother dreamed, while the sister acted. At the sight of Andrée, whose duties always kept her with the queen at that hour, he advanced, surprised, and almost frightened, which was increased when he perceived her gloomy look.

He questioned her, and she told him that she was about to leave the service of the queen, and go into a convent.

He clasped his hands, and cried, "What! you also, sister?"

"I also! what do you mean?"

"'Tis a cursed contact for us, that of the Bourbons. You wish to take religious vows; you, at once the least worldly of women, and the least fitted for a life of asceticism. What have you to reproach the queen with?"

"I have nothing to reproach her with; but you, Philippe, who expected, and had the right to expect, so much—why did not you remain at court? You did not remain there three days; I have been there as many years."

"She is capricious, Andrée."

"You, as a man, might put up with it. I, a woman, could not, and do not wish to do so."

"All this, my sister, does not inform me what quarrel you have had with her."

"None, Philippe, I assure you. Had you any when you left her? Oh, she is ungrateful!"

"We must pardon her, Andrée; she is a little spoiled by flattery, but she has a good heart."

"Witness what she has done for you, Philippe."

"What has she done?"

"You have already forgotten. I have a better memory, and with one stroke pay off your debts and my own."

"Very dear, it seems to me, Andrée—to renounce the world at your age, and with your beauty. Take care, dear sister, if you renounce it young, you will regret it old, and will return to it when the time will be passed, and you have outlived all your friends."

"You do not reason thus for yourself, brother. You are so little careful of your fortunes, that when a hundred others would have acquired titles and gold, you have only said—she is capricious, she is perfidious, and a coquette, and I prefer not to serve her. Therefore, you have renounced the world, though you have not entered into a monastery."

"You are right, sister; and were it not for our father——"

"Our father! Ah, Philippe! do not speak of him," replied Andrée, bitterly. "A father should be a support to his children, or accept their support. But what does ours do? Could you confide a secret to M. de Taverney, or do you believe him capable of confiding in you? M. de Taverney is made to live alone in this world."

"True, Andrée, but not to die alone."

"Ah, Philippe! you take me for a daughter without feeling, but you know I am a fond sister; and to have been a good daughter, required only to have had a father; but everything seems to conspire to destroy in me every tender feeling. It never happens in this world that hearts respond; those whom we choose prefer others."

Philippe looked at her with astonishment. "What do you mean?" said he.

"Nothing," replied Andrée, shrinking from a confidence. "I think my brain is wandering; do not attend to my words."

"But— —"

Andrée took his hand. "Enough on this subject, my dearest brother. I am come to beg you to conduct me to the convent of St. Denis; but be easy, I will take no vows. I can do that at a later period, if I wish. Instead of going, like most women, to seek forgetfulness, I will go to seek memory. It seems to me that I have too often forgotten my Creator. He is the only consolation, as He is really the only afflictor. In approaching Him more nearly, I shall do more for my happiness than if all the rich and great in this world had combined to make life pleasant to me."

"Still, Andrée, I oppose this desperate resolution, for you have not confided to me the cause of your despair!"

"Despair!" said she, with a disdainful air. "No, thank God, I am not despairing; no, a thousand times, no."

"This excess of disdain shows a state of mind which cannot last. If you reject the word 'despair,' I must use that of 'pique.'"

"Pique! do you believe that I am so weak as to yield up my place in the world through pique? Judge me by yourself, Philippe; if you were to retire to La Trappe, what would you call the cause of your determination?"

"I should call it an incurable grief."

"Well, Philippe, I adopt your words, for they suit me."

"Then," he replied, "brother and sister are alike in their lives: happy together, they have become unhappy at the same time." Then, thinking further remonstrance useless, he asked, "When do you want to go?"

"To-morrow, even to-day, if it were possible."

"I shall be ready whenever you require me."

Andrée retired to make her preparations. Soon she received this note from Philippe:

> "You can see our father at five o'clock this evening.
> You must be prepared for reproaches, but an adieu is indispensable."

She answered:

> "At five o'clock I will be with M. de Taverney all ready to start, and by seven we can be at St. Denis, if you will give me up your evening."

CHAPTER LV
THE MINISTER OF FINANCE

We have seen that the queen, before receiving Andrée, was smiling over a note from Madame de la Motte. She was, however, rendered serious by the interview with Mademoiselle de Taverney. Scarcely had she gone, when Madame de Misery came to announce M. de Calonne. He was a man of much intellect, but, foreseeing that disaster was hanging over France, determined to think only of the present, and enjoy it to the utmost. He was a courtier, and a popular man. M. de Necker had shown the impossibility of finding finances, and called for reforms which would have struck at the estates of the nobility and the revenues of the clergy; he exposed his designs too openly, and was overwhelmed by a torrent of opposition; to show the enemy your plan of attack is half to give them the victory. Calonne, equally alive to the danger, but seeing no way of escape, gave way to it. He completely carried with him the king and queen, who implicitly believed in his system, and this is, perhaps, the only political fault which Louis XVI was guilty of towards posterity. M. de Calonne was handsome, and had an ingratiating manner; he knew how to please a queen, and always arrived with a smile on his face, when others might have worn a frown.

The queen received him graciously, and said, "Have we any money, M. de Calonne?"

"Certainly, madame; we have always money."

"You are perfectly marvelous," replied she, "an incomparable financier, for you seem always ready when we want money."

"How much does your majesty require?"

"Explain to me first how you manage to find money, when M. Necker declared that there was none."

"M. Necker was right, madame; for when I became minister on the 3d of November, 1783, there were but one thousand and two hundred francs in the public treasury. Had M. Necker, madame, instead of crying out, 'There is no money,' done as I have done, and borrowed 100,000,000 the first year, and 125,000,000 the second, and had he been as sure as I am of a new loan of

80,000,000 for the third, he would have been a true financier. Every one can say there is no money, but not that there is plenty."

"That is what I compliment you on, sir; but how to pay all this?"

"Oh, madame, be sure we shall pay it," replied he, with a strange smile.

"Well, I trust to you," said the queen.

"I have now a project, madame," replied he, bowing, "which will put 20,000,000 into the pockets of the nation, and 7,000,000 or 8,000,000 into your own."

"They will be welcome, but where are they to come from?"

"Your majesty is aware that money is not of the same value in all the countries of Europe."

"Certainly. In Spain gold is dearer than in France."

"Your majesty is perfectly right. Gold in Spain has been for the last five or six years worth considerably more than in France; it results that the exporters gain on eight ounces of gold, that they send from here, about the value of fourteen ounces of silver."

"That is a great deal."

"Well, madame, I mean to raise the price of gold one-fifth of this difference, and where we have now thirty louis we shall then have thirty-two."

"It is a brilliant idea!" cried the queen.

"I believe it, and am happy that it meets your majesty's approbation."

"Always have such, and I am sure you will soon pay our debts."

"But allow me, madame, to return to what you want of me," said the minister.

"Would it be possible to have at present—I am afraid it is too much——"

Calonne smiled in an encouraging manner.

"500,000 francs?" continued the queen.

"Oh, madame, really your majesty frightened me; I was afraid it was something great."

"Then you can?"

"Assuredly."

"Without the king's knowledge?"

"Oh, madame, that is impossible. Every month all my accounts are laid before the king; however, he does not always read them."

"When can I have it?"

"What day does your majesty wish for it?"

"On the fifth of next month."

"Your majesty shall have it on the third."

"Thanks, M. de Calonne."

"My greatest happiness is to please your majesty, and I beg you never will allow yourself to be embarrassed for want of money." He rose, the queen gave him her hand to kiss, and then said, "After all, this money causes me some remorse, for it is for a caprice."

"Never mind; some one will gain by it."

"That is true; you have a charming mode of consoling one."

"Oh, madame, if we had none of us more reasons for remorse than you, we should all go straight to heaven."

"But it will be cruel to make the poor people pay for my caprices."

"Have no scruples, madame; it is not the poor who will pay."

"How so?" asked the queen, in some surprise.

"Because, madame, they have nothing to pay with."

He bowed and retired.

CHAPTER LVI
THE CARDINAL DE ROHAN

Hardly had M. de Calonne traversed the gallery, when Madame de la Motte was shown in to the queen.

"Madame," said she, "the cardinal is here." She then introduced him, and took her leave.

The cardinal, finding himself alone with the queen, bowed respectfully, without raising his eyes.

"Monsieur," said the queen, "I have heard of you what has effaced many wrongs."

"Permit me, madame," said he, trembling with real emotion, "to assure your majesty that these wrongs of which you speak I could explain in a few words."

"I do not forbid you to justify yourself," replied she, with dignity; "but if what you are about to say throws the smallest shade upon my family or country, you will only wound me still more. Let us leave this subject; and I will only see you under the fresh light, which shows you to me obliging, respectful, and devoted."

"Devoted until death," replied he.

"But," said Marie Antoinette, with a smile, "at present it is a question not of death, but of ruin; and I do not wish you devoted even so far. You shall live, and not be ruined, at least, not by me; for they say you are ruining yourself."

"Madame!"

"Oh! that is your own business; only, as a friend, I would counsel you to be economical—the king would like you better."

"I would become a miser to please your majesty."

"Oh, the king," replied she, with an accent on the word, "does not love misers either."

"I will become whatever your majesty desires," replied he, with a hardly-disguised passion.

"I said, then," continued she, "that you shall not be ruined for me. You have advanced money on my account, and I have the means of meeting the calls; therefore, regard the affair for the future as in my hands."

"To finish it, then, it only remains for me to offer the necklace to your majesty;" and drawing out the case, he presented it to her.

She took it, but did not open it, and laid it down by her side. She received kindly all his polite speeches, but as she was longing to be left alone with her diamonds, she began to answer somewhat absently.

He thought she was embarrassed, and was delighted, thinking it showed, at least, an absence of indifference. He then kissed her hand, and took leave, going away full of enthusiasm and hope.

Jeanne was waiting for him in the carriage, and received his ardent protestations with pleasure. "Well," said she, "shall you be Richelieu or Mazarin? Have her lips given you encouragement in ambition or love? Are you launched in politics or intrigue?"

"Do not laugh, dear countess; I am full of happiness."

"Already!"

"Assist me, and in three weeks I may be a minister."

"Peste! that is a long time; the next payment is in a fortnight."

"Ah! the queen has money, and will pay, and I shall have only the merit of the intention. It is too little; I would willingly have paid for this reconciliation with the whole sum."

"Make yourself easy," replied the countess; "you shall have this merit if you desire it."

"I should have preferred it; the queen would then have been under an obligation to me."

"Monseigneur, something tells me you will have this satisfaction. Are you prepared for it?"

"I have mortgaged all my revenue for the ensuing year."

"Then you have the money?"

"Certainly, for this payment; after that, I do not know what I shall do."

"Oh, this payment will give you three quiet months; who knows what may happen in three months?"

"That is true; but she said that the king wished me to incur no more debt."

"Two months in the ministry would set all straight."

"Countess!"

"Oh, do not be fastidious; if you do not assist yourself, others will."

"You are right. Where are you going now?"

"Back to the queen, to hear what she says of your interview."

"Good! I go to Paris."

"Why? You should go this evening to the 'jeu du roi;' it is good policy to keep your ground."

"No, countess; I must attend a rendezvous, for which I received a note this morning."

"A rendezvous?"

"Yes, and a serious one, by the contents of the note. Look."

"A man's writing," said the countess; and, opening the note, she read:

> "Monseigneur,—Some one wishes to see you about raising an important sum of money. This person will wait on you this evening, at Paris, to solicit the honor of an interview."

"Anonymous—some beggar?"

"No, countess; no beggar would expose himself to the risk of being beaten by my servants. Besides, I fancy I have seen the writing before. So au revoir, countess."

"Apropos, monseigneur, if you are going to get a windfall, some large sum, I understand we are to share."

"Countess, you have brought me luck; I shall not be ungrateful." And they separated.

The cardinal was full of happy dreams: the queen had received him kindly. He would place himself at the head of her party, and make it a popular one; he would protect her, and for her sake would abandon his slothful life, and live an active one.

As soon as he arrived at his hotel, he commenced burning a box full of love-letters; then he called his steward to order some economical reforms, and sat down to his history of English politics. Soon he heard a ring, and a servant entered to announce the person who had written to him that morning.

"Ask his name," said the cardinal.

The man, having inquired, returned and said:

"M. le Comte de Cagliostro."

"Let him come in."

The count entered.

"Mon Dieu!" cried the cardinal, "is it possible? Joseph Balsamo, who was supposed to have perished in the flames?"

"Yes, monseigneur, more alive than ever."

"But, sir, you have taken a new name."

"Yes, monseigneur; the other recalled too many painful recollections. Possibly, you yourself would not have opened your door to Joseph Balsamo."

"I! oh yes, sir."

"Then monseigneur has a better memory and more honesty than most men."

"Monsieur, you once rendered me a service."

"Am I not, monseigneur, a good specimen of the results of my elixir?"

"I confess it, sir; but you seem above humanity—you, who distribute health and gold to all."

"Health perhaps, monseigneur, but not gold."

"You make no more gold."

"No, monseigneur."

"Why?"

"Because I lost the parcel of an indispensable ingredient which Althotas discovered, but of which I never had the receipt. He has carried that secret with him to the grave."

"He is dead, then? How, could you not preserve the life of this man, so useful to you, as you have kept yourself through so many centuries?"

"Because I can guard against illness, but not against such accidents as kill before I can act."

"He died from an accident, then?"

"The fire in which you thought I died killed him; or rather he, weary of life, chose to die."

"It is strange."

"No, it is natural; I have a hundred times thought of ending my life."

"But you have not done so."

"Because I enjoy a state of youth, in which health and pleasure kept me from ennui; but he had chosen one of old age. He was a savant, and cared only for science; and thus youth, with its thousand pleasures, would have constantly drawn him from its study. An old man meditates better than a young one. Althotas died a victim to his love of science: I lead a worldly life, and do nothing—I live like a planet."

"Oh, sir, your words and appearance bring to me dreams of my youth. It is ten years since I saw you."

"Yes; but if you are no longer a fine young man, you are a prince. Do you remember the day when, in my cabinet, I promised you the love of the woman whose fair locks I consulted?"

The cardinal turned from pale to red. Terror and joy almost stopped the beating of his heart.

"I remember," said he.

"Ah, let me try if I can still play the magician. This fair child of your dreams— —"

"What is she doing now?"

"Ah, I suspect you yourself have seen her to-day; indeed, you have not long left her."

The cardinal could hardly stand.

"Oh, I beg, sir— —" he cried.

"Let us speak of something else," said Cagliostro, sitting down.

CHAPTER LVII
DEBTOR AND CREDITOR

"Now that we have renewed our acquaintance, let us converse," said Cagliostro.

"Yes," replied the cardinal, "about the money you wrote of; it was a pretext, was it not?"

"No, monsieur, a serious matter, as it concerns a sum of 500,000 francs."

"The sum which you lent me?" cried the cardinal, growing pale.

"Yes, monseigneur; I love to see so good a memory in a great prince like you."

The cardinal felt overwhelmed by the blow. At last, trying to smile, he said:

"I thought that Joseph Balsamo had carried his debt with him to the tomb, as he threw the receipt into the fire."

"Monseigneur," replied the count, "the life of Joseph Balsamo is as indestructible as the sheet on which you wrote. Death cannot conquer the elixir of life; fire is powerless against asbestos."

"I do not understand," said the cardinal.

"You soon will," replied Cagliostro, producing a folded paper, which he offered to the prince.

He, before opening it, cried, "My receipt!"

"Yes, monseigneur, your receipt."

"But I saw you burn it."

"True, I threw it on the fire, but by accident you had written on a piece of asbestos, so that the receipt remained uninjured among the cinders."

"Monsieur," said the cardinal, haughtily, for he thought this a proof that he had been suspected, "believe me, I should not have denied my debt, even without this paper; therefore you were wrong to deceive me."

"I deceived you?"

"Yes; you made me think the paper was destroyed."

"To leave you the calm enjoyment of 500,000 francs."

"But, sir, why have you left such a sum for ten years unclaimed?"

"I knew, monseigneur, that it was safe. Various events have deprived me of my wealth; but, knowing that I had this sum in reserve, I have waited patiently until the last moment."

"And has that arrived?"

"Alas! yes, monseigneur."

"So that you can really wait no longer?"

"No, monseigneur."

"You want it at once?"

"If it please you to pay it."

The cardinal was at first silent, through despair. Then he said, in a hoarse voice:

"M. le Comte, we unhappy princes of the earth do not improvise fortunes as quickly as you enchanters."

"Oh, monseigneur," said Cagliostro, "I would not have asked you for this sum, had I not known beforehand that you had it."

"I have 500,000 francs?"

"30,000 in gold, 11,000 in silver, and the rest in notes, which are in this buhl cabinet."

The cardinal turned white. "You knew this?"

"Yes, monseigneur, and I know you have made great sacrifices to obtain it. I have heard that you will pay heavily for it."

"Oh, it is too true!"

"But, monseigneur, during these ten years I have often been in want and embarrassment, yet I have kept this paper back, so as not to trouble you; therefore I do not think you can complain."

"Complain! oh, no, sir; when you graciously lent me such a sum, I must ever remain your debtor. But during those ten years there were twenty occasions when I could have repaid you with ease, while to-day the restitution you demand embarrasses me dreadfully. You, who know everything, who read even hearts, and penetrate the doors of cabinets, doubtless, know also the purpose for which this money was destined."

"You are wrong, monseigneur," said Cagliostro, coldly. "My knowledge has brought me so much misery and disappointment, that I no longer seek to penetrate the secrets of others. It concerned me to know whether you had this money, as I wished to claim it; but once having ascertained that, I did not trouble myself to think for what purpose it was destined. Besides, did I know it, it might seem so grave a matter as almost to force me to waive my claim, which really at present I cannot afford to do. Therefore, I prefer to be ignorant."

"Oh, monsieur," cried the cardinal, "do not think I wish to parade my embarrassments in order to elude my debt! You have your own interests to look to; they are guaranteed by this paper, which bears my signature—that is enough. You shall have your money, although I do not think there was any promise to pay."

"Your eminence is mistaken;" and opening the paper he read these words:

> "I acknowledge the receipt of 500,000 francs from M.
> Joseph Balsamo, which I will repay on demand.
> "Louis de Rohan."

"You see, monseigneur, that I only ask my right; besides, as this was a spontaneous loan by me to a man I hardly knew, the payment might have been equally spontaneous, without waiting for me to claim it. But you did not think so. Well, monseigneur, I withdraw this paper, and bid you adieu."

"No, count," replied the cardinal; "a Rohan must not receive lessons in generosity; besides, this is a mere question of honesty. Give me the paper, sir, and I will discharge my debt."

For a moment Cagliostro hesitated, for the pale face and distressed air of the cardinal inclined him to pity; but quickly hardening himself he handed him the paper. M. de Rohan went to the cabinet, and took out the money. "There," said he, "are your 500,000 francs; and I owe you 250,000 more for interest, which you shall have if you will give me time."

"Monseigneur," said Cagliostro, "I lent 500,000 francs to M. de Rohan, which he has paid me; he therefore owes me nothing more. I will take the notes with me, and send for the money. I thank you for your compliance with my request." Then, bowing, he left the room.

"Well," sighed M. de Rohan, "it is likely, at least, that the queen has the money, and no Joseph Balsamo will come and take it from her."

CHAPTER LVIII
FAMILY ACCOUNTS

It was the day before the first payment was due, and M. de Calonne had so much to do, that he had forgotten his promise. The queen had up to this time waited patiently, relying on his word; she now, however, was beginning to grow uneasy, when she received the following note:

> "This evening the business with which your majesty has charged me will be settled by the Council; the money will be with the queen to-morrow evening."

Marie Antoinette recovered all her gaiety directly.

After dinner the king went to the Council, but in a rather bad humor. The news from Russia was bad; a vessel had been lost; some of the provinces refused to pay the taxes; also a beautiful map of the world, made by himself, had that day split into two pieces. Vainly, therefore, M. de Calonne produced his accounts, with his usual smiling air; the king continued out of temper. For a long time he sat, as usual, drawing hieroglyphics on a piece of paper, whilst the foreign correspondence was being read, and paying little attention to what passed around him.

At last, however, M. de Calonne began to speak of the loan to be raised for the ensuing year. The king became attentive, and said, "Always borrowing; but how is it to be repaid? That is a problem, M. de Calonne, for you to solve."

"Sire, a loan is only turning a stream from one direction, to cause it to flow more abundantly in another. In deepening the channel, you only increase the supply; therefore, let us not think of paying, but only of obtaining present supplies." M. de Calonne then explained his plans, which were approved by his colleagues.

The king agreed, with a sigh.

"Now we have money," said M. de Calonne, "let us dispose of it;" and he handed a paper to the king, with a list of pensions, gifts, and payments to be made.

The king glanced at the total, — "1,900,000 francs for this — enormous!"

"But, sire, one item is 500,000 francs."

"Which?"

"The advance to the queen."

"To the queen! 500,000 francs to the queen!—impossible!"

"Pardon, sire, it is correct."

"But there must be a mistake; a fortnight ago her majesty received her money."

"Sire, but if her majesty has need of money; and we all know how well she employs it."

"No," cried the king; "the queen does not want this money; she said to me that she preferred a vessel to jewels. The queen thinks but of France, and when France is poor, we that are rich ought to lend to France; and if she does require this money, it will be a greater merit to wait for it; and I guarantee that she will wait."

The ministers applauded this patriotic speech of the king,—only M. de Calonne insisted.

"Really, monsieur," said the king, "you are more interested for us than we are for ourselves."

"The queen, sire, will accuse us of having been backward when her interests were concerned."

"I will plead your cause."

"But, sire, the queen never asks without necessity."

"If the queen has wants, they are, I trust, less imperious than those of the poor, and she will be the first to acknowledge it."

"Sire!"

"I am resolved," said the king; "and I fancy I hear the queen in her generosity thanking me for having so well understood her heart."

M. de Calonne bit his lips, and Louis, content with this personal sacrifice, signed all the rest without looking at them.

"Calonne, you shall tell the queen yourself."

"Oh! sire, I beg to resign to you the honor."

"So be it then. Ah! here she comes, let us meet her."

"I beg your majesty to excuse me," he replied, and retired quickly.

The king approached the queen—she was leaning on the arm of the Comte d'Artois, and seemed very gay.

"Madame," said the king, "have you had a pleasant walk?"

"Yes, sire. And you an agreeable council?"

"Yes, madame, I have gained you 500,000 francs."

"M. de Calonne has kept his word," thought the queen.

"Only imagine, madame," continued the king; "M. de Calonne had put down 500,000 francs for you, and I have struck it out,—a clear gain, therefore, of that sum."

"Struck it through!" cried the queen, turning pale; "but, sire— —"

"Oh! I am so hungry, I am going to supper;" and he went away delighted with his work.

"Brother," said the queen, "seek M. de Calonne for me."

At that moment a note from him was handed to her: "Your majesty will have learned that the king refused your grant. It was incomprehensible, and I retired from the council penetrated with grief."

"Read," said she, passing the note to the count.

"And there are people," said he, "who say that we squander the revenue! This is an extraordinary proceeding— —"

"Quite husbandlike," said the queen. "Adieu, brother."

"I condole with you," he replied; "and it is a lesson for me. I was going to make a request to-morrow for myself."

"Send for Madame de la Motte," said the queen, when she returned to her room.

CHAPTER LIX
MARIE ANTOINETTE AS QUEEN, AND MADAME DE LA MOTTE AS WOMAN

The courier despatched for Madame de la Motte, not finding her at home, went to the hotel of the Cardinal de Rohan to inquire if she were there.

The well-tutored Swiss replied that she was not, but that he could get any message transmitted to her.

The courier, therefore, left word for her to come to the queen as soon as possible. The man had hardly left the door before the message was delivered to Jeanne as she sat at supper with the cardinal. She set off immediately, and was at once introduced into the queen's chamber.

"Oh!" cried the queen on seeing her, "I have something to tell you. The king has refused me 500,000 francs."

"Mon Dieu!" murmured the countess.

"Incredible, is it not? He struck through the item; but it is useless to talk of it; you must return to Paris, and tell the cardinal that since he is so kind I accept the 500,000 francs he offered me. It is selfish, I know, but what can I do?"

"Oh! madame!" cried Jeanne, "we are lost—the cardinal no longer has the money."

The queen started.

"No money!" stammered she.

"No, madame; an unexpected creditor claimed this money from him. It was a debt of honor, and he paid it."

"The whole 500,000 francs?"

"Yes, madame."

"And he has no more?"

"No, madame, he told me this an hour and a half ago, and confessed to me that he had no other resources."

The queen leaned her head on her hands; then, after a few moments' reflection, she said:

"This, countess, is a terrible lesson for me, and a punishment for having done anything, great or small, without the king's knowledge. It was a folly; I had no need of this necklace."

"True, madame; but if the queen consulted only her absolute wants— —"

"I must consult before everything the tranquillity and happiness of my household. I renounce forever what has begun with so much annoyance. I will sacrifice my vanity on the altar of duty, as M. de Provence would say; and beautiful as this necklace is, you shall carry it back to MM. Bœhmer and Bossange."

"Carry it back?"

"Yes."

"But, madame, your majesty has already given 100,000 francs for it."

"Well, I shall gain all the rest that was to have been paid for it."

"But, madame, they will not like to return your money."

"I give it up on condition of their breaking the contract. Now, countess, that I have come to this determination, I feel at ease once more. This necklace brought with it cares and fears; diamonds cannot compensate for these. Take it away, countess; the jewelers must be satisfied; they will have their necklace, and 100,000 francs into the bargain."

"But M. de Rohan?"

"He only acted to give me pleasure, and when he is told it is my pleasure, not to have the necklace, he will understand me, I am sure; and if he is a good friend, he will approve and strengthen me in my sacrifice." Saying these words, the queen held out the casket to Jeanne.

She did not take it. "Why not ask for time, madame?"

"No, countess, it is humiliation. One may humiliate one's self for a person one loves, to save a living creature, were it only a dog; but only to keep some sparkling stones—never, countess; take it away."

"But, madame, it will surely become known that your majesty has had the jewels, and was obliged to return them."

"No one will know anything about it. The jewelers will surely hold their tongues for 100,000 francs. Take it away, countess, and thank M. de Rohan for his good-will towards me. There is no time to lose; go as soon as possible, and bring me back a receipt for them."

"Madame, it shall be done as you wish."

She first drove home, and changed her dress, which was too elegant for a visit to the jewelers. Meanwhile she reflected much; she thought still it was a fault for M. de Rohan to allow the queen to part with these jewels; and should she obey her orders without consulting him, would he not have reason to complain? Would he not rather sell himself than let the queen return them? "I must consult him," she thought; "but, after all, he never can get the money." She then took the necklace from the case, once more to look at and admire it. "1,600,000 francs in my possession; true, it is but for an hour. To carry away such a sum in gold I should want two horses, yet how easily I hold it here! But I must decide. Shall I go to the cardinal, or take it direct to the jewelers, as the queen ordered? And the receipt—in what form shall I get it, so as not to compromise the queen, the cardinal, or myself? Shall I consult— — Ah! if he loved me more, and could give me the diamonds."

She sat down again and remained nearly an hour in deep thought. Then she rose, with a strange look in her eyes, and rang the bell with a determined air.

She ordered a coach, and in a few minutes she reached the house of the journalist, M. Reteau de Villette.

CHAPTER LX
THE RECEIPT OF MM. BŒHMER AND BOSSANGE, AND THE GRATITUDE OF THE QUEEN

The result of Madame de la Motte's visit to M. Reteau de Villette appeared the next day. At seven o'clock in the morning she sent to the queen the following paper:

"We, the undersigned, acknowledge having received back again the diamond necklace sold to the queen for 1,600,000 francs, the diamonds not suiting her majesty, who has paid us for our loss and trouble 100,000 francs.

"Bœhmer and Bossange."

The queen, now tranquil about the whole affair, locked up the receipt, and thought no more of it.

But, in strange contradiction to this receipt, the jewelers received a visit two days after from M. de Rohan, who felt uneasy about the payment.

If the instalment had not been paid, he expected to find them naturally annoyed; but to his great satisfaction they received him with smiles.

"The queen has paid, then?" he asked.

"No, monseigneur, the queen could not procure the money, as the king had refused it to her; but she has guaranteed the debt, and that fully satisfies us."

"Ah! so much the better; but how? Through the countess?"

"No, monseigneur. On hearing of the king's refusal, which soon became public, we wrote to Madame de la Motte——"

"When?"

"Yesterday."

"And she replied?"

"By one word, 'Wait.' That evening we received from the queen, by a courier, a letter."

"A letter to you?"

"Or rather a guarantee, in due form."

"Let me see it."

"Oh! we would with pleasure, but her majesty enjoins that it is not to be shown to any one."

"Then you are safe?"

"Perfectly, monseigneur."

"The queen acknowledges the debt?"

"Fully."

"And engages to pay?"

"500,000 francs in three months, the rest in six;" and she adds, "let the affair rest between ourselves. You will have no cause to repent it."

"I am charmed that it is settled," said the cardinal.

We must now raise the veil, though, doubtless, our readers comprehend how Jeanne de la Motte had acted towards her benefactress, and how she had managed to satisfy both the queen and the jewelers by borrowing the pen of M. Reteau.

Three months were thus obtained for the completion of her design of crime and deception, and within three months everything would be arranged.

She went to M. de Rohan, and repeated to him what the jewelers had already told him.

He asked if the queen remembered his good intentions. She drew a picture of her gratitude, which enchanted him.

Her intention had been to sell some of the diamonds to the value of 100,000 crowns, and then pass over to England, where, when necessary, she could dispose of the remainder. But her first essay frightened her; some offered despicably small sums for the stones, others went into raptures, declaring they had never seen such diamonds but in the necklace of MM. Bœhmer and Bossange.

She abandoned this course, therefore, which she saw might soon bring about her ruin. She shut up the diamonds carefully, and resolved to wait. But her position was critical. A few words of explanation between the queen and the cardinal, and all would be discovered. She consoled herself by thinking that the cardinal was too much in love not to fall into all the snares she might lay for him.

One thought alone occupied her—how to prevent their meeting. That he would not be long satisfied without an interview she knew—what should she do? Persuade him to ask for one, and offend the queen by his presumption?—but then the queen would speak her anger out, and all would come to light. She must compromise her, and endeavor so to close her lips. But if they met by chance, what remained for her but flight? That was easy; a few hours would suffice. Then, again, she thought of the name she would leave behind her, and bear with her; no longer a woman of rank, but a thief, whom justice only does not reach, because she is too far off. No, she would not fly, if she could help it. She would try what audacity and skill could do, remain here and act between them. "To prevent them from meeting—that is the difficulty, as he is in love, and a prince, who has a right to see the queen; and she is now grateful and will no longer fly from him; but if I excite him to too open an admiration and disgust her, I alienate them more than ever. She will take fire easily, but what I want is something to make the queen tremble as well as him; something which would give me power to say, 'If you accuse me, I will accuse you and ruin you—leave me my wealth, and I will you your honor.' This is what I must seek for, and what I must find."

CHAPTER LXI
THE PRISONER

Meanwhile a different scene was passing in the Rue St. Claude, where M. de Cagliostro had lodged Oliva in the old house, to keep her from the pursuit of the police. There she lived, retired, and almost happy: Cagliostro lavished care and attentions on her, and she liked being protected by this great lord, who asked nothing from her in return. Only what did he want? she often asked herself, uselessly, for he must have some object. Her amour propre made her decide that after all he was in love with her; and she began to build castles in the air in which we must confess poor Beausire now very rarely had a place. Therefore the two visits a week paid to her by Cagliostro were always eagerly looked forward to, and between them she amused herself with her dreams, and playing the great lady. However, her books were soon read through, at least such as suited her taste, and pictures and music soon wearied her. She soon began to regret her mornings passed at the windows of the Rue Dauphine, where she used to sit to attract the attention of the passers-by; and her delightful promenades in the Quartier St. Germain, where so many people used to turn to look after her. True, the police-agents were formidable people, but what availed safety if she was not amused; so she first regretted her liberty, and then regretted Beausire.

Then she began to lose her appetite for want of fresh air, for she had been used to walk every day.

One day, when she was bemoaning her fate, she received an unexpected visit from Cagliostro. He gave his accustomed signal, and she opened the door, which was always kept bolted, with an eagerness which showed her delight; and, seizing his hands, she cried, in an impatient voice, "Monsieur, I am ennuyée here."

"This is unlucky, my dear child."

"I shall die here."

"Really?"

"Yes."

"Well," said he, soothingly, "do not blame me, blame the lieutenant of police, who persecutes you."

"You exasperate me with your sang froid, monsieur; I would rather you flew in a passion."

"Confess, mademoiselle, that you are unreasonable," said he, seating himself.

"It is all very well for you to talk," replied she; "you come and go as you like, you breathe the fresh air, your life is full of pleasure. I vegetate in the space to which you have limited me, and your assistance, is useless to me if I am to die here."

"Die!" said the count, smiling.

"You behave very badly to me; you forget that I love passionately."

"M. Beausire?"

"Yes, Beausire, I love him. I always told you so. Did you think I had forgotten him?"

"So little did I think so, mademoiselle, that I bring you news of him."

"Ah!"

"He is a charming person, young and handsome, is he not?"

"Full of imagination and fire, rather rough toward me, but that is his way of showing his love."

"Therefore I wished to take you back to him."

"You did not wish that a month ago."

"No, but when I see how you love him."

"Ah! you are laughing at me."

"Oh, no, you have resisted all my advances so well."

"Yes, have I not?"

"It was your love for him."

"But yours, then, was not very tenacious."

"No, I am neither old enough nor ugly enough, neither poor enough nor foolish enough, to run the risk of a refusal; and I saw that you would always have preferred Beausire."

"Oh, but," cried the coquette, using her eyes, which had remained idle so long, "this famous compact which you proposed to me, the right of always giving me your arm, of visiting me when you liked; did that give you no hope?"

Cagliostro did not reply, but turned his eyes as if dazzled by her glances.

"Let us return to Beausire," she said, piqued at his indifference; "why have you not brought him here? it would have been a charity. He is free—"

"Because," replied Cagliostro, "Beausire has too much imagination, and has also embroiled himself with the police."

"What has he done?"

"Oh, a delightful trick, a most ingenious idea; I call it a joke, but matter-of-fact people—and you know how matter-of-fact M. de Crosne can be—call it a theft."

"A theft!" cried Oliva, frightened. "Is he arrested?"

"No, but he is pursued."

"And is he in danger?"

"That I cannot tell you; he is well hunted for, and if you were together, the chances of his being taken would be doubled."

"Oh, yes, he must hide, poor fellow; I will hide too; let me leave France, monsieur. Pray render me this service; for if I remain shut up here, I shall end by committing some imprudence."

"What do you call imprudence?"

"Oh, just getting some fresh air."

"I do not want to prevent your getting fresh air; you would lose your beauty, and M. Beausire would love you no longer. Open the windows as much as you like."

"Oh, I see I have offended you; you care no more about me."

"Offended me—how?"

"Because you had taken a fancy to me, and I repulsed you. A man of your consequence, a handsome man like you, has a right to be angry at being rejected by a poor girl like me. But do not abandon me, sir, I entreat;" and she put her arms round his neck.

"Poor little thing," said he, kissing her forehead; "do not be afraid; I am not angry or offended. Indeed, were you to offer me your love, I should refuse you, so much do I desire to inspire pure sentiments. Besides, I should think you influenced more by gratitude than love; so we will remain as we are, and I will continue to protect you."

Oliva let his hand fall, humiliated, and duped by the pretended generosity of Cagliostro. "Oh, I shall say henceforth," she cried, "that there are men superior to what I ever thought."

"All women are good," thought Cagliostro, "if you only touch the right chord.—From this evening," he said aloud, "you shall move to other rooms, where the windows look on Menilmontant and the Bellevue. You need not fear to show yourself to the neighbors; they are all honest, simple people, who will never suspect you. Only keep a little back from the window, lest any one passing through the street should see you. At least you will have air and sunshine."

Oliva looked pleased.

"Shall I conduct you there now?"

"Oh, yes."

He took a light, and she followed him up a staircase to the third story, and entered a room, completely furnished, and ready for occupation.

"One would think it was prepared for me," she said.

"Not for you, but for myself; I like this place, and often come here to sleep. Nothing shall be wanting to make you comfortable, and your femme-de-chambre shall attend you in a quarter of an hour." And he left the room.

The poor prisoner sat down by her elegant bed, murmuring, "I understand nothing of all this."

CHAPTER LXII
THE LOOK OUT

Oliva went to bed, and slept better. She admired the count, whom she did not in the least understand. She could no longer think him timid; she did not suspect that he was only cold and insensible. She felt pleased at the perfect safety in which he assured her she was; and in the morning she examined her new rooms, and found them nobly and luxuriously furnished, and enjoyed immensely her privilege of going out into the balcony, filled with flowers, and where she got sunshine and fresh air, although she drew back whenever she saw any one approaching, or heard a carriage coming. There were not many, however, in the Rue St. Claude. She could see the château of Menilmontant, the great trees in the cemetery, myriads of houses of all colors; and she could see the fields beyond, full of children at play, and the peasants trotting along the roads on their donkeys. All this charmed Oliva, who had always a heart of love for the country, since she had left Taverney Maison-Rouge. At last, getting tired of this distant view, she began to examine the houses opposite to her. In some, she saw birds in cages; and in one, hung with yellow silk curtains, and ornamented with flowers, she thought she could distinguish a figure moving about. She called her femme-de-chambre to make inquiries about them; but the woman could only show her mistress all the churches, and tell her the names of the streets; she knew nothing of the neighbors. Oliva therefore sent her away again, and determined to watch for herself.

She saw some open their doors, and come out for a walk, and others variously occupied. At last she saw the figure of a woman seat herself in an armchair, in the room with the yellow curtains, and abandon her head for an hour and a half to a hair-dresser, while he built up one of those immense edifices worn at that time, in which minerals, vegetables, and even animals, were introduced. At last, it was complete: Oliva thought she looked pretty, and admired her little foot, encased in a rose-colored slipper, which rested on another chair. She began to construct all sorts of romances about this lady, and made various movements to attract her attention, but she never turned her eyes that way, as that room had never before been occupied, and she began to despair. The lady was, of course, Jeanne de Valois, who was deeply absorbed in devising some scheme for preventing the queen and the cardinal from meeting. At last, Oliva, turning suddenly round, knocked over a flower-pot which fell from the balcony with a crash: at the sound the lady turned and saw her, and clasping her hands she called out, "The Queen;" but looking again, she murmured, "Oh! I sought for a means to gain my end, and I have found one." Then, hearing a sound behind her, Oliva turned and saw Cagliostro, and came in directly.

CHAPTER LXIII
THE TWO NEIGHBORS

Cagliostro recommended her using the greatest circumspection, and, above all, not to make friends with her neighbors; but she did not feel disposed to relinquish the intercourse which she hoped for with her fair neighbor opposite. She, however, promised to obey him; but he was no sooner gone than she returned to her balcony, hoping to attract her attention again. Nor was she disappointed, for Jeanne, who was watching for her, acknowledged her with a bow and by kissing her hand. This went on for two days. Jeanne was ever ready to wave her a good morning, or an adieu when she went out.

Cagliostro, at his next visit, informed Oliva that an unknown person had paid a visit to her hotel.

"What do you mean?" cried Oliva.

"A very pretty and elegant lady presented herself here, and asked the servant who inhabited this story, and wished to see you. I fear you are discovered; you must take care, the police have female spies as well as male, and I warn you, that if M. de Crosne claims you, I cannot refuse to give you up."

Oliva was not at all frightened, she recognized the portrait of her opposite neighbor, and felt delighted at this advance, but she dissembled with the count, and said, "Oh! I am not at all frightened; no one has seen me; she could not have meant me."

"But she said a lady in these rooms."

"Well, I will be more careful than ever, and, besides, this house is so impenetrable."

"Yes, without climbing the wall, which is not easy, or opening the little door with a key like mine, which I never lend, no one can come in, so I think you are safe."

Oliva overwhelmed the count with thanks and protestations, but at six o'clock the next morning she was out in the balcony. She had not long to wait before Jeanne appeared, who, after looking cautiously up and down the street, and observing that all the doors and windows were still closed, and that everything was quiet, called across, "I wish to pay you a visit, madame; is it impossible to see you?"

"Alas, yes!" said Oliva.

"Can I send a letter?"

"Oh, no!"

Jeanne, after a moment's thought, left her balcony, but soon returned with a cross-bow, with which she shot a little wooden ball right through the open window of Oliva's room.

She picked it up and found wrapped round it the following note:

"You interest me, beautiful lady. I find you charming, and love you only by having seen you. Are you a prisoner? I vainly tried to obtain admission to you. Does the enchanter who guards you never let any one approach you? Will you be my friend? If you cannot go out, you can at least write, and as I go out when I please, wait till you see me pass, and then throw out your answer. Tie a thread to your balcony, and attach your note to it; I will take it off and fasten mine on, and in the dark no one will observe us. If your eyes have not deceived me, I count on a return of my affection and esteem, and between us we will outwit any one.

"Your Friend."

Oliva trembled with joy when she read this note. She replied as follows:

"I love you as you love me. I am a victim of the wickedness and cruelty of men; but he who keeps me here is a protector and not a tyrant; he comes to see me nearly every day. I will explain all this some day; but, alas! I cannot go out; I am locked up. Oh! if I could but see you; there is so much we cannot write.

"Your friend,

"Oliva Legay."

Then, when evening came, she let the thread fall over the balcony. Jeanne, who was below, caught it, and half an hour afterwards attached to it the following answer:

"You seem generally alone. How is your house secured— with a key? Who has this key? Could you not borrow or steal it? It would be no harm, but would procure you a few hours of liberty, or a few walks with a friend, who would console you for all your misfortune."

Oliva devoured this eagerly. She had remarked that when the count came in he put down his lantern and the key on a chiffonier. So she prepared some wax to take the impression of the key at his first visit. This she accomplished without his once turning to look at her, and as soon as he was gone, she put it into a little box, and lowered it to Jeanne, with a note.

The next day she received the following answer:

"My Dearest,

"To-night, at eleven o'clock, you will descend and unlock the door, when you will find yourself in the arms of your faithful friend."

Oliva felt more charmed than with the most tender love-letter that she had ever received. At the appointed time she went down and met Jeanne, who embraced her tenderly, and made her get into a carriage that waited a little way off; they remained out two hours, and parted with kisses and protestations of affection. Jeanne learned the name of Oliva's protector; she feared this man, and determined to preserve the most perfect mystery as to her plans. Oliva had confided everything to her about Beausire, the police, and all. Jeanne gave herself out for a young lady of rank, living here secretly, without the knowledge of her friends. One knew all, the other nothing. From this day, then, it was no longer necessary to throw out notes; Jeanne had her key, and carried off Oliva whenever she pleased. "M. de Cagliostro suspects nothing?" she often asked Oliva.

"Oh! no," she would reply; "I do not think he would believe it if I told him."

A week passed thus.

CHAPTER LXIV
THE RENDEZVOUS

When Charny arrived at his estates, the doctor ordered him to keep within doors, and not receive visitors; orders which he rigorously obeyed, to the great disappointment of all the young ladies in the neighborhood, who were most anxious to see this young man, reputed to be at once so brave and so handsome. His malady, however, was more mental than bodily; he was devoured by regrets, by longings, and by ennui; so, after a week, he set off one night on horseback, and, before the morning, was at Versailles. He found a little house there, outside the park, which had been empty for some time; it had been inhabited by one of the king's huntsmen, who had cut his throat, and since then the place had been deserted. There Charny lived in profound solitude; but he could see the queen from afar when she walked in the park with her ladies, and when she went in again he could see her windows from his own, and watch her lights every evening until they disappeared; and he even fancied he could see her shadow pass before the window. One evening he had watched all this as usual, and after sitting two hours longer at his window, was preparing to go to bed, for midnight was striking from a neighboring clock, when the sound of a key turning in a lock arrested his attention. It was that of a little door leading into the park, only twenty paces from his cottage, and which was never used, except sometimes on hunting-days. Whoever it was that entered did not speak, but closed it again quietly, and entered an avenue under his windows. At first Charny could not distinguish them through the thick wood, though he could hear the rustling of dresses; but as they emerged into an open space, and bright moonlight, he almost uttered a cry of joy in recognizing the tournure of Marie Antoinette, and a glimpse of her face; she held in her hand a beautiful rose. Stifling his emotion, he stepped down as quietly as possible into the park, and hid behind a clump of trees, where he could see her better. "Oh!" thought he, "were she but alone, I would brave tortures, or death itself, that I might once fall on my knees before her, and tell her, 'I love you!'" Oh, were she but menaced by some danger, how gladly would he have risked his life to save hers. Suddenly the two ladies stopped, and the shortest, after saying a few words to her companion in a low voice, left her. The queen, therefore, remained alone, and Charny felt inclined to run towards her; but he reflected that the moment she saw him she would take fright, and call out, and that her cries would first bring back her companion, and then the guards; that his retreat would be discovered, and he should be forced to leave it. In a few minutes the other lady reappeared, but not alone. Behind her came a man muffled up in a large cloak, and whose face was concealed by a slouch hat.

This man advanced with an uncertain and hesitating step to where the queen stood, when he took off his hat and made a low bow. The surprise which Charny felt at first soon changed into a more painful feeling. Why was the queen in the park at this time of night? Who was this man who was waiting for her, and whom she had sent her companion to fetch? Then he remembered that the queen often occupied herself with foreign politics, much to the annoyance of the king. Was this a secret messenger from Schoenbrunn, or from Berlin? This idea restored him to some degree of composure. The queen's companion stood a few steps off, anxiously watching lest they should be seen; but it was as necessary to guard against spies in a secret political rendezvous as in one of love. After a short time Charny saw the gentleman bow to the ground, and turn to leave, when the companion of the queen said to him, "Stop." He stopped, and the two ladies passed close to Charny, who could even recognize the queen's favorite scent, vervain, mixed with mignonette. They passed on, and disappeared. A few moments after the gentleman passed; he held in his hand a rose, which he pressed passionately to his lips. Did this look political? Charny's head turned; he felt a strong impulse to rush on this man and tear the flower from him, when the queen's companion reappeared, and said, "Come, monseigneur." He joined her quickly, and they went away. Charny remained in a distracted state, leaning against the tree.

CHAPTER LXV
THE QUEEN'S HAND

When Charny reentered the house, he felt overwhelmed by what he had seen—that he should have discovered this retreat, which he had thought so precious, only to be the witness of a crime, committed by the queen against her conjugal duty and royal dignity. This man must be a lover; in vain did he try to persuade himself that the rose was the pledge of some political compact, given instead of a letter, which might have been too compromising. The passionate kiss which he had seen imprinted on it forbade this supposition. These thoughts haunted him all night and all the next day, through which he waited with a feverish impatience, fearing the new revelations which the night might bring forth. He saw her taking her ordinary walk with her ladies, then watched the lights extinguished one by one, and he waited nervously for the stroke of midnight, the hour of the rendezvous of the preceding night. It struck, and no one had appeared. He then wondered how he could have expected it; she surely would not repeat the same imprudence two nights following. But as these thoughts passed through his mind, he heard the key turn again and saw the door open. Charny grew deadly pale when he recognized the same two figures enter the park. "Oh, it is too much," he said to himself, and then repeated his movements of the night before, swearing that, whatever happened, he would restrain himself, and remember that she was his queen. All passed exactly as the night before: the confidante left and returned with the same man; only this time, instead of advancing with his former timid respect, he almost ran up to the queen, and kneeled down before her. Charny could not hear what he said, but he seemed to speak with passionate energy. She did not reply, but stood in a pensive attitude; then he spoke again, and at last she said a few words, in a low voice, when the unknown cried out, in a loud voice, so that Charny could hear, "Oh! thanks, your majesty, till tomorrow, then." The queen drew her hood still more over her face, and held out both her hands to the unknown, who imprinted on them a kiss so long and tender that Charny gnashed his teeth with rage. The queen then took the arm of her companion and walked quickly away; the unknown passed also. Charny remained in a state of fury not to be described; he ran about the park like a madman: at last he began to wonder where this man came from; he traced his steps to the door behind the baths of Apollo. He comes not from Versailles, but from Paris, thought Charny, and to-morrow he will return, for he said, "to-morrow." Till then let me devour my tears in silence, but to-morrow shall be the last day of my life, for we will be four at the rendezvous.

CHAPTER LXVI
WOMAN AND QUEEN

The next night the door opened at the same time, and the two ladies appeared. Charny had taken his resolution—he would find out who this lover was; but when he entered the avenue he could see no one—they had entered the baths of Apollo. He walked towards the door, and saw the confidante, who waited outside. The queen, then, was in there alone with her lover; it was too much. Charny was about to seize this woman, and force her to tell him everything; but the rage and emotion he had endured were too much for him—a mist passed over his eyes, internal bleeding commenced, and he fainted. When he came to himself again, the clock was striking two, the place was deserted, and there was no trace of what had passed there. He went home, and passed a night almost of delirium. The next morning he arose, pale as death, and went towards the Castle of Trianon just as the queen was leaving the chapel. All heads were respectfully lowered as she passed. She was looking beautiful, and when she saw Charny she colored, and uttered an exclamation of surprise.

"I thought you were in the country, M. de Charny," she said.

"I have returned, madame," said he, in a brusque and almost rude tone.

She looked at him in surprise; then, turning to the ladies, "Good morning, countess," she said to Madame de la Motte, who stood near.

Charny started as he caught sight of her, and looked at her almost wildly. "He has not quite recovered his reason," thought the queen, observing his strange manner. Then, turning to him again, "How are you now, M. de Charny?" said she, in a kind voice.

"Very well, madame."

She looked surprised again; then said:

"Where are you living?"

"At Versailles, madame."

"Since when?"

"For three nights," replied he, in a marked manner.

The queen manifested no emotion, but Jeanne trembled.

"Have you not something to say to me?" asked the queen again, with kindness.

"Oh, madame, I should have too much to say to your majesty."

"Come," said she, and she walked towards her apartments; but to avoid the appearance of a tête-à-tête, she invited several ladies to follow her. Jeanne, unquiet, placed herself among them; but when they arrived, she dismissed Madame de Misery, and the other ladies, understanding that she wished to be alone, left her. Charny stood before her.

"Speak," said the queen; "you appear troubled, sir."

"How can I begin?" said Charny, thinking aloud; "how can I dare to accuse honor and majesty?"

"Sir!" cried Marie Antoinette, with a flaming look.

"And yet I should only say what I have seen."

The queen rose. "Sir," said she, "it is very early in the morning for me to think you intoxicated, but I can find no other solution for this conduct."

Charny, unmoved, continued, "After all, what is a queen?—a woman. And am I not a man as well as a subject?"

"Monsieur!"

"Madame, anger is out of place now. I believe I have formerly proved that I had respect for your royal dignity. I fear I proved that I had an insane love for yourself. Choose, therefore, to whom I shall speak. Is it to the queen, or the woman, that I shall address my accusation of dishonor and shame?"

"Monsieur de Charny," cried the queen, growing pale, "if you do not leave this room, I must have you turned out by my guards!"

"But I will tell you first," cried he, passionately, "why I call you an unworthy queen and woman! I have been in the park these three nights!"

Instead of seeing her tremble, as he believed she would on hearing these words, the queen rose, and, approaching him, said, "M. de Charny, your state excites my pity. Your hands tremble, you grow pale; you are suffering. Shall I call for help?"

"I saw you!" cried he again; "saw you with that man to whom you gave the rose! saw you when he kissed your hands! saw you when you entered the baths of Apollo with him!"

The queen passed her hands over her eyes, as if to make sure that she was not dreaming.

"Sit down," said she, "or you will fall."

Charny, indeed, unable to keep up, fell upon the sofa.

She sat down by him. "Be calm," said she, "and repeat what you have just said."

"Do you want to kill me?" he murmured.

"Then let me question," she said. "How long have you returned from the country?"

"A fortnight."

"Where do you live?"

"In the huntsman's house, which I have hired."

"At the end of the park?"

"Yes."

"You speak of some one whom you saw with me."

"Yes."

"Where?"

"In the park."

"When?"

"At midnight. Tuesday, for the first time, I saw you and your companion."

"Oh, I had a companion! Do you know her also?"

"I thought just now I recognized her, but I could not be positive, because it was only the figure—she always hid her face, like all who commit crimes."

"And this person to whom you say I gave a rose?"

"I have never been able to meet him."

"You do not know him, then?"

"Only that he is called monseigneur."

The queen stamped her foot.

"Go on!" said she. "Tuesday I gave him a rose— —"

"Wednesday you gave him your hands to kiss, and yesterday you went alone with him into the baths of Apollo, while your companion waited outside."

"And you saw me?" said she, rising.

He lifted his hands to heaven, and cried, "I swear it!"

"Oh, he swears!"

"Yes. On Tuesday you wore your green dress, moirée, with gold; Wednesday, the dress with great blue and brown leaves; and yesterday, the same dress that you wore when I last kissed your hand. Oh, madame, I am ready to die with grief and shame while I repeat that, on my life, my honor, it was really you!"

"What can I say?" cried the queen dreadfully agitated. "If I swore, he would not believe me."

Charny shook his head.

"Madman!" cried she, "thus to accuse your queen—to dishonor thus an innocent woman! Do you believe me when I swear, by all I hold sacred, that I was not in the park on either of those days after four o'clock? Do you wish it to be proved by my women—by the king? No; he does not believe me."

"I saw you," replied he.

"Oh, I know!" she cried. "Did they not see me at the ball at the Opera, at Mesmer's, scandalizing the crowd? You know it—you, who fought for me!"

"Madame, then I fought because I did not believe it; now I might fight, but I believe."

The queen raised her arms to heaven, while burning tears rolled down her cheeks.

"My God," she cried, "send me some thought which will save me! I do not wish this man to despise me."

Charny, moved to the heart, hid his face in his hands.

Then, after a moment's silence, the queen continued:

"Sir, you owe me reparation. I exact this from you. You say you have seen me three nights with a man; I have been already injured through the resemblance to me of some woman, I know not whom, but who is like her unhappy queen; but you are pleased to think it was me. Well, I will go with you into the park; and if she appears again, you will be satisfied? Perhaps we shall see her together; then, sir, you will regret the suffering you have caused me."

Charny pressed his hands to his heart.

"Oh, madame, you overwhelm me with your kindness!"

"I wish to overwhelm you with proofs. Not a word, to any one, but this evening, at ten o'clock, wait alone at the door of the park. Now go, sir."

Charny kneeled, and went away without a word.

Jeanne, who was waiting in the ante-chamber, examined him attentively as he came out. She was soon after summoned to the queen.

CHAPTER LXVII
WOMAN AND DEMON

Jeanne had remarked the trouble of Charny, the solicitude of the queen, and the eagerness of both for a conversation.

After what we have already told of the meetings between Jeanne and Oliva, our readers will have been at no loss to understand the scenes in the park. Jeanne, when she came in to the queen, watched her closely, hoping to gather something from her; but Marie Antoinette was beginning to learn caution, and she guarded herself carefully. Jeanne was, therefore, reduced to conjectures. She had already ordered one of her footmen to follow M. de Charny; the man reported that he had gone into a house at the end of the park.

"There is, then, no more doubt," thought Jeanne; "it is a lover who has seen everything, it is clear. I should be a fool not to understand. I must undo what I have done."

On leaving Versailles, she drove to the Rue St. Claude; there she found a superb present of plate, sent to her by the cardinal. She then drove to his house, and found him radiant with joy and pride. On her entrance he ran to meet her, calling her "Dear countess," and full of protestations and gratitude.

"Thank you also, for your charming present. You are more than a happy man; you are a triumphant victor."

"Countess, it frightens me; it is too much."

Jeanne smiled.

"You come from Versailles?" continued he.

"Yes."

"You have seen her?"

"I have just left her."

"And she said nothing?"

"What do you expect that she said?"

"Oh, I am insatiable."

"Well, you had better not ask."

"You frighten me. Is anything wrong? Have I come to the height of my happiness, and is the descent to begin?"

"You are very fortunate not to have been discovered."

"Oh! with precautions, and the intelligence of two hearts and one mind— —"

"That will not prevent eyes seeing through the trees."

"We have been seen?"

"I fear so."

"And recognized?"

"Oh, monseigneur, if you had been—if this secret had been known to any one, Jeanne de Valois would be out of the kingdom, and you would be dead."

"True; but tell me quickly. They have seen people walking in the park; is there any harm in that?"

"Ask the king."

"The king knows?"

"I repeat to you, if the king knew, you would be in the Bastile. But I advise you not to tempt Providence again."

"What do you mean, dear countess?"

"Do you not understand?"

"I fear to understand," he replied.

"I shall fear, if you do not promise to go no more to Versailles."

"By day?"

"Or by night."

"Impossible!"

"Why so, monseigneur?"

"Because I have in my heart a love which will end only with my life."

"So I perceive," replied she, ironically; "and it is to arrive more quickly at this result that you persist in returning to the park; for most assuredly, if you do, your love and your life will end together."

"Oh, countess, how fearful you are—you who were so brave yesterday!"

"I am always brave when there is no danger."

"But I have the bravery of my race, and am happier in the presence of danger."

"But permit me to tell you — —"

"No, countess, the die is cast. Death, if it comes; but first, love. I shall return to Versailles."

"Alone, then."

"You abandon me?"

"And not I alone."

"She will come?"

"You deceive yourself; she will not come."

"Is that what you were sent to tell me?"

"It is what I have been preparing you for."

"She will see me no more?"

"Never; and it is I who have counseled it."

"Madame, do not plunge the knife into my heart!" cried he, in a doleful voice.

"It would be much more cruel, monseigneur, to let two foolish people destroy themselves for want of a little good advice."

"Countess, I would rather die."

"As regards yourself, that is easy; but, subject, you dare not dethrone your queen; man, you will not destroy a woman."

"But confess that you do not come in her name, that she does not throw me off."

"I speak in her name."

"It is only a delay she asks?"

"Take it as you wish; but obey her orders."

"The park is not the only place of meeting. There are a hundred safer spots—the queen can come to you, for instance."

"Monseigneur, not a word more. The weight of your secret is too much for me, and I believe her capable, in a fit of remorse, of confessing all to the king."

"Good God! impossible."

"If you saw her, you would pity her."

"What can I do then?"

"Insure your safety by your silence."

"But she will think I have forgotten her, and accuse me of being a coward."

"To save her."

"Can a woman forgive him who abandons her?"

"Do not judge her like others."

"I believe her great and strong. I love her for her courage and her noble heart. She may count on me, as I do on her. Once more I will see her, lay bare my heart to her; and whatever she then commands, I will sacredly obey."

Jeanne rose. "Go, then," said she, "but go alone. I have thrown the key of the park into the river. You can go to Versailles—I shall go to Switzerland or Holland. The further off I am when the shell bursts the better."

"Countess, you abandon me. With whom shall I talk of her?"

"Oh! you have the park and the echoes. You can teach them her name!"

"Countess, pity me; I am in despair."

"Well, but do not act in so childish and dangerous a manner. If you love her so much, guard her name, and if you are not totally without gratitude, do not involve in your own ruin those who have served you through friendship. Swear to me not to attempt to see or speak to her for a fortnight, and I will remain, and may yet be of service to you. But if you decide to brave all, I shall leave at once, and you must extricate yourself as you can."

"It is dreadful," murmured the cardinal; "the fall from so much happiness is overwhelming. I shall die of it."

"Suffering is always the consequence of love. Come, monseigneur, decide. Am I to remain here, or start for Lausanne?"

"Remain, countess."

"You swear to obey me."

"On the faith of a Rohan."

"Good. Well, then, I forbid interviews, but not letters."

"Really! I may write?"

"Yes."

"And she will answer."

"Try."

The cardinal kissed Jeanne's hand again, and called her his guardian angel. The demon within her must have laughed.

CHAPTER LXVIII
THE NIGHT

That day, at four o'clock, a man on horseback stopped in the outskirts of the park, just behind the baths of Apollo, where M. de Rohan used to wait. He got off, and looked at the places where the grass had been trodden down. "Here are the traces," thought he; "it is as I supposed. M. de Charny has returned for a fortnight, and this is where he enters the park." And he sighed. "Leave him to his happiness. God gives to one, and denies to another. But I will have proof to-night. I will hide in the bushes, and see what happens."

As for Charny, obedient to the queen's commands, he waited for orders; but it was half-past ten, and no one appeared. He waited with impatient anxiety. Then he began to think she had deceived him, and had promised what she did not mean to perform. "How could I be so foolish—I, who saw her—to be taken in by her words and promises!" At last he saw a figure approaching, wrapped in a large black mantle, and he uttered a cry of joy, for he recognized the queen. He ran to her, and fell at her feet.

"Ah, here you are, sir! it is well."

"Ah, madame! I scarcely hoped you were coming."

"Have you your sword?"

"Yes, madame."

"Where do you say those people came in?"

"By this door."

"At what time?"

"At midnight each time."

"There is no reason why they should not come again to-night. You have not spoken to any one."

"To no one."

"Come into the thick wood, and let us watch, I have not spoken of this to M. de Crosne. I have already mentioned this creature to him, and if she be not arrested, he is either incapable, or in league with my enemies.

It seems incredible that any one should dare to play such tricks under my eyes, unless they were sure of impunity. Therefore, I think it is time to take the care of my reputation on myself. What do you think?"

"Oh, madame! allow me to be silent! I am ashamed of all I have said."

"At least you are an honest man," replied the queen, "and speak to the accused face to face. You do not stab in the dark."

"Oh, madame, it is eleven o'clock! I tremble."

"Look about, that no one is here."

Charny obeyed.

"No one," said he.

"Where did the scenes pass that you have described?"

"Oh, madame! I had a shock when I returned to you; for she stood just where you are at this moment."

"Here!" cried the queen, leaving the place with disgust.

"Yes, madame; under the chestnut tree."

"Then, sir, let us move, for they will most likely come here again."

He followed the queen to a different place. She, silent and proud, waited for the proof of her innocence to appear. Midnight struck. The door did not open. Half an hour passed, during which the queen asked ten times if they had always been punctual.

Three-quarters struck—the queen stamped with impatience. "They will not come," she cried; "these misfortunes only happen to me;" and she looked at Charny, ready to quarrel with him, if she saw any expression of triumph or irony: but he, as his suspicions began to return, grew so pale and looked so melancholy, that he was like the figure of a martyr.

At last she took his arm, and led him under the chestnut tree. "You say," she murmured, "that it was here you saw her?"

"Yes, madame."

"Here that she gave the rose?" And the queen, fatigued and wearied with waiting and disappointment leaned against the tree, and covered her face with her hands, but Charny could see the tears stealing through. At last she raised her head:

"Sir," said she, "I am condemned. I promised to prove to you to-day that I was calumniated; God does not permit it, and I submit. I have done what no other woman, not to say queen, would have done. What a queen! who cannot reign over one heart, who cannot obtain the esteem of one honest man. Come, sir, give me your arm, if you do not despise me too much."

"Oh, madame!" cried he, falling at her feet, "if I were only an unhappy man who loves you, could you not pardon me?"

"You!" cried she, with a bitter laugh, "you love me! and believe me infamous!"

"Oh, madame!"

"You accuse me of giving roses, kisses, and love. No, sir, no falsehoods! you do not love me."

"Madame, I saw these phantoms. Pity me, for I am on the rack."

She took his hands. "Yes, you saw, and you think it was I. Well, if here under this same tree, you at my feet, I press your hands, and say to you, 'M, de Charny, I love you, I have loved, and shall love no one else in this world, may God pardon me'—will that convince you? Will you believe me then?" As she spoke, she came so close to him that he felt her breath on his lips. "Oh!" cried Charny, "now I am ready to die."

"Give me your arm," said she, "and teach me where they went, and where she gave the rose,"—and she took from her bosom a rose and held it to him. He took it and pressed it to his heart.

"Then," continued she, "the other gave him her hand to kiss."

"Both her hands," cried Charny, pressing his burning lips passionately on hers.

"Now they visited, the baths—so will we; follow me to the place." He followed her, like a man in a strange, happy dream. They looked all round, then opened the door, and walked through. Then they came out again: two o'clock struck. "Adieu," said she; "go home until to-morrow." And she walked away quickly towards the château.

When they were gone, a man rose from among the bushes. He had heard and seen all.

CHAPTER LXIX
THE CONGÉ

The queen went to mass the next day, which was Sunday, smiling and beautiful. When she woke in the morning she said, "It is a lovely day, it makes me happy only to live." She seemed full of joy, and was generous and gracious to every one. The road was lined as usual on her return with ladies and gentlemen. Among them were Madame de la Motte and M. de Charny, who was complimented by many friends on his return, and on his radiant looks. Glancing round, he saw Philippe standing near him, whom he had not seen since the day of the duel.

"Gentlemen," said Charny, passing through the crowd, "allow me to fulfil an act of politeness;" and, advancing towards Philippe, he said, "Allow me, M. de Taverney, to thank you now for the interest you have taken in my health. I shall have the honor to pay you a visit to-morrow. I trust you preserve no enmity towards me."

"None, sir," replied Philippe.

Charny held out his hand, but Philippe, without seeming to notice it, said, "Here comes the queen, sir." As she approached, she fixed her looks on Charny with that rash openness which she always showed in her affections, while she said to several gentlemen who were pressing round her, "Ask me what you please, gentlemen, for to-day I can refuse nothing." A voice said, "Madame." She turned, and saw Philippe, and thus found herself between two men, of whom she almost reproached herself with loving one too much and the other too little.

"M. de Taverney, you have something to ask me; pray speak——"

"Only ten minutes' audience at your majesty's leisure," replied he, with grave solemnity.

"Immediately, sir—follow me." A quarter of an hour after, Philippe was introduced into the library, where the queen waited for him.

"Ah! M. de Taverney, enter," said she in a gay tone, "and do not look so sorrowful. Do you know I feel rather frightened whenever a Taverney asks for an audience. Reassure me quickly, and tell me that you are not come to announce a misfortune."

"Madame, this time I only bring you good news."

"Oh! some news."

"Alas, yes, your majesty."

"There! an 'alas' again."

"Madame, I am about to assure your majesty that you need never again fear to be saddened by the sight of a Taverney; for, madame, the last of this family, to whom you once deigned to show some kindness, is about to leave the court of France forever."

The queen, dropping her gay tone, said, "You leave us?"

"Yes, your majesty."

"You also!"

Philippe bowed. "My sister, madame, has already had that grief; I am much more useless to your majesty."

The queen started as she remembered that Andrée had asked for her congé on the day following her first visit to Charny in the doctor's apartments. "It is strange," she murmured, as Philippe remained motionless as a statue, waiting his dismissal. At last she said abruptly, "Where are you going?"

"To join M. de la Pérouse, madame."

"He is at Newfoundland."

"I have prepared to join him there."

"Do you know that a frightful death has been predicted for him?"

"A speedy one," replied Philippe; "that is not necessarily a frightful one."

"And you are really going?"

"Yes, madame, to share his fate."

The queen was silent for a time, and then said, "Why do you go?"

"Because I am anxious to travel."

"But you have already made the tour of the world."

"Of the New World, madame, but not of the Old."

"A race of iron, with hearts of steel, are you Taverneys. You and your sister are terrible people—you go not for the sake of traveling, but to leave me. Your sister said she was called by religions duty; it was a pretext. However, she wished to go, and she went. May she be happy! You might be happy here, but you also wish to go away."

"Spare us, I pray you, madame; if you could read our hearts, you would find them full of unlimited devotion towards you."

"Oh!" cried the queen, "you are too exacting; she takes the world for a heaven, where one should only live as a saint; you look upon it as a hell — and both fly from it; she because she finds what she does not seek, and you because you do not find what you do seek. Am I not right? Ah! M. de Taverney, allow human beings to be imperfect, and do not expect royalty to be superhuman. Be more tolerant, or, rather, less egotistical." She spoke earnestly, and continued: "All I know is, that I loved Andrée, and that she left me; that I valued you, and you are about to do the same. It is humiliating to see two such people abandon my court."

"Nothing can humiliate persons like your majesty. Shame does not reach those placed so high."

"What has wounded you?" asked the queen.

"Nothing, madame."

"Your rank has been raised, your fortune was progressing."

"I can but repeat to your majesty that the court does not please me."

"And if I ordered you to stay here?"

"I should have the grief of disobeying your majesty."

"Oh! I know," cried she impatiently, "you bear malice; you quarreled with a gentleman here, M. de Charny, and wounded him; and because you see him returned to-day, you are jealous, and wish to leave."

Philippe turned pale, but replied, "Madame, I saw him sooner than you imagine, for I met him at two o'clock this morning by the baths of Apollo."

It was now the queen's time to grow pale, but she felt a kind of admiration for one who had retained so much courtesy and self-command in the midst of his anger and grief. "Go," murmured she at length, in a faint voice, "I will keep you no longer."

Philippe bowed, and left the room, while the queen sank, terrified and overwhelmed, on the sofa.

CHAPTER LXX
THE JEALOUSY OF THE CARDINAL

The cardinal passed three nights very different to those when he went to the park, and which he constantly lived over again in his memory. No news of any one, no hope of a visit; nothing but a dead silence, and perfect darkness, after such brightness and happiness. He began to fear that, after all, his sacrifice had been displeasing to the queen. His uneasiness became insupportable. He sent ten times in one day to Madame de la Motte: the tenth messenger brought Jeanne to him. On seeing her he cried out, "How! you live so tranquilly; you know my anxiety, and you, my friend, never come near me."

"Oh, monseigneur, patience, I beg. I have been far more useful to you at Versailles than I could have been here."

"Tell me," replied he, "what does she say? Is she less cruel?"

"Absence is equal pain, whether borne at Versailles or at Paris."

"Oh, I thank you, but the proofs— —"

"Proofs! Are you in your senses, monseigneur, to ask a woman for proofs of her own infidelity?"

"I am not speaking of proofs for a lawsuit, countess, only a token of love."

"It seems to me that you are either very exacting or very forgetful."

"Oh! I know you will tell me that I might be more than satisfied. But judge by yourself, countess; would you like to be thrown on one side, after having received assurances of favor?"

"Assurances!"

"Oh, certainly, I have nothing to complain of, but still— —"

"I cannot be answerable for unreasonable discontents."

"Countess, you treat me ill. Instead of reproaching me for my folly, you should try to aid me."

"I cannot aid you. I see nothing to do."

"Nothing to do?"

"No."

"Well, madame, I do not say the same."

"Ah, monseigneur, anger will not help you; and besides, you are unjust."

"No, countess; if you do not assist me any longer, I know it is because you cannot. Only tell me the truth at once."

"What truth?"

"That the queen is a perfidious coquette, who makes people adore her, and then drives them to despair."

Jeanne looked at him with an air of surprise, although she had expected him to arrive at this state, and she felt really pleased, for she thought that it would help her out of her difficult position. "Explain yourself," she said.

"Confess that the queen refuses to see me."

"I do not say so, monseigneur."

"She wishes to keep me away lest I should rouse the suspicions of some other lover."

"Ah, monseigneur!" cried Jeanne in a tone which gave him liberty to suspect anything.

"Listen," continued he; "the last time I saw her, I thought I heard steps in the wood——"

"Folly!"

"And I suspect——"

"Say no more, monseigneur. It is an insult to the queen; besides, even if it were true that she fears the surveillance of another lover, why should you reproach her with a past which she has sacrificed to you?"

"But if this past be again a present, and about to be a future?"

"Fie, monseigneur, your suspicions are offensive both to the queen and to me."

"Then, countess, bring me a proof—does she love me at all?"

"It is very simple," replied Jeanne, pointing to his writing table, "to ask her."

"You will give her a note?"

"Who else would, if not I?"

"And you will bring me an answer?"

"If possible."

"Ah! now you are a good creature, countess."

He sat down, but though he was an eloquent writer, he commenced and destroyed a dozen sheets of paper before he satisfied himself.

"If you go on so, you will never have done," said Jeanne.

"You see, countess, I fear my own tenderness, lest I displease the queen."

"Oh," replied Jeanne, "if you write a business letter, you will get one in reply. That is your own affair."

"You are right, countess; you always see what is best." He then wrote a letter, so full of loving reproaches and ardent protestations, that Jeanne, when he gave it to her to read, thought, "He has written of his own accord what I never should have dared to dictate."

"Will it do?" asked he.

"If she loves you. You will see to-morrow: till then be quiet."

"Till to-morrow, then."

On her return home Jeanne gave way to her reflections. This letter was just what she wanted. How could the cardinal ever accuse her, when he was called on to pay for the necklace? Even admitting that the queen and cardinal met, and that everything was explained, how could they turn against her while she held in her hands such proofs of a scandalous secret? No, they must let her go quietly off with her fortune of a million and a half of francs. They would know she had stolen the diamonds, but they never would publish all this affair; and if one letter was not enough, she would have seven or eight. The first explosion would come from the jewelers, who would claim their money. Then she must confess to M. de Rohan, and make him pay by threatening to publish his letters. Surely they would purchase the honor of a queen and a prince at the price of a million and a half! The jewelers once paid, that question was at an end; Jeanne felt sure of her fortune. She knew that the cardinal had a conviction so firm that nothing could shake it, that he had met the queen. There was but one living witness against her, and that one she would soon cause to disappear. Arrived at this point, she went to the window and saw Oliva, who was watching in her balcony. She made the accustomed sign for her to come down, and Oliva replied joyfully. The great thing now was to get rid of her. To destroy the instrument that has served them is the constant endeavor of those who intrigue; but here it is that they generally fail; they do not succeed in doing so before there has been time to disclose the secret. Jeanne knew that Oliva would not be easy to get rid of, unless she could think of something that would induce her to fly willingly. Oliva, on her part, much as she enjoyed her nocturnal promenades at first, after so much confinement, was already beginning to weary of them, and to sigh once more for liberty and Beausire.

The night came, and they went out together; Oliva disguised under a large cloak and hood, and Jeanne dressed as a grisette; besides which the carriage bore the respectable arms of Valois, which prevented the police, who alone might have recognized Oliva, from searching it.

"Oh! I have been so ennuyée," cried Oliva, "I have been expecting you so long."

"It was impossible to come and see you, I should have run, and made you run, a great danger."

"How so?" said Oliva, astonished.

"A terrible danger at which I still tremble. You know how ennuyée you were, and how much you wished to go out."

"Yes; and you assisted me like a friend."

"Certainly; I proposed that we should have some amusement with that officer who is rather mad, and in love with the queen, whom you resemble a little; and endeavor to persuade him that it was the queen he was walking with."

"Yes," said Oliva.

"The first two nights you walked in the park, and you played your part to perfection; he was quite taken in."

"Yes," said Oliva, "but it was almost a pity to deceive him, poor fellow, he was so delightful."

"Yes, but the evil is not there. To give a man a rose, to let him kiss your hands, and call you 'your majesty,' was all good fun; but, my little Oliva, it seems you did not stop here."

Oliva colored.

"How?" stammered she.

"There was a third interview."

"Yes," replied Oliva, hastily, "you know, for you were there."

"Excuse me, dear friend; I was there, but at a distance. I neither saw nor heard what passed within, I only know what you told me, that he talked and kissed your hands."

"Oh, mon Dieu!" murmured Oliva.

"You surely could not have exposed us both to such a terrible danger without telling me of it."

Oliva trembled from head to foot.

Jeanne continued. "How could I imagine that you, who said you loved M. Beausire, and were courted by a man like Count Cagliostro, whom you refused; oh! it cannot be true."

"But where is the danger?" asked Oliva.

"The danger! Have we not to manage a madman, one who fears nothing, and will not be controlled. It was no great thing for the queen to give him her hand to kiss or to give him a rose; oh, my dear child, I have not smiled since I heard this."

"What do you fear?" asked Oliva, her teeth chattering with terror.

"Why, as you are not the queen, and have taken her name, and in her name have committed a folly of this kind, that is unfortunately treason. He has no proof of this—they may be satisfied with a prison or banishment."

"A prison! banishment!" shrieked Oliva.

"I, at least, intend to take precautions and hide myself."

"You fear also?"

"Oh! will not this madman divulge my share also? My poor Oliva, this trick of yours will cost us dear."

Oliva burst into tears.

"Oh!" she cried, "I think I am possessed of a demon, that I can never rest: just saved from one danger, I must rush into another. Suppose I confess all to my protector?"

"A fine story to confess to him, whose advances you refused, that you have committed this imprudence with a stranger."

"Mon Dieu! you are right."

"Soon this report will spread, and will reach his ears; then do you not think he will give you up to the police? Even if he only send you away, what will become of you?"

"Oh! I am lost."

"And M. Beausire, when he shall hear this——?"

Oliva started, and wringing her hands violently, cried out, "Oh, he would kill me; but no, I will kill myself. You cannot save me, since you are compromised also."

"I have," replied Jeanne, "in the furthest part of Picardy, a little farm. If you can gain this refuge, you might be safe."

"But you?"

"Oh, once you were gone, I should not fear him."

"I will go whenever you like."

"I think you are wise."

"Must I go at once?"

"Wait till I have prepared everything to insure safety; meanwhile, hide yourself, and do not come near the window."

"Oh yes, dear friend."

"And to begin, let us go home, as there is no more to say."

"How long will your preparations take?"

"I do not know, but remember henceforth, until the day of your departure I shall not come to the window. When you see me there, you will know that the day has arrived, and be prepared."

They returned in silence. On arriving, Oliva begged pardon humbly of her friend for bringing her into so much danger through her folly.

"I am a woman," replied Jeanne, "and can pardon a woman's weakness."

CHAPTER LXXI
THE FLIGHT

Oliva kept her promise, and Jeanne also. Oliva hid herself from every one, and Jeanne made her preparations, and in a few days made her appearance at the window as a sign to Oliva to be ready that evening for flight.

Oliva, divided between joy and terror, began immediately to prepare. Jeanne went to arrange about the carriage that was to convey her away. Eleven o'clock at night had just struck when Jeanne arrived with a post-chaise to which three strong horses were harnessed. A man wrapped in a cloak sat on the box, directing the postilions. Jeanne made them stop at the corner of the street, saying, "Remain here—half an hour will suffice—and then I will bring the person whom you are to conduct with all possible speed to Amiens. There you will give her into the care of the farmer who is my tenant; he has his instructions."

"Yes, madame."

"I forgot—are you armed? This lady is menaced by a madman; he might, perhaps, try to stop her on the road."

"What should I do?"

"Fire on any one who tries to impede your journey."

"Yes, madame."

"You asked me seventy louis; I will give you a hundred, and will pay the expenses of the voyage which you had better make to London. Do not return here; it is more prudent for you to go to St. Valery, and embark at once for England."

"Rely on me, madame."

"Well, I will go and bring the lady."

All seemed asleep in that quiet house. Jeanne lighted the lamp which was to be the signal to Oliva, but received no answering sign. "She will come down in the dark," thought Jeanne; and she went to the door, but it did not open. Oliva was perhaps bringing down her packages. "The fool!"

murmured the countess, "how much time she is wasting over her rubbish!" She waited a quarter of an hour—no one came; then half-past eleven struck. "Perhaps she did not see my signal," thought Jeanne; and she went up and lighted it again, but it was not acknowledged. "She must be ill," cried Jeanne, in a rage, "and cannot move." Then she took the key which Oliva had given her; but just as she was about to open the door, she thought, "Suppose some one should be there? But I should hear voices on the staircase, and could return. I must risk something." She went up, and on arriving outside Oliva's door she saw a light inside and heard footsteps, but no voices. "It is all right," she thought; "she was only a long time getting ready." "Oliva," said she softly, "open the door." The door opened, and Jeanne found herself face to face with a man holding a torch in his hand.

"Oliva," said he, "is this you?" Then, with a tone of admirably-feigned surprise, cried, "Madame de la Motte!"

"M. de Cagliostro!" said she in terror, feeling half inclined to run away; but he took her hand politely, and begged her to sit down.

"To what do I owe the honor of this visit, madame?"

"Monsieur," said she, stammering, "I came—I sought— —"

"Allow me, madame, to inquire which of my servants was guilty of the rudeness of letting you come up unattended?"

Jeanne trembled.

"You must have fallen to the lot of my stupid German porter, who is always tipsy."

"Do not scold him, I beg you, sir," replied Jeanne, who could hardly speak.

"But was it he?"

"I believe so. But you promise me not to scold him?"

"I will not; only, madame, will you now explain to me— —"

Jeanne began to gather courage.

"I came to consult you, sir, about certain reports."

"What reports?"

"Do not hurry me, sir; it is a delicate subject."

"Ah! you want time to invent," thought he.

"You are a friend of M. le Cardinal de Rohan?"

"I am acquainted with him, madame."

"Well, I came to ask you ——"

"What?"

"Oh, sir, you must know that he has shown me much kindness, and I wish to know if I may rely upon it. You understand me, sir? You read all hearts."

"You must be a little more explicit before I can assist you, madame."

"Monsieur, they say that his eminence loves elsewhere in a high quarter."

"Madame, allow me first to ask you one question. How did you come to seek me here, since I do not live here?" Jeanne trembled. "How did you get in? — for there are neither porter nor servants in this part of my hotel. It could not be me you sought here — who was it? You do not reply; I must aid you a little. You came in by the help of a key which you have now in your pocket. You came to seek a young woman whom from pure kindness I had concealed here."

Jeanne trembled visibly, but replied, "If it were so, it is no crime; one woman is permitted to visit another. Call her; she will tell you if my friendship is a hurtful one."

"Madame, you say that because you know she is not here."

"Not here! Oliva not here?"

"Oh you do not know that — you, who helped her to escape!"

"I!" cried Jeanne; "you accuse me of that?"

"I convict you," replied Cagliostro; and he took a paper from the table, and showed her the following words, addressed to himself:

> "Monsieur, and my generous protector, forgive me for leaving you; but above all things I love M. Beausire. He came and I follow him. Adieu! Believe in my gratitude!"

"Beausire!" cried Jeanne, petrified; "he, who did not even know her address?"

"Oh, madame, here is another paper, which was doubtless dropped by M. Beausire." The countess read, shuddering:

> "M. Beausire will find Mademoiselle Oliva, Rue St. Claude, at the corner of the boulevard. He had better come for her at once; it is time. This is the advice of a sincere friend."

"Oh!" groaned the countess.

"And he has taken her away," said Cagliostro.

"But who wrote this note?"

"Doubtless yourself."

"But how did he get in?"

"Probably with your key."

"But as I have it here, he could not have it."

"Whoever has one can easily have two."

"You are convinced," replied she, "while I can only suspect." She turned and went away, but found the staircase lighted and filled with menservants. Cagliostro called out loudly before them, "Madame la Comtesse de la Motte!" She went out full of rage and disappointment.

CHAPTER LXXII
THE LETTER AND THE RECEIPT

The day arrived for the payment of the first 500,000 francs. The jewelers had prepared a receipt, but no one came with the money in exchange for it. They passed the day and night in a state of cruel anxiety. The following day M. Bœhmer went to Versailles, and asked to see the queen; he was told that he could not be admitted without a letter of audience. However, he begged so hard, and urged his solicitations so well among the servants, that they consented to place him in the queen's way when she went out. Marie Antoinette, still full of joy from her interview with Charny, came along, looking bright and happy, when she caught sight of the somewhat solemn face of M. Bœhmer. She smiled on him, which he took for a favorable sign, and asked for an audience, which was promised him for two o'clock. On his return to Bossange, they agreed that no doubt the money was all right, only the queen had been unable to send it the day before. At two o'clock Bœhmer returned to Versailles.

"What is it now, M. Bœhmer?" asked the queen, as he entered. Bœhmer thought some one must be listening, and looked cautiously around him.

"Have you any secret to tell?" asked the queen, in surprise. "The same as before, I suppose—some jewels to sell. But make yourself easy; no one can hear you."

"Ahem!" murmured Bœhmer, startled at his reception.

"Well, what?"

"Then I may speak out to your majesty?"

"Anything; only be quick."

"I only wished to say that your majesty probably forgot us yesterday."

"Forgot you! what do you mean?"

"Yesterday the sum was due——"

"What sum?"

"Pardon me, your majesty, if I am indiscreet. Perhaps your majesty is not prepared. It would be a misfortune; but still — —"

"But," interrupted the queen, "I do not understand a word of what you are saying. Pray explain yourself."

"Yesterday the first payment for the necklace was due."

"Have you sold it, then?"

"Certainly, your majesty," replied Bœhmer, looking stupefied.

"And those to whom you have sold it have not paid, my poor Bœhmer? So much the worse; but they must do as I did, and, if they cannot pay, send it you back again."

The jeweler staggered like a man who had just had a sunstroke. "I do not understand your majesty," he said.

"Why, Bœhmer, if ten purchasers were each to send it back, and give you 100,000 francs, as I did, you would make a million, and keep your necklace also."

"Your majesty says," cried Bœhmer, ready to drop, "that you sent me back the necklace!"

"Certainly. What is the matter?"

"What! your majesty denies having bought the necklace?"

"Ah! what comedy is this, sir?" said the queen, severely. "Is this unlucky necklace destined to turn some one's brain?"

"But did your majesty really say that you had returned the necklace?"

"Happily," replied the queen, "I can refresh your memory, as you are so forgetful, to say nothing more." She went to her secretaire, and, taking out the receipt, showed it to him, saying, "I suppose this is clear enough?"

Bœhmer's expression changed from incredulity to terror. "Madame," cried he, "I never signed this receipt!"

"You deny it!" said the queen, with flashing eyes.

"Positively, if I lose my life for it. I never received the necklace; I never signed the receipt. Were the headsman here, or the gallows, I would repeat the same thing!"

"Then, sir," said the queen, "do you think I have robbed you? do you think I have your necklace?"

Bœhmer drew out a pocket-book, and in his turn produced a letter. "I do not believe," said he, "that if your majesty had wished to return the necklace, you would have written this."

"I write! I never wrote to you; that is not my writing."

"It is signed," said Bœhmer.

"Yes, 'Marie Antoinette of France.' You are mad! Do you think that is the way I sign? I am of Austria. Go, M. Bœhmer; you have played this game unskilfully; your forgers have not understood their work."

"My forgers!" cried the poor Bœhmer, ready to faint at this new blow. "You suspect me?"

"You accuse me, Marie Antoinette?" replied she.

"But this letter?"

"This receipt? Give it me back, and take your letter; the first lawyer you ask will tell you how much that is worth." And taking the receipt from his trembling hands, and throwing the letter indignantly down, she left the room.

The unfortunate man ran to communicate this dreadful blow to his partner, who was waiting in the carriage for him; and on their way home their gestures and cries of grief were so frantic as to attract the attention of every passer-by. At last they decided to return to Versailles.

Immediately they presented themselves they were admitted by the order of the queen.

CHAPTER LXXIII
"ROI NE PUIS, PRINCE NE DAIGNE, ROHAN JE SUIS"[B]

"Ah!" cried the queen, immediately they entered, "you have brought a reinforcement, M. Bœhmer; so much the better."

Bœhmer kneeled at her feet, and Bossange followed his example.

"Gentlemen," said she, "I have now grown calm, and an idea has come into my head which has modified my opinion with regard to you. It seems to me that we have both been duped."

"Ah, madame, you suspect me no longer. Forger was a dreadful word."

"No, I do not suspect you now."

"Does your majesty suspect any one else?"

"Reply to my questions. You say you have not these diamonds?"

"No, madame, we have not."

"It then matters little to you that I sent them—that is my affair. Did you not see Madame de la Motte?"

"Yes, madame."

"And she gave you nothing from me?"

"No, madame; she only said to us, 'Wait.'"

"But this letter—who brought it?"

"An unknown messenger, during the night."

She rang, and a servant entered.

"Send for Madame de la Motte. And," continued the queen to M. Bœhmer, "did you see M. de Rohan?"

"Yes, madame; he paid us a visit in order to ask."

"Good!" said the queen. "I wish to hear no more now; but if he be mixed up with this affair, I think you need not despair. I think I can guess what Madame de la Motte meant by saying 'Wait.' Meanwhile, go to M. de Rohan, and tell him all you have told us, and that I know it."

The jewelers had a renewed spark of hope; only Bossange said that the receipt was a false one, and that that was a crime.

"True," replied Marie Antoinette, "if you did not write it, it is a crime; but to prove this I must confront you with the person whom I charged to return you the jewels."

"Whenever your majesty pleases; we do not fear the test."

"Go first to M. de Rohan; he alone can enlighten you."

"And will your majesty permit us to bring you his answer?"

"Yes; but I dare say I shall know all before you do."

When they were gone she was restless and unquiet, and despatched courier after courier for Madame de la Motte.

We will, however, leave her for the present, and follow the jewelers in their search after the truth.

The cardinal was at home, reading, with a rage impossible to describe, a little note which Madame de la Motte had just sent him, as she said, from Versailles. It was harsh, forbidding any hope, ordering him to think no more of the past, not to appear again at Versailles, and ending with an appeal to his loyalty not to attempt to renew relations which were become impossible.

"Coquette, capricious, perfidious!" cried he. "Here are four letters which she has written to me, each more unjust and tyrannical than the other. She encouraged me only for a caprice, and now sacrifices me to a new one."

It was at this moment that the jewelers presented themselves. Three times he refused them admittance, and each time the servant came back, saying that they would not go without an audience. "Let them come in, then," said he.

"What means this rudeness, gentlemen? No one owes you anything here."

The jewelers, driven to despair, made a half-menacing gesture.

"Are you mad?" asked the cardinal.

"Monseigneur," replied Bœhmer, with a sigh, "do us justice, and do not compel us to be rude to an illustrious prince."

"Either you are not mad, in which case my servants shall throw you out of the window; or you are mad, and they shall simply push you out of the door."

"Monseigneur, we are not mad, but we have been robbed."

"What is that to me? I am not lieutenant of police."

"But you have had the necklace in your hands, and in justice — —"

"The necklace! is it the necklace that is stolen?"

"Yes, monseigneur."

"Well, what does the queen say about it?"

"She sent me to you."

"She is very amiable; but what can I do, my poor fellows?"

"You can tell us, monseigneur, what has been done with it."

"I?"

"Doubtless."

"Do you think I stole the necklace from the queen?"

"It is not the queen from whom it was stolen."

"Mon Dieu! from whom, then?"

"The queen denies having had it in her possession."

"How! she denies it? But I thought you had an acknowledgment from her."

"She says it is a forged one."

"Decidedly, you are mad!" cried the cardinal.

"We simply speak the truth."

"Then she denied it because some one was there."

"No, monseigneur. And this is not all: not only does the queen deny her own acknowledgment, but she produced a receipt from us, purporting that we had received back the necklace."

"A receipt from you?"

"Which also is a forgery, M. le Cardinal—you know it."

"A forgery, and I know it!"

"Assuredly, for you came to confirm what Madame de la Motte had said; and you knew that we had sold the necklace to the queen."

"Come," said the cardinal, "this seems a serious affair. This is what I did: first, I bought the necklace of you for her majesty, and paid you 100,000 francs."

"True, monseigneur."

"Afterwards you told me that the queen had acknowledged the debt in writing, and fixed the periods of payment."

"We said so. Will your eminence look at this signature?"

He looked at it, and said directly, "'Marie Antoinette of France:' you have been deceived, gentlemen; this is not her signature; she is of the House of Austria."

"Then," cried the jewelers, "Madame de la Motte must know the forger and the robber."

The cardinal appeared struck with this. He acted like the queen; he rang, and said, "Send for Madame de la Motte." His servants went after Jeanne's carriage, which had not long left the hotel.

M. Bœhmer continued, "But where is the necklace?"

"How can I tell?" cried the cardinal; "I gave it to the queen. I know no more."

"We must have our necklace, or our money," cried the jewelers.

"Gentlemen, this is not my business."

"It is Madame de la Motte," cried they in despair, "who has ruined us."

"I forbid you to accuse her here."

"Some one must be guilty; some one wrote the forged papers."

"Was it I?" asked M. de Rohan, haughtily.

"Monseigneur, we do not wish to say so."

"Well, who then?"

"Monseigneur, we desire an explanation."

"Wait till I have one myself."

"But, monseigneur, what are we to say to the queen? For she accused us at first."

"What does she say now?"

"She says that either you or Madame de la Motte has the necklace, for she has not."

"Well," replied the cardinal, pale with rage and shame, "go and tell her—no, tell her nothing; there is scandal enough. But to-morrow I officiate at the chapel at Versailles: when I approach the queen, come to us; I will ask her again if she has the necklace, and you shall hear what she replies; if she denies it before me, then, gentlemen, I am a Rohan, and will pay." And with these words, pronounced with an indescribable dignity, he dismissed them.

[B] The motto of the Rohans.

CHAPTER LXXIV
LOVE AND DIPLOMACY

The next morning, about ten o'clock, a carriage bearing the arms of M. de Breteuil entered Versailles. Our readers will not have forgotten that this gentleman was a personal enemy of M. de Rohan, and had long been on the watch for an opportunity of injuring him. He now requested an audience from the king, and was admitted.

"It is a beautiful day," said Louis to his minister; "there is not a cloud in the sky."

"Sire, I am sorry to bring with me a cloud on your tranquillity."

"So am I," replied the king, "but what is it?"

"I feel very much embarrassed, sire, more especially as, perhaps, this affair naturally concerns the lieutenant of police rather than myself, for it is a sort of theft."

"A theft! well, speak out."

"Sire, your majesty knows the diamond necklace?"

"M. Bœhmer's, which the queen refused?"

"Precisely, sire," said M. de Breteuil; and ignorant of all the mischief he was about to do, he continued, "and this necklace has been stolen."

"Ah! so much the worse. But diamonds are very easy to trace."

"But, sire, this is not an ordinary theft; it is pretended that the queen has kept the necklace."

"Why, she refused it in my presence."

"Sire, I did not use the right word; the calumnies are too gross."

"Ah!" said the king with a smile, "I suppose they say now that the queen has stolen the necklace."

"Sire," replied M. Breteuil, "they say that the queen recommenced the negotiation for the purchase privately, and that the jewelers hold a paper signed by her, acknowledging that she kept it. I need not tell your majesty how much I despise all such scandalous falsehoods."

"They say this!" said the king, turning pale. "What do they not say? Had the queen really bought it afterwards, I should not have blamed her. She is a woman, and the necklace is marvelously beautiful; and, thank God, she could still afford it, if she wished for it. I shall only blame her for one thing, for hiding her wishes from me. But that has nothing to do with the king, only with the husband. A husband may scold his wife if he pleases, and no one has a right to interfere. But then," continued he, "what do you mean by a robbery?"

"Oh! I fear I have made your majesty angry."

The king laughed. "Come, tell me all; tell me even that the queen sold the necklace to the Jews. Poor woman, she is often in want of money, oftener than I can give it to her."

"Exactly so; about two months ago the queen asked for 500,000 francs, and your majesty refused it."

"True."

"Well, sire, they say that this money was to have been the first payment for the necklace. The queen, being denied the money, could not pay— —"

"Well!"

"Well, sire, they say the queen applied to some one to help her."

"To a Jew?"

"No, sire; not to a Jew."

"Oh! I guess, some foreign intrigue. The queen asked her mother, or some of her family, for money."

"It would have been better if she had, sire."

"Well, to whom, then, did she apply?"

"Sire, I dare not— —"

"Monsieur, I am tired of this. I order you to speak out at once. Who lent this money to the queen?"

"M. de Rohan."

"M. de Rohan! Are you not ashamed to name to me the most embarrassed man in my kingdom?"

"Sire," said M. de Breteuil, lowering his eyes.

"M. de Breteuil, your manner annoys me. If you have anything to say, speak at once."

"Sire, I cannot bring myself to utter things so compromising to the honor of my king and queen."

"Speak, sir; if there are calumnies, they must be refuted."

"Then, sire, M. de Rohan went to the jewelers, and arranged for the purchase of the necklace, and the mode of payment."

"Really!" cried the king, annoyed and angry.

"It is a fact, sire, capable of being proved with the greatest certainty. I pledge my word for this."

"This is most annoying," said the king; "but still, sir, we have not heard of a theft."

"Sire, the jewelers say that they have a receipt signed by the queen, and she denies having the necklace."

"Ah!" cried the king, with renewed hope; "she denies it, you see, M. de Breteuil."

"Oh, sire! I never doubted her majesty's innocence. I am indeed unfortunate, if your majesty does not see all my respect for the purest of women."

"Then you only accuse M. de Rohan?"

"Yes, sire. And appearances demand some inquiry into his conduct. The queen says she has not the necklace—the jewelers say they sold it to her. It is not to be found, and the word 'theft' is used as connected both with the queen and M. de Rohan."

"You are right, M. de Breteuil; this affair must be cleared up. But who is that passing below? Is it not M. de Rohan going to the chapel?"

"Not yet, sire; he does not come till eleven o'clock, and he will be dressed in his robes, for he officiates to-day."

"Then I will send for him and speak to him."

"Permit me to advise your majesty to speak first to the queen."

"Yes, she will tell me the truth."

"Doubtless, sire."

"But first tell me all you know about it."

M. de Breteuil, with ingenious hate, mentioned every particular which he thought could injure M. de Rohan. They were interrupted by an officer, who approached the king, and said, "Sire, the queen begs you will come to her."

"What is it?" asked the king, turning pale. "Wait here, M. de Breteuil."

CHAPTER LXXV
CHARNY, CARDINAL, AND QUEEN

At the same moment as M. de Breteuil asked for an audience of the king, M. de Charny, pale and agitated, begged one of the queen. He was admitted, and touching tremblingly the hand she held out to him, said in an agitated voice, "Oh! madame, what a misfortune!"

"What is the matter?"

"Do you know what I have just heard? What the king has perhaps already heard, or will hear to-morrow."

She trembled, for she thought of her night with Charny, and fancied they had been seen. "Speak," said she; "I am strong."

"They say, madame, that you bought a necklace from M. Bœhmer."

"I returned it," said she quickly.

"But they say that you only pretended to do so, when the king prevented you from paying for it by refusing you the money, and that you went to borrow the amount from some one else, who is your lover."

"And," cried the queen, with her usual impetuous confidence, "you, monsieur—you let them say that?"

"Madame, yesterday I went to M. Bœhmer's with my uncle, who had brought some diamonds from the Indies, and wished to have them valued. There we heard this frightful story now being spread abroad by your majesty's enemies. Madame, I am in despair; if you bought the necklace, tell me; if you have not paid, tell me; but do not let me hear that M. de Rohan paid for you."

"M. de Rohan!"

"Yes, M. de Rohan, whom they call your lover—whom they say lent the money—and whom an unhappy man, called Charny, saw in the park in Versailles, kneeling before the queen, and kissing her hand."

"Monsieur," cried Marie Antoinette, "if you believe these things when you leave me, you do not love me."

"Oh!" cried the young man, "the danger presses. I come to beg you to do me a favor."

"What danger?"

"Oh, madame! the cardinal paying for the queen dishonors her. I do not speak now of the grief such a confidence in him causes to me. No; of these things one dies, but does not complain."

"You are mad!" cried Marie Antoinette, in anger.

"I am not mad, madame, but you are unhappy and lost. I saw you in the park—I told you so—I was not deceived. To-day all the horrible truth has burst out. M. de Rohan boasts, perhaps——"

The queen seized his arm. "You are mad," repeated she, with inexpressible anguish. "Believe anything—believe the impossible—but, in the name of heaven, after all I have said to you, do not believe me guilty. I, who never even thought of you without praying to God to pardon me for my fault. Oh, M. de Charny! if you do not wish to kill me, do not tell me that you think me guilty."

Charny wrung his hands with anguish. "Listen," said he, "if you wish me to serve you efficaciously."

"A service from you?—from you, more cruel than my enemies? A service from a man who despises me? Never, sir—never."

Charny approached, and took her hands in his. "This evening it will be too late. Save me from despair, by saving yourself from shame."

"Monsieur!"

"Oh, I cannot pick my words with death, before me! If you do not listen to me, we shall both die; you from shame, and I from grief. You want money to pay for this necklace."

"I?"

"Do not deny it."

"I tell you——"

"Do not tell me that you have not the necklace."

"I swear!"

"Do not swear, if you wish me to love you. There remains one way to save at once your honor and my love. The necklace is worth 1,600,000 francs—you have paid 100,000. Here is the remainder; take it, and pay."

"You have sold your possessions—you have ruined yourself for me! Good and noble heart, I love you!"

"Then you accept?"

"No; but I love you."

"And let M. de Rohan pay. Remember, madame, this would be no generosity towards me, but the refinement of cruelty."

"M. de Charny, I am a queen. I give to my subjects, but do not accept from them."

"What do you mean to do, then?"

"You are frank. What do the jewelers say?"

"That as you cannot pay, M. de Rohan will pay for you."

"What does the public say?"

"That you have the necklace hidden, and will produce it when it shall have been paid for; either by the cardinal, in his love for you, or by the king, to prevent scandal."

"And you, Charny; in your turn, I ask, what do you say?"

"I think, madame, that you have need to prove your innocence to me."

The Prince Louis, Cardinal de Rohan, was at that moment announced by an usher.

"You shall have your wish," said the queen.

"You are going to receive him?"

"Yes."

"And I?"

"Go into my boudoir, and leave the door ajar, that you may hear. Be quick—here he is."

M. de Rohan appeared in his robes of office. The queen advanced towards him, attempting a smile, which died away on her lips.

He was serious, and said, "Madame, I have several important things to communicate to you, although you shun my presence."

"I shun you so little, monsieur, that I was about to send for you."

"Am I alone with your majesty?" said he, in a low voice. "May I speak freely?"

"Perfectly, monseigneur. Do not constrain yourself," said she aloud, for M. de. Charny to hear.

"The king will not come?"

"Have no fear of the king, or any one else."

"Oh, it is yourself I fear," said he, in a moved voice.

"Well, I am not formidable. Say quickly and openly what you have to say. I like frankness, and want no reserve. They say you complain of me; what have you to reproach me with?"

The cardinal sighed.

CHAPTER LXXVI
EXPLANATIONS

"Madame," said the cardinal, bowing, "you know what is passing concerning the necklace?"

"No, monsieur; I wish to learn it from you."

"Why has your majesty for so long only deigned to communicate with me through another? If you have any reason to hate me, why not explain it?"

"I do not know what you mean. I do not hate you; but that is not, I think, the subject of our interview. I wish to hear all about this unlucky necklace; but first, where is Madame de la Motte?"

"I was about to ask your majesty the same question."

"Really, monsieur, if any one knows, I think it ought to be you."

"I, madame! why?"

"Oh! I do not wish to receive your confessions about her, but I wish to speak to her, and have sent for her ten times without receiving any answer."

"And I, madame, am astonished at her disappearance, for I also sent to ask her to come, and, like your majesty, received no answer."

"Then let us leave her, monsieur, and speak of ourselves."

"Oh no, madame; let us speak of her first, for a few words of your majesty's gave me a painful suspicion; it seemed to me that your majesty reproached me with my assiduities to her."

"I have not reproached you at all, sir."

"Oh! madame, such a suspicion would explain all to me; then I should understand all your rigor towards me, which I have hitherto found so inexplicable."

"Here we cease to understand each other, and I beg of you not to still further involve in obscurity what I wished you to explain to me."

"Madame," cried the cardinal, clasping his hands, "I entreat you not to change the subject; allow me only two words more, and I am sure we shall understand each other."

"Really, sir, you speak in language that I do not understand. Pray return to plain French; where is the necklace that I returned to the jewelers?"

"The necklace that you sent back?"

"Yes; what have you done with it?"

"I! I do not know, madame."

"Listen, and one thing is simple; Madame de la Motte took away the necklace, and returned it to the jewelers in my name. The jewelers say they never had it, and I hold in my hands a receipt which proves the contrary; but they say the receipt is forged; Madame de la Motte, if sincere, could explain all, but as she is not to be found, I can but conjecture. She wished to return it, but you, who had always the generous wish to present me the necklace, you, who brought it to me, with the offer to pay for it——"

"Which your majesty refused."

"Yes. Well, you have persevered in your idea, and you kept back the necklace, hoping to return it to me at some other time. Madame de la Motte was weak; she knew my inability to pay for it, and my determination not to keep it when I could not pay; she therefore entered into a conspiracy with you. Have I guessed right? Say yes. Let me believe in this slight disobedience to my orders, and I promise you both pardon; so let Madame de la Motte come out from her hiding-place. But, for pity's sake, let there be perfect clearness and openness, monsieur. A cloud rests over me; I will have it dispersed."

"Madame," replied the cardinal, with a sigh, "unfortunately it is not true. I did not persevere in my idea, for I believed the necklace was in your own hands; I never conspired with Madame de la Motte about it, and I have it no more than you say you or the jewelers have it."

"Impossible! you have not got it?"

"No, madame."

"Is it not you who hide it?"

"No, madame."

"You do not know what has become of it?"

"No, madame."

"But, then, how do you explain its disappearance?"

"I do not pretend to explain it, madame; and, moreover, it is not the first time that I have had to complain that your majesty did not understand me."

"How, sir?"

"Pray, madame, have the goodness to retrace my letters in your memory."

"Your letters!—you have written to me?"

"Too seldom, madame, to express all that was in my heart."

The queen rose.

"Terminate this jesting, sir. What do you mean by letters? How can you dare to say such things?"

"Ah! madame, perhaps I have allowed myself to speak too freely the secret of my soul."

"What secret? Are you in your senses, monsieur?"

"Madame!"

"Oh! speak out. You speak now like a man who wishes to embarrass one before witnesses."

"Madame, is there really any one listening to us?"

"No, monsieur. Explain yourself, and prove to me, if you can, that you are in your right senses."

"Oh! why is not Madame de la Motte here? she could aid me to reawaken, if not your majesty's attachment, at least your memory."

"My attachment! my memory!"

"Ah, madame," cried he, growing excited, "spare me, I beg. It is free to you to love no longer, but do not insult me."

"Ah, mon Dieu!" cried the queen, turning pale: "hear what this man says."

"Well, madame," said he, getting still more excited, "I think I have been sufficiently discreet and reserved not to be ill-treated. But I should have known that when a queen says, 'I will not any longer,' it is as imperious as when a woman says, 'I will.'"

"But, sir, to whom, or when, have I said either the one or the other?"

"Both, to me."

"To you! You are a liar, M. de Rohan. A coward, for you calumniate a woman; and a traitor, for you insult the queen."

"And you are a heartless woman and a faithless queen. You led me to feel for you the most ardent love. You let me drink my fill of hopes— —"

"Of hopes! My God! am I mad, or what is he?"

"Should I have dared to ask you for the midnight interviews which you granted me?"

The queen uttered a cry of rage, as she fancied she heard a sigh from the boudoir.

"Should I," continued M. de Rohan, "have dared to come into the park if you had not sent Madame de la Motte for me?"

"Mon Dieu!"

"Should I have dared to steal the key? Should I have ventured to ask for this rose, which since then I have worn here on my heart, and burned up with my kisses? Should I have dared to kiss your hands? And, above all, should I have dared even to dream of sweet but perfidious love."

"Monsieur!" cried she, "you blaspheme."

"Mon Dieu!" exclaimed the cardinal, "heaven knows that to be loved by this deceitful woman I would have given my all, my liberty, my life."

"M. de Rohan, if you wish to preserve either, you will confess immediately that you invented all these horrors; that you did not come to the park at night."

"I did come," he replied.

"You are a dead man if you maintain this."

"A Rohan cannot lie, madame; I did come."

"M. de Rohan, in heaven's name say that you did not see me there."

"I will die if you wish it, and as you threaten me; but I did come to the park at Versailles, where Madame de la Motte brought me."

"Once more, confess it is a horrible plot against me."

"No."

"Then believe that you were mistaken—deceived—that it was all a fancy."

"No."

"Then we will have recourse," said she, solemnly, "to the justice of the king."

The cardinal bowed.

The queen rang violently. "Tell his majesty that I desire his presence."

The cardinal remained firm. Marie Antoinette went ten times to the door of the boudoir, and each time returned without going in.

At last the king appeared.

CHAPTER LXXVII
THE ARREST

"Sire," cried the queen, "here is M. de Rohan, who says incredible things, which I wish him to repeat to you."

At these unexpected words the cardinal turned pale. Indeed, it was a strange position to hear himself called upon to repeat to the king and the husband all the claims which he believed he had over the queen and the wife.

But the king, turning towards him, said, "About a certain necklace, is it not, sir?"

M. de Rohan took advantage of the king's question, and chose the least of two evils. "Yes, sire," he murmured, "about the necklace."

"Then, sir, you have brought the necklace?"

"Sire— —"

"Yes, or no, sir."

The cardinal looked at the queen, and did not reply.

"The truth, sir," said the queen, answering his look. "We want nothing but the truth."

M. de Rohan turned away his head, and did not speak.

"If M. de Rohan will not reply, will you, madame, explain?" said the king. "You must know something about it; did you buy it?"

"No."

M. de Rohan smiled rather contemptuously.

"You say nothing, sir," said the king.

"Of what am I accused, sire?"

"The jewelers say they sold the necklace either to you or the queen. They show a receipt from her majesty— —"

"A forged one," interrupted the queen.

"The jewelers," continued the king, "say that in case the queen does not pay, you are bound to do so by your engagements."

"I do not refuse to pay, sire. It must be the truth, as the queen permits it to be said." And a second look, still more contemptuous than the first, accompanied this speech.

The queen trembled, for she began to think his behavior like the indignation of an honest man.

"Well, M. le Cardinal, some one has imitated the signature of the Queen of France," said the king.

"The queen, sire, is free to attribute to me whatever crimes she pleases."

"Sir," said the king, "instead of justifying yourself, you assume the air of an accuser."

The cardinal paused a moment, and then cried, "Justify myself?— impossible!"

"Monsieur, these people say that this necklace has been stolen under a promise to pay for it; do you confess the crime?"

"Who would believe it, if I did?" asked the cardinal, with a haughty disdain.

"Then, sir, you think they will believe— —"

"Sire, I know nothing of what is said," interrupted the cardinal; "all that I can affirm is, that I have not the necklace; some one has it who will not produce it; and I can but say, let the shame of the crime fall on the person who knows himself guilty."

"The question, madame, is between you two," said the king. "Once more, have you the necklace?"

"No, by the honor of my mother, by the life of my son."

The king joyfully turned towards the cardinal. "Then, sir, the affair lies between you and justice, unless you prefer trusting to my clemency."

"The clemency of kings is for the guilty, sire; I prefer the justice of men!"

"You will confess nothing?"

"I have nothing to say."

"But, sir, your silence compromises my honor," cried the queen.

The cardinal did not speak.

"Well, then, I will speak," cried she. "Learn, sire, that M. de Rohan's chief crime is not the theft of this necklace."

M. de Rohan turned pale.

"What do you mean?" cried the king.

"Madame!" murmured the cardinal.

"Oh! no reasons, no fear, no weakness shall close my mouth. I would proclaim my innocence in public if necessary."

"Your innocence," said the king. "Oh, madame, who would be rash enough, or base enough, to compel you to defend that?"

"I beg you, madame," said the cardinal.

"Ah! you begin to tremble. I was right: such plots bear not the light. Sire, will you order M. de Rohan to repeat to you what he has just said to me."

"Madame," cried the cardinal, "take care; you pass all bounds."

"Sir," said the king, "do you dare to speak thus to the queen?"

"Yes, sire," said Marie Antoinette; "this is the way he speaks to me, and pretends he has the right to do so."

"You, sir!" cried the king, livid with rage.

"Oh! he says he has letters— —"

"Let us see them, sir," said the king.

"Yes, produce them," cried the queen.

The cardinal passed his hands over his burning eyes, and asked himself how heaven could ever have created a being so perfidious and so audacious; but he remained silent.

"But that is not all," continued the queen, getting more and more excited: "M. le Cardinal says he has obtained interviews— —"

"Madame, for pity's sake," cried the king.

"For modesty's sake," murmured the cardinal.

"One word, sir. If you are not the basest of men; if you hold anything sacred in this world; if you have proofs, produce them."

"No, madame," replied he, at length, "I have not."

"You said you had a witness."

"Who?" asked the king.

"Madame de la Motte."

"Ah!" cried the king, whose suspicions against her were easily excited; "let us see this woman."

"Yes," said the queen, "but she has disappeared. Ask monsieur what he has done with her."

"Others have made her disappear who had more interest in doing so than I had."

"But, sir, if you are innocent, help us to find the guilty."

The cardinal crossed his hands and turned his back.

"Monsieur," cried the king, "you shall go to the Bastile."

"As I am, sire, in my robes? Consider, sire, the scandal will commence, and will fall heavily on whomsoever it rests."

"I wish it to do so, sir."

"It is an injustice, sire."

"It shall be so." And the king looked round for some one to execute his orders. M. de Breteuil was near, anticipating the fall of his rival; the king spoke to him, and he cried immediately, "Guards! arrest M. le Cardinal de Rohan."

The cardinal passed by the queen without saluting her; then, bowing to the king, went towards the lieutenant of the guards, who approached timidly, seeming to wait for a confirmation of the order he had received.

"Yes, sir," said M. de Rohan, "it is I whom you are to arrest."

"Conduct monsieur to his apartment until I have written the order;" said the king.

When they were alone, the king said, "Madame, you know this must lead to a public trial, and that scandal will fall heavily on the heads of the guilty."

"I thank you, sire; you have taken the only method of justifying me."

"You thank me."

"With all my heart; believe me, you have acted like a king, and I as a queen."

"Good," replied the king, joyfully; "we shall find out the truth at last, and when once we have crushed the serpent, I hope we may live in more tranquillity." He kissed the queen, and left her.

"Monsieur," said the cardinal to the officer who conducted him, "can I send word home that I have been arrested?"

"If no one sees, monseigneur."

The cardinal wrote some words on a page of his missal, then tore it out, and let it fall at the feet of the officer.

"She ruins me," murmured the cardinal; "but I will save her, for your sake, oh! my king, and because it is my duty to forgive."

CHAPTER LXXVIII
THE PROCÈS-VERBAL

When the king reentered his room he signed the order to consign M. de Rohan to the Bastile. The Count de Provence soon came in and began making a series of signs to M. de Breteuil, who, however willing, could not understand their meaning. This, however, the count did not care for, as his sole object was to attract the king's attention. He at last succeeded, and the king, after dismissing M. de Breteuil, said to him, "What was the meaning of all those signs you were making just now? I suppose they meant something."

"Undoubtedly, but——"

"Oh, you are quite free to say or not."

"Sire, I have just heard of the arrest of M. de Rohan."

"Well, and what then? Am I wrong to do justice even on him?"

"Oh no, brother; I did not mean that."

"I should have been surprised had you not taken part somehow against the queen. I have just seen her, and am quite satisfied."

"Oh, sire, God forbid that I should accuse her! The queen has no friend more devoted than myself."

"Then you approve of my proceedings? which will, I trust, terminate all the scandals which have lately disgraced our court."

"Yes, sire, I entirely approve your majesty's conduct, and I think all is for the best as regards the necklace——"

"Pardieu, it is clear enough. M. de Rohan has been making himself great on a pretended familiarity with the queen; and conducting in her name a bargain for the diamonds, and leaving it to be supposed that she had them. It is monstrous. And then these tales never stop at the truth, but add all sorts of dreadful details which would end in a frightful scandal on the queen."

"Yes, brother, I repeat as far as the necklace is concerned you were perfectly right."

"What else is there, then?"

"Sire, you embarrass me. The queen has not, then, told you?"

"Oh, the other boastings of M. de Rohan? The pretended correspondence and interviews he speaks of? All that I know is, that I have the most absolute confidence in the queen, which she merits by the nobleness of her character. It was easy for her to have told me nothing of all this; but she always makes an immediate appeal to me in all difficulties, and confides to me the care of her honor. I am her confessor and her judge."

"Sire, you make me afraid to speak, lest I should be again accused of want of friendship for the queen. But it is right that all should be spoken, that she may justify herself from the other accusations."

"Well, what have you to say?"

"Let me first hear what she told you?"

"She said she had not the necklace; that she never signed the receipt for the jewels; that she never authorized M. de Rohan to buy them; that she had never given him the right to think himself more to her than any other of her subjects; and that she was perfectly indifferent to him."

"Ah! she said that— —?"

"Most decidedly."

"Then these rumors about other people— —"

"What others?"

"Why, if it were not M. de Rohan, who walked with the queen— —"

"How! do they say he walked with her?"

"The queen denies it, you say? but how came she to be in the park at night, and with whom did she walk?"

"The queen in the park at night!"

"Doubtless, there are always eyes ready to watch every movement of a queen."

"Brother, these are infamous things that you repeat, take care."

"Sire, I openly repeat them, that your majesty may search out the truth."

"And they say that the queen walked at night in the park?"

"Yes, sire, tête-à-tête."

"I do not believe any one says it."

"Unfortunately I can prove it but too well. There are four witnesses: one is the captain of the hunt, who says he saw the queen go out two following nights by the door near the kennel of the wolf-hounds; here is his declaration signed."

The king, trembling, took the paper.

"The next is the night watchman at Trianon, who says he saw the queen walking arm in arm with a gentleman. The third is the porter of the west door, who also saw the queen going through the little gate; he states how she was dressed, but that he could not recognize the gentleman, but thought he looked like an officer; he says he could not be mistaken, for that the queen was accompanied by her friend, Madame de la Motte."

"Her friend!" cried the king, furiously.

"The last is from the man whose duty it is to see that all the doors are locked at night. He says that he saw the queen go into the baths of Apollo with a gentleman."

The king, pale with anger and emotion, snatched the paper from the hands of his brother.

"It is true," continued the count, "that Madame de la Motte was outside, and that the queen did not remain more than an hour."

"The name of the gentleman?" cried the king.

"This report does not name him; but here is one dated the next day, by a forester, who says it was M. de Charny."

"M. de Charny!" cried the king. "Wait here; I will soon learn the truth of all this."

CHAPTER LXXIX
THE LAST ACCUSATION

As soon as the king left the room, the queen ran towards the boudoir, and opened the door; then, as if her strength failed her, sank down on a chair, waiting for the decision of M. de Charny, her last and most formidable judge.

He came out more sad and pale than ever.

"Well?" said she.

"Madame," replied he, "you see, everything opposes our friendship. There can be no peace for me while such scandalous reports circulate in public, putting my private convictions aside."

"Then," said the queen, "all I have done, this perilous aggression, this public defiance of one of the greatest nobles in the kingdom, and my conduct being exposed to the test of public opinion, does not satisfy you?"

"Oh!" cried Charny, "you are noble and generous, I know— —"

"But you believe me guilty—you believe the cardinal. I command you to tell me what you think."

"I must say, then, madame, that he is neither mad nor wicked, as you called him, but a man thoroughly convinced of the truth of what he said—a man who loves you, and the victim of an error which will bring him to ruin, and you— —"

"Well?"

"To dishonor."

"Mon Dieu!"

"This odious woman, this Madame de la Motte, disappearing just when her testimony might have restored you to repose and honor—she is the evil genius, the curse, of your reign; she whom you have, unfortunately, admitted to partake of your intimacy and your secrets."

"Oh, sir!"

"Yes, madame, it is clear that you combined with her and the cardinal to buy this necklace. Pardon if I offend you."

"Stay, sir," replied the queen, with a pride not unmixed with anger; "what the king believes, others might believe, and my friends not be harder than my husband. It seems to me that it can give no pleasure to any man to see a woman whom he does not esteem. I do not speak of you, sir; to you I am not a woman, but a queen; as you are to me, not a man, but a subject. I had advised you to remain in the country, and it was wise; far from the court, you might have judged me more truly. Too ready to condescend, I have neglected to keep up, with those whom I thought loved me, the prestige of royalty. I should have been a queen, and content to govern, and not have wished to be loved."

"I cannot express," replied Charny, "how much your severity wounds me. I may have forgotten that you were a queen, but never that you were the woman most in the world worthy of my respect and love."

"Sir, I think your absence is necessary; something tells me that it will end by your name being mixed up in all this."

"Impossible, madame!"

"You say 'impossible'; reflect on the power of those who have for so long played with my reputation. You say that M. de Rohan is convinced of what he asserts; those who cause such convictions would not be long in proving you a disloyal subject to the king, and a disgraceful friend for me. Those who invent so easily what is false will not be long in discovering the truth. Lose no time, therefore; the peril is great. Retire, and fly from the scandal which will ensue from the approaching trial; I do not wish that my destiny should involve yours, or your future be ruined. I, who am, thank God, innocent, and without a stain on my life—I, who would lay bare my heart to my enemies, could they thus read its purity, will resist to the last. For you might come ruin, defamation, and perhaps imprisonment. Take away the money you so nobly offered me, and the assurance that not one movement of your generous heart has escaped me, and that your doubts, though they have wounded, have not estranged me. Go, I say, and seek elsewhere what the Queen of France can no longer give you—hope and happiness. From this time to the convocation of Parliament, and the production of witnesses must be a fortnight; your uncle has vessels ready to sail—go and leave me; I bring misfortunes on my friends." Saying this, the queen rose, and seemed to give Charny his congé.

He approached quickly, but respectfully. "Your majesty," cried he, in a moved voice, "shows me my duty. It is here that danger awaits you, here that you are to be judged, and, that you may have one loyal witness on your side, I remain here. Perhaps we may still make your enemies tremble before the majesty of an innocent queen, and the courage of a devoted man. And if you wish it, madame, I will be equally hidden and unseen as though I went. During a fortnight that I lived within a hundred yards of you, watching your every movement, counting your steps, living in your life, no one saw me; I can do so again, if it please you."

"As you please," replied she; "I am no coquette, M. de Charny, and to say what I please is the true privilege of a queen. One day, sir, I chose you from every one. I do not know what drew my heart towards you, but I had need of a strong and pure friendship, and I allowed you to perceive that need; but now I see that your soul does not respond to mine, and I tell you so frankly."

"Oh, madame," cried Charny, "I cannot let you take away your heart from me! If you have once given it to me, I will keep it with my life; I cannot lose you. You reproached me with my doubts—oh, do not doubt me!"

"Ah," said she, "but you are weak, and I, alas, am so also."

"You are all I love you to be."

"What!" cried she, passionately, "this abused queen, this woman about to be publicly judged, that the world condemns, and that her king and husband may, perhaps, also in turn condemn, has she found one heart to love her?"

"A slave, who venerates her, and offers her his heart's blood in exchange for every pang he has caused her!"

"Then," cried she, "this woman is blessed and happy, and complains of nothing!"

Charny fell at her feet, and kissed her hands in transport. At that moment the door opened, and the king surprised, at the feet of his wife, the man whom he had just heard accused by the Comte de Provence.

CHAPTER LXXX
THE PROPOSAL OF MARRIAGE

The queen and Charny exchanged a look so full of terror, that their most cruel enemy must have pitied them.

Charny rose slowly, and bowed to the king, whose heart might almost have been seen to beat.

"Ah!" cried he, in a hoarse voice, "M. de Charny!"

The queen could not speak—she thought she was lost.

"M. de Charny," repeated the king, "it is little honorable for a gentleman to be taken in the act of theft."

"Of theft?" murmured Charny.

"Yes, sir, to kneel before the wife of another is a theft; and when this woman is a queen, his crime is called high treason!"

The count was about to speak, but the queen, ever impatient in her generosity, forestalled him.

"Sire," said she, "you seem in the mood for evil suspicions and unfavorable suppositions, which fall falsely, I warn you; and if respect chains the count's tongue, I will not hear him wrongfully accused without defending him." Here she stopped, overcome by emotion, frightened at the falsehood she was about to tell, and bewildered because she could not find one to utter.

But these few words had somewhat softened the king, who replied more gently, "You will not tell me, madame, that I did not see M. de Charny kneeling before you, and without your attempting to raise him?"

"Therefore you might think," replied she, "that he had some favor to ask me."

"A favor?"

"Yes, sire, and one which I could not easily grant, or he would not have insisted with so much less warmth."

Charny breathed again, and the king's look became calmer. Marie Antoinette was searching for something to say, with mingled rage at being obliged to lie, and grief at not being able to think of anything probable to say. She half hoped the king would be satisfied, and ask no more, but he said:

"Let us hear, madame, what is the favor so warmly solicited, which made M. de Charny kneel before you; I may, perhaps, more happy than you, be able to grant it."

She hesitated; to lie before the man she loved was agony to her, and she would have given the world for Charny to find the answer. But of this he was incapable.

"Sire, I told you that M. de Charny asked an impossible thing."

"What is it?"

"What can one ask on one's knees?"

"I want to hear."

"Sire, it is a family secret."

"There are no secrets from the king—a father interested in all his subjects, who are his children, although, like unnatural children, they may sometimes attack the honor and safety of their father."

This speech made the queen tremble anew.

"M. de Charny asked," replied she, "permission to marry."

"Really," cried the king, reassured for a moment. Then, after a pause, he said, "But why should it be impossible for M. de Charny to marry? Is he not noble? Has he not a good fortune? Is he not brave and handsome? Really, to refuse him, the lady ought to be a princess, or already married. I can see no other reason for an impossibility. Therefore, madame, tell me the name of the lady who is loved by M. de Charny, and let me see if I cannot remove the difficulty."

The queen, forced to continue her falsehood, replied:

"No, sire; there are difficulties which even you cannot remove, and the present one is of this nature."

"Still, I wish to hear," replied the king, his anger returning.

Charny looked at the queen—she seemed ready to faint. He made a step towards her and then drew back. How dared he approach her in the king's presence?

"Oh!" thought she, "for an idea—something that the king can neither doubt nor disbelieve." Then suddenly a thought struck her. She who has dedicated herself to heaven the king cannot influence. "Sire!" she cried, "she whom M. de Charny wishes to marry is in a convent."

"Oh! that is a difficulty; no doubt. But this seems a very sudden love of M. de Charny's. I have never heard of it from any one. Who is the lady you love, M. de Charny?"

The queen felt in despair, not knowing what he would say, and dreading to hear him name any one. But Charny could not reply: so, after a pause, she cried, "Sire, you know her; it is Andrée de Taverney."

Charny buried his face in his hands; the queen pressed her hand to her heart, and could hardly support herself.

"Mademoiselle de Taverney? but she has gone to St. Denis."

"Yes, sire," replied the queen.

"But she has taken no vows."

"No, but she is about to do so."

"We will see if we can persuade her. Why should she take the vows?"

"She is poor," said the queen.

"That I can soon alter, madame, if M. de Charny loves her."

The queen shuddered, and cast a glance at the young man, as if begging him to deny it. He did not speak.

"And I dare say," continued the king, taking his silence for consent, "that Mademoiselle de Taverney loves M. de Charny. I will give her as dowry the 500,000 francs which I refused the other day to you. Thank the queen, M. de Charny, for telling me of this, and ensuring your happiness."

Charny bowed like a pale statue which had received an instant's life.

"Oh, it is worth kneeling again for!" said the king.

The queen trembled, and stretched out her hand to the young man, who left on it a burning kiss.

"Now," said the king, "come with me."

M. de Charny turned once, to read the anguish in the eyes of the queen.

CHAPTER LXXXI
ST. DENIS

The queen remained alone and despairing. So many blows had struck her that she hardly knew from which she suffered most. How she longed to retract the words she had spoken, to take from Andrée even the chance of the happiness which she still hoped she would refuse; but if she refused, would not the king's suspicions reawaken, and everything seem only the worse for this falsehood? She dared not risk this—she must go to Andrée and confess, and implore her to make this sacrifice; or if she would only temporize, the king's suspicions might pass away, and he might cease to interest himself about it. Thus the liberty of Mlle. de Taverney would not be sacrificed, neither would that of M. de Charny; and she would be spared the remorse of having sacrificed the happiness of two people to her honor. She longed to speak again to Charny, but feared discovery; and she knew she might rely upon him to ratify anything she chose to say. Three o'clock arrived—the state dinner and the presentations; and the queen went through all with a serene and smiling air. When all was over she changed her dress, got into her carriage, and, without any guards, and only one companion, drove to St. Denis, and asked to see Andrée. Andrée was at that moment kneeling, dressed in her white peignoir; and praying with fervor. She had quitted the court voluntarily, and separated herself from all that could feed her love; but she could not stifle her regrets and bitter feelings. Had she not seen Charny apparently indifferent towards her, while the queen occupied all his thoughts? Yet, when she heard that the queen was asking for her, she felt a thrill of pleasure and delight. She threw a mantle over her shoulders, and hastened to see her; but on the way she reproached herself with the pleasure that she felt, endeavoring to think that the queen and the court had alike ceased to interest her.

"Come here, Andrée," said the queen, with a smile, as she entered.

CHAPTER LXXXII
A DEAD HEART

"Andrée," continued the queen, "it looks strange to see you in this dress; to see an old friend and companion already lost to life, is like a warning to ourselves from the tomb."

"Madame, no one has a right to warn or counsel your majesty."

"That was never my wish," said the queen; "tell me truly, Andrée, had you to complain of me when you were at court?"

"Your majesty was good enough to ask me that question when I took leave, and I replied then as now, no, madame."

"But often," said the queen, "a grief hurts us which is not personal; have I injured any one belonging to you? Andrée, the retreat which you have chosen is an asylum against evil passions; here God teaches gentleness, moderation and forgiveness of injuries. I come as a friend, and ask you to receive me as such."

Andrée felt touched. "Your majesty knows," said she, "that the Taverneys cannot be your enemies."

"I understand," replied the queen; "you cannot pardon me for having been cold to your brother, and, perhaps, he himself accuses me of caprice."

"My brother is too respectful a subject to accuse the queen," said Andrée, coldly.

The queen saw that it was useless to try and propitiate Andrée on this subject; so she said only, "Well, at least, I am ever your friend."

"Your majesty overwhelms me with your goodness."

"Do not speak thus; cannot the queen have a friend?"

"I assure you, madame, that I have loved you as much as I shall ever love any one in this world." She colored as she spoke.

"You have loved me; then you love me no more? Can a cloister so quickly extinguish all affection and all remembrance? if so, it is a cursed place."

"Do not accuse my heart, madame, it is dead."

"Your heart dead, Andrée? you, so young and beautiful."

"I repeat to you, madame, nothing in the court, nothing in the world, is any more to me. Here I live like the herb or the flower, alone for myself. I entreat you to pardon me; this forgetfulness of the glorious vanities of the world is no crime. My confessor congratulates me on it every day."

"Then you like the convent?"

"I embrace with pleasure a solitary life."

"Nothing remains which attracts you back to the world?"

"Nothing!"

"Mon dieu!" thought the queen; "shall I fail? If nothing else will succeed, I must have recourse to entreaties; to beg her to accept M. de Charny—heavens, how unhappy I am!—Andrée," she said, "what you say takes from me the hope I had conceived."

"What hope, madame?"

"Oh! if you are as decided as you appear to be, it is useless to speak."

"If your majesty would explain— —"

"You never regret what you have done?"

"Never, madame."

"Then it is superfluous to speak; and I yet hoped to make you happy."

"Me?"

"Yes, you, ingrate; but you know best your inclinations."

"Still, if your majesty would tell me— —"

"Oh, it is simple; I wished you to return to court."

"Never!"

"You refuse me?"

"Oh, madame, why should you wish me?—sorrowful, poor, despised, avoided by every one, incapable of inspiring sympathy in either sex! Ah, madame, and dear mistress, leave me here to become worthy to be accepted by God, for even He would reject me at present."

"But," said the queen, "what I was about to propose to you would have removed all these humiliations of which you complain. A marriage, which would have made you one of our great ladies."

"A marriage?" stammered Andrée.

"Yes."

"Oh, I refuse, I refuse!"

"Andrée!" cried the queen, in a supplicating voice.

"Ah, no, I refuse!"

Marie Antoinette prepared herself, with a fearfully-palpitating heart, for her last resource; but as she hesitated, Andrée said, "But, madame, tell me the name of the man who is willing to think of me as his companion for life."

"M. de Charny," said the queen, with an effort.

"M. de Charny?"— —

"Yes, the nephew of M. de Suffren."

"It is he!" cried Andrée, with burning cheeks, and sparkling eyes; "he consents— —"

"He asks you in marriage."

"Oh, I accept, I accept, for I love him."

The queen became livid, and sank back trembling, whilst Andrée kissed her hands, bathing them with her tears. "Oh, I am ready," murmured she.

"Come, then!" cried the queen, who felt as though her strength was failing her, with a last effort to preserve appearances.

Andrée left the room to prepare. Then Marie Antoinette cried, with bitter sobs, "Oh, mon Dieu! how can one heart bear so much suffering? and yet I should be thankful, for does it not save my children and myself from shame?"

CHAPTER LXXXIII
IN WHICH IT IS EXPLAINED WHY THE BARON DE TAVERNEY GREW FAT

Meanwhile Philippe was hastening the preparations for his departure. He did not wish to witness the dishonor of the queen, his first and only passion. When all was ready, he requested an interview with his father. For the last three months the baron had been growing fat; he seemed to feed on the scandals circulating at the court—they were meat and drink to him. When he received his son's message, instead of sending for him, he went to seek him in his room, already full of the disorder consequent on packing. Philippe did not expect much sensibility from his father, still he did not think he would be pleased. Andrée had already left him, and it was one less to torment, and he must feel a blank when his son went also. Therefore Philippe was astonished to hear his father call out, with a burst of laughter, "Oh, mon Dieu! he is going away, I was sure of it, I would have bet upon it. Well played, Philippe, well played."

"What is well played, sir?"

"Admirable!" repeated the old man.

"You give me praises, sir, which I neither understand nor merit, unless you are pleased at my departure, and glad to get rid of me."

"Oh! oh!" laughed the old man again, "I am not your dupe. Do you think I believe in your departure?"

"You do not believe? really, sir, you surprise me."

"Yes, it is surprising that I should have guessed. You are quite right to pretend to leave; without this ruse all, probably, would have been discovered."

"Monsieur, I protest I do not understand one word of what you say to me."

"Where do you say you go to?"

"I go first to Taverney Maison Rouge."

"Very well, but be prudent. There are sharp eyes on you both, and she is so fiery and incautious, that you must be prudent for both. What is your address, in case I want to send you any pressing news?"

"Taverney, monsieur."

"Taverney, nonsense! I do not ask you for the address of your house in the park; but choose some third address near here. You, who have managed so well for your love, can easily manage this."

"Sir, you play at enigmas, and I cannot find the solution."

"Oh, you are discreet beyond all bounds. However, keep your secrets, tell me nothing of the huntsman's house, nor the nightly walks with two dear friends, nor the rose, nor the kisses."

"Monsieur!" cried Philippe, mad with jealousy and rage, "will you hold your tongue?"

"Well, I know it all—your intimacy with the queen, and your meetings in the baths of Apollo. Mon Dieu! our fortunes are assured forever."

"Monsieur, you cause me horror!" cried poor Philippe, hiding his face in his hands. And, indeed, he felt it, at hearing attributed to himself all the happiness of another. All the rumors that the father had heard, he had assigned to his son, and believed that it was he that the queen loved, and no one else; hence his perfect contentment and happiness.

"Yes," he went on, "some said it was Rohan; others, that it was Charny; not one that it was Taverney. Oh, you have acted well."

At this moment a carriage was heard to drive up, and a servant entering, said, "Here is mademoiselle."

"My sister!" cried Philippe.

Then another servant appeared, and said that Mademoiselle de Taverney wished to speak to her brother in the boudoir. Another carriage now came to the door.

"Who the devil comes now?" muttered the baron; "it is an evening of adventures."

"M. le Comte de Charny," cried the powerful voice of the porter at the gate.

"Conduct M. le Comte to the drawing-room; my father will see him; and I will go to my sister—What can he want here?" thought Philippe, as he went down.

CHAPTER LXXXIV
THE FATHER AND THE FIANCÉE

Philippe hastened to the boudoir, where his sister awaited him. She ran to embrace him with a joyous air.

"What is it, Andrée?" cried he.

"Something which makes me happy. Oh! very happy, brother."

"And you come back to announce it to me."

"I come back for ever," said Andrée.

"Speak low, sister; there is, or is going to be, some one in the next room who might hear you."

"Who?"

"Listen."

"M. le Comte de Charny," announced the servant.

"He! oh, I know well what he comes for."

"You know!"

"Yes, and soon I shall be summoned to hear what he has to say."

"Do you speak seriously, my dear Andrée?"

"Listen, Philippe. The queen has brought me suddenly back, and I must go and change my dress for one fit for a fiancée." And saying this, with a kiss to Philippe, she ran off.

Philippe remained alone. He could hear what passed in the adjoining room. M. de Taverney entered, and saluted the count with a recherché though stiff politeness.

"I come, monsieur," said Charny, "to make a request, and beg you to excuse my not having brought my uncle with me, which I know would have been more proper."

"A request?"

"I have the honor," continued Charny, in a voice full of emotion, "to ask the hand of Mademoiselle Andrée, your daughter."

The baron opened his eyes in astonishment—"My daughter?"

"Yes, M. le Baron, if Mademoiselle de Taverney feels no repugnance."

"Oh," thought the old man, "Philippe's favor is already so well-known, that one of his rivals wishes to marry his sister." Then aloud, he said, "This request is such an honor to us, M. le Comte, that I accede with much pleasure; and as I should wish you to carry away a perfectly favorable answer, I will send for my daughter."

"Monsieur," interrupted the count, rather coldly, "the queen has been good enough to consult Mademoiselle de Taverney already, and her reply was favorable."

"Ah!" said the baron, more and more astonished, "it is the queen then——"

"Yes, monsieur, who took the trouble to go to St. Denis."

"Then, sir, it only remains to acquaint you with my daughter's fortune. She is not rich, and before concluding——"

"It is needless, M. le Baron; I am rich enough for both."

At this moment the door opened, and Philippe entered, pale and wild looking.

"Sir," said he, "my father was right to wish to discuss these things with you. While he goes up-stairs to bring the papers I have something to say to you."

When they were left alone, "M. de Charny," said he, "how dare you come here to ask for the hand of my sister?" Charny colored. "Is it," continued Philippe, "in order to hide better your amours with another woman whom you love, and who loves you? Is it, that by becoming the husband of a woman who is always near your mistress, you will have more facilities for seeing her?"

"Sir, you pass all bounds."

"It is, perhaps; and this is what I believe, that were I your brother-in-law, you think my tongue would be tied about what I know of your past amours."

"What you know?"

"Yes," cried Philippe, "the huntsman's house hired by you, your mysterious promenades in the park at night, and the tender parting at the little gate."

"Monsieur, in heaven's name——"

"Oh, sir, I was concealed behind the baths of Apollo when you came out, arm in arm with the queen."

Charny was completely overwhelmed for a time; then, after a few moments, he said, "Well, sir, even after all this, I reiterate my demand for the hand of your sister. I am not the base calculator you suppose me; but the queen must be saved."

"The queen is not lost, because I saw her on your arm, raising to heaven her eyes full of happiness; because I know that she loves you. That is no reason why my sister should be sacrificed, M. de Charny."

"Monsieur," replied Charny, "this morning the king surprised me at her feet— —"

"Mon Dieu!"

"And she, pressed by his jealous questions, replied that I was kneeling to ask the hand of your sister. Therefore if I do not marry her, the queen is lost. Do you now understand?"

A cry from the boudoir now interrupted them, followed by another from the ante-chamber. Charny ran to the boudoir; he saw there Andrée, dressed in white like a bride: she had heard all, and had fainted. Philippe ran to where the other cry came from; it was his father, whose hopes this revelation of the queen's love for Charny had just destroyed; struck by apoplexy, he had given his last sigh. Philippe, who understood it, looked at the corpse for a few minutes in silence, and then returned to the drawing-room, and there saw Charny watching the senseless form of his sister. He then said, "My father has just expired, sir; I am now the head of the family; if my sister survive, I will give her to you in marriage."

Charny regarded the corpse of the baron with horror, and the form of Andrée with despair. Philippe uttered a groan of agony, then continued, "M. de Charny, I make this engagement in the name of my sister, now lying senseless before us; she will give her happiness to the queen, and I, perhaps, some day shall be happy enough to give my life for her. Adieu, M. de Charny— —" and taking his sister in his arms, he carried her into the next room.

CHAPTER LXXXV
AFTER THE DRAGON, THE VIPER

Oliva was preparing to fly, as Jeanne had arranged, when Beausire, warned by an anonymous letter, discovered her and carried her away. In order to trace them, Jeanne put all her powers in requisition—she preferred being able to watch over her own secret—and her disappointment was great when all her agents returned announcing a failure. At this time she received in her hiding-place numerous messages from the queen.

She went by night to Bar-sur-Aube, and there remained for two days. At last she was traced, and an express sent to take her. Then she learnt the arrest of the cardinal. "The queen has been rash," thought she, "in refusing to compromise with the cardinal, or to pay the jewelers; but she did not know my power."

"Monsieur," said she to the officer who arrested her, "do you love the queen?"

"Certainly, madame."

"Well, in the name of that love I beg you to conduct me straight to her. Believe me, you will be doing her a service."

The man was persuaded, and did so. The queen received her haughtily, for she began to suspect that her conduct had not been straightforward. She called in two ladies as witnesses of what was about to pass.

"You are found at last, madame," said the queen; "why did you hide?"

"I did not hide, madame."

"Run away, then, if that pleases you better."

"That is to say, that I quitted Paris. I had some little business at Bar-sur-Aube, and, to tell the truth, I did not know I was so necessary to your majesty as to be obliged to ask leave for an absence of eight days."

"Have you seen the king?"

"No, madame."

"You shall see him."

"It will be a great honor for me; but your majesty seems very severe towards me—I am all trembling."

"Oh, madame, this is but the beginning. Do you know that M. de Rohan has been arrested?"

"They told me so, madame."

"You guess why?"

"No, madame."

"You proposed to me that he should pay for a certain necklace; did I accept or refuse?"

"Refuse."

"Ah!" said the queen, well pleased.

"Your majesty even paid 100,000 francs on account."

"Well, and afterwards?"

"Afterwards, as your majesty could not pay, you sent it back to M. Bœhmer."

"By whom?"

"By me."

"And what did you do with it?"

"I took it to the cardinal."

"And why to the cardinal instead of to the jewelers, as I told you?"

"Because I thought he would be hurt if I returned it without letting him know."

"But how did you get a receipt from the jewelers?"

"M. de Rohan gave it to me."

"But why did you take a letter to them as coming from me?"

"Because he gave it to me, and asked me to do so."

"It is, then, all his doing?"

"What is, madame?"

"The receipt and the letter are both forged."

"Forged, madame!" cried Jeanne, with much apparent astonishment.

"Well, you must be confronted with him to prove the truth."

"Why, madame?"

"He himself demands it. He says he has sought you everywhere, and that he wishes to prove that you have deceived him."

"Oh! then, madame, let us meet."

"You shall. You deny all knowledge of where the necklace is?"

"How should I know, madame?"

"You deny having aided the cardinal in his intrigues?"

"I am a Valois, madame."

"But M. de Rohan maintained before the king many calumnies, which he said you would confirm."

"I do not understand."

"He declares he wrote to me."

Jeanne did not reply.

"Do you hear?" said the queen.

"Yes, madame."

"What do you reply?"

"I will reply when I have seen him."

"But speak the truth now."

"Your majesty overwhelms me."

"That is no answer."

"I will give no other here;" and she looked at the two ladies. The queen understood, but would not yield; she scorned to purchase anything by concession.

"M. de Rohan," said the queen, "was sent to the Bastile for saying too much; take care, madame, that you are not sent for saying too little."

Jeanne smiled. "A pure conscience can brave persecution," she replied; "the Bastile will not convict me of a crime I did not commit."

"Will you reply?"

"Only to your majesty."

"Are you not speaking to me?"

"Not alone."

"Ah! you fear scandal, after being the cause of so much to me."

"What I did," said Jeanne, "was done for you."

"What insolence!"

"I submit to the insults of my queen."

"You will sleep in the Bastile to-night, madame!"

"So be it; I will first pray to God to preserve your majesty's honor."

The queen rose furiously, and went into the next room.

"After having conquered the dragon," she said, "I can crush the viper!"

CHAPTER LXXXVI
HOW IT CAME TO PASS THAT M. BEAUSIRE WAS TRACKED BY THE AGENTS OF M. DE CROSNE

Madame de la Motte was imprisoned as the queen had threatened, and the whole affair created no little talk and excitement through France. M. de Rohan lived at the Bastile like a prince: he had everything but liberty. He demanded to be confronted with Madame de la Motte as soon as he heard of her arrest. This was done. She whispered to him, "Send every one away, and I will explain." He asked this, but was refused; they said his counsel might communicate with her. She said to this gentleman that she was ignorant of what had become of the necklace, but that they might well have given it to her in recompense for the services she had rendered the queen and the cardinal, which were well worth a million and a half. The cardinal turned pale on hearing this repeated, and felt how much they were in Jeanne's power. He was determined not to accuse the queen, although his friends endeavored to convince him that it was his only way to prove his innocence of the robbery. Jeanne said that she did not wish to accuse either the queen or the cardinal, but that, if they persisted in making her responsible for the necklace, she would do so to show that they were interested in accusing her of falsehood. Then M. de Rohan expressed all his contempt for her, and said that he began to understand much of Jeanne's conduct, but not the queen's. All this was reported to Marie Antoinette. She ordered another private examination of the parties, but gained nothing from it. Jeanne denied everything to those sent by the queen; but when they were gone she altered her tone, and said, "If they do not leave me alone I will tell all." The cardinal said nothing, and brought no accusations; but rumors began to spread fast, and the question soon became, not "Has the queen stolen the necklace?" but "Has she allowed some one else to steal it because she knew all about her amours?" Madame de la Motte had involved her in a maze, from which there seemed no honorable exit; but she determined not to lose courage. She began to come to the conclusion that the cardinal was an honest man, and did not wish to ruin her, but was acting like herself, only to preserve his honor. They strove earnestly but ineffectually to trace the necklace. All opinions were against Jeanne, and she began to fear that, even if she dragged down the queen and cardinal, she should be quite overwhelmed under the ruins she had caused; and she had not even at hand the fruits of her dishonesty to corrupt her judges with. Affairs were in this state when a new episode changed the face of things. Oliva and M. Beausire were living, happy and rich, in a country house, when one day Beausire, going out hunting, fell into the company of two of the agents of M. de Crosne, whom he had scattered all over the country. They recognized Beausire immediately, but, as it was Oliva whom they most wanted, they did not arrest him there, but only joined the chase. Beausire, seeing two strangers, called the huntsman, and asked who they were. He replied that he did not know, but, if he had permission, would send them away. On his questioning them, they said they were friends of that gentleman, pointing to M. Beausire. Then the man brought them to him, saying, "M. de Linville, these gentlemen say they are friends of yours."

"Ah, you are called De Linville now, dear M. Beausire!"

Beausire trembled; he had concealed his name so carefully. He sent away the huntsman, and asked them who they were.

"Take us home with you, and we will tell you."

"Home?"

"Yes; do not be inhospitable." Beausire was frightened, but still feared to refuse these men who knew him.

CHAPTER LXXXVII
THE TURTLES ARE CAGED

Beausire, on entering the house, made a noise to attract Oliva's attention, for, though he knew nothing about her later escapades, he knew enough about the ball at the Opera, and the morning at M. Mesmer's, to make him fear letting her be seen by strangers. Accordingly, Oliva, hearing the dogs bark, looked out, and, seeing Beausire returning with two strangers, did not come to meet him as usual. Unfortunately the servant asked if he should call madame. The men rallied him about the lady whom he had concealed; he let them laugh, but did not offer to call her. They dined; then Beausire asked where they had met him before. "We are," replied they, "friends of one of your associates in a little affair about the Portuguese embassy."

Beausire turned pale.

"Ah!" said he: "and you came on your friend's part?"

"Yes, dear M. Beausire, to ask for 10,000 francs."

"Gentlemen," replied Beausire, "you cannot think I have such a sum in the house."

"Very likely not, monsieur; we do not ask for impossibilities. How much have you?"

"Not more than fifty or sixty louis."

"We will take them to begin with."

"I will go and fetch them," said Beausire. But they did not choose to let him leave the room without them, so they caught hold of him by the coat, saying:

"Oh no, dear M. Beausire, do not leave us."

"But how am I to get the money if I do not leave you?"

"We will go with you."

"But it is in my wife's bedroom."

"Ah," cried one of them, "you hide your wife from us!"

"Are we not presentable?" asked the other. "We wish to see her."

"You are tipsy, and I will turn you out!" said Beausire.

They laughed.

"Now you shall not even have the money I promised," said he, emboldened by what he thought their intoxication; and he ran out of the room.

They followed and caught him; he cried out, and at the sound a door opened, and a woman looked out with a frightened air. On seeing her, the men released Beausire, and gave a cry of exultation, for they recognized her immediately who resembled the Queen of France so strongly.

Beausire, who believed them for a moment disarmed by the sight of a woman, was soon cruelly undeceived.

One of the men approached Oliva, and said:

"I arrest you."

"Arrest her! Why?" cried Beausire.

"Because it is M. de Crosne's orders."

A thunderbolt falling between the lovers would have frightened them less than this declaration.

At last Beausire said, "You came to arrest me?"

"No; it was a chance."

"Never mind, you might have arrested me, and for sixty louis you were about to leave me at liberty."

"Oh no, we should have asked another sixty; however, for one hundred we will do so."

"And madame?"

"Oh, that is quite a different affair."

"She is worth two hundred louis," said Beausire.

They laughed again, and this time Beausire began to understand this terrible laugh.

"Three hundred, four hundred, a thousand—see, I will give you one thousand louis to leave her at liberty!"

They did not answer.

"Is not that enough? Ah, you know I have money, and you want to make me pay. Well, I will give you two thousand louis; it will make both your fortunes!"

"For 100,000 crowns we would not give up this woman. M. de Rohan will give us 500,000 francs for her, and the queen 1,000,000. Now we must go. You doubtless have a carriage of some kind here; have it prepared for madame. We will take you also, for form's sake; but on the way you can escape, and we will shut our eyes."

Beausire replied, "Where she goes, I will go; I will never leave her."

"Oh, so much the better; the more prisoners we bring M. de Crosne, the better he will be pleased."

A quarter of an hour after, Beausire's carriage started, with the two lovers in it. One may imagine the effect of this capture on M. de Crosne. The agents probably did not receive the 1,000,000 francs they hoped for, but there is reason to believe they were satisfied. M. de Crosne went to Versailles, followed by another carriage well guarded. He asked to see the queen, and was instantly admitted. She judged from his face that he had good news for her, and felt the first sensation of joy she had experienced for a month.

"Madame," said M. de Crosne, "have you a room here where you can see without being seen?"

"Oh yes—my library."

"Well, madame, I have a carriage below, in which is some one whom I wish to introduce into the castle unseen by any one."

"Nothing more easy," replied the queen, ringing to give her orders.

All was executed as he wished. Then she conducted M. de Crosne to the library, where, concealed from view behind a large screen, she soon saw enter a form which made her utter a cry of surprise. It was Oliva, dressed in one of her own favorite costumes—a green dress with broad stripes of black moirée, green satin slippers with high heels, and her hair dressed like her own. It might have been herself reflected in the glass.

"What says your majesty to this resemblance?" asked M. de Crosne, triumphantly.

"Incredible," said the queen. She then thought to herself, "Ah! Charny; why are you not here?"

"What does your majesty wish?"

"Nothing, sir, but that the king should know."

"And M. de Provence see her? shall he not, madame?"

"Thanks, M. de Crosne, you hold now, I think, the clue to the whole plot."

"Nearly so, madame."

"And M. de Rohan?"

"Knows nothing yet."

"Ah!" cried the queen; "in this woman, doubtless, lies all his error."

"Possibly, madame; but if it be his error it is the crime of some one else."

"Seek well, sir; the honor of France is in your hands."

"Believe me worthy of the trust. At present, the accused parties deny everything. I shall wait for the proper time to overwhelm them with this living witness that I now hold."

"Madame de la Motte?"

"Knows nothing of this capture. She accuses M. de Cagliostro of having excited the cardinal to say what he did."

"And what does M. de Cagliostro say?"

"He has promised to come to me this morning. He is a dangerous man, but a useful one, and attacked by Madame de la Motte, I am in hopes he will sting back again."

"You hope for revelations?"

"I do."

"How so, sir? Tell me everything which can reassure me."

"These are my reasons, madame. Madame de la Motte lived in the Rue St. Claude, and M. de Cagliostro just opposite her. So I think her movements cannot have been unnoticed by him; but if your majesty will excuse me, it is close to the time he appointed to meet me."

"Go, monsieur, go; and assure yourself of my gratitude."

When he was gone the queen burst into tears. "My justification begins," said she; "I shall soon read my triumph in all faces; but the one I most cared to know me innocent, him I shall not see."

M. de Crosne drove back to Paris, where M. de Cagliostro waited for him. He knew all; for he had discovered Beausire's retreat, and was on the road to see him, and induce him to leave France, when he met the carriage containing Beausire and Oliva. Beausire saw the count, and the idea crossed his mind that he might help them. He therefore accepted the offer of the police-agents, gave them the hundred louis, and made his escape, in spite of the tears shed by Oliva; saying, "I go to try and save you." He ran after M. de Cagliostro's carriage, which he soon overtook, as the count had stopped, it being useless to proceed. Beausire soon told his story; Cagliostro listened in silence, then said, "She is lost."

"Why so?" Then Cagliostro told him all he did not already know—all the intrigues in the park.

"Oh! save her," cried Beausire; "and I will give her to you, if you love her still."

"My friend," replied Cagliostro, "you deceive yourself; I never loved Mademoiselle Oliva; I had but one aim—that of weaning her from the life of debauchery she was leading with you."

"But——" said Beausire.

"That astonishes you—know that I belong to a society whose object is moral reform. Ask her if ever she heard from my mouth one word of gallantry, or if my services were not disinterested."

"Oh, monsieur! but will you save her?"

"I will try, but it will depend on yourself."

"I will do anything."

"Then return with me to Paris, and if you follow my instructions implicitly, we may succeed in saving her. I only impose one condition, which I will tell you when I reach home."

"I promise beforehand. But can I see her again?"

"I think so, and you can tell her what I say to you." In two hours they overtook the carriage containing Oliva, and Beausire bought for fifty louis permission to embrace her, and tell her all the count had said. The agents admired this violent love, and hoped for more louis, but Beausire was gone. Cagliostro drove him to Paris.

We will now return to M. de Crosne.

This gentleman knew a good deal about Cagliostro, his former names, his pretensions to ubiquity and perpetual regeneration, his secrets in alchemy and magnetism, and looked upon him as a great charlatan.

"Monsieur," said he to Cagliostro, "you asked me for an audience; I have returned from Versailles to meet you."

"Sir, I thought you would wish to question me about what is passing, so I came to you."

"Question you?" said the magistrate, affecting surprise. "On what?"

"Monsieur," replied Cagliostro, "you are much occupied about Madame de la Motte, and the missing necklace."

"Have you found it?" asked M. de Crosne, laughing.

"No, sir, but Madame de la Motte lived in the Rue St. Claude— —"

"I know, opposite you."

"Oh, if you know all about Oliva, I have nothing more to tell you."

"Who is Oliva?"

"You do not know? Then, sir, imagine a young girl very pretty, with blue eyes, and an oval face, a style of beauty something like her majesty, for instance."

"Well, sir?"

"This young girl led a bad life; it gave me pain to see it; for she was once in the service of an old friend of mine, M. de Taverney—but I weary you."

"Oh no, pray go on."

"Well, Oliva led not only a bad life, but an unhappy one, with a fellow she called her lover, who beat and robbed her."

"Beausire," said the magistrate.

"Ah! you know him. You are still more a magician than I am. Well, one day when Beausire had beaten the poor girl more than usual, she fled to me for refuge; I pitied her, and gave her shelter in one of my houses."

"In your house!" cried M. de Crosne in surprise.

"Oh! why not? I am a bachelor," said Cagliostro, with an air which quite deceived M. de Crosne.

"That is then the reason why my agents could not find her."

"What! you were seeking this little girl? Had she then been guilty of any crime?"

"No, sir, no; pray go on."

"Oh! I have done. I lodged her at my house, and that is all."

"No, sir, for you just now associated her name with that of Madame de la Motte."

"Only as neighbors."

"But, sir, this Oliva, whom you say you had in your house, I found in the country with Beausire."

"With Beausire? Ah! then I have wronged Madame de la Motte."

"How so, sir?"

"Why just as I thought I had hopes of reforming Oliva, and bringing her back to an honest life, some one carried her away from me."

"That is strange."

"Is it not? And I firmly believed it to be Madame de la Motte. But as you found her with Beausire, it was not she, and all her signals and correspondence with Oliva meant nothing."

"With Oliva?"

"Yes."

"They met?"

"Yes, Madame de la Motte found a way to take Oliva out every night."

"Are you sure of this?"

"I saw and heard her."

"Oh, sir, you tell me what I would have paid for with one thousand francs a word. But you are a friend of M. de Rohan?"

"Yes."

"You ought to know how far he was connected with this affair."

"I do not wish to know."

"But you know the object of these nightly excursions of Madame de la Motte and Oliva?"

"Of that also I wish to be ignorant."

"Sir, I only wish to ask you one more question. Have you proofs of the correspondence of Madame de la Motte and Oliva?"

"Plenty."

"What are they?"

"Notes which Madame de la Motte used to throw over to Oliva with a cross-bow. Several of them did not reach their destination, and were picked up either by myself, or my servants, in the street."

"Sir, you will be ready to produce them, if called upon?"

"Certainly; they are perfectly innocent, and cannot injure any one."

"And have you any other proofs of intimacy?"

"I know that she had a method of entering my house to see Oliva. I saw her myself, just after Oliva had disappeared, and my servants saw her also."

"But what did she come for, if Oliva was gone?"

"I did not know. I saw her come out of a carriage at the corner of the street. My idea was that she wished to attach Oliva to her, and keep her near her."

"And you let her do it?"

"Why not? She is a great lady, and received at court. Why should I have prevented her taking charge of Oliva, and taking her off my hands?"

"What did she say when she found that Oliva was gone?"

"She appeared distressed."

"You suppose that Beausire carried her off?"

"I suppose so, for you tell me you found them together. I did not suspect him before, for he did not know where she was."

"She must have let him know herself."

"I think not, as she had fled from him. I think Madame de la Motte must have sent him a key."

"Ah! what day was it?"

"The evening of St. Louis."

"Monsieur, you have rendered a great service to me and to the state."

"I am happy to hear it."

"You shall be thanked as you deserve. I may count on the production of the proofs you mention?"

"I am ready, sir, to assist justice at all times."

As Cagliostro left, he muttered, "Ah, countess! you tried to accuse me—take care of yourself."

Meanwhile, M. de Breteuil was sent by the king to examine Madame de la Motte. She declared that she had proofs of her innocence, which she would produce at the proper time; she also declared, that she would only speak the truth in the presence of the cardinal. She was told that the cardinal laid all the blame upon her. "Tell him then," she said, "that I advise him not to persist in such a foolish system of defense."

"Whom then do you accuse?" asked M. Breteuil.

"I accuse no one," was her reply.

A report was spread at last that the diamonds were being sold in England by M. Reteau de Villette. This man was soon found and arrested, and brought over and confronted with Jeanne. To her utter confusion, he acknowledged that he had forged a receipt from the jewelers, and a letter from the queen at the request of Madame de la Motte. She denied furiously, and declared that she had never seen M. Reteau. M. de Crosne produced as witness a coachman, who swore to having driven her, on the day named, to the house of M. Reteau. Also, one of the servants of M. de Cagliostro deposed to having seen this man on the box of Jeanne's carriage on the night that she came to his master's house. Now, Jeanne began to abuse the count, and accused him of having inspired M. de Rohan with the ideas inimical to the royal dignity. M. de Rohan defended him, and Jeanne at once plainly accused the cardinal of a violent love for the queen. M. de Cagliostro requested to be incarcerated, and allowed to prove his innocence publicly. Then the queen caused to be published all the reports made to the king about the nocturnal promenades, and requested M. de Crosne to state all that he knew about it. This public avowal overturned all Jeanne's plans, and she denied having assisted at any meetings between the queen and the cardinal. This declaration would have cleared the queen, had it been possible to attach any credence to what this woman said. While Jeanne continued to deny that she had ever been in the park, they brought forward Oliva at last, a living witness of all the falsehoods of the countess. When Oliva was shown to the cardinal the blow was dreadful. He saw at last how infamously he had been played upon. This man, so full of delicacy and noble passions, discovered that an adventuress had led him to insult and despise the Queen of France; a woman whom he loved, and who was innocent. He would have shed all his blood at the feet of Marie Antoinette to make atonement. But he could not even acknowledge his mistake without owning that he loved her—even his excuse would involve an offense; so he was obliged to keep silent, and allow Jeanne to deny everything. Oliva confessed all without reserve. At last Jeanne, driven from every hold, confessed that she had deceived the cardinal, but declared that it was done with the consent of the queen, who watched and enjoyed the scene, hidden behind the trees. To this story she kept; the queen could never disprove it, and there were plenty of people willing to believe it true.

CHAPTER LXXXVIII
THE LAST HOPE LOST

Here the affair therefore rested, for Jeanne was determined to share the blame with some one, as she could not turn it from herself. All her calculations had been defeated by the frankness with which the queen had met, and made public, every accusation against her.

At last Jeanne wrote the following letter to the queen:

"Madame,

"In spite of my painful position and rigorous treatment, I have not uttered a complaint; all that has been tried to extort avowals from me has failed to make me compromise my sovereign. However, although persuaded that my constancy and discretion will facilitate my release from my present position, the friends of the cardinal make me fear I shall become his victim. A long imprisonment, endless questions, and the shame and despair of being accused of such crimes, begin to exhaust my courage, and I tremble lest my constancy should at last give way. Your majesty might end all this by a few words to M. de Breteuil, who could give the affair in the king's eyes any color your majesty likes without compromising you. It is the fear of being compelled to reveal all which makes me beg your majesty to take steps to relieve me from my painful position. I am, with profound respect,

"Your humble servant,

"Jeanne de la Motte."

Jeanne calculated either that this letter would frighten the queen, or, what was more probable, would never reach her hands, but be carried by the messenger to the governor of the Bastile, where it could hardly fail to tell against the queen. She then wrote to the cardinal:

"I cannot conceive, monseigneur, why you persist in not speaking plainly. It seems to me that your best plan would be to confide fully in our judges. As for me, I am resolved to be silent if you will not second me; but why do you not speak? Explain all the circumstances of this mysterious affair, for if I were to speak first, and you not support me, I should be sacrificed to the vengeance of her who wishes to ruin us. But I have written her a letter which will perhaps induce her to spare us, who have nothing to reproach ourselves with."

This letter she gave to the cardinal at their last confrontation. He grew pale with anger at her audacity, and left the room. Then Jeanne produced her letter to the queen, and begged the Abbé Lekel, chaplain of the Bastile, who had accompanied the cardinal, and was devoted to him, to take charge of it and convey it to the queen. He refused to take it. She declared that if he did not she would produce M. de Rohan's letters to the queen. "And take care, sir," added she, "for they will cause his head to fall on the scaffold."

At this moment the cardinal reappeared.

"Madame," said he, "let my head fall, so that I have the satisfaction of seeing also the scaffold which you shall mount as a thief and a forger. Come, Abbé." He went away, leaving Jeanne devoured with rage and disappointment at her failures at every turn.

CHAPTER LXXXIX
THE BAPTISM OF THE LITTLE BEAUSIRE

Madame de la Motte had deceived herself on all points, Cagliostro upon none. Once in the Bastile, he saw a good opportunity for working at the ruin of the monarchy, which he had been trying to undermine for so many years. He prepared the famous letter, dated from London, which appeared a month after. In this letter, after attacking king, queen, cardinal, and even M. de Breteuil, he said, "Yes, I repeat, now free after my imprisonment, there is no crime that would not be expiated by six months in the Bastile. They ask me if I shall ever return to France? Yes, I reply, when the Bastile becomes a public promenade. You have all that is necessary to happiness, you Frenchmen; a fertile soil and genial climate, good hearts, gay tempers, genius, and grace. You only want, my friends, one little thing—to feel sure of sleeping quietly in your beds when you are innocent."

Oliva kept her word faithfully to Cagliostro, and uttered no word that could compromise him. She threw all the blame on Madame de la Motte, and asserted vehemently her own innocent participation in what she believed to be a joke, played on a gentleman unknown to her. All this time she did not see Beausire, but she had a souvenir of him; for in the month of May she gave birth to a son. Beausire was allowed to attend the baptism, which took place in the prison, which he did with much pleasure, swearing that if Oliva ever recovered her liberty he would make her his wife.

CHAPTER XC
THE TRIAL

The day at last arrived, after long investigations, when the judgment of the court was to be pronounced. All the accused had been removed to the Conciergerie, to be in readiness to appear when called on. Oliva continued to be frank and timid; Cagliostro, tranquil and indifferent; Reteau, despairing, cowardly, and weeping; and Jeanne, violent, menacing, and venomous. She had managed to interest the keeper and his wife, and thus obtain more freedom and indulgences.

The first who took his place on the wooden stool, which was appropriated for the accused, was Reteau, who asked pardon with tears and prayers, declared all he knew, and avowed his crimes. He interested no one; he was simply a knave and a coward. After him came Madame de la Motte. Her appearance produced a great sensation; at the sight of the disgraceful seat prepared for her, she, who called herself a Valois, threw around her furious looks, but, meeting curiosity instead of sympathy, repressed her rage. When interrogated, she continued, as before, to throw out insinuations, stating nothing clearly but her own innocence. When questioned as to the letters which she was reported to have said passed between the queen and the cardinal, she answered that she did not wish to compromise the queen, and that the cardinal was best able to answer this question himself. "Ask him to produce them," said she; "I wish to say nothing about them." She inspired in nearly all a feeling of distrust and anger. When she retired, her only consolation was the hope of seeing the cardinal in the seat after her; and her rage was extreme when she saw it taken away, and an armchair brought for his use. The cardinal advanced, accompanied by four attendants, and the governor of the Bastile walked by his side. At his entrance he was greeted by a long murmur of sympathy and respect; it was echoed by loud shouts from without—it was the people who cheered him. He was pale, and much moved. The president spoke politely to him, and begged him to sit down. When he spoke, it was with a trembling voice, and a troubled and even humble manner. He gave excuses rather than proofs, and supplications more than reasons, but said little, and seemed to be deserted by his former eloquence. Oliva came next. The wooden stool was brought back for her.

Many people trembled at seeing this living image of the queen sitting there as a criminal. Then Cagliostro was called, but almost as a matter of form, and dismissed immediately. The court then announced that the proceedings were concluded, and the deliberations about to begin. All the prisoners were locked for the night in the Conciergerie. The sentence was not pronounced till the following day. Jeanne seated herself early at the window, and before long heard a tremendous shouting from the crowd collected to hear the sentence. This continued for some time, when she distinctly heard a passer-by say, "A grand day for the cardinal!" "For the cardinal," thought Jeanne; "then he is acquitted;" and she ran to M. Hubert, the keeper, to ask, but he did not know. "He must be acquitted!" she said; "they said it was a grand day for him. But I——"

"Well, madame," said he, "if he is acquitted, why should you not be acquitted also?"

Jeanne returned to the window. "You are wrong, madame," said Madame Hubert to her; "you only become agitated, without perfectly understanding what is passing. Pray remain quiet until your counsel comes to communicate your fate."

"I cannot," said Jeanne, continuing to listen to what passed in the street.

A woman passed, gaily dressed, and with a bouquet in her hand. "He shall have my bouquet, the dear man!" said she. "Oh, I would embrace him if I could!"

"And I also," said another.

"He is so handsome!" said a third.

"It must be the cardinal," said Jeanne; "he is acquitted."

And she said this with so much bitterness that the keeper said, "But, madame, do you not wish the poor prisoner to be released?"

Jeanne, unwilling to lose their sympathy, replied, "Oh, you misunderstand me. Do you believe me so envious and wicked as to wish ill to my companions in misfortune? Oh no; I trust he is free. It is only impatience to learn my own fate, and you tell me nothing."

"We do not know," replied they.

Then other loud cries were heard. Jeanne could see the crowd pressing round an open carriage, which was going slowly along. Flowers were thrown, hats waved; some even mounted on the steps to kiss the hand of a man who sat grave and half frightened at his own popularity. This was the cardinal. Another man sat by him, and cries of "Vive Cagliostro!" were mingled with the shouts for M. de Rohan. Jeanne began to gather courage from all this sympathy for those whom she chose to call the queen's victims; but suddenly the thought flashed on her, "They are already set free, and no one has even been to announce my sentence!" and she trembled. New shouts now drew her attention to a coach, which was also advancing, followed by a crowd; and in this Jeanne recognized Oliva, who sat smiling with delight at the people who cheered her, holding her child in her arms. Then Jeanne, seeing all these people free, happy, and fêted, began to utter loud complaints that she was not also liberated, or at least told her fate.

"Calm yourself, madame," said Madame Hubert.

"But tell me, for you must know."

"Madame."

"I implore you! You see how I suffer."

"We are forbidden, madame."

"Is it so frightful that you dare not?"

"Oh no; calm yourself."

"Then speak."

"Will you be patient, and not betray us?"

"I swear."

"Well, the cardinal is acquitted."

"I know it."

"M. de Cagliostro and Mademoiselle Oliva are also acquitted, M. Reteau condemned to the galleys— —"

"And I?" cried Jeanne, furiously.

"Madame, you promised to be patient."

"See—speak—I am calm."

"Banished," said the woman, feebly.

A flash of delight shone for a moment in the eyes of the countess; then she pretended to faint, and threw herself into the arms of Madame Hubert. "What would it have been," thought she, "if I had told her the truth!"

"Banishment!" thought Jeanne; "that is liberty, riches, vengeance; it is what I hoped for. I have won!"

CHAPTER XCI
THE EXECUTION

Jeanne waited for her counsel to come and announce her fate; but, being now at ease, said to herself, "What do I care that I am thought more guilty than M. de Rohan? I am banished—that is to say, I can carry away my million and a half with me, and live under the orange trees of Seville during the winter, and in Germany or England in the summer. Then I can tell my own story, and, young, rich, and celebrated, live as I please among my friends."

Pleasing herself with these notions, she commenced settling all her future plans, the disposal of her diamonds, and her establishment in London. This brought to her mind M. Reteau. "Poor fellow!" thought she, "it is he who pays for all; some one must suffer, and it always falls on the humblest instrument. Poor Reteau pays now for his pamphlets against the queen; he has led a hard life of blows and escapes, and now it terminates with the galleys." She dined with M. and Madame Hubert, and was quite gay; but they did not respond, and were silent and uneasy. Jeanne, however, felt so happy that she cared little for their manner towards her. After dinner, she asked when they were coming to read her sentence.

M. Hubert said they were probably waiting till she returned to her room. She therefore rose to go, when Madame Hubert ran to her and took her hands, looking at her with an expression of so much pity and sympathy, that it struck her for a moment with terror. She was about to question her, but Hubert took her hand, and led her from the room. When she reached her own apartment, she found eight soldiers waiting outside; she felt surprised, but went in, and allowed the man to lock her up as usual. Soon, however, the door opened again, and one of the turnkeys appeared.

"Will madame please to follow me?" he said.

"Where?"

"Below."

"What for? What do they want with me?"

"Madame, M. Viollet, your counsel, wishes to speak to you."

"Why does he not come here?"

"Madame, he has received letters from Versailles, and wishes to show them to you."

"Letters from Versailles," thought Jeanne; "perhaps the queen has interested herself for me, since the sentence was passed. Wait a little," she said; "Till I arrange my dress." In five minutes she was ready. "Perhaps," she thought, "M. Viollet has come to get me to leave France at once, and the queen is anxious to facilitate the departure of so dangerous an enemy."

She followed the turnkey down-stairs, and they entered a room, which looked like a vault; it was damp, and almost dark.

"Sir," said she, trying to overcome her terror, "where is M. Viollet?"

The man did not reply.

"What do you want?" continued she; "have you anything to say to me? you have chosen a very singular place for a rendezvous."

"We are waiting for M. Viollet," he replied.

"It is not possible that M. Viollet should wish for me to wait for him here." All at once, another door, which Jeanne had not before observed, opened, and three men entered. Jeanne looked at them in surprise, and with growing terror. One of them, who was dressed in black, with a roll of papers in his hand, advanced, and said:

"You are Jeanne de St. Rémy de Valois, wife of Marie Antoine, Count de la Motte?"

"Yes, sir."

"Born at Fontette, on the 22d of July, 1756?"

"Yes, sir."

"You live at Paris, Rue St. Claude?"

"Yes, sir; but why these questions?"

"Madame, I am the registrar of the court, and I am come to read to you the sentence of the court of the 31st of May, 1786."

Jeanne trembled again, and now looked at the other two men; one had a gray dress with steel buttons, the other a fur cap on and an apron, which seemed to her spotted with blood. She drew back, but the registrar said, "On your knees, madame, if you please."

"On my knees?" cried Jeanne; "I, a Valois!"

"It is the order, madame."

"But, sir, it is an unheard-of thing, except where some degrading sentence has been pronounced; and banishment is not such."

"I did not tell you you were sentenced to banishment," said he gravely.

"But to what, then?"

"I will tell you, madame, when you are on your knees."

"Never!"

"Madame, I only follow my instructions."

"Never! I tell you."

"Madame, it is the order that when the condemned refuse to kneel, they should be forced to do it."

"Force—to a woman!"

"There is no distinction in the eyes of justice."

"Ah!" cried Jeanne, "this is the queen's doings; I recognize the hands of an enemy."

"You are wrong to accuse the queen; she has nothing to do with the orders of the court. Come, madame, I beg you to spare me the necessity of violence, and kneel down."

"Never!" and she planted herself firmly in a corner of the room.

The registrar then signed to the two other men, who, approaching, seized her, and in spite of her cries dragged her into the middle of the room. But she bounded up again.

"Let me stand," said she, "and I will listen patiently."

"Madame, whenever criminals are punished by whipping, they kneel to receive the sentence."

"Whipping!" screamed Jeanne; "miserable wretch, how dare you——"

The men forced her on her knees once more, and held her down, but she struggled so furiously that they called out, "Read quickly, monsieur, for we cannot hold her."

"I will never hear such an infamous sentence," she cried; and indeed she drowned his voice so effectually with her screams, that although he read, not a word could be heard.

He replaced his papers in his pocket, and she, thinking he had finished, stopped her cries. Then he said, "And the sentence shall be executed at the place of executions, Cour de Justice."

"Publicly!" screamed she.

"Monsieur de Paris, I deliver you this woman," said the registrar, addressing the man with the leathern apron.

"Who is this man?" cried Jeanne, in a fright.

"The executioner," replied the registrar.

The two men then took hold of her to lead her out, but her resistance was so violent that they were obliged to drag her along by force, and she never ceased uttering the most frantic cries. They took her thus into the court called Cour de Justice, where there was a scaffold and which was crowded with spectators. On a platform, raised about eight feet, was a post garnished with iron rings, and with a ladder to mount to it. This place was surrounded with soldiers. When she appeared, cries of "Here she is!" mingled with much abuse, were heard from the crowd. Numbers of the partisans of M. de Rohan had assembled to hoot her, and cries of "A bas la Motte, the forger!" were heard on every side, and those who tried to express pity for her were soon silenced.

Then she cried in a loud voice, "Do you know who I am? I am of the blood of your kings. They strike in me, not a criminal, but a rival; not only a rival, but an accomplice. Yes," repeated she, as the people kept silence to listen, "an accomplice. They punish one who knows the secrets of——"

"Take care," interrupted the registrar.

She turned and saw the executioner with the whip in his hand. At this sight she forgot her desire to captivate the multitude, and even her hatred, and sinking on her knees she said, "Have pity!" and seized his hand; but he raised the other, and let the whip fall lightly on her shoulders. She jumped up, and was about to try and throw herself off the scaffold, when she saw the other man, who was drawing from a fire a hot iron. At this sight she uttered a perfect howl, which was echoed by the people.

"Help! help!" she cried, trying to shake off the cord with which they were tying her hands. The executioner at last forced her on her knees, and tore open her dress; but she cried, with a voice which was heard through all the tumult, "Cowardly Frenchmen! you do not defend me, but let me be tortured; oh! it is my own fault. If I had said all I knew of the queen I should have been——"

She could say no more, for she was gagged by the attendants: then two men held her, while the executioner performed his office. At the touch of the iron she fainted, and was carried back insensible to the Conciergerie when the crowd gradually dispersed.

CHAPTER XCII
THE MARRIAGE

On the same day at noon the king entered a drawing-room, where the queen was sitting in full dress, but pale through her rouge, and surrounded by a party of ladies and gentlemen. He glanced frequently towards the door. "Are not the young couple ready? I believe it is noon," he said.

"Sire, M. de Charny is waiting in the gallery for your majesty's orders," said the queen, with a violent effort.

"Oh! let him come in." The queen turned from the door. "The bride ought to be here also," continued the king, "it is time."

"Your majesty must excuse Mademoiselle de Taverney, if she is late," replied M. de Charny, advancing; "for since the death of her father she has not left her bed until to-day, and she fainted when she did so."

"This dear child loved her father so much," replied the king, "but we hope a good husband will console her. M. de Breteuil," said he, turning to that gentleman, "have you made out the order of banishment for M. de Cagliostro?"

"Yes, sire."

"And that De la Motte. Is it not to-day she is to be branded?"

At this moment, Andrée appeared, dressed in white like a bride, and with cheeks nearly as white as her dress. She advanced leaning on her brother's arm. M. de Suffren, leading his nephew, came to meet her, and then drew back to allow her to approach the king.

"Mademoiselle," said Louis, taking her hand, "I begged of you to hasten this marriage, instead of waiting until the time of your mourning had expired, that I might have the pleasure of assisting at the ceremony; for to-morrow I and the queen commence a tour through France." And he led Andrée up to the queen, who could hardly stand, and did not raise her eyes. The king then, putting Andrée's hand into Philippe's, said, "Gentlemen, to the chapel,"—and they began to move. The queen kneeled on her prie Dieu, her face buried in her hands, praying for strength. Charny, though pale as death, feeling that all eyes were upon him, appeared calm and strong.

Andrée remained immovable as a statue; she did not pray—she had nothing to ask, to hope for, or to fear. The ceremony over, the king kissed Andrée on the forehead, saying, "Madame la Comtesse, go to the queen, she wishes to give you a wedding present."

"Oh!" murmured Andrée to Philippe, "it is too much; I can bear no more; I cannot do that."

"Courage, sister, one effort more."

"I cannot, Philippe; if she speaks to me, I shall die."

"Then, you will be happier than I, for I cannot die."

Andrée said no more, but went to the queen. She found her in her chair with closed eyes and clasped hands, seeming more dead than alive, except for the shudders which, shook her from time to time. Andrée waited tremblingly to hear her speak; but, after a minute, she rose slowly, and took from the table a paper, which she put into Andrée's hands. Andrée opened it, and read:

> "Andrée, you have saved me. My honor comes from you; my life belongs to you. In the name of this honor, which has cost you so dear, I swear to you that you may call me sister without blushing. This paper is the pledge of my gratitude, the dowry which I give you. Your heart is noble and will thank me for this gift.
>
> "MARIE ANTOINETTE DE LORRAINE D'AUTRICHE."

Andrée looked at the queen, and saw tears falling from her eyes; she seemed expecting an answer, but Andrée, putting the letter in the fire, turned and left the room. Then Charny, who was waiting for her, took her hand, and they, each pale and silent, left the room. Two traveling-carriages were in the courtyard; Andrée got into one, and then said:

"Sir, I believe you go to Picardy."

"Yes, madame."

"And I to where my mother lies dead. Adieu, monsieur."

Charny bowed, but did not reply, and Andrée drove off.

Charny himself, after giving his hand to Philippe, got into the other, and also drove off.

Then Philippe cried, in a tone of anguish, "My task is done!" and he too vanished.